"Through my musician's perspective, Barbara Thornburgh Carlton's epic tale resonates deeply. But this is a universal story of perseverance, set in a beautifully drawn era with empathy, passion and warm humor. Prepare to be drawn in and captivated by Carlton's vivid imagery and musical sensibility. I cannot recommend it enough!"

—**ALOYSIA FRIEDMANN,** *Violinist and Founder of the Orcas Island Chamber Music Festival*

"*The Well-Tempered Violinist,* Book One of The Gift, is a breathtaking testament to the enduring power of dreams and a young woman's journey, not just to master an instrument, but to find her voice in a world that often seeks to silence it. Barbara Thornburgh Carlton's exquisite prose paints a vivid portrait of a world on the brink of change, where the delicate notes of a violin can transcend the struggles of a tumultuous era.

"This novel is a triumph that will resonate with anyone who has ever dared to pursue a passion against all odds and linger in your heart long after you turn the final page. Highly recommended for anyone who appreciates the beauty of music and the strength of the human spirit."

—**JOHN LARGESS,** *Violist, Miró Quartet*

"Barbara's Carlton's formidable epic *The Well-Tempered Violinist*, Book One of The Gift, begins at the dawn of modernism as young Marthe Adler, a highly talented violinist, struggles to overcome the obstacles blocking on her path toward a deserved world class career. Society's limits stretch and fall one by one in a groundswell of inevitable change and heroic personal determination.

"Carlton captures Germany's highly sophisticated musical life in the early 1900s and weaves in multiple rich characters to reflect the deep-seated conflicts and prejudices of the time with compelling and imaginative storytelling that keeps the reader wanting more.

"In all, it is a human and universal story. In the same way, music speaks to us all."

—**YVES ABEL,** *Principal Conductor, San Diego Opera*

"With intimate imagery and sensual sensitivity, Barbara Thornburgh Carlton masterfully weaves a story of grit and grace around the gifted young violinist Marthe Adler. Carlton's keen awareness of formalities and traditions of early twentieth-century Germany brings vivid historical and musical authenticity to Marthe's struggles and victories, balanced with the tenderness of human bonds.

"Heart-warming yet chilling, *The Well-Tempered Violinist* lives up to its title with each turn of the page."

—**LISA BERGMAN,** *Classical KING Radio Host and Concert Pianist*

THE WELL-TEMPERED VIOLINIST

1905-1911

BARBARA T. CARLTON

Helping talented writers
publish exceptional books.

This is a work of fiction. References to real people, events, establishments, organizations, or locales are intended only to provide a sense of authenticity and are used fictitiously. All other characters, and all incidents and dialogue are drawn from the author's imagination and are not to be construed as real.

The Well-Tempered Violinist
Copyright © 2025 Barbara Thornburgh Carlton

Printed in the United States of America

For information, address: Acorn Publishing LLC
3943 Irvine Blvd. Ste. 218, Irvine, CA 92602

www.AcornPublishingLLC.com

Cover Design by Damonza

ISBN-13: 979-8-88528-134-8 (hardcover)
ISBN-13: 979-8-88528-133-1 (paperback)
Library of Congress Control Number (LCCN): 2025911181

AUTHOR'S NOTE

In 2014 I discovered chamber music.

It had, of course, been there all along. I grew up with classical music, but had never experienced chamber music as I did that June on Orcas Island, Washington, when, by pure good luck, a family vacation coincided with a special concert series of the Orcas Island Chamber Music Festival: the Miró Quartet, playing the complete Beethoven string quartets. On a whim, we decided to attend, only to learn the series had been sold out for months. Yet our good luck held: each night by curtain time, cancelled tickets became ours.

The Miró Quartet's musicianship was brilliant, Beethoven's music profound. Together they expressed the full range of human emotion through the intimate transparency of four stringed instruments. We soon learned that a string quartet is a high-wire undertaking without a safety net, and that, among the world's string quartets, the Miró Quartet ranks with the finest.

After each concert, OICMF hosted a reception where ordinary people like us, who squeaked in on cancellations and wore hiking clothes to concerts (not having packed anything else), could actually talk with the musicians, a privilege most organizations reserve for major donors. The members of the Miró answered my nightly barrage of questions about their work and their art with endless patience and unfailing grace.

I was hooked.

Like Alice in Wonderland, I fell down a magical rabbit hole that first June evening in 2014. But, unlike Alice, I opened a door that led to a world of endless richness and depth, drama and beauty. I learned more about the enormous commitment and discipline required to become a musician. I learned more about women musicians' historical struggles to gain respect, opportunity, and recognition. One question led to another, and another, and another, and eventually all those questions demanded to become a story. The Gift is the result.

This story takes place in a real city, in a real country, in real history, all as vivid as I can make them. But it is entirely fictional; though real historical figures may make a cameo appearance from time to time, any resemblance to any real individual of any period is entirely coincidental.

Barbara Thornburgh Carlton

DEDICATION

To the people who make everything worthwhile:

Lauren, who loves to read

Ian, who loves to make music

and

Barry, who has loved me through all of it

✦

And to the Miró Quartet,

who opened the door:

(in alphabetical order)

Daniel Ching,

Will Fedkenheuer,

Joshua Gindele,

John Largess

TABLE OF CONTENTS

Prologue: The Lost World, February 1949 1

Before: 1905–1906

1 Finding Purpose, November 1905–September 1906 9

Year One: The Fledgling, 1906–1907

2 Fall, September 1906 29

3 Fall, October–November 1906 45

4 Fall, December 1906 53

5 Winter, January–April 1907 70

6 Spring, April–June 1907 90

Year Two: Fortress Music, 1907–1908

7 Summer, June–September 1907 103

8 Fall, September–October 1907 111

9 Fall, October–December 1907 130

10 Winter, December 1907–April 1908 154

11 Spring, April–June 1908 166

Year Three: Dangerous Ideas, 1908–1909

12 Summer, June–September 1908 175

13 Fall, September–December 1908 179

14 December 1908 201

15 Winter, January–April 1909 209

16 Spring, April–June 1909 226

Year Four: A Tempering Fire, 1909–1910

17 Summer, June–September 1909 247

18 Fall, September–December 1909 259

19 December 1909 281

20 Winter, December 1909–April 1910 292

21 Spring, April–June 1910 312

22 The Solo Recital, June 1910 335

The Future: 1910–1911

23 Debut, June 1910–April 1911 353

PROLOGUE:
THE LOST WORLD

February 1949, Heidelberg

In the very beginning was the sound, bright and rich, with an edge of darkness.

I knew it before birth, my mother said, for whenever my father played, I became still in her womb, as if I were mesmerized.

In the sitting room of our house in Eberlinstrasse, I became the audience, propped with pillows before I could sit up, listening to my father and his friends play string quartets on Saturday nights—for love, he said, not money, for he was a banker, though as a young man he had studied with the famous Schradieck in Hamburg. Later, he told me I never fussed, never had to be removed, but remained transfixed, no matter how rough the music nor how often they repeated it. So perhaps my mother was right.

✦　✦　✦

The second beginning was my fourth birthday, when my baby sister Anni stuck her fist into my birthday cake when no one was looking and my grandparents gave me a music box that played "Papageno's Magic Bells" from *The Magic Flute,* which I listened to until everyone but me was sick of it. Best of all, my father gave me my own small violin and began to teach me its mysteries. First, the names of the strings and their personalities: A, sensible and even-tempered; D, cheerful and impetuous; down to G, serious and thoughtful; up to E, nervous and temperamental, with a tendency to squeak. How to tune them, how to find the notes and make them pure instead of scratchy. He turned exercises and drills into games and improvised harmony to my children's songs, something different every time. *Alle Meine Entchen,* All My Ducklings. *Bruder Jakob,* a round. *Kleines Mädchen,* Little Girl—my favorite, because it was about *me.*

I practiced every afternoon for my evening lesson. Occasionally, with nerves like caterpillars in my stomach, I played for the applause and praise of my father's friends. I might have thought all children were as docile as myself, if not for Anni. Anni's temper tantrums, Anni thundering up and down the stairs, Anni meddling with my toys and often breaking them. I couldn't imagine where my parents had found her, or why. Someday, I thought—preferably soon—she would run off to become a pirate and leave us in peace.

The pirate would surely come to no good. But I dreamed I would become a famous violinist and lead an exotic and sophisticated life on the concert stages of the world.

✦   ✦   ✦

When I outgrew my first violin, Anni inherited it and my father began to teach her—at least, he tried. Anni never practiced and she hated lessons of all kinds. The experiment was short-lived and a spectacular failure.

I felt horribly smug for weeks.

My father and I shared a secret language, a world full of treasures where Anni couldn't stick in her fat little fist and grab anything and where my mother didn't care to go. A bond grew between us as between two fibers of the same tree, pure and deep.

✦   ✦   ✦

On my ninth birthday, he told me I needed more methodical training, by which he meant Frau Buchwald, who lived in the next block and taught violin and piano. I refused. He insisted that she was very nice and liked children.

She looked as though she liked children, all right—for breakfast.

"You'll be fine," he said. But just to be safe, he bribed me with a new three-quarter size violin.

In fairness, I never did notice any children go mysteriously missing from our neighborhood, but Frau Buchwald was old and stout and her house smelled of boiled cabbage. No games lightened her endless drills, including basic piano technique, which I disliked. Her annual recitals were terrifying: first the wait, then the ordeal, playing from memory while trying to control shaking hands and sweaty fingers. Last, the reward: punch served in little porcelain cups and tea cakes on tiny old-fashioned plates.

✦ ✦ ✦

I had just turned thirteen and graduated to a full size violin when Frau Buchwald told my father I needed an advanced teacher. Again, I protested. By then I played last at recitals and quite liked being the best. Frau Buchwald was never warm and cuddly, but she was familiar and safe. She had not, in the end, eaten me for breakfast.

"You want to be a great violinist, don't you?" my father asked.

My face must have given away my secret.

"I thought so," he said. "You need someone strict, but temperament and personality matter, too. You can audition for different teachers and decide on the best fit."

"I have to *audition*?"

"I mean, you'll audition each other. You can't learn from a teacher you dislike. Herr Schradieck was relentlessly demanding, but he never made me feel stupid. I'd have worked my fingers to the bone for him."

"Surely *that's* not necessary!" my mother snapped. "Music is just a pastime, after all."

"It is *not*!" Mother never did understand me at all.

"Sarah." My father never raised his voice, but his tone was firm. "A gift is a gift. Our duty is to nurture it. Where it will take her, who can say?"

". . . waste of money," Mother muttered under her breath, but she said nothing more.

✦ ✦ ✦

Herr Jäger, my first audition, was old, terrifying, and expensive and reminded me of a bird of prey. Herr Mendel, my second, was nearly as wide as he was tall and told my father a girl could never master his virtuosic training. *Ridiculous*, I thought. Surely, he'd heard of Fanny Mendelssohn? And Nannerl Mozart?

Herr Wilhelm Dietrich, my third, played in the Köln Sinfonia, but he was newly graduated from the Köln Conservatory, so his price was affordable. As for my being a girl, he never once mentioned it. He taught in his flat on Johann-Christoph-Strasse in the Braunsfeld district, not far from our house. Mother forbade me to take the streetcar by myself, or to be alone in his flat with him. So, she went with me every week and waited in his sitting room while I had my lesson and instructions.

Herr Dietrich, who besides being young was both handsome and single, treated me with formal respect, always *Fräulein* this, *Fräulein* that. I wished my mother had more trust in me, so I could begin to abuse it; I thought if she were not so constantly, annoyingly present, Herr Dietrich might fall in love with me. It was both easy and pleasant to imagine my grown-up self married to a handsome professional violinist and I spent quite a lot of time doing it. In truth, I'm sure he was exceedingly grateful for my mother's stony presence in his sitting room and, to my great regret at the time, he never once overstepped the bounds of propriety, then or later.

Just as my father had described Schradieck, Herr Dietrich left no imperfection uncorrected. But he was kind. He might address me as an adult, but he knew I wasn't one, and never betrayed impatience or anger. He was funny, too, which put him a step above old Schradieck in my opinion; my father never mentioned his teacher having a sense of humor. Herr Dietrich approved of the technique Frau Buchwald had hammered into me and only rarely had to touch my hand to correct me. I considered making more mistakes, in hopes of getting more such corrections, but I also wanted to please him; anyway, Mother was always right there, watching. So, I mostly concentrated on doing my best.

Herr Dietrich had broader horizons than Frau Buchwald and assigned me French, Russian, and Italian pieces. I couldn't say how, but they were *different* from German music in some mysterious way. I felt I was playing them only on the surface, as if in their melodies, moods, rhythms, and harmonies, they contained worlds that were hidden from me.

Then he decided to push me.

"Every violinist should know how to play the viola," he said. "Few do, fewer still are good at it. We'll just drill a few minutes a day on my old one when you're here."

I protested.

"It was Mozart's favorite instrument, you know," he said, opening a battered case and handing me the viola and bow. They felt huge, heavy, and awkward in my hands.

"Trust me," he said.

Of course, I wanted to trust him and I also felt my mother's stern eyes on my back. I sighed and tried to maneuver the cumbersome thing up under my ear.

"It will feel odd," he said—a gross understatement. "But if it's good enough for Mozart, it's good enough for us."

He explained it. I tried a scale. I couldn't find a single note. I was afraid I would cry in front of him, then die on the spot of humiliation.

"That was fine for the first time," he said. "You learned the fundamentals of the violin so long ago you don't remember how hard it was, or how long it took. One more time, then we'll carry on with the rest of your lesson."

He drilled me on the viola a bit every week. I grew more comfortable with it over time and even took it home to practice on. But I always felt a wave of relief when I shut it back in its case and returned to the violin.

At Herr Dietrich's annual recital, I found myself at the beginning, rather than the end, where I thought I surely belonged—until I heard his other students. Annoyed, but also inspired, I thought, if I practiced hard (and why wouldn't I, being hopelessly in love, in spite of the viola business?), I would one day play as well as these men, from the teenage boy whose blond hair stubbornly resisted his mother's attempts to tame it to a distinguished-looking man with gray hair and a massive mustache.

At least I was relieved to have no romantic competition among Herr Dietrich's other students.

✦ ✦ ✦

My fantasy future crumbled two years later when Herr Dietrich married a woman named Gerda Hoffmann, to whom his mother's cousin had introduced him at a party. She was kind to me, but in my darkest heart I knew she couldn't possibly be worthy of him. It took a long, long time for my disillusionment to fade.

Still, once Frau Dietrich was safely in charge, my mother no longer felt the need to shepherd me across town to every lesson. I'm sure she was happy to be rid of this burdensome chore. I was thrilled, even though my hopes of becoming Frau Dietrich had been brutally dashed to pieces.

I began to nurture another dream, instead, one that grew from a seed Herr Dietrich himself planted in my head: my road to becoming a famous violinist would lead first of all through four years of training at the Köln Conservatory.

✦ ✦ ✦

March 1906, Köln

Both of these beginnings came before the real one, like the prologue in fiction.

The third beginning, the real one, is now: a cold March morning a month past my eighteenth birthday, before the grand front door of one of the grandest houses in Köln. Herr Dietrich keeps a firm grip on my elbow, probably to keep me from running away. In my other hand, I carry my violin in its case. This house, on Leopoldstrasse in the heart of the Lindenthal district, belongs to Herr Ferdinand Kurtz, president of the Bank of Köln. My father's bank.

Yes. It begins here.

The violin I carry is my father's, because he is dead.

Before:

1905–1906

1

FINDING PURPOSE
NOVEMBER 1905–SEPTEMBER 1906

November 1905

My father was struck down in the street by a horseless carriage.

Doctor Goldmann could do nothing for him. In desperation, Mother called a rabbi, a stranger to me and a nice enough man, but he could do nothing either, except offer traditional comfort and counsel, neither of which was at all helpful. I never cared much about religion before, but after that I was done with it for good.

In three days our family's comfortable life shattered, leaving a widow and two girls with an uncertain future. Mother wailed for days, out of fear, I think, as much as grief. Anni slammed her bedroom door shut so hard that it cracked. She hurled books and who knows what else against it for a solid hour. Only later did I hear her sobbing on the other side of the wall.

I couldn't summon the strength to do either.

✦ ✦ ✦

I have one year left in secondary school. Anni has three. Our house in Eberlinstrasse isn't paid off. Within two months it's sold, including most of the furniture and the piano, and the proceeds invested for us by a friend of my father's. We move what little is left into a nearby flat at Forty-six Hildegardstrasse whose walls, dressed in ancient wallpaper, breathe out a faded, musty air of benign old age.

My dream of attending Conservatory suddenly looks as unattainable as the moon.

9

Through these suffocating weeks, I still pretend to take violin lessons. I arrive, make some wretched attempt, and end up in a blubbering heap on the floor. Frau Dietrich steps in at these times, although she's pregnant with her first child and feels chronically ill. Not so long ago I'd have been jealous. But now, as she sits with her arm around me week after week on the little sofa where my mother used to sit, she feels more like an older, wiser friend than the wife of my teacher. Herr Dietrich, for his part, quietly withdraws to the bedroom, there being no other place in their flat to withdraw to, and shuts the door to wait out the hour.

✦　✦　✦

"Marthe. Listen to me."

It's been five weeks. Gerda's voice is gentle. "Everyone grieves sometimes. It's natural, essential. It won't last forever. You'll always miss your father— I know I miss mine—"

"Your father—?"

"Six years ago. An accident. I won't go into it. But I've been where you are. Trust me. You'll miss him, but I promise he'll come to live within you. Someday, you'll begin to feel alive again. Your ability will return. When it does, you'll continue to grow as an artist, deeper, because you've known grief, and higher, because he'll walk beside you. You *must* persevere. Wil and I have discussed this. He says he'll teach you without charge, if necessary, when you're able to pick yourself up and carry on. And then—"

"He can't do that! You're going to have a baby!" Even in my self-absorbed haze, I can't believe he would do something so foolish.

Gerda studies me with a small, quizzical smile.

"He's determined that you not give up," she says. "Now, with the terrible loss you've had and the challenges any artist faces, especially a woman, it may seem an easy choice. Quit, let the violin go, think of it as something you used to do, irrelevant to your life as an adult. Put it away in a closet, find some other path through life. Like freezing to death. Give up, go to sleep. Be honest, you've thought it, haven't you?"

"Yes," I mutter, not looking her in the eye. "What's the point? There's no place for a woman violinist, except teaching beginners. Like Frau Buchwald. And—no, thank you."

"I'll leave the professional counseling to the professional," she says.

10

"I'll only say that even I, and I'm no musician, can tell your gift is extraordinary. And the more extraordinary the gift, the more dedication is required—from you and from your teachers—to bring it to its highest level."

A gift is a gift, my father said. I don't believe in gifts anymore.

"When I was small, my father and I used to go on long Sunday walks through the parks around Köln," Gerda says. "I liked autumn best, when you could kick the leaves and see the colors of the sky though the bare branches of trees. He taught me the names of all the plants. We planned the garden we would have one day. The flowers we'd plant along little brick paths, a cherry tree in each corner, a sundial in the center. A huge oak for shade, with branches big enough to hang a swing from. In summer we would sit on the swing in the shade of the oak, smell the flowers, and watch the shadow progress around the sundial. We lived in a flat, you see. The garden was always in our imagination."

I try not to sniffle.

"For months after the accident, I couldn't look at a park, or a garden. I could hardly go out. It was the first autumn, I think, when I saw bare branches in the Rheinpark and through them the spires of the cathedral across the river, that I first heard his voice." She's speaking more to herself than to me, but her arm is still firmly around my shoulders. "It said, *Look, sweetheart, isn't it beautiful? And the smell of leaf mould, and cooling earth* . . . all the things we used to notice together. It was such a quiet feeling. Melancholy, yes, but also alive, touching so many things at once. I felt so close to him, where before he had felt so far away. Since then, he's stayed close by me, especially when I'm outdoors . . ." Her voice trails off.

"I hope to take our baby for long walks in the parks," she says finally. "Teach him the names of plants and see if my father's voice will speak through mine sometimes. And someday I *will* have a garden and we'll plant things together in it. That's my dream, anyway." She smiles a quick, self-conscious smile, having perhaps revealed more of herself than she meant to.

"It's a wonderful dream," I say. "You'll do it, I know you will."

The doorbell rings. It's time for the boy with the untamable blond hair. I ask Gerda to tell Herr Dietrich I'll do better next time and I try to leave without letting my fellow student see my face. I'm sure he thinks I'm terribly rude.

✦　✦　✦

Later I remember the neglected garden behind our house in Eberlinstrasse. No one's soul was ever soothed there. It was no one's dream. My mother grew vegetables in it, nothing more.

I wish the Dietrichs could have bought our house, and in that unloved bit of earth Gerda could bring to life the dream she and her father cherished. I wish her child could grow up to run along the brick paths she would lay there among the flowers she would plant; climb the cherry trees she would nurture in its corners to reach their ripening fruit; devour cherries, red juice dribbling down the front of dirt-encrusted clothes, while swinging on the wooden seat hanging from her spreading oak as the summer sun slowly cast its lengthening shadow across the sundial she would place to mark its heart.

✦ ✦ ✦

March 1906

My real recovery begins two months after we move, when my mother says one day while I'm trying to practice, "Why are you playing that old thing? Take your father's violin, for heaven's sake. He told you to, remember? If you're not going to use it, I'll sell it. Go on, make some space in the closet! Or I just might."

He did tell me this, in one of his last lucid moments. *Play it*, he said. *Don't let her sell it. Promise!* I promised, but after we moved, I didn't touch it. I couldn't bear to.

But Mother's threat frightens me. I dig the case out at once from the shelf where I stuffed it during the move and take it into my room for safekeeping. The next day, I take a few deep breaths and open it.

My father's violin nestles in its fitted black lining, waiting. Its red-amber wood glows in the dim light of my room. A fresh wave of raw emotion washes over me. When I pull myself together enough to lift it out of the case, it feels warm in my hands and seems to vibrate, as if making sound is more natural to it than being silent.

One of the last things he ever touched. If he's anywhere, he is here, in his beloved violin. The bond between them wasn't one-sided, I'm sure of it. He sometimes said a fine instrument remembers the hands that play it, as the wood remembers the tree it came from.

The unknown luthier who made this violin believed that, too. He paid homage to the tree in a way I've never seen on any other violin. Down the center of the scroll, between the flutes, he carved in low relief a tiny pattern of maple leaves, to honor the wood from which the back, at least, was most likely made. The carving is so delicate it might easily be overlooked, but it always fascinated me, for the luthier's gift of imagination, the skill of his hand in the carving.

I run my finger over the leaves. Their familiarity gives me a little confidence. The strings are still good. It hasn't been so long, really. I tune them, take my time, rosin the bow. Finally, feeling scared, I raise my father's violin to my shoulder for the first time and draw his bow across the open A.

Bright and rich, with a dark edge. Memories flood into my head. Images. Sounds. Only after I regain a bit of self-control do I try again. I play several scales, the timbre of every note so beautifully and terribly familiar. A kind of calm settles over me. My father becomes present in some way I don't understand and he and I proceed to play music on his violin together. The next day I put away my old violin, the inexpensive one he gave me before I started with Herr Dietrich. I have no idea what happened to it after that.

✦   ✦   ✦

Herr Dietrich approves of my father's violin. He says the sound suits my personality. I begin to make progress. As I approach my last term in secondary school, he starts pushing me to apply to the Köln Conservatory. I dreamed of this for years, yet now I doubt myself. We can't afford it. And why bother, when no orchestra will ever hire a woman, gift or no gift?

At the end of my last lesson before the spring holiday, Gerda, now nearly seven months pregnant, walks in and sits down heavily on the sofa.

"Wil tells me you're being obstinate about applying to Conservatory for next year," she says. She knows this already, of course. She's generally home and their flat is very small.

"Obstinate? Realistic. I have no future there."

"You certainly won't know that unless you try it."

"Why should I?"

"You have other plans?"

"No. I've had other things to think about."

"What will you do, then? Get married?"

"Do you know anyone who's looking?"

"Be serious. This is the modern age. No one has any guarantee of marriage at all."

"You did."

"Didn't you know? I'm a nurse. I worked two shifts a week at the hospital until two months ago. Every woman today, married or not, should have some means to support herself. If you want to go into nursing, I'll help you get started. Or you could become a schoolteacher. Or work in your father's bank. All honorable professions for women. But you know you belong in Conservatory."

I saw enough of nurses in three days to last me a lifetime. And teaching school . . . I like my teachers, but that path holds no charm for me. The bank? No. But—

"What's the point? They probably don't even admit women. And if I finish, no orchestra will hire me. Because I'm a woman. The same old problem."

"The Conservatory has admitted women students for several years," Herr Dietrich says. "I had six in my class ten years ago. And women faculty. As to career opportunities, that is changing."

"Hmph."

"Well, slowly. But it is. A few orchestras around Europe include women. Not many yet, and not here, but there'll be more. And there are other opportunities besides orchestras, you know. A solo career, say. Teaching, I might say from personal experience, despite its, ahem, occasional head-aches, can be exceedingly rewarding. And a decent living."

I think of Frau Buchwald. "I don't want to teach children."

"My dear," he says with exaggerated patience, "without Conservatory training, that is precisely whom you will spend your life teaching."

"Anyway, I can't pay for it," I say.

"Ah!" he says. "That reminds me. Just this week I heard about a Conservatory scholarship that seems tailored precisely for you."

"Scholarship?" I say as if I'd never heard the word before.

"The Bank of Köln set it up. Your father's bank. For music students who are children of its employees. Living or otherwise—the employees, that is, not the children. Full tuition. You'd only have to pay your expenses."

Is it my imagination, or is he blushing ever so slightly?

"I never heard of anything like that before," I say.

"I believe it's new," he says. "And in good time. Three or four of your current pieces would be suitable for Conservatory and scholarship auditions. The Schubert, the Mozart, the Spohr. We'll polish them over the next month. You might as well apply, anyway. Nothing to lose. Everything to gain."

"If you get in, you can always say no," Gerda says in a reasonable tone. "And then I'll put you in touch with the nursing superintendent at the hospital."

I open my mouth to raise another objection. But I can't think of one. A tiny bit of my old ambition, still warm under the banked ashes of months of turmoil, flares back to life. Maybe there's a chance I *could*—Herr Dietrich seems to think so, but—expenses—

"Oh, and another thing," Herr Dietrich says. "I have a student for you."

They both laugh at my startled expression.

"A member of the Sinfonia Board of Directors asked me to find him a young woman violinist to teach his daughter," he explains. "She's fifteen and being raised the old-fashioned way, all governesses and private tutors and so on."

"Ridiculous way to raise a modern girl, even a rich one," Gerda snorts. "It ought to be illegal."

"I gather it's her career destiny to become a society matron," he says. "Like her mother. Throw large parties, wear the latest fashions, that sort of thing. Still, to her credit, she wants to learn to play the violin. I told Herr Kurtz I have an extremely talented student—and discreet, which is even more important—who will fit the bill nicely. He's commanded us to come to his home at ten o'clock next Saturday morning so the family can interview you. Be here by nine-thirty and we'll walk over together so I can fill you in on the way. Wear your best dress."

"So the family can interview me? The whole family?"

"The girl's parents. You don't suppose she's allowed to choose for herself, do you?"

Gerda makes a disgusted face. I laugh, in spite of myself.

The doorbell rings. The untamable-haired boy is late. I wonder if that was by arrangement.

"See you Saturday at nine-thirty, then," Herr Dietrich says as he gets up to answer the door.

"Er—"

"Best dress, remember," Gerda says.

"Right," I say.

I spend the entire streetcar ride home trying to sort out what just happened. Somehow, I might have a student to teach and a chance to go to Conservatory after all. For more understanding than that, I guess I'll just have to wait and see.

✦ ✦ ✦

Saturday morning is cold but unusually fine for March: a pale early spring sun, crisp early spring air. Herr Dietrich and I walk past blocks of shops and flats and through a couple of parks into Lindenthal, the domain of bankers and their wealthiest clients, where every mansion we pass is bigger and more ostentatious than the one before.

"Herr Kurtz is president of the Bank of Köln," Herr Dietrich says.

"The scholarship sponsor?"

"The same. Madame Kurtz—"

"Madame?"

"Madame is French. Herr Kurtz told me most emphatically she detests being called 'Frau Kurtz,' or even 'Herrin.' Says it sounds dumpy. She sticks to 'Madame.' As you should also."

"Does she speak German?"

"Oh, yes. Madame is very prominent in Köln society. Gives and attends the best parties, shops in Paris. I gather she's raising Katerina in the same mold. A pity, really. Gerda can be a bit militant at times, but she's right—a modern girl should be educated to do more than entertain."

"They sound dreadful!"

"Herr Kurtz is actually quite decent, for someone as rich as he is. You won't see much of him—very busy man and all that. Madame is in charge at home and very sure of her position, I would say."

"You've met her?"

"At Sinfonia events. Attractive, but, well, French." As if being French speaks for itself. "I have complete confidence in your ability to charm her and everyone else, or I wouldn't have recommended you."

"Why aren't they hiring you?"

"A male music teacher for a wealthy, overprotected teenage girl? Surely, you're joking. As it is, Madame will likely observe your lessons for some time, until she comes to trust you. But they'll pay you well."

"I keep forgetting that. How much should I ask for?"

"If they give you a chance to ask, I'd say twenty marks per hour lesson. But I doubt they will. And they won't haggle. Their offer will be a good one. You can accept it."

I begin to wonder if any amount of money could be worth dealing with a spoiled rich teenager and her Gorgon mother.

"You are absolutely capable of this. Gerda and I have complete faith in you. I've met Katerina. She's young for her age, having been ridiculously sheltered, but quite charming. Sweet, even. Her circumstances aren't her fault, you know. She wears her status gently, as her father does. You'll see. Here we are!"

We turn in at the largest and grandest mansion yet, with Greek columns gracing the porch and a vast front door with stained-glass panels on either side. The front walk passes between formal arrays of still-dormant flower beds ringed with little hedges, perfectly trimmed, and a single small, bare willow tree perfectly centered on each side. A garden for standing up straight in. I try to ignore my pounding heart.

"Ready, then?" Herr Dietrich gives me a jaunty smile, which I don't manage to return, and taps the brass door knocker three times.

We wait.

At last footsteps click inside. The door opens enough to reveal a severe-looking woman in a black dress.

"Herr Dietrich and Fräulein Adler to see Madame and Fräulein Kurtz," he says.

"Wait here," the woman says as she turns away, leaving us on the porch.

"Very smooth," I say.

"Dealing with the Sinfonia Board teaches one a great deal about rich people," he says.

"I'm not sure I want to know."

"Just be your charming, unaffected self. You'll have them eating out of your hand," he says. "Well, maybe not immediately. But soon."

More clicking footsteps. The stone-faced housekeeper returns.

"This way," she says.

We follow her into a large entry hall where a stairway with an elaborate wrought iron railing curves up to the second floor, then through a door at the left into a lavishly furnished sitting room containing scarcely a single straight line. Carpets and upholstery swirl with vines, leaves, and flowers in greens and golds. Every lampshade is a mosaic of stained glass. Carved wood trim curves around the top of every door and window. I feel as though I've walked into a jungle made of wood, cloth, and glass. A handsome parlor grand piano, which looks as if it gets very little use, stands in one corner.

"You may sit here," the housekeeper says, indicating two small bentwood chairs. She closes the door behind her as she leaves for more important business.

We wait for what feels like a long time. Herr Dietrich appears quite relaxed, but he's not the one being examined. I try to distract myself by studying the room.

"All the rage in Paris, I hear," Herr Dietrich says.

"I've never seen anything like it," I say.

"Nor I," he says.

Finally, footsteps sound in the entry. Madame Kurtz sails into the room with Katerina in her wake. Madame is as tall as Herr Dietrich, with pale blonde hair piled on top of her head and a light blue silk morning dress over a high-necked ivory-colored blouse covered with lace. Katerina, behind her, is similarly dressed, but her blonde hair is pulled simply back into a single plait.

"Herr Dietrich."

"Good morning, Madame. May I introduce my pupil, Fräulein Marthe Adler."

I can feel Madame judging my hair, my clothes, my features. Her cool glance slides to my violin case, which looks even more battered than usual in this luxurious room.

"Fräulein." She doesn't smile. "Katerina, sit over there."

Katerina sits, studying me with evident interest. I try a small smile, which she returns.

"How long have you studied violin, Fräulein?"

"Fourteen years, Madame. My father was my first teacher."

"And how long with Herr Dietrich?"

"Five years, Madame."

"You are in the Conservatory, I'm told?"

"I—ah—hope to attend next year, Madame. I plan to apply and also apply for the new scholarship." I color slightly, not daring to look at Herr Dietrich.

"I did not know the Conservatory accepts women."

"Herr Dietrich assures me it does, Madame, and has for some time."

"Do you consider yourself capable at the instrument?"

What a question!

"I have much yet to learn, of course. But I am capable now, yes."

I feel like an actress, playing the role of a capable violinist.

"You can teach a beginner?"

"Of course, Madame." Is she trying to insult me, or is she always like this?

"What method will you use?"

"My own training in the Wandel Method was very effective, Madame. The books are available at every violin shop. They cover basic exercises, theory, and easy student pieces. Very step-by-step."

"This meets your approval, Herr Dietrich?"

"Of course," he says.

"Herr Dietrich has assured us of your skill," Madame continues. "He has also commended your discretion. I insist on discretion. The position of our family in this city will allow for no breaches of trust. None. You understand this?"

"Yes, Madame." I wonder how many skeletons are buried under these parquet floors.

"*Parlez-vous Français?*"

"*Un peu, Madame.* I am much better at German, of course."

"You are a Jew?"

"It is my heritage, yes."

"I will have no Yiddish spoken here. Is that understood?"

"Yes, Madame." Especially since I don't speak it. But I can see what she is.

"Good. I suppose you can't help the circumstances of your birth."

I say nothing.

"Your father is dead, I believe?"

"He died last year."

"I am sorry to hear it." Her tone conveys no sympathy.

I risk a look beyond her to Katerina, whose pale cheeks have turned pink.

"We have purchased Katerina a violin. Katerina—" Katerina suddenly sits up straighter "—go and get it. We will see if Fräulein Adler approves."

Katerina leaves the room. Madame glances out the window to the front walk.

"Ah. Herr Kurtz is back." I hear the front door open and close and a heavy step in the entry. The next moment a large man in a dark suit fills the doorway.

"Hello, my dear. Ah, Dietrich. So good of you to come by. This must be Fräulein Adler. Very pleased to meet you! I understand we shall be hearing great things from you at Conservatory next year." He kisses his wife on the cheek, shakes Herr Dietrich's hand and then to my surprise shakes my hand also. His smile seems completely genuine, as if we're the high point of his morning.

"Have I missed the conversation, then? My apologies. The usual Saturday morning tiny tempest at the bank. We're like the swans, you know. We glide serenely above the water, but below it we're always paddling furiously—ah, hello, sweetheart. You've brought your new violin to show the professionals, I see. I should probably have consulted you before, Dietrich, but I went over to Karol's Violins in the Hauptstrasse and he assured me this one was the best in store. Let's have it out, sweetheart, and take a look at it."

Katerina lifts the violin out of its old-fashioned case and hands it to Herr Dietrich, who inspects it closely, nods, and hands it to me.

"What do you think, Fräulein?" he asks.

I think this old violin is gorgeous, that's what I think. Its wood is a lustrous golden color; the book-matched seam on its back is perfect. Its scroll, I note with perverse pride, is carved in the traditional, ordinary pattern. I wonder how much it cost.

"It's exquisite," I say. "Do you know its provenance?"

"Karol said it was late eighteenth century, German-made. I suppose he would know."

"He would," Herr Dietrich says.

I glance at Herr Dietrich. He nods imperceptibly.

"May I try it?" I ask.

Katerina hands me the bow. I tune and test, adjust the bow's tension and draw across the open A string. The note reverberates through the sitting room, bright and sweet, and is quickly absorbed by all the upholstery. Herr Dietrich's face mirrors my own thrill at the beauty of its tone. I play a scale. An arpeggio. A few bars of my Mozart sonata.

"It's all right, then?" Herr Kurtz rocks forward on his feet, as if he's eager to get on with things.

"It's more than all right, Herr Kurtz," I say. "It's magnificent."

"Oh, excellent!" he says. "I'll tell old Karol next time I'm in the Hauptstrasse. The professionals approve. I love music, you know, but I never played an instrument myself. My talent seems to lie in underwriting orchestras. Never mind. Art takes money. It's a fact of life. But I'm glad Katerina has an interest. I'm sure she'll learn well from you, Fräulein."

Madame Kurtz clears her throat. "We covered everything but the price," she says.

"Ah. Of course. Fräulein, we're prepared to pay you thirty marks per hour lesson. I trust that's satisfactory?"

"Thirty—er, yes, that will be more than satisfactory."

"And we can begin next Saturday at this same time, if that suits you."

"I can begin this morning, if you would like me to."

"Very generous! But next Saturday will be superb."

"As you wish," I say.

"Well then. Have we missed anything? No? Then we'll see you out and let you get on with your day."

I return the violin and bow to the case and step back. Katerina catches my eye, smiles at me and latches the case. As Madame sweeps imperiously past her, I hear her say in a low voice, "Clean it."

"Yes, Mamá," Katerina says.

They ascend the curving stair with the ornate railing to the second floor. Herr Kurtz sees us to the front door himself and waves us out, all smiles.

Herr Dietrich and I are busily dissecting the interview on our walk back to his flat when I realize that my new pupil did not speak one word to me the entire time we were there.

✦ ✦ ✦

"Bourgeois!" Anni sniffs that evening at dinner.

"Language, Anni!" Mother says.

"All right, filthy rich, pretentious bourgeois," Anni says. I'm sure she has no idea what it means.

"The other two were nice, though," I say.

"Give thanks for small favors, then. Snobs like her run the world," she says with the confident certainty of a sheltered fourteen-year-old.

"I hope I can just ignore her," I say.

"And aren't you doing those Conservatory auditions soon?" Anni says. "Same problem, different faces. The admissions committee will be a lineup of arrogant old fossils. They'll sneer down their noses at you, because you have the *gall*—" she glances at Mother, who seems for the moment to have given up "—to say, 'I'm as good as anyone else. I *deserve* to be here.' What right have they got to look down on you? None! You take Papa's violin in there and blow the suspenders off them. That's my advice."

"Nothing to it," I say, wondering when Anni turned into such a firebrand. Her outlook and vocabulary will get her into trouble one of these days, and not just with our mother.

But later I think about what she said and I realize she's right. I deserve a chance, both to prove I can teach Katerina Kurtz and to prove I belong in the Conservatory, starting with two approaching auditions: one to get in and the other for the Bank of Köln scholarship.

In truth, I'd be more apprehensive about these auditions if I hadn't just endured my interview with Madame Kurtz. The self-pity I'd permitted myself to wallow in begins to give way to a slow-burning anger. Over the next weeks, fanned by Anni's outburst, anger begins to scorch its way into my playing.

Herr Dietrich notices and is pleased, whether or not he suspects the source.

If I can hold onto that anger until my auditions in July, I'll be ready.

✦　✦　✦

April 1906

True to Herr Dietrich's prediction, I give Katerina her first Saturday lessons with Madame Kurtz sitting stiffly on an uncomfortable-looking chair with a very high back, observing our proceedings like a well-dressed vulture. She's quiet, at least, doing embroidery, thumbing through a fashion magazine, or writing notes in a little book, which I assume is for policing Katerina when she practices. I wonder if all of the girl's other tutors are kept under such scrutiny, or if it's a special privilege reserved just for me.

Our lessons don't take place in the opulent sitting room where I had my interview, but in a smaller sitting room just behind it, equipped with simpler furniture, a second parlor grand piano, and French windows overlooking a large, immaculately landscaped rear garden just beginning to show signs of life. I can't look at it without thinking of Gerda.

Katerina is an attentive pupil. No doubt conscious of her mother hovering in the background, she doesn't speak conversationally, but only asks questions. Intelligent questions, I'm happy to see. She may be overindulged and undereducated, but she's far from stupid. However, as I suspected would happen, she doesn't practice much between lessons, so her progress is slow. The first sounds any beginner makes on a violin, even one as magnificent as hers, are demoralizing, to say the least, and besides, I gather her social calendar is quite demanding. Still, her smile and her voice are always warm and friendly.

Herr Dietrich's other prediction fails: Madame will not eat out of my hand, not in this world or the next. She remains as cold as stone and barely looks at me as I enter and leave.

I wonder if she has the little sitting room disinfected after each of my visits.

✦　✦　✦

July 1906

The jury of old fossils at my audition contains a surprise: two of the six are women. I can barely see them past the footlights at the edge of the stage in the Conservatory's main recital hall, but I tell myself it's a good sign; maybe this world is not as monolithic as I feared. Herr Dietrich has driven me like a racehorse until I'm as prepared as I can possibly be. My nerves, however, are wound tighter than they've ever been, accompanied by a large colony of caterpillars, several hundred of which have been crawling around in my stomach ever since breakfast.

I know these caterpillars well. They've accompanied every recital I've ever played, right back to my father's friends. Today, they've brought along a lot of their relatives, so many I wonder how my stomach even has room for all of them. I breathe deeply, the way Herr Dietrich taught me, and take my time getting my balance centered, willing myself to become still.

It works, not as well as I dared to hope, but a lot better than it might have. My pieces aren't perfect, but I don't make any real flub until I'm well into them, so I'm able to recover and go on. They allow me to play all three all the way through, a good sign, then they thank me and I leave. My caterpillars and I come back a week later. Feeling slightly more confident because I've already done it once, I play my three pieces again for the Bank of Köln scholarship, not with fewer mistakes, but with different ones. I have no idea if I played well enough. I try to put the whole business out of my mind.

Naturally, that doesn't work.

Two weeks after that, when I return home from teaching Katerina, I find three letters waiting for me on the kitchen table. One contains a birth announcement for Thomas Wilhelm Dietrich, born in late June. My heart begins to race when I see the emblem of the Conservatory on the other two.

When my shaking hands finally manage to slit the envelopes, one letter informs me of my acceptance and the other congratulates me on my Bank of Köln scholarship, covering full tuition for four years. I sink into a kitchen chair and stare at them, rereading first one, then the other. It takes me several readings to comprehend them. I'd scarcely dared to allow myself to hope for admittance, let alone the scholarship. It seemed impossible. And yet it has happened.

I'm going to have my chance.

✦ ✦ ✦

For two days I feel euphoric and weightless. As reality sinks in I begin to feel heavier, until by the end of the week my euphoria yields to anxiety and weightlessness to dread. I resort to giving myself stern daily lectures in the mirror in an attempt to keep my determination from slipping.

I can hardly imagine what the old fossils threw at the foolhardy first woman to attend the Köln Conservatory, or what courage she must have had, but she did it, and if she did it, I can follow her example. I must expect opposition. I will overcome it. Challenges. I will meet them. Setbacks. I will persevere. I will *not*, I tell myself in the mirror, under *any* circumstances, let Herr Dietrich down.

Whatever the Conservatory throws at me, I will endure.

Year One:
The Fledgling
1906–1907

2

FALL, SEPTEMBER 1906

Monday morning.

Above the bustling traffic of Mecklenburgstrasse, the huge front doors of the Köln Conservatory stand open. Students laden with instrument cases and shoulder bags surge past me up a broad flight of stairs and disappear through them as I pause at the bottom, case in hand, bag slung over my shoulder, trying to fire up my determination hot enough to temper my nerves.

Every other new student feels the same way, I tell myself, and always has.

I paid more attention than usual to my appearance today, not that there's much to be done with it. Other than my one good dress, which I wore to my auditions, I have two dresses to choose from, so I chose the less-worn one, and my less-worn shoes, and I wrestled with my hair until my bun didn't have too many ends sticking out. I brought neither hat nor coat—less to carry. Soon enough the weather will turn and I won't have a choice.

In the foyer I join a sea of young men filing into the recital hall. Many stare at me, most with frank curiosity, a few (is it only because I expect it?) with something like resentment.

I tell myself to get used to it.

Inside the hall I spot a cluster of young women down in one corner. I feel the heat of dozens of pairs of men's eyes trained on me as I walk with what I hope looks like confidence down the steps toward them. I think of Madame Kurtz and hold my head high, though not so high as to risk falling.

"Hello!" the woman nearest me says as I sit down. "Are you the first-year?"

"Yes," I say.

"We heard there was only going to be one," she says. "I'm Rosamunde Apfelbaum. Call me Ros. Second-year, cello. My brother Felix is starting, too. That's him, down in front, the tall one with dark hair. You'll be playing ensemble with Berit and me." She taps the woman next to her, who is talking to the woman on her other side.

"Berit. Here's the new girl. Er—?"

"Marthe Adler," I say. "Violin."

"Damn," Berit says. "I mean, welcome and all, but I was really hoping for a violist. Or a pianist. We spent last fall's ensemble having to borrow Käthe—down there with the red hair—for trios. She's a year ahead, but the only woman violist we have, so she's always in demand."

"There must be plenty of violists here," I say, looking around.

"Men, playing with women?" Berit sounds amused. "God, the horror! The pillars would crack and the roof would fall in! It's scandalous enough that we have classes together. No, no, my dear, you step back in time when you enter the portals of the Conservatory."

"To the Dark Ages," Ros says. "We begged the faculty last year. Got nowhere. Never mind that we all grew up playing at home with brothers and fathers. At least, I did."

"And uncles and cousins," Berit says. "But at least the rule keeps things simple."

"Well, I sort of play viola." It's not a complete lie, thanks to Herr Dietrich's insistent drilling, just a wild exaggeration.

"No piano, then?" Berit says.

"Only a little," I say, wondering if it's too late to go back to Frau Buchwald.

"Never mind," she says. "Here they come."

In the general applause as the faculty file onto the stage, I feel a hard *thunk* on my back. I turn around to see a thin young man with blond hair and a very expensive suit in the seat behind me. He kicks the back of my seat again.

"Do you mind?" I say under cover of the noise.

"Not a bit, Fräulein," he says with a big smile. He elbows his seatmate and they both laugh. "Better pay attention, Fräulein," he says, pointing to the stage as the applause ends.

I glance at Ros, but she's watching the stage and hasn't seen.

I recognize the two women faculty members from my auditions.

"The taller one is Professorin Wolff," Ros whispers. "She teaches women string players and pianists, *very* occasionally advanced male students, and she's assistant provost. You'll get to know the Wolff very well and good luck ahead of time. The other is Professorin Hensel. She teaches women wind players." Ros points to a pair of twins sitting at the end of our row with identical plaits rolled up into buns. "She's a bit more honey than vinegar. Or so they say."

Good luck ahead of time, is it? I study Professorin Wolff while the provost makes his speech. A stern face dominated by a pair of straight, dark eyebrows. Dark hair parted in the center and pulled severely back into a bun, a hairstyle many years past its prime. An equally severe dark gray dress. Professorin Hensel, plump and gray-haired, looks significantly more cheerful, but, as my father used to say, never judge character by appearance.

The provost's welcome is long, but not very exciting. Every time there is applause, the young man behind me kicks my seat again. Ros and Berit don't notice. I feel my face flushing with the effort to ignore the anger building in my chest.

Finally, the greeting is over. We're dismissed to our first classes and Conservatory begins.

✦ ✦ ✦

My earliest days are consumed with trying to learn my way around the Conservatory's maze of corridors and stairwells, from the common room and lockers on the ground floor to the classrooms on the second; from the faculty studios on the third floor to the practice rooms in the basement.

The first thing I learn is that in this entire labyrinth, there is no toilet assigned to women, not even near the common room. There is exactly one such facility in the entire place, namely the public one near the foyer by the recital hall. It's large enough, to be sure, designed for the usual rush at intermissions, but it's a several-minute walk from wherever I happen to be during breaks, which are never quite long enough. Welcome to the world of men, I think, as I plan my day around these expeditions.

Most of my fellow first-years seem pleasant enough. I struggle to remember names, though they all seem to know mine by the first afternoon. Some keep their distance, whether out of shyness or resentment I can't tell. One, the same young man who kept kicking my chair at the Welcome, flirts with me every time he sees me. He has a wildly inflated idea of his own charm and I don't like him. I'm carefully polite to him, but give him only minimal responses.

Our first classes plunge headlong into theory, ear training, and history. Wherever I sit, this same young man, whose name, according to the roll call, is Reinhold von Marburg, slides into a seat behind me as the lesson begins and kicks the back of my chair anytime he can do it without being caught. I ask him to stop. He just laughs. He seems to enjoy tormenting me in class as much as he enjoys flirting with me in the corridors. After the third day, I realize I need a strategy, short of sitting in the very back row.

So, the next time he sits down behind me, I turn to the young man next to me and say, "I'm so sorry, I've just realized I can't see over this fellow in front of me. Would you mind trading places with me?"

He says, "Of course not," and we switch seats. It takes just long enough that by the time we're settled, the professor has begun lecturing about the Greek Modes, or perfect fifths, or whatever, and no more switching of seats is possible. It works. I make a habit of it. As a bonus, when my seatmate is quite tall, I suspect that Reinhold von Marburg, who is not, might have some difficulty seeing the chalkboard on which the Greek Modes or perfect fifths are being explained.

Quite often, whether by coincidence or not, my tall, friendly seatmate turns out to be Ros's brother, Felix Apfelbaum.

The professors fall into three camps. Some, mostly younger ones, treat me exactly like everyone else. Some ignore me entirely. A few put me front and center, call on me often, ask me the most difficult questions, try to embarrass me. At such times, I remember my anger at the contempt of Madame Kurtz and further back to Herr Mendel's patronizing disdain. Eventually, I come to think of it not as anger, but as fire.

I burn a mountain of fire in my early days at Conservatory, but I persevere.

✦ ✦ ✦

Wednesday morning.

Nothing about my first visit to the studio of Professorin Wolff suggests that it will become any kind of refuge within the hard world of the Conservatory.

"May I inspect your violin?" she says when I walk in. The words suggest a polite request, but the tone is a command. I open my case and hand it over. She examines it minutely from one end to the other, frowns at the decorated scroll, takes it over to the window to peer inside. I wait, afraid she's about to tell me I have to buy another violin, which of course I can't.

"What is its provenance?"

"It belonged to my father, Professorin," I say. "He studied in Hamburg, with Schradieck. Before that, I don't know."

"Schradieck? He played professionally, then?"

"No, Professorin, only as an amateur. For love, not money, he said."

"Ah."

She hands it back to me.

"The bow." I hand it over.

She examines it just as minutely, then returns it. "No doubt you are aware of this," she says, "but it is rare to find an embellished instrument of this extraordinary quality."

"Emb—?"

"The scroll," she says. "The instrument is unsigned, which is also odd, but I was struck by its tone in your audition. Bright and resonant, with a dark edge. A perfect second violin for ensemble work. Your bow, on the other hand, is quite good, make no mistake, fine for now and for a long time to come. But it is not of quite the same quality as the instrument. Someday, you may wish to replace it."

"I'll remember that, Professorin," I say, though it seems a singularly useless and unaffordable piece of information.

"In the *distant* future," she says.

"Yes, Professorin."

She hands me a score, a Ludwig Spohr sonata. "Sight-read," she says.

I'm not good at sight-reading. Even though the sonata is fairly straightforward, I have a difficult time. I expect at any moment she'll stop me, maybe throw me out of her studio, but she lets me flounder through it.

We move on to several exercises, all of which lie at the outer edges of my ability. By the time my lesson is over, I'm exhausted and have a low opinion of my prospects for survival.

"Have the Spohr first movement by next week," she says by way of dismissal, "and the exercises."

"Yes, Professorin." I pack up, feeling like a used dishcloth, but still determined to be pleasant. I spot a photograph on the Professorin's desk, a portrait of a young woman in clothing of forty years ago who bears some resemblance to the Professorin herself. I admire it and inquire who it is.

"Perhaps one day I will tell you," the Professorin snaps. "Good day."

✦　✦　✦

Wednesday afternoon.

Among the men, Fall term chamber ensembles involve complex negotiations, but for the women it's simple. The woodwind and piano students work together and the four third- and fourth-year string players have the luck to form a quartet: Magde Oberländer, first violin; Hildreth von Prinzenburg, second violin—which chafes her no end, Ros says, but Magde has seniority, so Hildreth must bide her time; the ever-in-demand Käthe Lagersdorf, viola; and on cello, Ursula Wagner, who claims distant kinship with the composer Richard Wagner, although she's apparently never produced any actual proof.

That leaves Berit, Ros and me to play trios. I expect one for two violins and cello, since that's what we have.

"Why?" Professorin Wolff glares at me from under her eyebrows. "Your application says you play viola, does it not?"

"I have some familiarity with it, yes," I say. "I'm far from expert."

"You will improve," she says.

Unfortunately, the fact that I don't own a viola is no impediment; the Conservatory owns instruments for just such situations. So now I have two instrument cases, plus my bag of books and scores to manage on the streetcar every day. In what I choose to interpret as a kindness, the Professorin at least assigns a trio with a viola part I can manage, a middle period Haydn clearly composed for recreation. It's short, no part of it over ten minutes, and even starts off slow, to ease me into it. On a violin, it would be downright easy. But I'll take manageable and be grateful for it.

If Ros and Berit are annoyed at having their talents wasted in this way, they're kind enough not to show it.

✦ ✦ ✦

That night, I ask Mother about the history of my father's violin.

"That old thing?" she says. "No idea."

But the Professorin's question sticks in my mind. *He played professionally, then?* As if that would be the expected path for anyone with Schradieck's training and a professional level, if unusual, instrument. Was that my father's goal? His dream? If so, what happened to it? What happened to him, that he became a banker instead?

I never thought to ask him. Mother doesn't know. Schradieck was before her time, she says. His parents are dead. He had no siblings. There is no one left living who knows the answer.

Not until much later does it occur to me that the Wolff's comment about my bow may mean she thinks I have a future with the violin, that someday I'll not only play well enough to need a better bow than my father's, but be able to afford it.

This is a very encouraging, if short-lived, thought.

The first weekend, after Katerina's lesson and after I've practiced all my other assignments until my fingers hurt and my neck is sore, I start on the Haydn Trio. It's been over a year since Herr Dietrich last drilled me on the viola. Still, if he hadn't insisted back in the beginning, I'd be far worse off now. I must remember to thank him for being such an ogre. He'll say *I told you so*, but he did tell me so, and he was right.

It takes me an hour to remember where my fingers go. I set aside the Trio and practice scales and arpeggios until, even with the mute on, I expect Mother and Anni to pound on my door and scream at me to stop. It takes two more frustrating hours before it starts to feel right. Of course, when I return to the violin, my hand feels unnaturally scrunched up. I alternate, trying to reach a point where I adapt readily to either instrument with a minimum of trial and error. In the end, I fall into bed, my body exhausted, my fingers utterly confused.

✦ ✦ ✦

Berit, Ros and I try to give the piece some coherence in a practice room

35

before our next session with Professorin Wolff. Between adapting to the viola and my new-girl nerves, I'm definitely the weak link. Berit has nearly all the showy parts, to the extent there are any, while Ros and I mostly have harmony, but they're both really good, where I feel very rough. My pitches are vague at best and I miss a lot of notes altogether.

"You're doing fine," Ros assures me as we pack up. "I'd hate for someone to switch me to double bass on no notice."

"Agreed," Berit says. "It'll just take extra practice, that's all."

"Clearly," I say.

On the second Wednesday afternoon in Professorin Wolff's studio, we try again. I spent the evening before on basic drills more than the part itself and that helps somewhat; my pitches are better, though not perfect. The Wolff stops us every two measures with some objection, which rattles me so that I'm playing worse by the session's end, even though the objections aren't all aimed at me. Far from it. Still. I'm exhausted by the time we finish.

"Tell you what," Ros says afterward. "Let's rehearse at my house Saturday afternoon. Stay for dinner, of course."

"I was hoping you'd ask," Berit says. "That was such fun last year."

"Are you sure?" I ask, taken aback. "Won't that be an imposition on your family?"

"No, of course not," she says, looking surprised. "It's lots more comfortable than a practice room. And more relaxed. Come at two."

"Perfect," Berit says. "I'll come early to catch up with your grandmother."

"I'll be there," I say. "What can I bring?"

Ros looks surprised again. "Bring your viola," she says.

"And your score," Berit says.

"Right," I say. "I meant to contribute to dinner."

"That's sweet," Ros says. "But not necessary. We're off to Theory now. See you Saturday."

"Thanks!" I call after them.

Ros turns and waves before they turn the corner and disappear.

✦　✦　✦

From Ros's streetcar stop I walk half a block up Josephine-Lang-Strasse to her house, through piles of leaves the overhanging elm trees have shed faster than the residents can rake them. Number Thirty-four looks solid and respectable, set back from the street behind a generous front garden, which must be lovely in summer. Just now, it's blanketed in leaves from two cherry trees that flank the walk.

"You're early!" Ros says, holding the door open for me. Somewhere nearby, I hear instruments being tuned. "Berit's in the kitchen, catching up with my grandmother. Felix invited his group to rehearse here, too. They've commandeered the sitting room. Felix! Come out, everyone, and say hello to Marthe!"

The tuning stops. Before I even have time to feel flustered, four young men appear in the wide sitting room doorway. Felix, of course, I know from my last-minute seat exchange strategy. The others look familiar, but I don't know their names.

"Welcome!" Felix says. "This is Eduard Desjardins, our second violin. Franz Herzberg, viola. Arnold Blum, cello."

They're a motley-looking lot in their well-worn baggy trousers, suspenders, and rumpled shirts in place of the suits they wear to school, except for Eduard, who even in baggy trousers manages to look well-dressed. Franz looks about fifteen, seriously underfed, with under-combed hair and discreet patches on his clothes. Arnold has a pleasant, open face and inclines toward plumpness.

"I'd been looking out for a chance to say hello," Arnold says. "It's been a little hectic so far. Maybe things will smooth out sooner or later."

"Dream on!" Ros laughs.

"I had the benefit of Ros's complaining all last year," Felix says. "Anyway, where are you all going to rehearse?"

"Upstairs in Papa's office," Ros says. "We'll leave the door open to help build your concentration."

"See you at dinner, then," Felix says. The four of them disappear back into the sitting room and the tuning resumes.

"We need to collect Berit," Ros says. "Come on, you can meet my mother and Oma Judith."

I follow Ros down a passage toward smells of chocolate and ginger into a large kitchen with several windows overlooking the back garden. Berit is deep in conversation across the kitchen table from a small woman with silver plaits wrapped about her head. A plump black-haired girl leans over the sink, up to her elbows in dishwater. A stouter, older version of Ros looks up from kneading dough at a wooden counter.

"You must be Marthe!" she says. "At last, Ros brings you home!"

"Mama, it's only the second weekend! I couldn't have brought her much sooner, could I?"

"Doesn't matter. Marthe, dear, consider yourself at home here, starting right now. Dinner's at six, girls. You're staying, of course." It's not a question.

"That's so kind—" I begin.

"And you need something to keep you going up there. Ros, take the tray up, will you? The boys already have theirs."

"I thought I noticed crumbs on their shirts," Ros says, picking up a tray on the sideboard.

"Hot chocolate and ginger biscuits," Frau Apfelbaum says. "It's a bit cool in Papa's office at this time of year. Just don't spill anything on his work, all right?"

"We'll try," Ros says. "Berit, are you ready?"

"Sure," Berit says.

The older woman stands, limping slightly and leaning on a cane, her extended hand a small landscape of prominent bones and roping veins. Its appearance deceives; her grip is surprisingly strong.

"I'm Judith," she says in a gravelly voice. "Call me Oma. Everyone around here does. I'll find out all about you at dinner. Go on, Berit. Get busy. I want to hear some music this afternoon!"

"You're not likely to hear more than two bars at a time, Oma," Ros says. "And some competition from downstairs."

"Chaos!" Oma Judith says. "I *love* a living house. Now, get going."

In a small back corner room upstairs, three chairs and music stands crowd between a large desk, an even larger drawing table, two wooden file cabinets (one for large flat things and one regular), and piles of papers, books, and odd objects on the floor. Books about architecture and more piles of paper jostle for space on floor-to-ceiling shelves. It feels cozy, like a tree house, with a view of the back garden and the house next door through the yellow foliage of an elm tree.

"Papa's retreat," Ros says, setting the tray down carefully on the desk. "He works in here, but sometimes he says he just comes in to think."

"Great place for thinking," Berit says, pouring the hot chocolate into mugs and handing them around. "D'you suppose he'd let me borrow it?"

"We *are* borrowing it," Ros says. "Try a ginger biscuit. Watch out for crumbs."

Once fortified, we begin to rehearse the trio in earnest. We start. We stop. We start again.

"From measure four."

"From measure ten."

"Let's slow that down."

"I was flat. Let me try again." That's always me. I feel anxious about holding the others back. Berit hasn't really mastered her more complicated line yet, but her sight-reading is really good. I tell her so.

"There are fairly predictable patterns," she says, "so that helps. And a little pretending, so we don't get hung up. No fear, we'll have it to perfection long before the end of term. We'll do at least two, maybe three, since they're so short."

"Hm," I say, taking the opportunity to stretch my fingers.

They're patient and generous, yet I frequently feel like I'm eavesdropping on a private conversation. After working together for a year, Ros and Berit have a level of intuitive communication that I lack. I want it. Badly. But I know the only way to get it is to work, work, and work some more, observe closely, and learn to read their subtle gestures of head and body.

I wonder how many women before us have wanted this opportunity and been prevented from having it? How many sisters were just as gifted as their brothers, maybe more so, and got nowhere, got married off, their gifts claimed by brothers or husbands, or worse, forcibly abandoned and left to rot? The thought drives my concentration on my unwieldy instrument and the music in front of me with such ferocity that my hand cramps.

"Relax, Marthe, you're tying yourself in a knot," Ros says.

I massage my hand and try to relax.

By the end of the afternoon, the viola is beginning to feel a little more natural. My fingers are tired from stretching, my arms are tired from the added weight of both instrument and bow and my neck aches, but the part is beginning to come along.

✦ ✦ ✦

In the Apfelbaum dining room, ten chairs have been squeezed around a table built for no more than eight. Delicious smells roll in from the kitchen every time the door opens. My stomach growls. I hope no one notices. The ginger biscuits suddenly seem a long time ago and I barely remember eating lunch at home.

"Places, everyone!" Frau Apfelbaum calls from the kitchen. "Ros, Felix! A little help?"

"Coming!"

"Over here, Marthe," Oma Judith says, patting the seat beside her. "Time to find out everything about you. Berit, here, on my other side."

Ros and Felix carry stacks of soup plates and a loaf of dark bread to the sideboard. Frau Apfelbaum follows with a large tureen, from which she serves up a rich, paprika-scented goulash. I notice just in time that Herr Apfelbaum and Oma Judith are waiting and set my fork down. Franz notices a moment too late and tries to chew without being obvious.

We raise our glasses.

"To music and the new musicians among us!" Herr Apfelbaum says.

Oma Judith says, "Good appetite!" and at last we begin.

No one says much for a few minutes, but conversations soon build around the table. Felix and his friends gossip about school. Herr Apfelbaum's day featured an argument between a difficult builder and an even more difficult client.

"So," Oma Judith says, turning to me, "how *did* you come to hurl yourself into the Conservatory maelstrom, anyway?"

Conversations stop. Heads turn my way. Under nine pairs of sympathetic eyes, I say more than I intend to about my mother and my sister. About my father. Oma Judith nods.

"The only thing harder than getting through Conservatory," she says, "is getting through it without having your family behind you. If you need one, join ours. Always room for one more, right, Lidia?"

"Right," Frau Apfelbaum says.

"Er—"

"You're going to make it, though," Berit says. "Conservatory isn't easy for anyone and they add a few extra tortures for women, like the toilet business, but you have all the nerve and discipline you need. And talent, obviously."

"Of course, you will," Ros says. "Because you also have us. And we're the best. Right, Berit?"

"That, too, yes."

"We're on your heels, though," Felix says. "We'll be playing circles around you before long. Right, gentlemen?"

"Good *luck*," Ros says. Laughter erupts around the table.

"Ros and Berit are being heroically patient as I try to become a violist," I say.

"That's harsh," Felix says. "And right at the beginning, too. Have you had much viola?"

"Not enough," I say. "I'm lucky my teacher insisted, or I'd be in much deeper trouble right now."

"I can—I mean, if you need any help, I could—I mean, I could give you some tips, if you want—I mean—" Franz breaks off helplessly and blushes to the roots of his hair. "I mean, switching is hard. I studied violin first, but I've done nearly all viola since I was ten. I can help you if you want—that's all."

"Yes, please!" I say.

Franz must be terribly shy—he looks like he wants to crawl under the table. I almost want to laugh, but of course I don't. It's hard to imagine he switched to viola at such a young age. He barely looks big enough for it now.

"And what about you young men?" Oma says.

They're a mixed lot. Arnold comes from a long line of accountants in Aachen, west of Köln. His first cello, at age four, was a viola with a pin attached to the end. He intends to marry his childhood sweetheart, a girl named Alma, as soon as he finishes Conservatory and gets a job. Eduard's father works in the French Consulate in Köln and he has an uncle who plays double bass in the National Orchestra of France. Franz is the eldest son of a goldsmith. He switched to the viola after his mother died and a teacher told him a violist is never out of work, just as Herr Dietrich told me.

"I like viola better, anyway," Franz says. "It doesn't squeak."

After a magnificent strudel of new fall apples, the noise level increases as people sit back, relaxed and full. Oma Judith and Herr Apfelbaum discuss events in Palestine and the latest news from Bohemia, where she apparently grew up. I could eavesdrop here for hours; it's about as much like my house as I am like Kaiser Wilhelm. But too soon, it's time to go home. Everyone crowds in and out of the kitchen, helping to clear the table, and then we gather our cases and bags to leave.

"Same time next Saturday," Ros says as Berit and I step out onto the front porch. "Looks like a full house on weekends this term. All the better."

All seven of us head back to the streetcar stop, full of chatter, music, food, and good company.

I don't say much. This idea, a family you can just join if you need to — and what a family! The noise and energy at the dinner table, yet how attentively everyone listened when I spoke. How fond of each other Ros and Felix seem to be. Oma Judith. A father.

At the streetcar stop, Ros and Felix say, "Goodnight, everyone!" and start back down the street toward their house, arguing with each other in a friendly way.

"Good night!"

"Good night!"

One streetcar after another arrives. Finally only Franz and I are left.

"Thanks for offering to help me with the viola," I say. "I'll need it."

"Oh—ah, sure. Any time," Franz says. He holds his case in front of him like a shield. My streetcar comes rattling up the block.

"Good night, then," I say as I climb aboard.

When I glance out the window, Franz isn't looking at me. He's staring back down the street, past the pools of light cast by the streetlamps and the shadows of trees, in the direction of the Apfelbaums' house.

✦ ✦ ✦

I hear familiar raised voices all the way from the stairs. When I open our front door, Mother and Anni stop screeching at each other long enough to see it's me before starting again. Something about Anni's low marks, Anni's late hours, Anni's irresponsible attitude and the disreputable company she keeps seem to have set Mother off. Again. Her tirades have grown in frequency and vitriol since my father's death and it's always worse in the evening when she's been drinking. Her face is flushed, her hair falling out of its pins. Anni's face, by contrast, is white with anger.

"Excuse me, don't let me interrupt," I say, edging past them into my bedroom, where I shut the door and set down my case and bag.

A moment later, I hear Anni's door slam. Mother hurls a few parting phrases through it and then her bedroom door slams, too. It takes a minute or two for the reverberations to die down in the flat, or maybe they're just in my head, and then a cold, hard-edged silence takes over, broken only by the occasional voices of passersby on the street below my window.

I get ready for bed and sit down to study a little theory before going to sleep. I'm trying to memorize the difference between the Lydian and Mixolydian modes when there's a tap at my door and Anni sticks her head in.

"I saw your light was still on," she says, crossing to my bed and flopping down on it.

"Come in, won't you?" I say.

"God, you're lucky!" she says. "Out all day and half the night."

"It's not even ten."

"She's been like that all afternoon and all this evening," Anni says. "Carping and carping and niggling at me, trying to get under my skin."

"Sounds like she succeeded beyond her dreams," I say.

Anni pulls my pillow over her head. "I shouldn't let her get to me like that," she says, very muffled.

"I can't blame you," I say. "She's impossible, especially at night."

"You know she's been making Bärenfang?" Anni says.

"That stuff with vodka and honey?" I shudder. "Ugh. No wonder she was out of control. What started it, anyway?"

"The usual. You heard the main themes. She repeated herself for several hours, right through dinner. Honestly, she was just so wound up, she couldn't stop. It's a good thing you came in when you did. It threw her off long enough for me to get away."

"Glad to help," I say.

I suddenly feel very tired. I sag back into my chair and study Anni's rumpled form draped over my bed. When did she stop being a little girl? I must not have looked at her properly for the last several months. She and Mother have always argued, even when Anni was small. She wants what she wants and she says what she thinks, while Mother has all the subtlety of a brick wall.

It's worse since Papa died, of course. Even though it's been almost a year, we're all still raw, less forgiving, when we should forgive each other more. We should comfort each other, but somehow we end up pushing each other away. And I've been concentrating so single-mindedly on school, I haven't been present in body or mind to be of help to anyone.

"I'm so sorry, Anni," I say.

She rolls over to stare at me. "What for?" she says. "You're not making her drink that filthy stuff."

"Just . . . for not being here. Even when I'm here, I'm not here. And I'm afraid it's going to get worse. I have a feeling Conservatory's going to be like, I don't know, like . . ."

"Like riding a tiger?" Anni says. "I expect so. I'm glad you're doing it, though."

"You are?"

"Why wouldn't I be? It's where you belong. When you're a famous violinist, you can support me in the style I deserve."

"Ah. The truth comes out. Sorry to disappoint you, but I may not even be able to support myself in the style I deserve. I hope that doesn't change your mind about my belonging there."

"No." She rolls onto her back. "If I were that good at something, I'd go where I belonged."

"You're good at lots of things!"

"Not like that. I haven't figured it out yet. You know what I'd like to be when I grow up, if I could be anything I wanted?"

"A pirate?" It slips out before I can stop it.

Anni sits up and stares at me. "How did you know?"

"Just a guess."

"Well, not many job advertisements for pirates these days. I'll have to come up with something else. Anyway, it's late. Good night."

"Good night, Anni," I say. "See you in the morning."

"Right." She slides off my bed and slips out the door. I try to return to the Mixolydian mode, but I can't concentrate. I give up before long, turn out the light, and go to bed.

3

FALL, OCTOBER–NOVEMBER 1906

The Professorin appears to enjoy her job of culling the herd. Never mind that I'm a herd of only one. Her assignments are brutal, her microscopic attention to detail exhausting. I imagine she's waiting for me to crack, burst into tears, give up, run away. In truth, a voice of doubt whispers daily in my ear, suggesting exactly these possibilities. I know my fellow first-years aren't being subjected to this level of rigor, because I ask them and they tell me. They're astonished at Professorin Wolff's assignments. They shake their heads at my anecdotes. Ros and Berit, though, only nod wisely.

"She did the same to us," Ros says. "Still doing it, in fact."

"Just wait till next year," Berit says.

They've invited me to lunch at the Café Max Bruch, named for a Köln native son who is now a big name in Berlin, just across Mecklenburg-strasse from the Conservatory. Students crowd its tables, debating the merits of Bach versus Schubert or strings versus winds while downing enough inexpensive coffee to keep debating all night. I needed a break, they said, and a bit of encouragement regarding the Professorin and her methods.

"But here's the thing," Ros says. "She's survived in the music world for twenty years. In her mind, she does us no favors by coddling us. She's tough as steel and she wants to make us tough as steel, too."

"I feel more like a twig," I say.

"She wouldn't have admitted you if she didn't think you could handle it," Berit says.

"Such a comfort," I say.

"You're going to be fine," Ros says. "I've heard you play in class. You're playing rings around most of the men. Just don't let up for a minute. The Wolff will make you work for every note, but it will be worth it."

"Right," I say.

In those moments when I contemplate quitting, and there are several in those first few weeks, I think of what Ros and Berit said, and I tell myself in the mirror, *They're doing it. They believe in you. You can do it, too.*

Knowing I'm being toughened up to survive in a male world fuels my fire and my fire drives me to practice, hours and hours, until my fingers hurt. It drives me on Wednesdays through my morning lesson and our afternoon trio session. It drives me to review past lessons on top of preparing for the next and studying for other classes. By the fourth week, Professorin Wolff and I seem to approach the beginning of an understanding: I'm not going to break and I'll attempt anything she throws at me. I won't be perfect, but I'll do my best.

She doesn't stop pushing for an instant. Neither do I. I sense I'm slowly earning her respect and she begins, slowly, to show it, in the tone of her voice, in occasionally correcting without criticism, and in rare, hard-won words of praise.

Ros wasn't just trying to cheer me up. As the weeks progress, I realize I really do have better technique and greater musicality than most of my classmates. Every day I'm grateful for Herr Dietrich's patient, exacting encouragement. It isn't long before my classmates begin to observe this also. A few, mostly friends of Marburg, retreat into jealousy and even hostility. But most begin to show me genuine respect. The language we're learning is meant to connect us, after all. We must rely on each other to speak it as fluently as possible. Their respect begins to open up something inside me: a sense of possibility that in this world there may be a place for a woman who works hard at her gift.

There may, after all, be a place for me.

✦ ✦ ✦

September becomes October. October accelerates into November. I immerse myself in classes: History, Theory, Ear Training. I practice in the basement where the temperature requires fingerless gloves. On Wednesdays Professorin Wolff tears me apart: mornings in my private lesson, and afternoons with Berit and Ros in our Haydn trios, plural, for, as Berit predicted, the first is quickly followed by a second.

Saturday mornings I give Katerina her lessons under the cold, bored eye of her mother. On my streetcar ride to Lindenthal and my walk up Leopoldstrasse under its now-bare linden trees, I always reprise the same internal debate. On the one hand, Katerina's interest seems genuine, and she's making real progress. Moreover, she might one day be my calling card into Köln's upper class, where private music teachers can make a living. My hours in the rarified world of the Kurtz home, though it's quite clear I'm only a servant, balances my distinctly un-rarified existence the rest of the week. Even Madame has her uses: she fuels my essential fire every single time I see her, and I need all the fire I can get.

On the other hand, subjecting myself to Madame's character-building hostility is about as enticing as a weekly flogging. I never open that wrought iron front gate without asking myself if the ordeal is worth it.

But it *is* worth it, above all, for the thirty marks left for me in an envelope on the entry hall table, where everyone pretends to ignore it until I pick it up. I need those marks for my expenses, and I give fifteen marks a week to my mother to help run the household. Our little broken family is holding its own, but every mark helps. And nowhere else would I, as a beginning teacher, earn thirty marks for an hour's lesson.

Yes. It's worth it. Perhaps Madame has been placed in my path for some greater purpose, to stiffen my spine for Conservatory and whatever comes after it. Perhaps I should be thanking her, although it would probably choke me.

Saturday afternoons I rehearse with the others in Herr Apfelbaum's study, where our second Haydn Trio, slightly longer and more showy, comes together more smoothly than the first. Franz, as good as his word, helps me with fingerings and bowing, and, once he's less scared of me, words of encouragement. He even helps me coax a better tone than I'd thought possible from the battered old school viola. In any normal conversation, Franz ties up in a knot of nerves and shyness. But when he becomes the resident viola expert, he's confident, patient, a man on solid ground. His voice becomes softer and deeper. Occasionally he even touches my hand without embarrassment to guide it—until he realizes he's done it and turns bright red. His help, as much as anything else, secures the trios under my fingers.

I look forward most of all to Saturday night dinners with Ros's family, Felix's quartet, and other friends, young and old, who often drop in. The Apfelbaums' table seems to possess an infinite capacity for expansion. Conversations swirl around it in all sorts of directions: architecture (modern, ancient, in Köln, elsewhere); Zionism and philosophy (pet topics of Oma Judith's); painting (which Frau Apfelbaum studied before her children were born); international affairs. I don't have much to add, but every time I get up to help clear the table, my world is bigger than it was when I sat down.

On Sundays my world shrinks to the walls of our flat. I study. I practice. I try to ignore the constant friction between Anni and Mother and I try to avoid calling attention to myself. I try to rest, too, but as the weeks pass, I feel fatigue beginning to set in.

✦ ✦ ✦

One cold, gray Saturday morning in November, when I follow the Kurtz's unsmiling housekeeper into the little sitting room, I'm surprised to see Madame, not in her usual chair, but dressed to go out, her expression reminiscent of eating lemons. Katerina's face, by contrast, belies her unusually demure pose, as if she had been, say, sneaking chocolates—very expensive chocolates.

"The winter holidays are coming," Madame says. "I have a great many preparations to oversee for the season. We will host several parties for the most important families in Köln and every detail will require my supervision. Therefore, I will not be attending Katerina's lessons for the time being. I shall stop in from time to time, as I am able. I expect you to write down Katerina's assignments so I may review them and I expect you not to engage in foolish gossip just because I am not present. And I expect you to leave this door open. Is that clear?"

"Yes, Madame." So that's why Katerina looks so pleased! I've thought from the beginning she must chafe under her mother's constant lurking presence.

"Good." Madame sweeps out of the room.

Katerina and I stare after her as her skirts swish around the open door and disappear. Her footsteps recede up the stairs. A door closes above us. We look at each other for what seems like the first time.

"Well!" I say. "Shall we begin?"

Katerina buries her face in her hands before looking up with an expression of great anxiety.

"Oh, Marthe," she says, her voice low, but urgent and intense. "I've been waiting six months to tell you how sorry I am that my mother's been so horrible to you! I don't dare say anything to her and there's no point, anyway. Believe me, it's not personal. She's driven away so many governesses and tutors, I've lost count. Really, you're so magnificent, just floating above it all, always so dignified. I wanted to tell you while we had the chance—"

The door upstairs opens again and we hear footsteps on the stairs.

"Yes, Fräulein," she says abruptly in a bright, carrying voice. "I worked on the A major scale and the Bach exercises. Shall I try them first?"

"Umm, why yes, let's hear them," I say.

She winks at me and raises her violin.

"Katerina," Madame says, appearing in the open doorway with a broad hat now pinned over her piled-up hair and a navy blue coat with a fur collar over her dress. "I am going to Galérie Française. I will be back in a couple of hours. Frau Schmidt will be here."

"Yes, Mamá. Have a good time," Katerina says.

Madame turns and leaves without another word. We hear the front door open and close. Katerina draws a deep breath.

"At last! We still need to be careful," she says in her low voice. "Schmidt's expected to spy on us, of course. But what a relief to have Mamá gone! Anyway, as I was saying, you've been so kind, and so patient, and I'm so sorry you've had to put up with her. And so embarrassed."

"Your mother does have her, ah, ideas."

"Ideas. That's a nice way to put it. Look, you don't have to pretend. I know she's an arrogant snob. She does have some nice qualities, once you get to know her, but—"

"I somehow doubt I'll reach that level of acquaintance," I say.

Katerina makes a face.

"No. She doesn't like Jews. It makes me ashamed. Papá says people are people. He has a lot of Jews who work for him at the bank. They're intelligent and they're kind, he says. Just a different religion. So what? It's some stupid prejudice she brought with her from France. I'm sorry, I truly am. Can you forgive me for being related to her?"

"You don't seem to share her opinions."

"On lots of things. She's stuck in the world she grew up with. I want to be educated, for one thing. I don't want to be just a hostess my whole life. I see you, you're not much older than me, and you're out in the world. I'd like to be there, too. It must be so exciting to go to school!"

"Sometimes," I say.

"Anyway, I hope we can at least get better acquainted without her breathing down our necks all the time."

"I would like that," I say.

A door closes somewhere in the house. We look at each other and both start to giggle. I reach hastily for my case and take out my own violin.

"Well then," I say again, my voice equally bright and carrying, "what would you like to play next?"

✦ ✦ ✦

Madame does indeed poke her head in from time to time, but not often. For she is the empress of her domain, commanding preparations for the holidays, a task I'm sure she finds more to her taste than policing her daughter's music lessons. She has, as Katerina said, conscripted Frau Schmidt as her deputy, but Frau Schmidt, too, is busy with preparations and also, she doesn't care. So, although we're constantly on the alert for approaching footsteps, we enjoy a degree of autonomy I hadn't previously dreamed possible.

Katerina has excellent hearing. She raises her voice on some technical point well before I hear any hint of someone approaching. I could learn deviousness from her. I expect in this house it's an essential survival skill.

Although our surreptitious conversations necessarily cut into our lesson time, Katerina begins learning faster with far more enthusiasm. Her desire is real, clearly. Her tone is much improved; if she perseveres, she may someday do justice to the beautiful instrument her father bought her.

She's worked her way through all the scales, major and minor, and their attendant arpeggios. She's completed the first Wandel Method book and has made a good start on the second. She wants to learn Christmas carols to play at her mother's parties; happily, her choices reflect the German midwinter preoccupation with snow and holly. I'm anxious that

50

she play them well, since they'll inevitably reflect on me.

In bits and snippets, always with one ear toward the open door, I learn a bit about her and she about me. She's always had tutors and never been to school ("unless you count Frau Engelmann's Finishing School—deportment, making small talk, stupid things like that"). She would love to go for walks around the city, or even just through the park, by herself. She's always wanted a sister.

"They're overrated," I say.

Most of all, she's desperate to have someone—anyone, even her violin teacher—to talk to. Anni and I are as different as summer and winter and, when I'm home, I'm rarely out of my room, but I can't imagine having no one at all to talk to.

She wants to know about my family, how we manage without my father. My struggles at the Conservatory.

"You're very brave," she says.

"Foolhardy, more like," I say.

"I should think all the young men would be after you," she says. "Imagine, so few girls and all those boys!"

"I don't have to imagine it," I say. "Thirty in my year, a hundred twenty altogether, with eleven women. But everyone's overwhelmed just trying to survive. No one has time for much else."

"Would you play something for me?" she says. "I know you must be so talented, and here you're stuck demonstrating my little beginner exercises for me."

"Maybe you could come to our December recital," I say. "You might find it inspiring."

"Oh, I'd love that!" Her eyes shine at the prospect, though whether the music or the musicians are the greater draw I wouldn't care to guess. "I'll ask Papá. I doubt Mamá would be interested, but—"

"Not if I were there, probably not."

She blushes. An embarrassing pause follows, during which I regret being petty.

"But now? Could you play something now?"

I look over my shoulder at the open door. I would actually like to stretch my fingers a little past the mild demands of Wandel No. 2 and I've thought for some time that hearing real music close up might inspire

Katerina to work harder. I'm quite sure Madame would not approve, but I don't know where she is. So, I pick up my violin, tune it while I think a bit, and then launch into a slow movement of a Mozart violin sonata, not being warmed up for anything fast. About ten bars in—

"Fräulein, we are not paying you to practice!"

I stop, wink at Katerina, who jumps up to defend me, and turn to face Madame, who has magically appeared in the doorway.

"Of course, Madame." I can feel my expression, so earnest and innocently sincere any sentient person should suspect it. "I am merely demonstrating a technique to Fräulein Katerina. It is the *legato*: smooth, like the finest silk." I demonstrate a couple of measures of *legato* for Madame and turn back to Katerina. "Does it make more sense now?" I ask.

"Yes, Fräulein, I will try it again," Katerina says, very solemnly.

Madame stares at me with icicles in her eyes before she turns to leave.

"You will remember your place, Fräulein."

"Yes, Madame." I offer a little curtsy to her retreating back for emphasis.

"Indeed," I say, resuming our usual conspiratorial tone when the entry hall is empty once again, "I'm hardly likely ever to forget it."

Katerina buries her face in her hands and shakes her head. But we're both giggling, try as we might to suppress it.

4

FALL, DECEMBER 1906

December 1906

The Kurtz residence looks and smells like a forest fairy tale. I keep expecting elves to appear around every corner. Madame has applied the full force of her considerable energy to festooning every mantelpiece, shelf, and doorway with fir boughs cut in the woods outside of Köln and tied in place with red ribbons that flutter as I pass. Set among the boughs, enormous white candles wait to be lit for parties.

Through the open door of the large sitting room where I had my interview, I glimpse an enormous fir tree encrusted with glittering ornaments. It's even bigger and more lavishly decorated than the one in the window of Hegel's Department Store in the Neustadt. Clearly, no one is going to outdo Madame Kurtz in holiday spirit. As a bonus, her competitive determination continues to keep her too busy to police our lessons.

At her last lesson before my recital, Katerina is bubbling with news. The housekeeper's footsteps have barely died away when she pulls me down beside her on the sofa to giggle about her star turn at the family's most recent Christmas party.

"I played all the carols you taught me and people sang along! I was so nervous, but I didn't lose my place and, oh, it was *such* fun! And one of the young men sat down at the piano and played along with me! I thought that would make me lose my place for sure, but it didn't. You would have been so proud of me!"

"I am proud of you!" I say, and I mean it.

"We're having two more parties before Christmas, plus Christmas Eve, and I'm so excited, I'm going to play for all of them. I liked having someone at the piano, that made it even better! I'm going to make someone play with me every time. My debut! It's not the Conservatory, but it's a big enough stage for me. And speaking of the Conservatory—" her voice drops to a conspiratorial whisper "—Papá and I are going to attend your recital next week! I'm so excited, I'll finally get to hear you play. I can't wait! I'll be inspired—no, discouraged—no, inspired. Definitely! I wish I could come every night."

"That would be extreme. But I'm glad you're coming," I say. "I'm glad your father's coming, too." *And not Madame.* But I don't say it, of course.

"He said he has an interest. His scholarship, you know. And to hear the new talent."

I'd conveniently allowed myself to forget that it's only through the generosity of the Bank of Köln, meaning the generosity of Herr Kurtz, that I'm in school at all. Now is not the time to think about it, however; I don't need any more nerves than I already have.

"He'll hear plenty of talent, I think, even among the first- and second-years. You can tell me what you think afterward. So. Shall we begin?"

✦ ✦ ✦

The Monday, Tuesday, and Wednesday performances all go reasonably well. Some ensembles are more polished than others and everyone makes at least a few mistakes, but no one falls apart. The audiences are mostly families and friends, both forgiving and enthusiastic. On Thursday, our day at last, my viola case, shoulder bag, and a cumbersome bag containing my one good dress, my better shoes, and a hairbrush occupy two seats on the streetcar, earning me annoyed looks from other passengers. Ros, Berit, and I spend the afternoon rehearsing, then huddle over an early dinner at the Café Max Bruch.

The trios are so short we're going to do both. Once I managed to learn the first one, with Franz's help, the second was easier. I feel good about tonight, despite the restlessness of the usual pre-performance family of caterpillars in my stomach, which I seem to have eaten along with my dinner.

Back at school, where no one thought to include a women's dressing room, we're relegated to changing clothes in the stalls of the one and only women's toilet.

When we emerge, there is an awkward pause while we stare at each other. Somehow, I never thought to ask what they were wearing and they didn't ask me. Not that it matters; I only have what I have. But they're both wearing gowns. Simple gowns, to be sure, but flowing and elegant, with open necklines and sparkling necklaces, whereas I'm wearing a dark blue wool dress that looks a lot like my other dresses and that no one would under any circumstances mistake for a gown. No one would mistake my shoes for formal evening slippers, either. They're just decent shoes.

"Oh," Berit says. "I guess we should have talked about clothes. I thought you would know."

"I don't have anything else," I say.

"It doesn't matter now, anyway. We can't do anything about it," Ros says.

"What about your hair?" Berit says.

"I was going to brush it and put it up again," I say. My bun, as usual by this time of day, is falling out.

"I can put it up for you," Ros says. She's just finished doing her own hair. "I used to spend a lot of time playing with my hair. I decided at a young age I wanted to expand beyond wrapped plaits. Here, give me your brush."

"Do you have any jewelry?" Berit asks while Ros has a go at my hair. Berit herself has on a festoon-style necklace of garnets, arranged in delicate little swags around her neck and yet out of the way of her violin.

"I have a little brooch my grandmother gave me when I was small." I'm beginning to feel flustered.

"No earrings? No necklaces?"

"No."

"Hm." Berit looks put out. "You'll need them. Appearance matters, you know."

"Well, yes, I—"

"I didn't bring anything extra. Your neckline's too high for a necklace, anyway. But before next time, we'll have to work you over."

"I can't afford fancier clothes," I say. "We're barely getting by as it is."

"Let's not worry about it now," Ros says, managing to sound both soothing and practical. "There, that will stay put. You could play standing on your head if you wanted to. Lucky you had so many hairpins. Can you see the back of your head in the mirror?"

"No." I hate feeling embarrassed in front of these two, hate feeling inferior and poor.

"Trust me, it looks elegant. Here, Berit, let me do yours."

I wait as Ros gives Berit's dark hair the same treatment as mine, feeling self-conscious in my ordinary dress. How could I have neglected to ask them what I should wear? Only, what difference would it have made? I really can't afford new clothes, let alone expensive formal ones. I don't want my clothing to get more attention than my playing. I don't want people looking at me with pity. And now that's exactly what they'll do.

We return through the labyrinth to the waiting lounge, where the rest of tonight's ensembles, including Felix's, are already huddled in little groups, talking quietly among themselves. Everyone is dressed up in suits of varying degrees of sophistication. Felix and Arnold might be attending a Sinfonia concert or a wedding. Eduard looks very French, perfect in every detail and yet apparently achieved without effort. Franz looks the way I feel. His suit isn't patched, but it's clearly been worn for a long time.

"All ready?" Felix asks.

"Readier than you," Ros says to general laughter.

We occupy an empty corner and begin tuning. Across from us, a group of five students I don't know well are warming up on oboe, clarinet, horn, and bassoon, while the fifth compulsively flexes his fingers. In the remaining corner, a violinist, violist and cellist keep glancing at their pocket watches. The violinist mutters something to the others.

"I know," the cellist says. "Where the devil is he? The time was in the instructions."

On cue the lounge door swings open. Marburg walks in, dressed in a velvet suit and carrying his case.

"God, where have you been?" the violinist bursts out, loud enough to carry across the room.

"What are you on about? There's plenty of time," Marburg says with a lazy glance around the room. His eyes narrow when they get to me. I meet them with my own. I tell myself not to blush, not to give him the satisfaction of rattling me.

"Oh, it's you," he says, as if I were something that turned up on the bottom of his shoe.

"Good luck this evening," I say.

He looks me up and down without answering. My clothes, of course.

"Get over here and tune, will you?" the violist says. "We're up first, in case you'd forgotten."

Marburg will be happier than anyone if I fail. He knows I'm a better musician than he is; our relative abilities are abundantly clear after only one term. He may or may not have figured out it's because I work harder than he does, that his aristocratic name doesn't allow him to skip that part. But if I fail, his belief in his superiority will be confirmed.

For his own good, I am not going to let that happen.

Yes, I've been singled out for challenges no one else has. Maybe because I'm a woman, and poor, or maybe because everyone on this faculty knows I'm a better musician than nearly everyone else. I may be playing a school-issue viola instead of my father's violin. But Marburg's snub makes the heat rise in my face, just in time to make use of some properly channeled fire.

Just wait, Marburg. All of you. Just wait.

The stage manager pokes his head around the door and says, "Places! First and second ensembles to stage right." He doesn't bother to say *please*. I met Herr Schädler last summer at my audition. It was immediately clear that within his domain, which includes the stage and everything behind it, his authority is absolute. If you want to perform at this Conservatory, you do what he says, when he says to do it.

Even Marburg.

The two ensembles obediently gather their instruments and parts and leave. Herr Schädler shuts the door. Everyone takes a collective deep breath.

"Well," Felix says. "Now we wait."

Marburg's group is playing a Spohr quartet, a miniature concerto for first violin, in which the other three instruments play largely supporting parts. Marburg, to no one's surprise, is first violin. Only—

"He could have used a few more hours in the practice room, couldn't he?" Berit says.

"Definitely," Felix says.

"Hear how the other three are having to compensate?" Eduard says.

"Marburg should have been in a bigger group," Felix says. "Fifteen violins, at least." We clap our hands over our mouths to keep from laughing. I say nothing. My caterpillars shift from a slow waltz to a polka.

"There's no way the audience could miss that one," Franz says after one particularly noticeable slip.

"It's hard, though, having to go first," Arnold says.

"You have a kind heart, Blum," Franz says. "Save it for someone who deserves it."

So. I'm not the only person who dislikes Marburg.

They get through the three movements somehow. Marburg isn't getting lost, he's just sloppy, occasionally off the beat, his pitches occasionally sharp or flat. But they give a spirited build-up to the finale, three of them perfectly together and one . . . almost together.

Polite applause. A short break to roll the piano into place in center stage. The quintet enters. A pause while they adjust their chairs, then they, too, begin.

"They rehearsed," Franz says. "Such a radical idea."

The lounge door opens and Marburg's group walks in.

"Sounded great," Felix says.

"Thanks," the cellist says.

Marburg, looking the other way, appears not to have noticed. My grip tightens reflexively on my viola.

They pack up and leave. Marburg disappears first, letting the door close behind him. Felix jumps up to hold the door for the others.

"Damn, I'm glad that's over," the cellist says. "Thanks, Apfelbaum. Good luck, everyone." Felix closes the door behind him.

Franz wants to go sample the refreshments in the foyer at intermission, but the more experienced Berit advises against it.

"It'll wreck your concentration," she says. "Stay focused. There'll be more food afterward, anyway. Didn't you eat dinner?"

"Yes," Franz says. "But that was a long time ago."

"You'll live," Berit says. Then, to us, "Let's tune."

Ten minutes later, the door opens again.

"Places! Third and fourth ensembles to stage right," Herr Schädler says.

I've heard he never bothers to learn anyone's name. Students come, students go. In his empire, they're interchangeable.

We all stand up, stretch, collect our instruments and parts, and follow Herr Schädler up the hallway to his post at stage right. The boys settle into chairs. We line up: me first, then Ros, then Berit. My heart races. My caterpillars switch to line-dancing. I remember Marburg's expression when he saw my dress. He'll never know it, but he's one big reason I'll be good tonight.

"Ladies," Berit says from the back of the line, "we are going to make Papa Haydn proud!"

I smile in the dark.

The house lights dim. I feel different from last summer, when I waited to step out into these same footlights for my auditions. Now I feel so much more—

"Go!" Herr Schädler says.

The audience applauds politely above a little rippling murmur, maybe about my dress, or maybe it's my imagination. We bow, take our seats. Berit insisted we rehearse these details last week, largely for my benefit. I'm glad of it: I feel professional and ready, my dress momentarily forgotten. We wait, poised, still, our eyes on Berit, who pauses, nods, and then we're off.

In the Adagio of the second trio, something suddenly clicks into place. With no lessening of intensity, suddenly I no longer have to struggle to get the old viola to sound like a more exalted instrument. The music begins to flow. The rest of the trio tumbles out of us, slow, fast, loud, soft, Ros and I supporting Berit's line, the three of us supporting each other. It builds to its showy, satisfying conclusion and then, with a final flourish of our bows, it's finished.

For a second, the last notes reverberate through the still auditorium and then applause rises from the darkened seats. We did it! I can see Ros and Berit are pleased, and pleased with me. I've held my own. I've made the school viola sing.

I've proved I belong.

We stand, take our bows—this we also rehearsed. Then, Berit leading and me last, we exit the stage.

"The best by far!" Arnold says. The boys are lined up, waiting.

"Until now," Felix says with a poke at Ros.

"It's a fantastic way to spend twenty minutes, isn't it, ladies?" Ros says.

"The best!" I say.

"Yes, indeed!" Berit says. "Good luck to you, gentlemen!"

"Yes, good luck!"

"Good—"

"Go!" Herr Schädler says. The four of them walk out onto the stage.

"Let's watch," Ros says.

The boys have ambition, I'll say that for them. And they're good. *Very* good. They've chosen Beethoven's Opus 18 No. 3, the first string quartet the master ever wrote. I'd only ever heard snatches of it on Saturday afternoons; I had no idea they were learning something of this magnitude. I feel suddenly as if I accomplished very little this term. I watch the group on the stage, watch them watch each other, signal, turn pages at lightning speed. They look so young, yet sound so professional. After the first movement, I settle back into my chair and allow myself to be captivated by the music. Berit listens intently with her eyes closed, her face a study in concentration. Ros sits forward on her chair, staring fixedly at Felix, her face a study in pride and love. I wonder in passing if I've ever looked at Anni like that.

I'm pretty sure I have not.

✦　✦　✦

The Conservatory foyer, usually cavernously empty, eddies with students, parents, and friends milling about and chatting. Franz disappears toward a long refreshment table at one side and returns with a small plate piled with cookies in one hand and a cup of punch in the other, which he finishes in two swallows.

Oma Judith limps over and kisses each of us on both cheeks.

"Not a bad evening's concert," she says. "Not bad at all."

Other families crowd around: Berit's parents, Eduard's parents, even Arnold's parents and his sweetheart, Alma, who came by train from Aachen, and Franz's father and stepmother with Franz's two younger brothers and three younger sisters, all as thin as he is. At last, I spot Mother with Anni and drag them over to meet everyone. Frau Apfelbaum immediately takes Mother under her wing and soon they're conversing like old friends. Ros does the same with Anni, who looks delighted at the older girl's genuine interest. I marvel at this gift the Apfelbaums possess.

"You have improved, Fraülein." Professorin Wolff appears from the crowd.

"Thanks to your coaching, Professorin," I say.

"I confess I didn't think that viola could produce sound of such quality."

"Franz helped me get the most out of it."

"Franz?" Her eyes narrow.

"Herzberg. From the fourth ensemble. He was very kind."

"That group, eh? Hm. Anyhow, the trios were decent. Notes tomorrow morning, nine o'clock. Be prompt."

"Yes, Professorin," we say.

She turns to Berit's father. "Always good to see you," she says as they shake hands. She nods to our families, turns and strides away.

The boys stare after her.

"Is she always that cuddly?" Felix asks.

"She said we were decent," Ros says. "Translating, I'd say that means we were fantastic. You notice she didn't say *you* were decent."

"So much for maternal instinct," Felix says.

"You'll get more maternal instinct from the Kaiser," Ros says. "But if you want a hard-to-please perfectionist, she's the hardest-to-please there is."

"I'll bear it in mind," Felix says.

"Who was your coach, anyway?" Ros says. "You never mentioned."

"Professor Nodelmann," Felix says. "He didn't really get in our way. Made a few comments once in a while."

"He fell asleep once while he was coaching us," Eduard says. "At the Paris Conservatory, that would have got him thrown out. Here . . . puh! His comments weren't useful, either."

"Do you mean to tell me," Berit says, "that you four first-years put that quartet together in three months without even a proper coach?"

"More or less," Felix says.

"*Very* impressive," Berit says.

I duck away to try the cookies and nearly walk into Herr Dietrich and Gerda.

"Your viola playing has improved dramatically!" he says.

"I have you to thank for insisting I learn which end makes the noise," I say. "And Franz, over there, helped. And of course, Professorin Wolff."

"Ah, yes, the Wolff," Herr Dietrich says. "I never had her, of course. Is she as ferocious as her legend claims?"

"Not at all," I say. "More."

"You hide the teeth-marks well," Gerda says. "Anyhow, you were terrific. We were impressed overall, except for the first group's first violin."

"He's got more money than discipline," I say.

"That's young Marburg, isn't it?" Herr Dietrich says. "His father bragged at the last Sinfonia Board meeting that his son was starting here. I thought that might be the situation. You know him, then?"

"A bit," I say.

"Anyhow, well done," he says. "We're off now. Thomas is with my mother, and teething, speaking of teeth-marks. Not a happy time for either of them, I'm afraid."

Gerda hugs me and kisses my cheek. "I won't call the nursing school just yet, all right?" She winks and they disappear into the crowd.

I'm almost to the refreshment table when Katerina, her face shining with excitement, surges out of a knot of people toward me. Her father emerges behind her.

"You were fantastic!" she squeals.

"Clearly the bank's scholarship was well awarded," Herr Kurtz says. "But I was under the impression you were a violinist. Did you switch?"

I explain the limitations of having so few women.

"That is unfortunate," he says, "if perhaps useful in some ways. Surely the situation will change?"

"It depends on who begins next year," I say. "Or if they change the rules."

"We may hope," he says. "At any rate, we'll say goodbye until after the New Year—"

"Oh, no, Papá!" Katerina says. "I need one more lesson this Saturday, to be sure my Christmas carols are perfect! Please, Marthe, say you can come!"

"Of course," I say, wondering if I'll be awake by Saturday.

"Settled, then," Herr Kurtz says with an indulgent smile. "Katerina, my dear, are you ready?"

"See you Saturday!"

I see Katerina's head turning every which way, making sure she's seen every young man in the place, before she finally disappears.

"Good to keep sucking up," says a familiar voice behind me. I turn to see Marburg sauntering past. "Maybe they'll buy you a proper dress for the next recital."

I can't think of a single thing to say in response to this. I pull myself up to my full height, which is almost even with his, look him in the eye, and turn away. But I can feel heat rising on my neck and my face. When I reach the refreshment table I realize my teeth are clenched so tightly, I have to make a conscious effort to unclench them.

I pile a plate with cookies and head back. When I arrive, everyone is talking to somebody different and Felix is busy learning the names of every one of Franz's brothers and sisters.

The crowd thins. The euphoria of our success begins to ebb, leaving me sagging with tiredness. I see fatigue building in the others' faces, too.

"Remember," Berit says, "nine tomorrow morning with the Wolff. Bring your instruments."

"I'll be there," I say, suppressing a yawn. "By the way, how does she know your father?"

"She taught him when he was a student here," Berit says. "The story is, he showed enough promise that she wouldn't trust him to anyone else, even though she had barely started and wasn't much older than he was. She does teach men occasionally, you know, if she thinks they're exceptional enough. And tough enough. So, she's actually our family Wolff."

"Every family should have one," Ros says. "Stop that, Marthe, you'll get us all yawning."

"Too late," Felix says. "I was doing it already."

On the mostly empty streetcar on the way home with Mother and Anni, I lean against them, as if I were a little girl. Mother pats my shoulder, a gesture I had forgotten.

"You know what I said to the lady next to me?" Anni says. "While everyone was applauding after you finished, I said, 'That's my sister on viola. She's really a violinist, but she can play whatever they give her.'"

"Let's hope they don't give me a trumpet next."

"Gracious, no!" Mother says, shuddering.

"And the lady said, 'That's wonderful. That's what life is. I wish her all the best.'"

I reach out and give Anni the hug I've been meaning to give her for a long time.

I'm so tired I could fall asleep right here on the hard wooden seat, with screeching wheels and the clanging bell for a lullaby. Tired, but happy. It went well. I've made it this far. Then, on the heels of my happiness, the deep, empty place I've sealed off with the demands of daily life chooses this moment to crack open.

My father would have loved tonight, even if I was only playing a school viola and not his violin. Maybe he would have liked it even better, knowing I could meet the challenge. But he will never know.

I wonder if happiness and sadness will always walk hand in hand like this for me.

Well, let them. If that's the price of remembering him, I'll pay it. I know what he would say to me at this moment: *You're going to be just fine. You can do it. All you have to do is just not give up.*

At this moment, I believe him.

I survived the first term. I *will* make it through Conservatory. I'll play anything they give me.

Because that's what life is.

✦ ✦ ✦

We begin. The Wolff stops us, makes a correction. We begin again. If she's satisfied, we move on. If not, we play it again. And again. We play on. Another correction. Tempo. Phrasing. Who should be louder than whom. Infinitesimal adjustments. We play it again. It takes an hour and a half to get through the two trios.

"Now, then," she says as we pack up. "A word about next term."

Inwardly, I groan. I only stopped thinking about this term ten seconds ago.

"I need to start working on my solo recital for spring," Berit says.

Knowing Berit, she'll take something exceedingly difficult and make it look easy. But that means—

"Me, too," Ros says.

"In addition to an ensemble?" I ask, suspecting the answer.

"You heard them, Fräulein," the Wolff says. "You will work with me."

"But Orchestra's next term," I say. "I've never been able to play in an orchestra."

"Orchestra is for the men," the Wolff says in a tone of stating the obvious.

"But why? I know professional orchestras won't hire us. But it's absurd to bar us here at school."

"It is not considered proper," she says. "The presence of women would risk damage to the orchestra's reputation, not to mention distract the musicians. Moreover, as women do not play in professional orchestras, this training does them no good. Solo work is far more valuable."

"But I want—"

"It is not a matter of what you want and not open to discussion. Here are your solo assignments to begin over the holidays." She hands around scores; mine is a Mozart sonata.

"But—"

Professorin Wolff furrows her eyebrows and folds her arms in a posture I can only describe as menacing. "You object?"

"No, of course not," I say. "I love Mozart. I only want to be treated like every other student."

"And so you are, like every other *female* student," she says. "Now. Go home and rest, all of you. Be back here after the New Year with something to show me."

"Yes, Professorin," we say.

We pack up and file out.

"So, you wanted to be in the orchestra," Ros says as we descend the stairs.

"It looks like fun," I say. "And a whole different level of musicianship."

"We *could* stop by the library and see what they're playing next term," she says. "Just for curiosity's sake."

"Well . . ."

"You two go," Berit says. "See you over the holidays?"

"Yes!" we chorus.

"Berit wants to be a soloist, you know," Ros says as we head down to the basement. "It's so ironic, a woman soloist can play in front of an orchestra, that's perfectly respectable. But not in the sections."

"It's ridiculous," I say. "And unfair. It's how most musicians make a living. Why should it be closed to us?"

"Someday things will change," Ros says. "Here we are."

The library, currently deserted, occupies a dimly lit corner of the basement and is crowded with shelves packed to the ceiling with scores and individual parts. The notice board is covered with papers announcing obsolete schedules and past events.

"Here it is," Ros says. "Next term's assignments for first- and second-year orchestra."

It's a daunting list. Mozart's overture to *The Marriage of Figaro* and two symphonies, Beethoven No. 1 and Schubert, also No. 1.

"The thing is," Ros says, "Felix has been in youth orchestras for years and he always says that orchestra parts aren't as hard as solo work or small ensemble parts. Not trivial, by any means, but work you can learn pretty quickly, especially if you're lucky enough to be playing your preferred instrument."

"Are you saying I could just learn these violin parts?" I say. "But why, if they won't let me in?"

"You don't actually know if they won't let you in until you go sit in a chair and start playing. How brave do you feel?"

"You mean, just go and pretend I belong there? They'll throw me out of school!"

"They won't," she says. "Especially if you can already play the parts. I've heard the orchestra conductor, Zeidler, prefers teaching to arguing about rules and he loves a student who actually prepares."

"But the Wolff said—"

"The Wolff told you what the rule is. She didn't say you couldn't test it."

"What about you? Are you planning to infiltrate the orchestra, too?"

"I'm tempted," Ros says. "I didn't try it last year. I didn't feel secure and Berit didn't want to. I do have to work on my solos, though . . ."

I'm seized by a momentary recklessness. "I will if you will," I say.

Ros grins. "You're on," she says. "Let's find the parts. No one else will have theirs yet—most people won't bother until the start of the term."

We have a considerable search; the library's arcane organization reflects the disordered mind of its original librarian back in 1850. But at last, we find the parts we're looking for. I decide on the second violin part rather than the first, on the theory that I might have a better chance of surviving if I'm less conspicuous. We sign the register with our first initials and last names to make our subversion a little less obvious, slip the parts into our bags, and climb the stairs back up to the main floor.

"All these plus a Mozart sonata," I say. "I guess I won't sleep the whole break after all."

"Nor I," Ros says. "You'll have to come over, though. The holidays are fun."

"Are they?" I think of Mother and Anni, arguing about whatever it is this time.

Ros's glance suggests she understands all too well. "We'll work something out," she says.

"I'd like that," I say. "And—thanks for being my partner in crime. We'll take the orchestra by storm, whether the Wolff likes it or not."

"She'll come around," Ros says.

"They wouldn't throw both of us out of school—I hope."

"I'm guessing the old guard may try to bluff us, but if we hold our ground and look them in the eye, they'll back down and let us stay," she says.

"I hope you're right," I say.

Our footsteps echo on the marble floor of the foyer, where only last night we milled about with our families, feeling happy and accomplished. Now, we're starting over. Outside, we button our coats against cold winter sunshine that brightens the air but doesn't warm it. On the streetcar to Ehrenfeld, we talk of other things. The Christmas Market, which one need not be Christian to enjoy. Ros's cousins, arriving next week from Frankfurt.

"Come over any time," Ros says when we reach my stop. "Give Oma Judith someone else to talk to."

"I will," I say.

"Help keep things chaotic," she says. "Like Oma always says, we like a living house."

"I'll bring some chaos with me," I say.

I hop off the last step onto the sidewalk. The streetcar clangs away and I turn my footsteps up Hildegardstrasse, toward home.

✦ ✦ ✦

So, I don't sleep through the winter break after all, not all of it. The first few days, yes. I sleep so long and hard I wonder if I might be really ill, until Mother screeches at me to get my lazy self up and start making myself useful. By late afternoon I'm tired again, longing to crawl under my eiderdown and sleep some more. But my new assignments call. When I begin studying them, I immediately discover that the orchestra parts aren't noticeably easier than my sonata. For motivation, I imagine myself holding firm in the back of the second violins while some old fossil tries to force me to leave. If I can prove I know the parts when no one else does yet, I'll have a stronger chance of staying in that chair.

I hope.

✦   ✦   ✦

In an effort to be a better sister than I have been, I take Anni to the Christmas Market in the Neumarkt. Up and down we wander past rows of stalls, clutching cups of hot chocolate and admiring crafts of carved wood, knitted wool, and blown glass. On our third circuit, we linger before a stall of particularly fine woolens.

"Tell you what," I say, seized by a sudden impulse. "I'll buy us each a scarf. It's only going to get colder for the next few months and a wool scarf will last for years if you store it in your cedar box."

"Really? Can you afford—?"

I shrug. "Yes. No. Maybe. You mustn't risk pneumonia going to and from school, after all."

"Nor you," she says.

"Absolutely," I say.

"What about Mother?"

"Do you think she'd use one? She hardly ever goes out."

"If we buy ourselves presents, we ought to buy her something," Anni says. "You're right, though, maybe not a scarf. I know—earmuffs, for when you practice."

"That bad? But I'd have to buy them for the whole building. I can't believe people don't complain."

"It's all brick," she says. "They can't hear you. That's why you get such good sound."

"How do you know? Wait—never mind, don't tell me."

"I was hanging a picture. I broke off a piece of plaster and there was brick underneath," she says. "When the maintenance man fixed the plaster, he told me the whole building was brick. He even hung the picture for me. He was really nice."

"I don't remember that," I say.

"You're always gone. Let's get Mother a shawl. She can wear it at home and be cheap on the heat."

In short order we both sport velvety woolen mufflers around our necks, mine in shades of blue and gray and Anni's in bright red. A parcel under my arm contains a forest green shawl. We wander a bit more, indulge in a last hot chocolate and, lighter of heart and purse, head for home.

Later, I realize that, for all their daily locking of horns, it was Anni, not I, who suggested buying our mother a present.

✦　✦　✦

I enjoy a few visits to the Apfelbaums, but after the first two weeks the start of term looms closer and we all feel an increased need for serious practice. So, I stay home in my room most of the time, except for a walk in the early afternoon when the air is warmest, practicing and hoping Anni's friend the maintenance man is right about the walls. The main person who complains is Mother.

"Maybe we should have got the earmuffs," Anni says.

"Maybe so," I say. "At least she likes the shawl." Or so we infer. When we gave it to her, she kept repeating that we couldn't afford it, until I pointed out that we bought it with my earnings and Anni's savings and the least she could do was try it on. So, she threw it around her shoulders and humphed off to look in the mirror.

"It brings out your eyes," I said, which was true.

"Hmph," she said.

But she's worn it every waking minute since.

5

WINTER, JANUARY–APRIL 1907

January 1907

Monday morning.

Too soon, the church bells of Köln ring in the New Year. Too few days later, I'm back on the streetcar with my violin case, my Mozart sonata and three orchestra parts in my bag, my coat buttoned against the January cold, and my new scarf wound around my neck.

In the Conservatory, familiar faces, not strangers, fill the corridors. We greet each other by name, inquire after each other's holidays. Study groups form on the spot and include me. I don't feel nearly as much of an oddity as I felt before. Our new classes aren't any easier, but they seem less overwhelming. It feels right and good to be back.

A few students have left. Sadly, Marburg isn't one of them.

Still, my caterpillars are out in force and I have to keep unclenching my teeth. Ros presents a calm exterior, but I know she's nervous, too, by the way she toys with her food at lunch.

"There was quite a little crowd in the library this morning," she says. "I just happened to pass by. It seems everyone was trying to check out orchestra parts at the same time."

"Interesting," I say.

We both giggle.

"Who's concertmaster?" Berit asks.

"Bernd Meyer," Ros says.

"Lucky for you two," Berit says. "He's solid and his mother teaches violin. You'll have an ally."

"Good to know," I say.

"Good luck, then," Berit says.

"You think we're crazy, don't you?" I say.

"Yes," she says.

✦　✦　✦

Monday afternoon.

After studying the seating chart posted by the stage, Ros and I place chairs at the rear of our respective sections next to people without stand-mates. Several students already in their seats stare at us. Ros, over in the cello section, exchanges a few words with her stand-mate, who shrugs.

"Fräulein?" a startled voice says. It belongs to Leo Scheidel, a plump, shy second-year whose talent, Ros says, tends to be derailed by nerves. Which, I suspect, is how he ended up in the very back of the section, with no stand-mate if I hadn't miraculously appeared.

"I thought girls weren't in Orchestra." He looks genuinely confused.

"I'm trying out a new rule," I say. "I hope you don't mind if I sit here."

"Oh! No. I thought I wouldn't have anyone to sit by."

More people filter in, looking for their seats and doing double takes at me. I just smile back and begin tuning. Nearly everyone is seated when Reinhold von Marburg slouches in with a few of his friends. He stops when he sees me.

"What are *you* doing here?" he says in a voice loud enough that a dozen heads turn in our direction.

"Tuning," I say. "Oh, look, here comes the conductor."

"You're not allowed—"

"Places, everyone! Take your seats. Time to get started." Herr Zeidler, moving briskly for a man of his age and girth, steps up to the podium and raps on it with his baton.

"*Sir!*" Marburg says.

So much for being inconspicuous. I might be out before I even have a chance to start.

"Sir! Women are not allowed in Orchestra! I demand Fräulein Adler be removed." He catches a glimpse of Ros in the cello section. She ignores him.

"*Two* women! Sir, this violates the rules."

"What?" Herr Zeidler peers at Marburg as if he's babbling nonsense.

"*Women*, sir! Two *women* are attempting to force their way into Orchestra, against the rules and against all tradition." He casts a sweeping glance around to be sure more of us aren't hiding in other sections. A general mutter, followed by muffled laughter, runs through the orchestra.

"Really?" Herr Zeidler says, looking surprised. He glances around and spots Ros, then me. "Do you ladies have permission?"

"If you give it, Herr Zeidler," Ros says. "We're prepared, we've studied the parts, and we would like to stay."

"Studied the parts?" He looks from Ros to me.

"Yes, Herr Zeidler," I say. "We're prepared to rehearse."

Another wave of muttering, probably from the people who were crowding the library this morning.

"Demonstrate," Herr Zeidler says. "Play the Mozart."

"Yes, sir," I say. My part is already open to it. I play the opening bars at tempo, first the scurrying, intricate passage for the indispensable Figaro, followed by the more dignified theme of Count Almaviva.

Herr Zeidler holds up his hand to stop me. There is complete silence from the orchestra. I see a few open mouths out of the corner of my eye. He turns to Ros and signals. She responds with the cello part of the same passage.

"Who else has practiced this?" Herr Zeidler looks out over the orchestra. A few hands go up, including, I'm happy to see, those of Felix's quartet-mates and Meyer, the concertmaster. No one appears eager to be put on the spot. Felix, a few rows ahead of me in the first violins, turns to catch my eye and winks.

"Well, then," Herr Zeidler says, looking blandly at Marburg, whose face is turning red, "it appears the ladies are better prepared than most of you. Therefore, there is no time to be lost. Our concert is barely ten weeks away and we have much material to cover. If they can be patient while you catch up, they may stay as far as I'm concerned. Places, please, Herr, ah—"

"Marburg. I will report this!"

"If you wish. Sit down, Herr Marburg, so we can begin."

Marburg drops into his seat in the first violins and throws open the lid of his case, glowering. I realize I've been holding my breath and let it out. Leo gives me an admiring look. I flash him a small smile in return. I may yet be thrown out, but at least it didn't happen today.

What I don't realize is just how easily I've made an enemy.

✦　✦　✦

Wednesday morning.

"You did *what*?" Professorin Wolff pulls herself up to her full, rangy height and glares down at me under her beetling eyebrows.

"Herr Zeidler gave his permission," I say. "We had learned the parts already."

"*We*, Fräulein?"

"Ros Apfelbaum and I, Professorin. We both joined."

"I told you it was not done," the Wolff says. "The reputation of the Conservatory is at stake here. And, whether you realize it or not, your own reputation as well."

"Professorin, the reputation of the Conservatory is to produce top quality musicians, isn't it? You know Ros and I are capable of mastering the music. We spent the holiday learning our parts, as well as our solo work. And I've always wanted to be part of an orchestra. The other students seem to have no objections, er, most of them, anyway. If there are disciplinary problems, I'm sure Herr Zeidler can handle them. It is up to him, after all, and, as I said, he gave his permission."

"You have a full load of other work. You can't be allowed to drag down the quality of the orchestra because of your other commitments. Or allow your own work to suffer."

"We can do it," I say, sounding more optimistic than I feel, even though all the men are doing it and always have.

She glares at me for what seems like a full minute, then heaves a sigh that speaks eloquently of the intractability of young people and the imminent decline of civilization.

"We shall see, I suppose. I shall inform Herr Zeidler that he is not to allow you to slow the orchestra down in any way. I expect you'll come to your senses soon enough. Let me hear what you've done with the sonata."

So, she's already annoyed with me before my lesson even begins.

✦　✦　✦

Saturday morning.

Madame makes a show of returning to her high-backed chair, but as soon as we're safely underway, she departs for more important, or more congenial, business elsewhere. Katerina is improving dramatically, either because of my fine teaching or at the enticing prospect of playing duets with Otto von Marburg at the piano. Because it was he, she tells me in a giggling whisper, the better-looking elder brother of Reinhold, who played the piano with her at her first Christmas performance.

She further enlightens me in whispered snippets as the hour progresses, that he's just the most divine creature ever created, that they're passionately in love, that she will marry him as soon as she's allowed to, five years from now when she turns twenty-one, that the Marburgs are very nice once you get to know them, and that Reinhold himself is rather immature, but she's sure he'll grow up eventually.

"He's my age," I point out.

I debate whether to enlighten her. On the one hand, she poses no threat to him. Moreover, she's of his own class and a friend of his brother's, not to mention the daughter of an associate of his father. On the other hand . . .

No. I have little to gain and more to lose by revealing the dark underbelly of Prince Charming's unsatisfactory younger brother. Katerina wouldn't believe me, anyway. Not for the first time, I consider that the Kurtzes' choice to raise their daughter in a fairy tale tower won't serve her well in life. Or, maybe being rich is in itself sufficient protection from the Marburgs of this world.

I let it go.

✦ ✦ ✦

In the second week Felix suggests we—his quartet, Ros and I—meet in a large practice room and play the orchestra parts together. A *sinfonietta*, he calls it. No woodwinds or brass, naturally, but nonetheless it turns out to be an effective way to clarify cues and hear how the parts work together. Also, it's fun. Franz keeps us laughing with his wicked impersonations of everyone from Herr Zeidler on down. His Marburg impression is so diabolically perfect, I realize even more how widely disliked Marburg really is.

As the days pass, our *sinfonietta* rehearses longer and later after classes. One evening in mid-February we stay so long I'm afraid I'll miss my streetcar. The building isn't deserted, by any means; a muffled cacophony echoes in the basement corridors. But it's dark outside, and cold, and I'm tired and hungry. I bid a hasty goodbye to the others and head for the foyer, weighed down by my case and shoulder bag. I round the last corner and almost run into Reinhold von Marburg.

"Oh. Sorry!" I say somewhat breathlessly, and step to one side to go around him.

He steps sideways to block me.

"Well, hello, Fräulein Adler," he says. "My, you're here late, aren't you?"

"So are you," I say. "I have a streetcar to catch. Excuse me." I step to the other side. He blocks me again.

"It's not safe for a girl alone at this hour. Perhaps I should escort you. You can't be too careful, you know."

"I'll be fine. Excuse me, I need to go."

He continues to block me, staring at me in a way that makes me intensely uncomfortable.

"What do you want?" I say, my temper rising. I'm also beginning to feel something else: a little *drip-drip-drip* of fear.

"Want? Oh, I don't know, conversation, perhaps, or maybe . . ." He raises his hand as if he's going to touch my face, or—I reflexively grab his wrist with my free hand and push it away from my chest. My grip feels like iron, as if someone else's hand is keeping his hand away from me. His expression hardens.

"You're a bitch, Fräulein Adler," he says, his voice dripping with cold contempt. "And you don't belong here. You got in because someone felt sorry for you. A charity case, no better than a street urchin. Or a streetwalker. You and the other one, forcing your way into Orchestra where you don't belong. The Conservatory has been sullied by letting you in and the only thing that will make it clean again is for you to be gone. And the sooner the better." He wrenches his wrist out of my grip. I'm pleased to see I've left my handprint on it.

"Welcome to the twentieth century," I say as coolly as I can, though my heart is pounding. "If you want a men-only experience, I'd suggest a monastery. Or the army. I hear it's a great brotherhood, very manly. But if you're staying here—" I nod toward the back corridors without taking my eyes off of him "—I believe there are some practice rooms open."

"Why, you insolent—" He suddenly stops, his hand halfway raised again, as footsteps echo down the corridor behind me.

A moment later, Felix and Arnold round the corner. They stop at the sight of Marburg and me. Franz, Eduard, and Ros, directly behind, nearly trip over them. Their conversations switch off mid-sentence. We stand there, a startled tableau in the corridor for a beat or two, staring at each other.

"Oh, hello, Marburg," Felix says smoothly. "I see you're getting better acquainted with Fräulein Adler. She's been coaching us all through this week's class headaches, really a good person to have helping you. Theory, in particular."

Arnold looks blankly from Felix to me to Marburg. This is news to him, as it is to me.

"I didn't know you were kindling a romance," Felix continues. Marburg takes a step back. "Best of luck to you. Lord knows, none of us have got anywhere."

"I'm not!" Marburg says, flushing. He stuffs his hand in his pocket.

"No?! I was so sure of it!" Felix grins. "Always hanging around trying to get a word. Trying to sit close by in lectures. I misread all the signs. My most humble apologies. Well, in that case . . . Fräulein, didn't you say you had a streetcar to catch? We'll see you to the stop. Coming, everyone? Good night, then, Marburg. See you tomorrow!"

And the six of us, Felix and his violin on one side of me, Arnold and his cello on the other, and the remaining three behind me like some kind of honor guard, troop out the front door of the building, leaving Marburg glowering in the foyer.

Nobody says anything for half a block. My heart is still pounding, my free hand still shaking.

"I don't know what he would have done to me if you hadn't turned up." My voice trembles. "He hates me! I knew he didn't like me—always kicking my chair in lectures and trying to annoy me in the corridors. But I didn't know how much."

"I think he'll avoid you now, at least for a while. The last thing he wants is for a rumor to get started that he's in love with you. That might be the best insurance of all." Felix's voice is steady, but he's walking so fast the rest of us have trouble keeping up.

"I'm not sure that won't make him more dangerous. Honestly, I try not to be there late or alone anyway. That's just common sense. But I have to admit, I was scared in there. He was waiting for me, I'm sure of it."

"What did he do?" Felix demands.

I tell him. Everyone gasps. Behind me, Franz mutters, "Bastard!"

We've missed our streetcar, of course.

"Let's rehearse at our house, like last term," Ros says. "That solves Marthe's problem and it's more comfortable than the practice room."

"Great idea!" Franz says.

"You're just hungry," Felix says. "But I agree. Though I don't think Marburg will bother you when there are other people around. He'll want to make it obvious that you're beneath his notice. But you're right, on your own, it might be different. Maybe you should travel in a pack for the time being. Not that it's my place to give you advice."

"I'll walk with you whenever you need it," Arnold says. "You fellows, too, right?"

"Right," Franz and Eduard say.

"You'll end up protecting Franz," Felix says to me.

Franz punches him in the shoulder.

"I knew some people might not like a woman scholarship student who doesn't dress right in recitals," I say. "But I really didn't think I'd need bodyguards."

"Stupidest thing in the world." Felix shakes his head. "Typical bully, rich and spoiled rotten. He should put his energy into practicing. God knows, he could use it. Speaking of people who might have had a little help getting in."

When the Ehrenfeld streetcar finally comes, Ros, Felix and I climb in and talk about other things. Not until much later, when dinner is finished, Mother has gone to bed, and I'm in my own room with the door shut, do I allow myself to fall onto my bed, shaking all over, tears streaming down my face.

Five minutes later, a knock sounds on my door.

"Marthe!" Anni's voice. More knocking.

"Oh, for heaven's sake!" Anni blasts in like a wind and flops down beside me on my bed.

"What's wrong?" she demands.

I'm still snuffling and now I have hiccups. I don't know what to say.

"Bad day in the lions' den?" she suggests in a softer tone.

"You could say that."

"Tell me what happened."

I tell her.

"I was afraid of that," she says. "Bastard."

"Anni!" I hear my mother's voice coming out of my mouth. She ignores it.

"To be expected, though. No, really. You're so innocent, you think if you just work hard enough, men will respect you. Some do, to be fair. Your friends are all right. I wish I could have seen Felix put Shithead von Marburg in his place—"

"Anni! Where on earth did you pick up that awful—and how—oh, right, you met Felix after the recital."

"Is he in love with you?"

"No! He's just decent."

"Hm. So here's my theory." She settles back to instruct me while I try to stop my hiccups.

"When Ros started, she had Berit. They didn't push any boundaries, so they didn't have any extra trouble above the usual amount. This year, here you come, all by yourself. Most of your classmates are fine, but there are always one or two shitheads in every crowd."

I ignore the language. It feels cathartic, if I'm honest.

"So, Ros says to Felix, 'What would you do if I were the only girl in my class?' and Felix says, 'What do you mean?'"

"He's not stupid, Anni."

"No, just dense. All men are dense."

"How would *you* know?"

"Ros says, 'You'd look out for me, right?' He says he would. So, she says, 'This new girl, she's the only one. So, little brother—'"

"*Little*!"

"'—Look out for her, all right? Especially when she's not with us.' And he says he will."

"You should meet this Ros you've created," I say. "You seem to have a lot in common."

"Well, I know something about sisters. Then she says, 'And find other decent people and get them to help you. If enough decent people look out for her, she'll be all right. So, promise?' And he's a little bowled over—"

"I can see why."

"—and he promises." Anni looks very pleased with herself.

"I don't know," I say. "He certainly saved me this evening, though."

"But seriously, don't let Marburg get you cornered. He's over-privileged and mean, and he's bound to have friends sucking up to him. You should have some kind of weapon, honestly."

"I could hit him with my bag," I say. "Here, lift." I hand it to her. She falls off the bed.

"You could kill him with this. Be careful how you use it," she says, crawling back up. "Not that the world wouldn't be better off without Shithead von Marburg in it. Make it look like an accident. But seriously, be careful, all right? Watch out for yourself."

"We're going to the Apfelbaums' house for group practices from now on," I say.

"Good," she says.

We sit in silence for a while. My hiccups continue. I begin to think about getting ready for bed.

"Did I tell you I joined the fencing club at school?" Anni says.

"No. Does Mother know?"

"Sure. She disapproved, naturally. They just opened it to girls this term. The boys weren't terribly pleased when I came to the first meeting, but that's the new rule. They tried to intimidate me. Can you believe that?" She laughs. "You know what I told them?"

"I can sort of imagine," I say.

"I said, 'Look, shitheads—'"

"You didn't!" I laugh in spite of myself.

"Well, all right. I said, 'Gentlemen, my sister's in the Köln Conservatory. She's the only woman in her year. And she's going to make it, despite whatever the old fossils throw at her, because she's the toughest woman I know. Except for me. So, I'm going to be on your fencing team and if I'm the only girl here, fine, I'll fence any of you and anyone in my weight class on any other team and pretty soon I'll be good enough to beat you. Does anyone have a problem with that?' They all just shook their heads with their mouths hanging open. So, I'm a fencer now. When I'm suited up, you can't tell what sex I am, anyway. Well, except for the skirt."

"You—you said that?"

"More or less."

"I mean about me."

"I did. Because it's true, even if you don't think so."

"Being the toughest woman you know?"

"Except for me."

I sit slumped on my bed, digesting this.

"I don't feel tough. Right now, I feel like a used dishrag."

"If you weren't tough, you wouldn't even have tried. And you wouldn't be going back tomorrow, which you are. And you wouldn't be surviving Saturdays with that rich fluff-brain—"

"Katerina's all right. She's not stupid, just . . . shackled. Naive."

"—and putting up with her arrogant bitch mother. Say . . ." A wicked grin slowly fills Anni's face. "Have you ever considered what Shithead von Marburg would look like in Arrogant Bitch Kurtz's clothes?"

"No," I say, although now that she's suggested it, I suspect I will consider it, every time I see Marburg for the rest of all time. The picture, once imagined, is impossible to unimagine. I hiccup and giggle at the same time.

"Now, that's a secret weapon you can really use," Anni says. "Mental warfare. Like fencing. Except I get to jab people with foils. You should try it."

"That," I say, "I cannot imagine."

"You know," she says, "I'm not so sure you aren't tougher than me, actually."

"No."

"Because your toughness is all on the inside," Anni says. "I'm tough on the outside. But you—when someone attacks you, you try to rise above it. I can't do that. I have to fight them."

She slides off my bed.

"You're going to make it," she says. "You're going to rise above all the stupidity. You're going to graduate from the Conservatory and you're going to show the fossils and the shitheads what real class is. And you're going to play that damn violin better than anyone else."

She throws her arms around me and gives me a long, hard hug, then goes back to her own room, shutting my door behind her.

I stare after her, wondering if I ever actually knew my sister before tonight.

✦ ✦ ✦

"You two never have this sort of problem?" I ask Berit and Ros the next day.

"Last year we didn't push any limits," Ros says. "Come to that, I don't know why he's not picking on me for invading the orchestra, too."

"He's afraid of you," Berit says. "You're a year older. Your brother is in his year and is quite a bit bigger than he is. And quicker, judging by how he handled Marthe's predicament."

"Felix would never use violence," Ros says.

"Of course, not," Berit says. "But Marburg doesn't know that. Bullies are always cowards. I expect you're not done with him, Marthe. Just be careful."

"This is so stupid!" I say. "I'm here to study music like everyone else. Why should it matter to him?"

"It shouldn't, obviously. But it seems to," Berit says. "Now, as Ros says, you've pushed the limits and he's attacked you for it, so you can't back down. Ever. If you do, he wins, you see? You've started something. You'll have to finish it."

"Right," I say.

Two days after my encounter with Marburg, our *sinfonietta* gathers at the Apfelbaums', where we take over the sitting room and hammer away at the Beethoven symphony. It's a very Apfelbaum sitting room: shelves full of books and ceramics, walls hung with paintings, many by Ros's mother, a parlor grand piano, and a tiled fireplace with a massive hearth. A low ceiling makes it cozy and large windows look out over the snow-covered garden to the street beyond. It's an infinite improvement over the Conservatory basement.

By dinnertime, though, the savory, distracting aromas of beef, carrots and potatoes overwhelm our concentration.

"About time you all came over," Oma Judith growls as we gather about the table.

"Felix suggested it," I say. "I had a little trouble at school and I didn't want to stay into the evenings."

81

"Trouble?" Judith glares out from under her plaits. "What sort?"

I give the briefest possible summary, including Felix's improvisation and my gratitude.

"I explained a few things to him," Oma Judith says. "Such as, men are like little dogs. Present company excepted, of course. Everything's a threat to a little dog. Ros had Berit, but you're on your own and I knew when I met you, you'd be knocking things over sooner or later. I told him to look out for you. A few years from now, no one will care. There'll be plenty of women students right alongside the men. Then the problem will be keeping them out of each other's beds."

"Mother! Please!" Frau Apfelbaum says, but she sounds resigned.

"But for now, I'm not surprised you had trouble. Sad, but I've seen too much to be surprised."

"Why should anyone care?" Arnold says. "Marthe's really good! Isn't that the important thing?"

"It should be. Someday it will be," Oma Judith says. She sounds more confident than I feel. "For now, little men, little dogs. All the same."

I make a mental note to tell Anni.

✦ ✦ ✦

March 1907

I try never to walk alone in the corridors. But Marburg avoids me now, as if I have leprosy. In classes, he ignores me, and I him. It isn't a resolution, or even a truce, but it allows me to keep working. Right now, that's all I need.

Although Ros and I gave ourselves a head start over the holidays, the rest of the orchestra soon catches up. Leo turns out to be pleasant and Ros says she's helped her stand-mate with enough Theory homework to forestall any problems. A few people make rude comments, but only Marburg tries to persuade Herr Zeidler to expel us. As Berit predicted, Meyer, the concertmaster, becomes an ally. After he has a few private conversations with our more vocal opponents, they seem to quiet down. He never says anything directly to us, but his serious approach to his position gives him credibility in some ways as great as Herr Zeidler's.

My Mozart sonata, No. 17, is lovely, if not as deep as his later work.

There's no margin for error in even the simplest Mozart, so my weekly lessons involve tearing it apart phrase by phrase, with and without the piano, until the Wolff is satisfied.

For a whole month she doesn't mention the orchestra. I sense she's waiting for me to decide I don't belong there and quit. And yet, as I'm sure Herr Zeidler tells her, I keep not quitting.

At last, her curiosity gets the better of her patience. One day when the Mozart sonata has gone better than usual, she says, "Let me hear *The Marriage of Figaro* Overture."

I dig the part out of my bag. The overture is short, under five minutes, and she lets me play my part through without interruption. When I finish the triumphant final notes, she doesn't say anything for what seems like a full minute, just sits at her desk, drumming her fingers and studying me. I wait, trying not to fidget.

She heaves a deep sigh. "Clearly you have worked hard at this," she says.

"Yes, Professorin."

"And you intend to perform with the orchestra in its end of term concert, despite the risks."

"Yes, Professorin. Herr Zeidler has given permission."

"Fräulein Apfelbaum says the same. You remain aware, I trust, that professional orchestras are closed to you."

"For now," I say. "We're in the modern world, Professorin. This prejudice will fall. I want to be ready."

"I commend your optimism," she says. "I don't say it's fair. It's just how the world is."

"Yes, Professorin. I understand."

Another long silence, followed by another deep sigh.

"Again," she says.

This time, I get two measures in before she stops me to make a correction.

✦　✦　✦

"You need a black dress," the Wolff says the following week.

"Yes, Professorin," I say. "I don't have one, but I plan to ask Ros for advice."

"And black dress shoes."

"Yes, Professorin."

"Just so you know. I'm glad to see you don't waste money on frivolities. But proper clothing is essential, not only for the orchestra but for any performance, here or elsewhere."

"I don't have money to waste on essentials, let alone frivolities," I say. "But I'll find something."

Ros's advice is to try a nearby secondhand shop. I stop in on my way home one afternoon and inquire about a black gown. The proprietress sizes me up and leads me to a wall packed solid with nothing but black dresses.

"My sympathies," she says.

"I beg your pardon?"

"You are attending a funeral, I presume?"

"Oh! No, it's for a concert," I say. "I'm playing at the Conservatory."

"Ah," she says. "Well, not much in your size. Try these." She pulls a few dresses off the rack, hangs them up in the fitting room, and leaves me to it.

Only one comes anywhere close to fitting. Even I can see it's old-fashioned: meters of crepe with a high neck, leg-of-mutton sleeves, a ruffled skirt with a slight train. Another, also crepe, could pass for an evening gown, but was made for someone twice my size. Still, it looks less than thirty years old and has no train. Maybe with a belt . . . I cinch it with my hands, which makes it look even more voluminous.

"Ma'am, are you sure this is all of them?"

"You were expecting maybe Galérie Française?" she says.

"No, ma'am, just trying to find something that fits," I say, nettled. I can't imagine anyone doing this for fun.

"When do you need it?"

"In five weeks."

"Check back," she says. "We get new stock all the time."

I sigh. I'm not a gambler. I can buy something that doesn't fit and have it over with, or go through the ordeal again. But those awful dresses . . .

"Thanks, I'll try later," I say. I pull my own dress back on, hang up the others and leave.

Ros giggles when I tell her about my attempt.

"It's always a treasure hunt in the secondhand shops," she says. "Don't worry, you have time."

"I can't think of any way I'd rather spend it," I say.

On my third visit, a different clerk finds a crepe dress wedged in at the end of the rack that looks a lot like the first one, but with fewer ruffles and no train. It makes me look like a widowed housekeeper, but by now I'm sick of the whole farce and convinced I'll never find anything less dreadful I can afford. So, I buy it, and also black dress shoes that almost fit. I begrudge every mark of my purchase.

"There you go," the clerk says as I pick up my bags and walk out the door. "My sympathies."

"Thanks," I say as the door closes behind me.

✦　✦　✦

"Oh, my goodness!" Ros says. We're in the women's toilet by the recital hall an hour and a half before the performance, getting ready.

"I told you," I say. I stand before her in my widowed housekeeper's dress and black shoes, which now fit considerably worse than they did in the shop. "You should have seen the others."

"I can imagine," she says. "I did say it was a treasure hunt. Luckily, you're well in the back. No one will notice." She herself wears the black gown she wore for our fall recital, a simple, open-necked affair with long fitted sleeves and a full skirt to accommodate the cello. And her black shoes are actually pretty.

"I don't think it matters where we sit, we're going to stick out," I say. "I'll feel like I have a spotlight shining right on me. You look fantastic, though. Maybe people will be so dazzled by you they won't notice me."

"Never mind," she says. "Come over here so I can do your hair."

"At least my hair will look good. Honestly—do you think this was a good idea?"

Ros stops brushing my hair and spins me around to face her.

"Stop that. Of course, it was a good idea. Z singled you out for praise just last week, remember? You're just nervous. I am, too. Sure, we'll be conspicuous. People will be surprised. Some will hope we fail. But we're not going to. Once we get started, we'll forget everything else, just like always. As for your dress, repeat after me: nobody cares. Have you got that?

All right, turn around, let's finish your French roll."

I want her to be right, I really do. My caterpillars are hiking all over my stomach in hundreds of pairs of tiny, ill-fitting dress shoes, preparing to storm the bastions of Fortress Orchestra. Boiling oil or ridicule: I don't know which is worse.

At least, I'm not all alone.

✦　✦　✦

"You look nice," Leo says as we take our seats at the back of the second violins. He must have practiced this line, since it obviously isn't based on my actual appearance, except for my hair. Still, it won't do to be churlish.

"Thanks," I say. "So do you."

He blushes.

"Dear God, they let *housekeepers* play in orchestras now?"

My jaw clenches. Reinhold von Marburg, dressed in his usual velvet suit, saunters up from behind me on his way to his chair. I try to ignore him, but he parks himself in front of me, staring. I take a deep breath.

"Good luck tonight," I say.

He snorts, but at least he turns away and takes his seat, where he leans over and says something to his stand-mate. I can guess what it is.

"That was totally uncalled for!" Leo splutters. "Who does he think he is?"

"He thinks he's Reinhold von Marburg, but he doesn't know Reinhold von Marburg is an idiot," I say.

"He's just trying to rattle you," Leo says. "I know all about that. People used to rattle me a lot when I was younger. I'd get so upset I couldn't play at all. I like how you kept your temper."

"It's a good act," I say.

"Well," he shrugs, "if he makes you angry, you'll play better. That's what my teacher always said."

"It's true, now you remind me," I say. "I've had experience with that myself."

"Well . . . good luck!"

"You, too, Leo." I glance at the immaculately combed back of Marburg's head and feel my familiar rising heat. Suddenly, unbidden in my mind's eye, I see him again standing before me, contempt on his face, and

86

in place of his velvet suit, the light blue ruffles of Madame Kurtz's morning dress.

"What's so funny?" Leo says.

"Just something I thought of," I say.

Yes. A little well-placed mental warfare, the secret weapon for a great performance.

✦　✦　✦

The concert, after all, goes well. Once Herr Zeidler takes his place and raises his baton, there's no room in my universe for anything but the music. The sections are crisp, the tempi are lively, the soloists sound polished. The audience applauds with enthusiasm. Even at the back of the second violins, I can feel its energy.

I look for Ros at the intermission.

"See? Wasn't I right?" she says. I tell her about Marburg, and Leo's analysis. "I thought the second violins sounded a little extra fiery over there," she laughs. "Seriously, though, what a moron. But if his arrogance makes you play better, the joke's on him, isn't it?"

"By the look of things, I'll be playing better than anybody here, since he can't seem to leave me alone."

"Pour it into the Schubert," she says. "Lucky you can see the back of his head from where you sit, in case you need a little pick-me-up in the middle. And you *know*," she leans into my ear, "you already play better than most people here. Definitely better than him. Never let anyone tell you any different."

"I really—that means a lot to me, Ros," I say as Herr Schädler calls places. "Schubert it is, then. Back to the bastions of Fortress Orchestra! Good luck in the second half!"

"You, too," Ros grins.

The second half, not surprisingly, also goes well.

By the time Ros and I reach the foyer after changing back into our regular clothes, which is a great relief to both my self-respect and my feet, we have a hard time spotting our families in the crowd. We turn more than a few heads as we work our way toward them.

"We're celebrities," Ros says. "Wait for them to ask for our autographs."

"Or our heads on a platter," I say.

"You're such an optimist," she says. "Let's stop at the cookie table first. They won't last long with this crowd."

"Good idea." The staff is already replacing empty platters with new ones. A general muttering seems to follow us as we carry our loaded plates over to our families.

"How extraordinary! Who ever heard . . ."

"Ah, here you are!" Herr Zeidler has traded his baton for a glass of punch. "Well done, ladies. You held your own in a most professional way. If you maintain that level of preparedness, you will be most welcome back next year. Indeed, you might inspire the others to come a little better prepared themselves."

"We'll be there," we say.

"This business of women lacking ability, or being a distraction, is absurd, of course," he continues. "Your abilities and discipline are more than obvious. And I find my male students quite capable of distracting themselves regardless of who is seated beside them."

He drifts off in the direction of the punch bowl.

"So, in other words," Ros says, "if we come to the first rehearsal ready for the final performance, we can stay."

"Sounds right," I say. "But he said we can do it again!"

"That's my plan," she says.

"I'm glad you talked me into it," I say.

"I thought you talked *me* into it!" she says.

"But next time you'll be in the upper level orchestra," I say. "And I'll still be in this one . . . alone."

"You'll have Felix and the others to back you up. Not to mention Z himself. With any luck, you'll have a decent concertmaster. Besides, now you know you can do it. Don't worry so much!"

Our families surround us, everyone talking at once.

"A well-struck blow!" Oma Judith says, kissing my cheek. "Nothing like kicking a stupid rule in the teeth. We'll make it a modern world yet!"

"Oma," I say, struck by sudden inspiration, "have you met my sister Anni? I think you two have a lot in common."

"I haven't," Oma Judith says. "And why haven't I?"

"Anni!" I call over the noise. In less than a minute, Anni is telling Oma Judith about becoming a fencer and Oma Judith is giving Anni a rousing speech of encouragement in which she raps her cane frequently on the floor for emphasis, and in which I hear the phrase *little dogs* repeated more than once.

Ros catches my eye and winks.

Over by the refreshment table, a well-dressed man who looks vaguely familiar is poking his finger at the provost's chest. His voice carries, but I can't tell what he's saying. I lean over to Franz.

"You look like your plate needs refilling," I say. "And while you're at it, can you find out what that man is saying to the provost? Just curious."

Franz never needs a second suggestion to have a second helping. He's soon back with his plate piled with cookies.

"It's some bigwig ranting about women in the orchestra," he says.

"I suspected as much," I say. I help myself to one of Franz's cookies and turn to watch as the provost picks up two cookies from a nearby platter, offers one to his antagonist, and walks off with the other.

A few minutes later I spot the same man across the room, the cookie still in his hand, deep in conversation with Herr Kurtz. Beside him are two young men, the elder of whom is absorbing Katerina's earnest interest, and the younger of whom is Reinhold von Marburg.

"Is that him?" Anni says.

"Yes," I say. "In the velvet. That must be his brother, Otto, talking to Katerina."

"Shithead," she says.

"Anni!" I say, and we both giggle.

The younger Marburg, a glass of punch in his hand, glances idly around, clearly bored and resentful at not being the center of attention. We turn away before he glances in our direction, but it's too late: I've already imagined him for the second time this evening in Madame Kurtz's light blue morning dress.

6

SPRING, APRIL–JUNE 1907

April 1907

During my short spring holiday, I spend part of each day outdoors, walking. The chill morning air gives way to afternoon warmth that calls to the flowers in gardens and parks like a magician, pulling stems out of winter ground, blossoms out of their sheaths, leaflets from the bare branches of elm trees along Hildegardstrasse. As I wander, my mind wanders, too, free of the intense focus of the term.

In the evenings I make simple dinners for Mother and Anni, though I'm no cook: early vegetable soup, or sausage and roasted potatoes. It seems an inadequate atonement for my absences and my guilty pleasure of dining at the Apfelbaums' table, where ideas and conversation flow so freely.

In truth, I'm not looking forward to the spring term. The first-year men can return to small ensembles if they like, but I can't, because Ros and Berit are preparing their solo recitals. So, I'll be on my own with only the Wolff for company. No excuses to visit the Apfelbaums'. Outside of class, most of my time this spring I'll spend in a basement practice room by myself.

I suppose if I want a solo career, this will be a good taste of it.

✦ ✦ ✦

Wednesday morning.
I open the studio door and walk into the Wolff's lair. She hands me a score.

"Sight-read," she says.

So, I sight-read a Beethoven violin sonata, Opus 12 No. 1, not very well, for an exhausting hour.

"When you have the mechanics, we will add the piano," she says when I've finished mangling it. "Have the first movement by next week."

"Yes, Professorin," I say, wondering if this is possible. "Er—who is the pianist?"

"I am," the Wolff says. "Fortunately, you have fewer distractions this term."

"Yes, Professorin," I say, though I already miss them.

But by the next week, as I try to stay with the piano, I begin to grasp Beethoven's melodic ideas and structure, in which the piano is an equal voice, a part often more difficult than the violin's. The Wolff's command of the piano, as well as all the stringed instruments, astonishes me, especially in light of my own feeble attempts to master the basics. I wonder if she grew up playing all of them, or if she got to Conservatory and played anything they threw at her.

I just hope they don't throw a piano at me.

✦ ✦ ✦

I hope in vain. The following Wednesday, the Wolff hands me a book of basic piano study. My jaw drops.

"I would have given you this last term if not for your invasion of the orchestra," she says. "Now that you have more leisure, you need to bring your piano skills to an acceptable basic level."

"Oh," I say, wondering what, exactly, she means by *leisure* and what constitutes her idea of *an acceptable basic level*. "But I have no piano at home."

"No matter. Practice here will suffice. You must have basic skills in order to teach, as every professional does. That's all."

"I know scales and arpeggios," I say, hoping maybe that's enough.

"Good," she says. "Have the first five pages by next week."

"Yes, Professorin," I say as I stuff the piano book in my bag, along with the Beethoven.

Basic piano aside, I look forward to my lessons for the sheer emotional release of standing up to the Wolff. The Beethoven sonata is a half hour of technical and dramatic intensity, with a full range of complex emotions, from sweet and lyrical to pounding and virtuosic. The Wolff plays and snaps instructions and smacks her hand on the piano to keep time with the metronome and I play and play and play again. I meet her head on, like leaning into the wind on a mountaintop. By the end of the lesson, I'm exhausted. I flatter myself that I exhaust the Wolff, too.

The Wolff reveals nothing of herself. She never wastes time or energy on conversation. Her corrections are as exacting, not to say irascible, as ever. The one difference I observe, and only later do I understand its significance, is her occasional demand that I try a passage in different ways. "*Andante*, but slower." "Now the faster end of *andante*." "A little more *forte* just here." "Now *mezzo-forte*." And then (I never get over being surprised by this), "What do you think?"

✦　✦　✦

Midway through the term I meet Berit and Ros for a rare lunch at Café Max Bruch and mention my hope that we might resume our ensemble next fall.

"Unfortunately, no," Berit says. "We'll be in upper level ensembles next year. Magde Oberländer and Käthe Lagersdorf are graduating, so we'll be taking their places in the women's quartet with Hildreth and Ursula. At last, Hildreth will achieve her dream of being first violin."

"How will that even work?" I protest. "Two violins and two cellos?"

"Ursula claims to play viola," Ros says. "I have my doubts. I might end up coming to you for advice on how to play it myself."

"My advice would be, go to Franz."

"Very sensible," she says.

"At any rate," Berit says, "while I would vastly prefer playing children's songs with you to playing anything with Hildreth von Prinzenburg—"

"Not Berit's favorite person," Ros says.

"—who's going to be even more full of herself than usual, that isn't going to be possible. At least it's only one year and then she'll be gone."

"And by then you'll be a third year and we can do trios again," Ros says.

"But—that means next year I won't have an ensemble at all," I say.

"Depends on whether the next class has any women in it," Ros says. "We wondered the same thing last year. Lucky for us you showed up. Ask the Wolff. She's on the admitting committee, she'll know if any have applied."

"And if not . . ."

"You'll further your dream of a solo career," Berit says.

"You're the one with the dream of a solo career," I say. "At this point, I'm not so sure. I like ensembles. Plus, they're important for learning."

"Tell you what," Ros says. "We're out of time just now. Come over for dinner Saturday and have the treat of listening to the boys rehearse without having to do any rehearsing yourselves. They're sounding really good, actually."

"You sound surprised," Berit says.

"I don't know what else there is to discuss," I say, "but I'll never pass up an invitation to your house. I'll be there."

"Good," Ros says.

"See you then," Berit says.

We head across the street and back through the Conservatory's front doors.

The Wolff says no women have, so far, applied to join the Conservatory next year. When I point out that this leaves me with no ensemble, unless I'm allowed to play with the men, she merely says, "You'll be busy enough," and demands to hear the second movement of the Beethoven sonata. I don't get far before she stops me.

✦ ✦ ✦

Saturday afternoon.

I hear the sounds of a string quartet even before I push open the garden gate. The Apfelbaums' garden is presently a riot of daffodils and irises, and the ground under the cherry trees is littered with pink blossoms. Ros answers my knock and we watch from the sitting room door for a bit as the boys play something very fast.

"What is it?" I whisper.

"Mozart. *Spring*," she whispers back. "Appropriate, don't you think?"

"Quite." A cherry blossom falls out of my hair.

"Come on back," she says. We leave the boys and head for the kitchen, where Berit, Oma Judith, and Frau Apfelbaum are sharing a pot of tea. Dora, the maid, bends over the sink as usual. Ros and I pour our own tea from the pot and join them.

"I still can't believe that they're doing what they're doing without proper coaching," Berit says. "They should have complained right away and got someone else. I asked my father about Professor Nodelmann. He was teaching here when my father was a student. He cared somewhat then, but he clearly doesn't now. What they've done on their own is astonishing, but unfair. They deserve the best teacher, not the worst."

"They deserve the Wolff," I say.

The others laugh.

"I thought you liked them!" Ros says in mock indignation.

"Well, you can't deny she's a *very* good teacher."

"Marthe's right," Berit says. "My father knows most of the faculty. Many are more charming, but he says none of them can give you pedagogical whiplash like the Wolff."

"Pedagogical whiplash!" Oma Judith says. "Now *there's* a phrase. It makes me want to know her, it truly does."

A brief silence from the sitting room shifts into a series of short phrases, stopping and starting again.

"They're teaching themselves," Berit says. "And not doing half badly. Still. They deserve better."

"Damn right," Oma Judith says.

That evening, just as I'm thinking how pleasant it is to be back in my spot by Oma Judith, enjoying a chicken stew with potatoes and not paying much attention to the other conversations, Eduard says something and everything stops.

"Sorry, Eduard, did I hear you correctly?" Herr Apfelbaum says into the silence.

"Unfortunately, yes," Eduard says. "My father has been recalled to Paris. My mother and I will return after the end of the school year."

"What a shame, Eduard," Frau Apfelbaum says.

"It's the curse of being a diplomat's son," he says. "I spent two of my primary school years in Warsaw and one secondary year in Madrid. But Paris is home. I'll transfer to the Paris Conservatory. Even if Papá gets posted somewhere else after that, I'll stay, now I'm old enough. Mostly I feel bad about leaving our quartet. I really like playing quartets with you. I won't miss Nodelmann, though."

The table erupts in laughter.

"We don't miss him now," Felix says.

More laughter.

"What that means, though, if we want to keep going," Franz says, "is that we need an unattached violinist to take your place. Who do we know who might . . . ?"

"Marthe, of course!" Arnold says.

"What? Me?" I can feel myself turning red as all heads swivel in my direction. "But I can't!"

"Ros was telling us the other night about your predicament for next year," Felix says. "Most of the other fellows our year are either staying with the same ensembles or lost no time switching after last fall. Not mentioning any names. If you join us, it solves our problem and yours, too."

"And creates a big new one for me, called getting thrown out," I say. "Ask Ros and Berit how much luck they had getting permission to play in mixed ensembles. The old guard are afraid we'll create some sort of cataclysm if we get mixed up with you. A rupture of propriety so deep the whole school will fall in, and the rest of civilization right after it."

"Ah," Oma Judith says. "But you've played in their orchestra now. And the earth didn't open and swallow you up, or anyone else either. You joining the boys' quartet will be less horrific, because you've already proved the little dogs can touch noses with you and survive."

"The provost almost got swallowed up afterward," I say. "Remember, Franz? Marburg senior tried to bite his head off at the reception."

"You know, it's a fair point, though," Ros says.

I think of the Wolff's furrowed eyebrows and the thin, hard line of her mouth before she opens it to tear me to pieces.

"I can't," I say. I can't believe I'm arguing so hard against something I would very much like. "I'm on a scholarship. I can't afford to threaten it by rocking too many boats."

"On the contrary," Oma Judith says, "Your benefactor has every reason to expect that his scholarship is well spent. If you have no ensemble, you're not getting his money's worth. He also seems like a reasonably decent man, as men go—"

"I beg your pardon," Herr Apfelbaum says.

"—present company excepted, of course, as I was about to say. If you work him right, my dear, you'll have him *demanding* that you be allowed to play with these three upstanding young men. And the school policy will suddenly, miraculously, change."

In five minutes, I've gone from being happy and secure to being completely torn. "I—I can't," I say.

"You don't have to decide now, obviously," Felix says. "Tell you what. We've all got a lot to work on during the next few weeks, so what if you just come over during the summer and we play a few quartets, just for entertainment. No commitment. What do you say?"

He sounds so soothing, so casual. So persuasive. No commitment. Just for entertainment.

"Well," I say, "I guess I'd say that sounds like fun."

✦ ✦ ✦

June 1907

Ros lends me her black gown to perform my Beethoven sonata at the term's end. It's too big and the full skirt is too long, but it's infinitely better than last term's widowed housekeeper look. I accept with gratitude. I'm still stuck with the horrible black shoes, but at least nobody can see them. I don't slip them on until the very last possible moment and kick them off again directly afterward.

I invited Mother and Anni, but Mother said I couldn't possibly be serious, expecting her to come downtown on the streetcar to hear something that won't last half an hour and that she's heard me play every evening for three months in my room. So Anni comes without her. By contrast, the entire Apfelbaum family attends, even though neither Ros nor Felix is playing that evening, without once mentioning the short duration of my performance or more important commitments. Felix's quartet comes, too, and Arnold brings Alma, who is in town with his parents for his performance the next night.

My caterpillars turn up on schedule for a spring frolic involving a spirited game of tag in my stomach. Then Herr Schädler says, "Go!" and the Wolff and I take our places, make eye contact and begin. I find myself trusting the Wolff's training so that I not only enjoy the performance, it becomes a gift, an expression of gratitude to the few people in the world who really believe in me.

Afterward, in the foyer, once I'm back in my street clothes, the Wolff approaches, says, "Decent. Notes tomorrow, nine o'clock," and leaves.

"Is she always that rude?" Anni asks when the Wolff is safely out of hearing.

"Heavens, no! You caught her on a good day," I say.

"She was ecstatic about Marthe's performance, couldn't you tell?" Franz asks.

"She's not so bad when you get to know her, assuming you're serious about your work," Ros says.

"'Decent' from her would be a cannon salute from anyone else," Arnold says.

"And a pony," Franz adds.

"I see," Anni says.

"Marthe, dear, where's your mother?" Frau Apfelbaum asks.

I begin to invent a polite excuse, but Anni interrupts to explain in far less diplomatic terms.

"I see," Frau Apfelbaum says, pursing her lips tightly together, probably to keep from saying what she really thinks. She turns away to interrupt her husband's conversation with Eduard. Herr Apfelbaum hastens over to us.

"Join us for dinner down the street?" Herr Apfelbaum says. "You, too, Anni."

He read my mind. I was *not* looking forward to going straight home. Anni's face says the same. And I'm suddenly ravenous. Soon, the eleven of us are sitting around a long table at a restaurant I could never afford, solving the world's problems—although, thankfully, the future of Felix's quartet doesn't come up.

"No wonder you like hanging around them," Anni says afterward as we walk up Hildegardstrasse toward home. "If I were in your shoes, I'd never come home at all. Not just because they treated me to dinner, either."

"I feel like they've just taken me under their wing," I say.

"Good thing somebody has," she says. Then, after a pause, "The Wolff is formidable, isn't she?"

"Good word for her," I say. "Formidable, indeed."

✦ ✦ ✦

It's odd to be sitting in the audience with no caterpillars, no superhuman concentration, no worries about how many people want me to fail. Ros is more nervous on Felix's behalf than her own, which I find amusing, considering how polished the boys are and how crisp their performance.

"I still *cannot* believe they're doing that on their own," Berit says during the applause when they're finished.

A few days later, it's Ros's and Berit's turn.

Berit plays the Bach Violin Partita No. 2, a suite of dances that remember their origins only through their names and meters: Allemande, Courante, Sarabande, Gigue, and Chaconne.

Bach always seemed dry and complicated to me, although necessary for teaching things like counterpoint and how to play a three-part fugue. So, when Berit, in a gown of wine-red silk, her garnet necklace glinting in the footlights, walks to center stage, I sit back and prepare to be bored.

But I'm the opposite of bored. Under Berit's bow the partita is no dry exercise but an expression of disciplined passion, its emotions subtle but undeniable, the filigree of its lines elegant and cool. She moves with it, her eyes closed, her six months of work showing in every confident note.

By the time Berit finishes the Chaconne, I'm determined to play a partita myself.

Next Ros enters to play her Mendelssohn sonata, the full skirt of her deep blue-green gown flowing behind her, cello and bow in hand, the Wolff at her heels.

Ros has a challenge I don't: she faces the audience, not her pianist. Yet cellist and pianist are equal partners, a partnership based on heightened awareness and acute listening. Ros communicates with her body as well, while the Wolff plays almost entirely without looking at her hands, through the four contrasting movements in a variety of moods. Ros, I remind myself, was learning this last term along with our orchestra repertoire without showing any sign of cracking, though the Wolff must have been pushing her very hard, indeed.

With a pang of lingering guilt, I remember those Trios back in the fall, and how neither Berit nor Ros ever once mentioned that I, the new girl, was holding them back.

Afterward, the evening's performers all wear identical expressions of relief. Even the Wolff is unusually enthusiastic.

"Well done," she says. "Notes tomorrow, nine o'clock."

"'Well done?' Impressive," I say. "Fireworks *and* a trumpet fanfare!"

"And a pony and a large helping of ice cream," Felix says.

"We'll see what she says tomorrow morning," Ros says. "I expect her notes to be nothing short of excruciating."

"At least you get notes," Felix says.

"You need to trade Nodelmann in," Berit says. "I'm serious."

"You need the Wolff," Ros says.

"I was only joking," Felix says. "Anyway, lucky for us, the Wolff doesn't teach men."

"Only the best," Berit says. "Or the ones who want to be the best. That part's up to you."

"Ouch!"

"Think about it," Berit says. "Anyway, I'm going to go home and sleep."

"Me, too," Ros says and the party breaks up.

The last thing I hear is Franz and Arnold muttering behind me as we head out the front doors.

"... terrifying thought."

"Teeth marks ..."

"I'm not that brave."

"Or foolhardy. What a nightmare."

I smile to myself. *I'm* brave enough for the Wolff. Her plan to toughen me up must be working.

Year Two:

Fortress Music

1907-1908

7

SUMMER, JUNE–SEPTEMBER 1907

July 1907

Felix suggests I come over the first Saturday afternoon of summer, just to play a little, hear how we sound together. Just for fun, stay for dinner. But by Saturday morning, I'm convinced the whole business is a waste of time. Oma Judith's analysis doesn't allow for the massive inertia of the Conservatory, not to mention the whole world. A woman playing in public with three unrelated men? Sheer prejudice will destroy anyone who tries. So why take the time from my summer assignments, besides adding to my perpetual guilt for never being home?

Because the Apfelbaums are magnetic, that's why. They draw people to them like moths to light. Conversation, laughter, ideas whirl through the rooms of that house. *Chaos!* Oma Judith said once with a satisfied smile and a rap of her cane, but to me it feels like permission to be alive, to think about something bigger than anxiety, money, conflict, survival. Yes, I'm going to the Apfelbaums', because there I feel the heartbeat of a vibrant, living family. Well, and to play a little music. But only for fun.

Felix answers my knock and points me into the sitting room where the stands are set up and a large plate of still-warm anise cookies waits. Franz and Arnold arrive shortly after and the plate is soon empty.

"Now I remember why I wanted to be early," I say.

Felix disappears with the plate and returns with it piled high again.

Mid-cookie, an intense awkwardness seizes me, an acute awareness of being the outsider, the *female*. If this is an audition, I have nothing prepared. It's all pointless, anyway.

"This won't work," I say.

A beat of surprised silence follows.

"You can't stay today?" Arnold sounds disappointed.

"No, I mean, for school. Me, playing with you. They'll just never allow it."

"Well, that's jumping ahead," Felix says. "For now, it doesn't really matter, does it? I thought we could just try a few things, see how our instruments sound together."

"What about a round of scales in thirds?" Arnold says. "That way everybody stands out."

I sigh. I'm annoyed with myself. I should be thrilled. They're the best in our year, even with no proper coaching. They want me to play with them. All right, so it's pointless, but there's no harm in spending a Saturday afternoon at someone's house playing scales in thirds, is there? No one, not even an old fossil, if one were cluttering up the Apfelbaums' sitting room right now, could object to that. And yet I feel as though I'm being subversive, breaking some unwritten, unbreakable rule. It's stupid. I feel it anyway.

We tune.

Felix sets his metronome. "Nice and slow," he says.

We begin, Felix and Franz on the G, Arnold and I a third up on the B. Felix's violin sounds a little brighter than mine. Franz's old and well-used viola has a dark, rich sound that meshes well with everyone else's. Arnold's cello has a wonderful lower range, like a tiger's purr.

"Not bad!" Franz says when we're done. "We ought to form a quartet."

"There's a thought," Arnold says. "D Major next?"

"Now what?" Franz says after we finish D Major.

"Marthe, the second movement of your Beethoven was a theme and variations, wasn't it?" Felix says. "You play it and we'll try some harmony. It may not sound much like Beethoven, but it'll wake us up."

I play the deceptively simple initial theme with its straightforward harmonies. The others join in for the variations. The improvisation fragments as the variations range progressively further afield, with frequent additions of laughter and, "Oh, wrong direction!" "The great ones always go somewhere you don't expect!" And frequently, "Damn!"

We try a few more experiments, then Felix says, sounding almost shy, "If you'd like to come back next Saturday, we could try learning something."

I say yes, because here in his house I'm under the Apfelbaum spell, in which accomplishments seem possible and life is a thing to be enjoyed. And Felix just happens to have an easy early Haydn quartet ("We had this one lying around") and hands out the parts. Frau Apfelbaum eventually calls us in to dinner and Oma Judith says, "Sounded like the new girl was showing you all up!" And we laugh with her.

The conversation flies elsewhere. The next thing I know, I'm on the streetcar on the way home with a quartet to learn for next Saturday, thinking, "Well, it won't work for next year. But it's not a bad way to spend the summer. It most definitely is not."

The next Saturday it's fun again, and the Saturday after that. By the fourth Saturday, I begin to feel like less of an outsider and more like I've gained three brothers, and then I start to think about playing solos with no one but the Wolff for company all year, even more than I'll have to anyway for my recital, and the thought is burdensome, to say the least. I begin to wish that forming a quartet with them might really be a possibility. And, if I want to make it possible, how I should go about it.

Who would give or deny permission for this radical experiment? Their coach, I suppose, the notoriously inattentive Nodelmann, who doesn't care what they do or bother to stay awake while they're doing it. Or the Wolff. Another manner of beast altogether. Good luck trying to persuade *her*. Though if I somehow succeeded, I doubt the old fossils would overrule her. I believe they're as intimidated by her as most of the students.

But if Nodelmann wouldn't care, he also wouldn't teach me anything. That's a problem. However much I've suffered under the Wolff's exasperating perfectionism, I wouldn't trade it. Without real coaching, any ensemble, mixed or not, will be a waste of time.

I awaken one morning in July with the answer. Not that I just thought of it; Berit, Ros, and I have all said it, even if we weren't serious at the time.

I'll join them if we can persuade the Wolff to be our coach. She's taught men before under exceptional circumstances, and this certainly is one. I won't join them so much as bring them with me, to her.

And that means, as in the orchestra, it will be essential to have a quartet under our fingers before we ask her.

I also need the approval of Herr Kurtz. If he disapproves, no quartet for me. Or if he disapproves and I persist, that's the end of my scholarship and the end of my education with it. But I never see him during Katerina's lessons. Perhaps I should go to his office during the week, but the days pass and I don't.

✦   ✦   ✦

Anni spends her savings to attend a girls' fencing camp. For three weeks, Mother has no one to fight with but me, and I'm usually away or practicing. Without Anni's incendiary presence to spark an argument, our dinners together are dull, quiet affairs. I wish, even more than usual, that my father, or even his ghost, were sitting beside us. A spirit from the dead would bring more life to our table than we can provide on our own.

Only on the calendar has it been almost two years since he died. In my mind it seems like last week and also like forever.

I hear his voice in his violin, which, aside from necessity, is one reason I practice so much. I wonder if he talks to my mother and if so, what they say to each other. I wonder if they were happy together. I wonder how one defines happiness in this difficult world.

✦   ✦   ✦

"Throw us to the Wolff?"

Back in the Apfelbaums' sitting room on the third Saturday in July, we're tuning for another of the easy quartets that Felix just happened to have lying around.

"Like Faust's bargain," Franz says. "We sell our souls to the devil and he—she—makes us an amazing quartet."

"Still," Arnold says, "the Professorin's obviously a great coach, judging by the girls' recitals and your sonata, Marthe."

"Our teachers are good, too," Felix says. "Any of them would be a better coach than Nodelmann."

"But they don't teach, or coach, women," I say. "Also, the only way our little rebellion can succeed is for us to be the best. Not just the best in class. The best in Conservatory history. Professional level, more rigorous than any other students. And that means we need the Wolff."

"I don't feel any pressure at all," Franz says. "Do you, gentlemen?"

I ignore him. "And we need to choose an advanced quartet to learn, and we need to have the basics down before the beginning of term."

106

"Wait," Franz says. "You mean—*work?* You're as bad as she is."

"I learned from the best," I say. "Those are my conditions. Remember, I'm the one taking the risk here."

I begin tuning. Other than my little *plink, plink, plink,* the room is utterly silent. I wonder if they'll decide to back out. Find some male second violinist, play trios themselves, ask to join other ensembles as extra players. And, in the silence, I realize I don't want them to back out. Now that I've made the experiment seem possible in my own mind, now that I've decided I'm willing to challenge tradition for it, risk my scholarship for it, risk the wrath of the administration for it, risk my personal reputation for it, I want this quartet to *be.*

I wait. I tune. *Plink, plink, plink.*

"Fräulein Generalin is right," Felix says after what feels like several minutes. "We need to ask Professorin Wolff to coach us. And we can't show up the first week with nothing more than a great idea. We'll have to be prepared for her objections, and be prepared to play. We'll have to prove we're serious and professional, not just kids."

"Well, *I'm* doomed," Franz says.

"And another thing," I say. "I don't even like to mention it, but we'll have to be sure nothing we do gives anyone cause for objection. Anything unprofessional will give some old fossil an excuse to break us up. And kick me out."

"Goes without saying," Felix says.

"What about Alma?" I ask.

Arnold frowns, as if he's trying to imagine what possible objection Alma might have to his spending hours every week making eye contact with an unattached woman student. "I'll explain," he says. "She trusts me."

I doubt there's a man on the planet more trustworthy than Arnold.

"What about Herr Kurtz?" Felix asks.

"Er—" I *definitely* have to speak to Herr Kurtz. As soon as possible.

"If he says yes, I'm in if you two are," Felix says.

Franz and Arnold look at each other, shrug, and nod.

Just like that, we're a quartet.

It should feel exhilarating. A daring agreement, assuming Herr Kurtz gives his blessing and the Wolff gives hers. We'll be rebels. Conspicuous. Violating propriety. Risking disapproval. Well, I already know what that's like. Now that they've decided, I feel a little gnawing dread of the confrontations ahead, the criticisms, the insinuations—and I also feel like I ate caterpillars again.

"What'll we play?" Felix asks.

"May I suggest my namesake?" Ros says, appearing from nowhere with a tray bearing a pitcher of lemonade and four glasses.

"Were you eavesdropping?" Felix demands.

"Maybe," she says, setting down the tray. "Mama says if you're not playing, you must be dying of thirst. Anyway, *I* think Schubert's *Rosamunde* would be entirely fitting, since I brought Marthe over in the first place. I'm named for it, you know. Apparently, I was conceived after a particularly fine performance of it by the Berlin Quartet."

Franz and Arnold choke on their lemonade.

So, our first official act as a quartet is to buy full scores and our individual parts for Schubert's Quartet No. 13, *Rosamunde,* at Karol's Violins in the Hauptstrasse, bring them back to the Apfelbaums', and sight-read. It's chaos, but before our first session is over, we're in love.

"What's your student like?" Oma Judith says during dinner that night.

"Katerina? Sweet. Naive. Surprisingly unspoiled. Three years younger than me, an only child. We get along fine."

"A Papa's girl?"

"Probably. He bought her the best violin in Karol's shop, just to learn on. And he's brought her to our performances."

"So, if you want her father behind you when you storm the fortress of the little dogs, enlist her. At the very least, she can advise you how to persuade him. Most likely, all she has to do is say, *Papá, I want . . .* and your problem is solved."

"How do I persuade her that my playing music with three men I'm not related to is a good idea? She's had a very proper upbringing."

"Didn't you tell me she's boy-mad?"

"She's easily infatuated, yes," I say, thinking of Otto von Marburg.

"There's your answer," Oma Judith says. "Tell her next week. Ask her advice."

"I'm not infa—"

"Dear girl, I promise you, your Katerina would give anything not to be so wretchedly *proper*. You're her *knight*. You're doing things she can only dream of doing. And she in turn is your guide to the care and management of her father. Trust me, she's been managing him since the day she was born."

"How do you know all this?" I say. "You've never met her."

"When you're sixty-seven, you'll know a few things, too," she says.

But Madame hovers over Katerina's next lesson and the following week the Kurtzes depart for the Alps. I still have time, I tell myself, when they return.

✦ ✦ ✦

They return barely two weeks before school begins. I arrive for Katerina's lesson with my speech memorized, but then Madame perches on her chair for the first half hour, either to make sure Katerina attends to the lesson or to re-establish her authority, probably both. When she finally leaves, I've barely begun when she sweeps back in to remind Katerina of something or other, and she keeps interrupting in this way the entire rest of the hour. It's not until I'm packing up to leave that she finally considers it safe to disappear.

"Sorry!" Katerina whispers.

I take a deep breath again. In a low, hurried voice. I explain my problem as succinctly as possible.

"I need to be sure your father approves and understands I *need* ensemble training for my education. Because I can't afford to lose my scholarship. And also, the old foss—the administration might throw me out unless he insists."

"How exciting!" she says in an equally low, breathless voice. "I'll talk to him tonight."

I imagine the scene at the Kurtzes' dinner table.

"I don't think your mother would approve, either," I say.

"What do you take me for?" she says.

I pick up my envelope from the hall table and Katerina lets me out.

"Don't worry," she whispers to me as I step out the door.

"If you insist," I say as I head down the garden walk into the late summer sunshine.

✦ ✦ ✦

As we learn our parts, we inevitably do as much talking as playing.

"I'm not hearing the cello here; I think it should be a little louder."

"Now, there's an unusual harmony. Can we try that again?"

"I'm getting an introspective mood here. How about you?"

What I don't hear is Felix telling everyone else what to do. Everyone contributes. Everyone listens to everyone else—and to me. Somehow, I'd just assumed that in this group, as second violin, and a new member, and a woman, I wouldn't have much say in how we played it. I couldn't have been more wrong.

"Marthe, you're the bridge here. What do you think?"

"Marthe, do you think the first line is loud enough?"

"It's two to one on this passage. Marthe, what's your opinion?"

They listen. Often, they agree with me. If we disagree, we try it different ways. Sometimes we find more than one right way to play something, depending on our mood, or how we played something just before. Like the music itself, we're four equals and our partnership is based, not in hierarchy, but on mutual respect.

It gives me a lot to think about on my streetcar rides home.

8

FALL, SEPTEMBER–OCTOBER 1907

September 1907

Monday morning.

"Out of the question."

Felix, Franz, Arnold, and I stand in the Wolff's studio on the first day of fall term. She glares up at us from her chair, her eyebrows a solid, dark storm cloud across her forehead.

"I realize it's an unusual proposal—" Felix begins.

"It is against Conservatory policy. We do not permit mixed ensembles. Such an impropriety would damage the reputation of the Conservatory, not to mention the reputation of our women students. Both must be protected at all costs."

"The curriculum itself says the art of ensemble is essential to musicianship," I say. "And my benefactor, Herr Kurtz, approves. He considers that my education should not lack in any essential or be inferior in any way."

This is in fact not strictly true. When I finally explained my predicament to Herr Kurtz after Katerina's last lesson of the summer, he expressed grave doubts regarding the propriety of my solution. I finally persuaded him, with assurances that Professorin Wolff, besides being the most rigorous coach in the school, will be an unassailable chaperone and that we'll rehearse at the Apfelbaum home with Felix's mother and grandmother present at all times. Also, I have no other choice, because the first-year class has no women in it, and I deserve not to be treated as inferior, because I'm not, which he knows.

Whether my reasoned assurances persuaded him, or whether Katerina merely said, *Papá, I want . . .* I have no idea.

The Wolff studies me, her lips compressed into a thin line that matches her eyebrows.

"It's only for one term," I say. "Next term is orchestra, after all."

"Don't remind me," she snaps.

"I promised Herr Kurtz you would be our coach," I say. "Because we want the most rigorous training possible."

The Wolff's lip twitches slightly.

"And, of course, it is more proper than if I went with them to a male coach."

"I don't teach men," she says.

"You taught Berit Morgenthaler's father."

"That was an exceptional circumstance," she says.

"We're an exceptional circumstance," Felix says.

She frowns at him. "Who coached you last year?"

"Professor Nodelmann," Felix says.

"Really?" One eyebrow arches toward her hairline. She eyes him beadily, her head to one side. "I would not have expected it was he. You played decently."

With great effort, I stifle a giggle. Felix seizes the opening.

"Thank you, Professorin. Think how much better we would be under *your* coaching. And Fraülein Adler is the best in the year. We could reach professional standards with your help."

"However, as I said, it would violate the Conservatory's traditional standards of public performance, not to mention those of society at large," the Wolff says. "You have no idea the level of risk you would incur in forming a mixed ensemble. Not only the risk to your institution, but to yourselves. Particularly to you, Fraülein."

"And yet I'm sure you recall what happened when two women played in the orchestra last year, also in a break from tradition," Felix says.

"What do you mean, what happened?" The Wolff's eyebrows furrow deeply across her forehead.

"Nothing happened, Professorin. The Conservatory is still highly regarded, as far as I know."

She glares at him.

"Still," he continues, "a quartet might cause more comment, so if you prefer, we'll agree not to perform in public. What we need is essential ensemble training. And we want to learn from the best."

She stares up at us.

"Not perform? Why would I waste my time if you don't plan to perform?"

"We'd love to perform, obviously, once we've perfected it," Felix says. "If you permit us."

"It?" Her voice hints at a growl.

"We prepared a quartet over the summer, Professorin. It's coming along decently, we think."

"Hmph." She knows he did that on purpose. "And what quartet would that be, Herr Apfelbaum?"

"Schubert's *Rosamunde*, Professorin."

The Wolff's eyebrows shift.

"You have already begun preparing this?" she says.

We nod.

She sighs, closes her eyes and massages her temples with her fingertips.

We wait.

"I will hear it Wednesday afternoon," she says. "But I promise you nothing."

"Thank you, Professorin," we say and, feeling elated, hurry off to class.

✦　✦　✦

Wednesday afternoon.

On the way up the stairs to the Wolff's studio, a recital-level invasion of caterpillars stomps about in my stomach.

"Scales first," she says. "In unison. Begin with your lowest C and continue up. Major and relative minors."

"Scales?" Felix says. "I think we're all warmed up enough to start the Schubert."

I try and fail to catch his eye. The Wolff fixes him with a withering stare.

"Herr Apfelbaum, if you are inclined to argue, we need not continue."

"Oh, no, I didn't mean—sorry, I only wondered, why take rehearsal time with a warm-up exercise?"

113

"A reasonably legitimate question, as you are just starting. The operative phrase is, 'in unison.' I believe the exercise will speak for itself. Go."

We start off dishearteningly ragged. We watch each other closely for tempo and volume. About halfway through we begin to sound cleaner. By the end, we're not bad and I suspect our breathing has synchronized.

"Do this at least once a week," the Wolff says. "Especially if you've been apart for a time. You see why, I trust."

"Yes, Professorin," we say in unison.

"Now, Herr Apfelbaum, I will hear your Schubert, *if* you have no more questions."

"Er—no, Professorin," Felix says.

"Very well, then. Begin."

So, we begin. We play through *Rosamunde's* first movement.

"Again," she says.

We begin again.

"Stop! Too fast. Play it again. Stop! Too soft. Again. Stop! There is no balance. Who is in charge in this passage? Again. Stop! Did you practice with a metronome at all? The time for *rubato* is after you have mastered the work, not before. Again. Stop! Your fingering will not work, as you will discover in the next measure. Again!"

One bar. Two bars. A page. Two pages. By the end of two hours, we've plowed through four pages. We're exhausted. The others look as sweaty as I feel, partly from too many people in a too-small room and partly from the ordeal itself.

"Well," she says when our time is up. "It is not as bad as I expected. Not good yet, but not irredeemably hopeless. Your inner voices are strident when they should be sweet and sweet when they should be strident. Come back next week."

"Yes, Professorin. Thank you, Professorin," we chorus as we troop out the door.

As we turn the corner the others let out a long, collective sigh.

"You did that all last year?" Franz asks.

"And I already had an hour of it this morning," I say. "She's assigned me Schumann's Violin Sonata No. 2 this term. I've come to enjoy the intensity. Nothing else matters when you're with her."

"Something of the same pleasure as hurling yourself repeatedly against a wall," Felix says. "Not that I ever tried it until now. I thought Ros was exaggerating."

"Like being ripped to shreds, but in a good way," Arnold says.

"Or just being ripped to shreds," Franz says.

"And yet, she's allowing us to continue," Felix says. "Somehow we persuaded her."

"Because we're brilliant," Franz says. "Obviously."

"And we want her to keep being persuaded," I say. "So, this week we should focus on her corrections and practice the first and second movements. Work on fingerings and phrasing. The tempi will come."

"Yes, Fraülein Generalin!" Felix says.

"You're as bad as she is," Franz says.

"Or you could go back to Professor Nodelmann."

"No, no, we're fine."

"No, really, can't wait to get started."

"No!" None of us have ever heard Arnold raise his voice. Neither has he, by the look on his face.

"Marthe's right," he says. "If we're going to be accepted, we need to be the best. The best possible, anyway. Imagine what we could have done last year with the Wolff, instead of—"

At this moment, we pass the studio of Professor Nodelmann himself. We glance in through the half-open door to see the professor leaning well back in his chair, his feet up on his desk, sound asleep.

✦ ✦ ✦

"The little dogs aren't snapping at your ankles?"

Oma Judith and I are again leaning elbows on the Apfelbaums' kitchen table, she with a steaming mug of coffee in her hand, I with a cup of tea. *Come early*, she said last time. *I want to hear all about it.*

"Not yet," I say.

"The administration won't cross the Wolff," she says. "With your fellow students, it might be a different story. You may find you have a target on your back."

"Most don't seem to care," I say.

"Most won't care," she says. "Just don't be surprised if your scandalous behavior sparks a reaction."

115

"We're not doing anything scandalous! Besides, you were the one who said it was possible."

"And I was right, wasn't I?" she says. "You're doing it. And you have every right to do it. The only reason it's scandalous is because the Conservatory's policy and the conventions of polite society are idiotically bourgeois. The scandal is, you're proving just *how* bourgeois by refusing to be shackled by it. Never be afraid to kick a stupid rule in the teeth, as I said. Just don't be surprised if it kicks back."

"You didn't say that part before."

"Didn't think of it till just now." She laughs her cackling laugh.

I seriously doubt that.

"I know we need to be careful," I say. "We promised the Wolff we'd rehearse here with you and Frau Apfelbaum to chaperone. We're just practicing separately at school."

"Doesn't matter," she says. "Everyone will know about it inside of a week."

"Everyone already does," I say. "All the best-kept secrets at Conservatory are public knowledge."

"Any gossip yet?"

"Not that I've heard," I say.

"You'll be the last to know," Oma Judith says. She laughs again, although I don't think it's particularly funny.

"What do I do about it when I find out?"

"Hold your head up. Go about your business," she says. "Gossip is fire. Don't give it any more air than you can help. Now, go rehearse. I want to hear that quartet sing this afternoon."

"It's a little early for it to sing," I say. "It'll probably sound more like hiccups."

✦ ✦ ✦

I, as Oma Judith predicted, am the last person to hear the rumors, though I begin to notice people whispering as I pass in the corridors, particularly people I don't know well. I don't think anything of it—I am rather busy, after all—but there comes a Tuesday lunch break when I notice our usual discussion of *Rosamunde* seems strangely subdued. Felix finally clears his throat.

"Have you heard what people are saying?" he says.

"About what?"

"About you."

"No. Something ridiculous, I suppose."

Felix shakes his head. The others exchange uneasy glances.

"Am I a witch or something now?" Their expressions give me a little stab of anxiety.

"No." Felix drops his voice. "It's going around that you're sleeping with people. I mean, with us."

"I'm *what*?!"

"I'm sorry. It's stupid. I didn't think you'd have heard."

Oma Judith said to expect it, or something like it. But when he actually says it . . . I stare at my friends, slack-jawed. I can feel my face burning.

"You know who started it," Felix says.

"Let's see. Who around here does not like me?"

"Trust me, Marthe," Felix says. "Nearly everyone's *glad* you're here. If people had doubts at first, you've won them over with your ability and your discipline. They have no problem with our playing together. Absolutely none. Several have told me they're jealous, because you're *good*. And you're not afraid of the Wolff. She terrifies most of them. And you have her twice in one day."

"People respect a crazy person," Franz says.

"Thanks," I say.

"I think Marburg was waiting for you to buckle under the pressure and quit. That would save him the bother of making trouble for you. He doesn't know you very well, obviously. But you didn't quit. So now he's back on his hobby horse about women in the Conservatory, hoping the rumors will drive you out or get you thrown out. He dislikes us, too, because we're working with you."

"Speak for yourself," Franz says. "He dislikes me because I'm smarter and better-looking than he is."

"Not better-looking," Arnold says. "But definitely smarter. And a better musician."

"All right," Felix says. "He dislikes us because we're working with Marthe, except for Franz, who's smarter and may or may not be better-looking—"

"No," Arnold says.

"—and is definitely a better musician, even if he's just playing the triangle. Why Marburg dislikes women musicians, I can't fathom, considering how many great musicians have happened to be women."

"It's because he's an idiot," Franz says.

"Granted. So anyway, you didn't quit and now he's back to waging his own petty warfare against you. And us."

"It doesn't matter," Arnold says. "I say we just go about our business and ignore him."

"Absolutely," Felix says. He glances up at the large clock on the wall. "Including right now. We need to get to Theory."

I sigh and reach for my bag. It was too much to hope, I suppose, that Oma Judith would be wrong. Oma Judith is so very rarely wrong.

"Not that I didn't expect something like this," I say, "but I can't say I'm happier knowing what people are whispering about me. Just something else to rise above."

"That's the spirit!" Arnold says.

"Who sleeps, anyway?" I say.

"If it weren't this, it would be something else, or someone else," Felix says. "It's just because you're pushing the limits. You won't be the last. Five years from now, no one will care."

"I've heard that somewhere before," I say.

✦   ✦   ✦

Rumors, ugly little titters and sneers, wisps and coils of malicious gossip follow me around all week. I keep my head up. I pretend I don't know or care what people are saying. I have my Wednesday morning lesson with the Wolff and our Wednesday afternoon coaching session with the quartet. I stop talking to people in the corridors.

Felix and the others seem somehow able to ignore the whole sordid business. Perhaps it's not such a hard thing for them to be accused of sleeping with a woman they work with. Come to that, why should I care? After all, the history of music is rife with tales of affairs and rampant passions, and not just in modern times. So what if I'm not actually having the affairs? So what if passion is a language I don't speak, except to my violin?

Rumors, I tell myself, can only hurt me if I accept them as accusations rather than admissions of jealousy—but I can't make myself believe it. I'm not Anni, who can tell people to go to hell. I wish I could.

And what will happen when the rumors reach Herr Kurtz, as of course they will, sooner rather than later? What if he believes them?

Should I seize the offensive and defend myself to him? Should I tell Katerina? Since she dotes on Marburg's brother, would she believe me? Even if she does, even if she persuades her father that I'm innocent, Madame, who doesn't care if I'm innocent or not, would like nothing better than an excuse to throw me out of her house for good. The barest hint of scandal in my direction, meritless or not, would suffice.

Should I ask my mother? Ugh, no. Anni? She'd advise me to challenge Marburg to a duel, which would be worse than unhelpful.

No. When I think it over, I realize there's only one person I can turn to for advice.

✦　✦　✦

"Shh!" Gerda whispers. "Thomas is still napping. Come in, I'll make hot chocolate, just please don't make any loud noises!" We tiptoe into the little kitchen, where she puts a pot of milk on the stove to heat.

"Sorry," she says when we're settled at the kitchen table with our steaming mugs. "He's been awful lately, some days no nap at all. And then he's fretful when Wil gets home and wants to play with him. Wil's coming soon, by the way, if you want him."

I explain my predicament.

"Why not tell Kurtz yourself?" Gerda says. "Get ahead of it."

"I was hoping I wouldn't have to. It's so humiliating."

"Hm," Gerda says. "Let's see what Wil thinks. But other than playing the libertine without having the fun of being one, how's your term going?"

Thomas wakes up at this moment and sits on my lap chewing purposefully on my fingers while I tell Gerda the school gossip. She in turn is full of what Thomas has learned, which students have left, what the new ones are like.

A key turns in the lock. Herr Dietrich walks in, looking tired.

"Long rehearsal," he says as he drops his coat and violin case on the sofa. He picks Thomas out of my lap and raises him high over his head before tucking him into the crook of his arm. Thomas squeals and reaches for his father's hair. "To what do we owe the honor of your visit?"

I explain. The story grows more absurd and more onerous with every repetition.

"You're correct, Herr Kurtz will hear the rumor, if he hasn't already," Herr Dietrich says when I'm finished, "if for no other reason than because Marburg senior is also on the Sinfonia Board. And Kurtz is even more than normally averse to scandal of any kind. It's a problem, yes."

"But what can I *do*? I haven't done anything wrong. And yet if he cuts me off, there's no way I can continue at Conservatory."

"I'll talk to Kurtz after tonight's concert. But Gerda's right. You should tell him yourself, too." He hands Thomas back to Gerda and pulls himself out of his chair with some effort. "That boy's getting heavy," he says, shaking his head. He pats my shoulder as he passes. "Try not to worry," he says. "It will be all right."

"Will it?" I say to no one in particular after he's gone. I stand up to go. Gerda gives me a hug with her free arm.

"Yes," she says. "It will." But I don't believe her.

✦ ✦ ✦

The next morning, Herr Kurtz himself sits in on Katerina's lesson. Needless to say, I'm in a cold sweat the entire time. Katerina seems surprised but pleased at his presence and oblivious to the tension that envelops me. I wonder how much attention she really gets from her father these days, not that it's any of my business. She plays her exercises and her work in progress for him, not for me. I correct gently, making sure I never touch her, and make some new assignments. I say nothing nonessential and write everything down in Madame's notebook. Herr Kurtz sits gravely in the high-backed chair, seemingly relaxed, as I wish I were. By the end, I'm keeping my hands steady only with conscious effort.

At the end of the hour, I congratulate Katerina on another excellent lesson. I avoid looking at Herr Kurtz. He stays comfortably in his chair as we pack up our instruments.

"Katerina, my dear, would you excuse us for a moment?" he says. "I'd like a word with Fräulein Adler."

"Yes, Papá," Katerina says. "I'll see you next week, Fräulein."

"I'll look forward to it," I say with what I hope is a confident smile. This is our ritual for the benefit of Frau Schmidt, who has a way of happening to walk by just at this moment. But we usually exchange a conspiratorial wink and today we don't. She picks up her case and leaves. I turn to face Herr Kurtz, feeling sick.

"Please, Fräulein, sit down," he says, gesturing to the small sofa where my case and bag lie. I push them aside and sit carefully down, conscious of every motion: how my hands fold in my lap, how my knees press together. His voice is soft, not unkind.

"Fräulein, we have been very pleased with your instruction of Katerina. I had put her sudden desire to study the violin down to a passing fancy. I thought it would last a few months and then vanish, as these things do with young people. Yet it didn't. She has gained something lasting from your teaching, something good."

I don't mention that I thought the same thing, at the beginning.

"She works hard and has a genuine love for the instrument and the music," I say. "I enjoy teaching her."

"I have also been most impressed with your progress at the Conservatory," he continues. "You are clearly very gifted and you work hard, without which the gift would be worthless. You passed the audition. You survived the first year. You even, shall we say, persevered your way into the orchestra. That also impressed me. We are living in the modern world; the prejudices of the past must not limit us. This is my philosophy in banking, as well as the arts. Sadly, the arts don't share it. I doubt even I will be able to prevail upon Herr Reinecke to admit women players to the Sinfonia. Not soon, at any rate."

"If Herr Reinecke ever decides to hold blind auditions, I'll be there," I say.

"I'm sure it hasn't been easy," he says.

"I didn't expect it to be easy. But I've made it this far. I'll make it through."

"Yes," he says. "However, there is a problem."

"Sir?" I say, although I know what's coming. He pauses, as if he's hunting around for the right way to drop a load of bricks on my head.

"Word has reached me that you are accused of behaving . . . with indiscretion. I wish to know the truth. Any behavior which is, shall I say, unladylike, is impermissible. I refuse to tolerate any scandal in association with my name or my family. We have discussed this; I had thought you understood it."

"Of course, I understand it!" Indignation and a wave of pent-up anger spill out in my voice. "I've conducted myself as seriously as I know how, every minute of every day. Musicians work together. It's what music is. So, I've made friends at Conservatory, both men and the few women there are, and their families. And yes, this term I'm playing in a quartet with three men, because, as I told you, there are no other women and I deserve the same education everyone else has. But they're friends, like brothers. Not—" I choke on the words.

"Please continue," he says, studying me closely.

I suppose a banker is necessarily a judge of character. I take a deep breath.

"Not every student is as forward-looking as you are, or as my friends are. There's one—really, only one, although he has sycophants—who is obsessed with keeping women out of the professional world. He's hated my presence since the first day. He ignores the women in other years, but he's taunted me, harassed me, tried to intimidate me. He as much as told me he wants to drive me out. But I haven't quit. So now he's spreading rumors that I'm—that I'm—doing these things you're hearing. He hopes I'll quit, or you'll take away my scholarship. Because then I'd have to leave in disgrace. That would be a triumph for him."

I'm completely wound up now. I try to keep my voice under control but don't altogether succeed.

"I promise you, I promise on my word of honor, that I've done *nothing* outside the bounds of propriety. Ask my ensemble-mates, who are also having their good names dragged through the dirt. Ask the Apfelbaums to vouch for me. Ask my professors. Ask Professorin Wolff, who is coaching our quartet in addition to being my private instructor."

"And which student bears such animosity toward you?" Herr Kurtz asks.

I was afraid of this.

"I don't wish to be indiscreet, sir," I say.

"But I asked you for a name," he says.

"I don't know what good—"

"I insist," he says.

I tell him.

"I know you know his family. I know Katerina is a friend of his brother. I'm sure his actions don't represent the rest of his family—" a stretch, there, having seen his father in action with the provost "—and I don't know why he's so vicious to me, other than that I'm a woman. And . . . not rich."

"I see." He's quiet for a long time.

I sit on the sofa with my hands clenched in my lap, my knuckles white, my fingers falling asleep. I don't know what else to say. So, I just sit there.

"I must think," he says. "As I say, no hint of impropriety is permissible to me. In my position, scandal is a form of ruin."

"I understand, sir. I'm also at risk of being ruined by scandal. But I'm being smeared. As are my friends. If there's a real scandal—" I just thought of this "—it's that someone from such a fine family should discredit his family name in such a . . . an ignoble way."

"I see your point. You have sworn? Yes. In truth, I didn't want to believe it. It doesn't comport with my own observations of you and my judgment of your character, or Herr Dietrich's observations. Still. No hint of scandal . . . I must think." He uncrosses his ankles and rises from the straight-backed chair. The interrogation is finished.

"I will be in touch, Fräulein. In the meantime, continue to work hard."

"I will, sir." I decide not to add that it would be easier to work hard if I weren't consumed by fear for my future.

Herr Kurtz bows me courteously out of the sitting room. I precede him down the hall to the big front door, quietly pick up my envelope from the hall table, and slip it into my coat pocket. We both pretend not to notice this. He opens the door for me. I step through it onto the front porch, where, though the October air is cold, the sun has warmed the wall behind me.

I walk past the front garden and out through the gate to the street, where nearly bare branches arch overhead against a gray sky and the last autumn leaves lie glued to the sidewalk by rain. He didn't drop bricks on my head, anyway, and I defended myself as well as I could. Honestly, I was more coherent than I'd dared hope. Now all I can do is wait. Wait, and keep practicing.

On the way back down Leopoldstrasse, past the mansions of Lindenthal to the streetcar stop, I try to regain my equilibrium by breathing deeply and imagining Oma Judith giving Herr Kurtz a piece of her mind on my behalf.

✦　✦　✦

My hopefulness lasts through my afternoon rehearsal at the Apfelbaums, during which I say nothing about my morning, and into Sunday. I stay home and practice, emerging only to make dinner with Anni and my mother, who is full of some slight she imagines the new upstairs neighbor has committed against her.

I slice carrots and potatoes in silence as she grouches on about heavy footsteps at all hours and overwatered potted plants on the landing. Dinner is more of the same. I haven't enough spirit to contribute or argue. Anni is preoccupied and finally gives up on trying to change the subject.

After we've cleaned up, everyone vanishes into her respective bedroom; I to practice some more, Anni to study, or pretend to study, and Mother to do whatever it is she does in there. But as I face another week of Marburg's attempts to assassinate my character, the familiar sense of foreboding returns. What else can I do to defend myself? I can only think of one more thing. I would rather put my head into a lion's mouth, but I need to try to enlist the aid of the Wolff.

✦　✦　✦

Monday morning.

I arrive at school an hour before the first class, a little foggy from not sleeping well and getting up extra early. The three flights of stairs to the Wolff's studio seem unusually long and steep. I know she's in; I saw her studio light on from the street. I take my usual deep breath and knock on the door.

"Eh, who is it?" she barks.

"Marthe Adler, Professorin. May I come in?"

"Oh, all right," she says.

I open the door, step inside and close it behind me.

124

"It isn't Wednesday," she says. The smell of strong coffee fills the room from a large mug on her desk.

"No, Professorin. Please pardon my interruption. I must speak with you."

"Well?" she says.

"Professorin, I'm in danger of losing my scholarship." I rehearsed this opening phrase. If I can start cogently, maybe she'll listen all the way through. Her attention immediately focuses, as if I've started to play something.

"Why?"

Now the hard part. I explain, as succinctly as I can.

"You know me better than anyone here. You know how hard I work and you know my character. And you know my quartet-mates. You know this smear isn't true."

She is silent for a time, studying me. Her eyebrows furrow into one impressive line across her forehead. I meet her gaze, trying to look dignified rather than how I feel, which is pleading.

"And what do you want me to do about it?" she says.

"I don't know if you can do anything," I say. I thought about this last night while I was lying awake in bed. I could ask her to be my character witness to Herr Kurtz, like a beggar, and if she did it because I begged her to, I'd end up in her debt, her rescued waif, which seems unhealthy for a teacher-student relationship. I need her to choose to do it, which takes the risk that she will choose to let me go. She has the same aversion to scandal in her Conservatory; she said as much on the first day of term.

"I want you to know that, if I'm forced to leave, I'm innocent. I've been slandered. It will be the end of my training. I can't afford Conservatory without my scholarship. My personal reputation will be destroyed. And I'll have trouble getting private students, at least, any I would want."

She studies me some more. I try not to fidget.

"Who is it?"

"Who is—?"

"Who's the clever mastermind behind this plot against you?"

"I don't wish to be accused of finger-pointing."

"Very noble. Who?"

I say the despised name once more.

"Ah," she says, looking out the window. I'm almost certain I hear her mutter under her breath, *little prick.*

Pause.

"Are you prepared for Wednesday?" she says.

"Almost, Professorin. I plan to work on the Schumann today and tomorrow."

"Good. Watch out for the fingering we discussed in the first movement. It is somewhat unconventional."

"Yes, Professorin." It sounds like a dismissal. I pick up my case and bag.

"I will look forward to hearing it."

"I'll look forward to playing it for you," I say, hoping she means I'll still be around on Wednesday. "Thank you, Professorin, for your time."

"I warned you, if you recall," she says.

"Yes, Professorin."

I'm looking out the window before History starts when I happen to see the Wolff walk out the front door and up the street. Wouldn't it be excellent, I think, if she were going to beard Herr Kurtz in his den at the bank? But more likely she's only going to the apothecary to buy something for the headache I gave her. I turn my attention to the lesser Baroque composers and try unsuccessfully to put the whole ghastly business out of my mind.

I survive the week on nerves. Wednesday doesn't go particularly well. In the morning I plod through the Schumann Violin Sonata No. 2, bar by bar, fingering, fingering, fingering. In the afternoon, Felix, Franz, Arnold and I drill our way through the third movement of the *Rosamunde*. The Wolff doesn't mention my predicament or any conversation she might or might not have had with Herr Kurtz. Marburg doesn't come near me. I sense he's standing back, waiting for the little drama he's set in motion to play out, waiting for the day when I don't appear. I put my head down and try to work, with notably little success. As weeks go, it ranks among the worst.

✦ ✦ ✦

Saturday morning.

To my "Good morning, Frau Schmidt," the housekeeper responds, as always, with nothing. I walk back to the little sitting room, where Katerina and her father are waiting for me. My heart feels like it just stops. I can't read their faces at all.

"Good morning, Fräulein," Herr Kurtz says, inclining his head.

"Good morning, sir," I say.

"I thought you would like to know that I have decided to continue your scholarship," he says pleasantly, as though he were discussing the weather. "And to continue to retain you as Katerina's teacher."

My heart starts beating again, racing. My eyes sting with relief. I think I'm actually crying, which I try never to do in public. Katerina hugs me. It's the first time she's ever done that. Herr Kurtz doesn't reprimand her.

"I have been impressed by your character references," Herr Kurtz says. "Both personal and professional. As I said last week, they comport with my own judgment. However, I must stress—"

"Papá!" Katerina whirls to face him. "We talked about this last week, when you told me what Otto's father said, remember? Marthe can't control what people say about her. Anyone can say anything about anyone. People could say such things about *me*. And what could I do? Nothing! It's not fair. What matters is that we *know* Marthe. We know the truth. So, if anyone spreads more horrible rumors, you'll *know* they're false. Won't you, Papá?"

"Yes, sweetheart, I will know," he says.

I just stare. I've never heard Katerina stand up to either of her parents, or, indeed, say much more than "Yes, Papá," or "Yes, Mamá." I wonder, then, if the Wolff really did go to the bank and have her say, or if it turned out in the end that Herr Kurtz could deny his daughter nothing she really wanted.

Either way, my life isn't over. I should feel ecstatic, but at the moment I mostly feel numb and limp. Herr Kurtz smiles at me, nods, and departs. Katerina waits until his footsteps are receding up the stairs and then hugs me again.

"Poor Marthe!" she says. "Papá told me after our lesson last week that Herr Marburg said those awful things about you. I knew it was all just nasty, made-up nonsense and I told him so. I had to speak to him *very* firmly. I hope you haven't been too worried."

"Not too worried?" I say, sinking down onto the sofa. "What do you *think* I've been? You've saved my life, speaking up for me."

"Well, we girls have to stick together, right?" She giggles. "I practiced this week, too. I'm going to play with Otto again at Christmas, so I want to be extra-perfect."

Ah, there's my old familiar Katerina, bubbling up from behind the new, assertive Katerina I didn't recognize.

"Naturally," I say, unlatching my violin case rather slowly, to allow my pulse to return to something like normal. "So, I'll hear all the Christmas carols you've been working on, plus the Haydn, but first, let's have a couple of scales."

Katerina smiles delightedly, and so we begin.

✦ ✦ ✦

When I tell the others at our Saturday rehearsal, they whoop and cheer in congratulation. They look like they're about to whack me on the back until they remember that I'm a woman and that might not be the right gesture. Arnold gives me a tentative little punch on the shoulder. Ros comes in to see what the commotion is about and gives me a proper hug at the news.

"What rot!" she says. "Thank God that's all over."

The rest of the family echoes her sentiment at dinner, which I enjoy inordinately. Oma Judith has the last word.

"Ten years from now, no one will care. Every Conservatory and every university will have so many women students alongside the men, it'll be a whole different world. Free love and chaos!" She looks quite pleased at the prospect.

"Mother! Please!" Frau Apfelbaum says in her usual resigned tone.

That night I sleep well for the first time in weeks. I sleep so late on Sunday that Mother bangs on my door to see if I'm sick. I pull my pillow over my head.

"I'm fine," I call out. The pillow muffles my voice.

"Are you sure?" She opens the door and pulls my pillow off to feel my forehead. "Hmph. No fever. You've been acting so odd lately. Are you pregnant?"

I can't help it—I start to laugh. I roll over in bed in a tangle of sheets, trying to grab my pillow back out of her hands, and give way to it, laughing until tears come to my eyes at the complete absurdity of my existence. I laugh until I she gets annoyed and stomps out in a huff.

Anni barges in through the open door to see what the hysterics are about. I tell her the whole idiotic, miserable story. I hadn't before, since there was nothing she could do for me besides challenge Marburg to a duel, which I'm sure she would happily have done, but which would have ultimately just made things worse. She just shakes her head, regarding me with something like pity.

"What an utter jackass," she says.

"Little dog," I say. "Just a little dog in fancy clothes."

That starts Anni laughing and I start all over again, and we laugh for another long time. Whenever I begin to pull myself together, Anni barks a little yipping bark, and that sends us off again, tears streaming down our faces and hanging on to each other. Mother sticks her head in the door once or twice but leaves again, muttering that we've gone mad.

I've never felt closer to Anni than I do this morning.

✦　✦　✦

By Monday morning I've got my temperament back to normal, mostly, although I almost lose control again at the look on Marburg's face when he saunters into History and sees me. Out of the corner of my eye, I watch him stop and frown in my direction before ambling over to his usual seat. Felix, Franz, and Arnold find Marburg's reaction highly amusing. I keep a straight face with superhuman effort.

"Now you can get back to the important stuff," Felix says. "Like Schubert."

"And the lesser Baroque composers," Arnold says.

"A little revenge might be nice," Franz says, flexing his fingers and looking sideways at Marburg, who is whispering to his friends on the other side of the room.

"You sound like Anni. Yesterday she offered to challenge Marburg to a duel anyway, even though I've won, just to reinforce the point."

"Leave it," Felix says.

Franz has a dangerous look in his eye, but fortunately the professor arrives at that moment and we're soon back in the Baroque. By lunchtime, the routine of school has reasserted itself in my mind and I'm back to normal for real, except for the occasional stifled giggle.

After this, Marburg appears to decide I'm beneath his notice, which suits me very well. The Wolff doesn't seem surprised to see me on Wednesday morning.

She never mentions my early morning visit to her studio again.

9

FALL, OCTOBER–DECEMBER 1907

October 1907

By the middle of term, between hours of individual practice, rehearsals at the Apfelbaums', and our weekly coaching with the Wolff, after which we generally feel like mincemeat, *Rosamunde* is beginning to come together.

"Almost decent. But not quite," Franz always says afterward in an uncanny impression of the Wolff, though never where she can hear him.

"I wonder if there's any chance she'll let us perform it," Arnold says after one of our rehearsals. "I hear other groups rehearsing and we're better than they are. It doesn't seem fair, just because Marthe's not a man."

"We could all wear long dresses," Franz says. "Personally, I think I'd look good in one."

"I wouldn't," Arnold says.

"Much as I would love to see that," I say, "and I really would *love* to see that, somehow I don't think it would work."

"Agreed," Felix says. "I'm pretty sure I *wouldn't* want to see it, in any case. But maybe at least she'd let us perform for our families. I can't see why she'd object. Nothing to lose by asking, anyway. Who knows, it might shame her into letting us play in the recitals."

After our next session with the Wolff ("*Pianissimo*, not *piano*! Again, you are rushing! You must *feel* the *rubato* if you are going to use it and you must all feel it the same!"), Felix cautiously brings up the subject of performance.

"Professorin," he says, "we just want to thank you again for coaching us this term. We can tell we're doing better than other ensembles and we can see how much we've improved over last year. We wish we could have been so fortunate from the beginning. Last year, well, we didn't learn nearly as much."

She fixes him with her best stare, one eyebrow raised, and waits.

"I know we don't have permission to perform in the school recital, but our families would appreciate the opportunity to hear us. Could we perform *Rosamunde* just for them? Perhaps in one of the large practice rooms?"

The Wolff studies us all for a minute, her arms folded.

"It is undeniable," she finally says, sounding as if she would much prefer to deny it, "that you are making acceptable progress. Your unconventional membership has not proved as great an impediment as I feared."

"Marthe has more discipline than any of us," Felix says. I feel myself blush. "Her previous experience as your student is serving us all well in practice. It's like having your lieutenant among us."

The Wolff's lip twitches.

"I will consider it," she says.

"Thank you, Professorin," we say, and file out.

"Unconventional membership?" Franz says when we're safely downstairs. "Is *that* what we have? I had no idea!"

"Lieutenant?" I say.

"Well, I couldn't tell her you're the Generalin, could I?" Felix says. "She might think you were angling for her job."

"Nicely done, though," Arnold says. "I'll bet she says yes."

"Clever of you to put her in mind of Nodelmann," I say. "She doesn't respect him even a little. And I think she's not as high minded as she likes to seem."

"He won't come hear us play for our families," Arnold says.

"Of course not," I say. "He'll have to come to the class recitals, though. Whomever he's neglecting this year will be playing, which might just make her decide to put us in front of the whole school, and him, unconventional membership or not."

"My thought exactly," Felix says.

✦　✦　✦

"I have spoken to the provost," the Wolff says when we arrive the following week. "I have explained the exceptional circumstances and your acceptable progress. He has graciously permitted your ensemble to perform in the main program on the Tuesday evening of recital week, with the understanding that the official policy has not changed. It is unprecedented. I have taken a considerable risk in advocating for you. I expect thoroughgoing professionalism from all of you at all times. And I expect as professional a performance as possible, even though you are only in your second year."

"That's terrific news, Professorin!" Felix says. "We won't let you down."

"If you are planning to surprise me," she says, fixing us with one of her looks, "I suggest you exceed my expectations rather than otherwise."

"Yes, Professorin," we say in unison.

"Very well then," she says. "Toward that end, turn your chairs around."

We stare, mouths open.

"So you are facing away from each other," she adds helpfully.

"But how will we—" I begin.

"You will *listen*," she says. "You rely too much on visual cues. You are not listening properly. Go on, our time is already short."

My turned-around chair faces the Wolff's enormous framed diploma, which I've never really studied before. A broad, ornamental border surrounds several lines of impossibly elaborate script, which I decipher while the others are getting settled.

The Vienna Conservatory awards this Day, 15 June 1885, to MARIA ANNA WOLFF, its Diploma in Music with Emphasis in Violin, Piano, and Pedagogy. Several signatures follow.

If someone with this level of training is ever pleased with me, even a little, I must be doing very well, indeed.

Felix faces a wall with a painting on it. Arnold faces the piano. Franz's view is out the window. How are we supposed to—

"Begin."

It sounds ragged. She doesn't stop us, but lets us struggle on. A few pages in, it begins to tighten. I'm straining to hear every note, every nuance from the other three instruments, to try to stay with them. At the end of the first movement, we stop and look around at the Wolff for directions.

"Continue," she says.

We reach the end, finally. It's far from our best run-through, but it becomes less ragged as it progresses, and I feel my hearing sharpen, like an animal's. When we finish, we all turn around with identical expressions of surprise.

"Do this at least once a week," the Wolff says.

"Amazing," Felix says. "I've never encountered this technique before."

"Somehow, I'm not surprised," the Wolff says. "This is how you begin to think like a quartet. Four instruments, eight arms, one brain. Your emotions must be in perfect unison. Now, face front and do it again."

We do it again, listening to each other for all we're worth. I find I'm focusing on tinier details than before, hearing more subtle relationships between voices.

"Better," she says. "You must pay more attention to dynamics. Don't be fooled. They only look simple."

"All right, who said it looks simple?" Franz demands, glaring around at us.

The Wolff almost, but not quite, laughs. "Go. Get out of here. Use your ears this week."

"Yes, Professorin," we say as we pack up and leave.

"I wonder what that quartet octopus really looks like," Franz says as we head downstairs.

"Terrifying," Arnold says.

"I felt the difference, though," Felix says. "Didn't you?"

We all did.

"I wonder if she's right about us," he says. "Beginning to think like a quartet?"

"She didn't say we were," I point out. "She said this is how you do it. Besides, since when would the Wolff not be right? At least, where string quartets are concerned, or music generally, or human nature? Did I tell you what she called Marburg? She was muttering to herself, so she thought I wouldn't hear."

"What?" Franz says. I whisper it to them. They burst into such howls of laughter that heads turn in the corridor.

"You know, I have a sudden increased respect for the Wolff," Franz says. "An astute judge of character if ever there was one."

"Agreed," Felix and Arnold say together.

We continue down the corridor, my three brothers and I, stifling giggles on our way to the common room.

✦ ✦ ✦

At the Apfelbaums' table I meet painter friends of Frau Apfelbaum, young architects from Herr Apfelbaum's firm, friends from the neighborhood, and friends of Oma Judith whose debates revolve around Marxism, Zionism, and philosophy. The first weekend in November, after several hours of intense concentration on *Rosamunde*, I meet Ros's childhood friend, Johanna Weinenberg, who works in a fashionable dress shop near the Altstadt.

After we've praised Frau Apfelbaum's chicken stew with new apples and her trademark heavy dark bread, when smaller conversations have begun to eddy around the table, Johanna asks what I'm wearing to our recital.

I've wondered this myself for weeks and shoved the thought out of my mind, pretending I'm far too busy trying to learn the music to worry about what I'll wear while performing it. My last dress-buying experience will more than last me forever, but even I know I can't wear my widowed housekeeper dress to perform in the quartet. After the orchestra concert, I wanted to burn the ghastly thing, but we don't have a fireplace. I won't humiliate myself by even mentioning it to Johanna. Besides, she probably already knows.

"I don't know yet," I say. "I don't own a gown."

"You need one. Especially as I understand your ensemble is bending a few rules. Ros? Ideas?"

"Not overly fancy, but a nice fabric," Ros says promptly, as if she's been awaiting her cue.

Johanna nods. "Velvet? Silk? A bit of lace?"

"All-season," Ros says.

Something tells me they've rehearsed this.

Johanna: "Open neck, long sleeves. Not too puffy. Sleek shape."

Ros: "Not too slim. No hobbles."

Johanna: "God, never! Women have *died* because of hobbles."

Ros: "No train. They're a nightmare onstage and they get filthy."

Johanna: "Definitely not. What color?"

"Black," I say. "I don't want to stick out any more than—wait, why are we even pretending? I can't afford anything at all, let alone something custom-made."

Johanna ignores me, gets up from the table, and returns with a pad of paper and a pen from her bag. She turns over a fresh sheet and begins to sketch something. I throw Ros a panicked look. Ros shrugs with feigned innocence.

In twenty seconds Johanna sketches a woman holding a violin and a bow, wearing a long, slim gown, with long sleeves loose at the top and slim at the wrist. A lace panel flows down the front.

"It's beautiful," I say. "And the sleeves are perfect for performance. But, as I said, I can't afford anything new. I'll go back to the secondhand shop. I might have better luck this time."

The thought makes my stomach turn over in a most unpleasant way.

"I think materials for this would be about twenty marks," Johanna says. "Labor would be about the same. You could pay me a mark a month if you want, I don't care. And it's so simple, I can have it done in a few weeks, in plenty of time before your performance."

"But—"

"Come see me tomorrow," Johanna says. She fishes a card out of her pocket. "Be there at noon and we'll get started."

And because I'm in the Apfelbaums' world, I can't do anything but agree.

✦ ✦ ✦

The dress shop on Schwalbengasse in the Neumarkt isn't open on Sunday, perhaps because its usual clients don't need it to be, having nothing else to do during the week but buy clothes. I follow Johanna into the rear of the shop, past wooden mannequins modeling morning dresses, afternoon tea dresses, evening dresses, past shelves crowded with bolts of fabric and rolls of lace, past a dozen little tables bearing lamps with mosaic shades that would be perfectly at home in the Kurtz family's front sitting room.

In a back room she's propped the sketch she made last night against an easel next to several bolts of black fabric, a roll of black lace, a tape measure, and her sketchbook and pens. Somehow, I'm not surprised to see Ros here, too, sitting sideways on a sofa with her feet up.

"I couldn't resist," she says. "I hope you don't mind. I always love this part, putting the design together with fabrics and things."

"I'll rely on you," I say. "I'm out of my depth here."

"Today, we'll just get your measurements and choose a fabric," Johanna says. "If you like the sketch, I'll develop it from there."

I study the sketch again. I can't believe she came up with it in twenty seconds.

"It's amazing," I say. "Do you play? You knew exactly what would work."

"No," Johanna laughs. "But I know people who do."

"Johanna made mine," Ros says. "And Berit's."

"Ah," I say.

We settle on a mid-weight black satin and a black Belgian lace for the panel. Ros makes a few suggestions and Johanna draws more sketches to show the back, and how the skirt will allow me to move freely.

"You have to be able to dress yourself," she says. "So, it buttons up the side. Gowns with twenty little buttons up the back are for women with husbands. Or maids."

"I'm not likely ever to have either," I say. "Are you sure about this? I really do *not* have—"

"Satin charmeuse silk, black, three meters. Belgian lace, black, two meters. Labor, let's say two weeks, because it will be after hours. Just as I thought, about twenty marks each," she says. "And I'm serious, a mark a month is fine."

"But I can't ask you—"

"Look," Johanna says. "Ros says your performance with Felix and the others will be a first for the Conservatory and maybe in recorded history. You cannot look like a student and pull this off. You must look professional. Fair or not, that's just how the world is. Besides, do you have any idea how many little girls are being inspired by the example you and Ros and the others are setting? You're telling a whole generation of girls that they can *do* things. My little sister takes violin lessons. I want her to see you out there being magnificent. And looking magnificent. And if anyone asks you where you got your gown, you just tell them, all right?"

"I will," I promise. "Does your sister need a teacher? Maybe I could trade lessons for it."

"Not at present," Johanna says. "And I don't want you distracted. Maybe when you're out of Conservatory."

"Keep me in mind," I say.

"Come back in two weeks for a fitting."

"Right."

"Good! Now, go practice. I want my sister to be motivated, all right?"

She sees us out and locks the front door behind us.

"What did you think?" Ros says.

"Infinitely better than the secondhand shop," I say.

"Sounds like a low standard," Ros says.

"Too low, you're right," I say. "Actually, I'm overwhelmed, that's what I think. Just absolutely floored."

Ros looks very pleased with herself.

✦   ✦   ✦

December 1907

It's three weeks before I can go back for a fitting, which mainly involves a lot of pins, and another two weeks to finish, so our performance is drawing uncomfortably near before my gown is ready. Ros is already in her spot on the sofa when I arrive to take delivery.

"I couldn't wait for the performance!" she says.

She seems to be in an exceptionally good mood. My incredibly beautiful black gown hangs on a fancy wooden hanger in an alcove, waiting.

"I won't help you," Johanna says. "You have to be able to do it on your own. Shout if you have any problems."

Behind a curtain in the alcove, I change my well-worn dress for the silky creation before me. The side buttons work flawlessly. The length is perfect. The black lace down the front is perfect. The sleeves are perfect. I look at the young woman in the mirror, her hair in an untidy bun, a magnificent gown cascading down her body, her eyes unnaturally bright. I barely recognize her. I stare for a full minute before Johanna calls, "Come out! Let's have a look at you."

As I push back the curtain, I realize I still have a serious problem. My high button boots poke out from under the gown, looking utterly ludicrous. I don't own formal dress shoes and can't afford any, especially on top of forty marks for the gown. My feet begin to hurt just thinking of last winter's widowed housekeeper shoes. Even if I didn't dread putting them back on my feet, they're definitely not what this gown deserves, but I suppose they'll have to do. I step out into the fitting room, where Johanna and Ros have been conversing in low voices.

"Gorgeous!" Ros says. "Turn around!"

Johanna surveys me from top to bottom with a critical eye.

"There's plenty of room in the shoulders? The waist isn't too snug? The sleeves are long enough when your arms are extended?"

I extend my arms. Johanna seems satisfied.

"And my signature detail—check the left side."

It takes me a few seconds of fumbling, but at last my fingers find their way into a hidden pocket.

"For keys. Or whatever," she says.

I can only shake my head.

"And one last thing." Ros hands me a box. "A little donation to the cause from Oma Judith. Something for kicking a stupid rule in the teeth, she said."

Inside the box nestles a pair of black satin slippers, with small black bows and a delicate heel.

"I couldn't!" I say, shocked.

"You can't walk out and play Schubert in your high-buttons," Ros says. "And you can't hurt Oma's feelings, either, can you? You're stuck, my dear. You have no alternative but to be professionally, gorgeously dressed when you make history at the Conservatory, in spite of yourself. Put them on, I want to see the whole effect."

The whole effect is to make me look like someone else, someone who is a vast improvement over the normal me. I think I might start to cry.

"Don't," Johanna warns. "Not good for the silk. All right, take it off and I'll wrap it up for you."

"I'll come early and do your hair," Ros says.

"A mark a week," I say. "As long as it takes. It's worth it. It's worth every penny."

Johanna smiles. "Give my sister something to aim for," she says.

"I will," I say. "I promise."

✦　✦　✦

The following Saturday, when I come home after rehearsing at the Apfelbaums', I find my mother asleep in her armchair with her eternal mug of

Bärenfang on the table beside her. Usually when I find her here, I try to sneak past without waking her. Tonight, for some reason, I pat her shoulder.

"Mother, wake up." She stirs, but I have to shake her a little before she opens her eyes. "Mother. You'll be more comfortable in your own bed."

"Wha'?" she mumbles. "'m fine. Go on. Leave m' alone." Her eyes finally drag open, but have trouble focusing. "Go 'way, can't you? I said 'm fine."

I should leave her alone, but pity gets the better of my judgment. I pull her to her feet and half-carry her into her cluttered, musty bedroom. She's extraordinarily heavy, a limp, dead weight. I let her down as gently as I can onto her unmade bed, coax her to lie down, try to push her away from the edge, cover her with her eiderdown. She lies there, inert, breathing noisily. I watch her for a minute, feeling guilty for not taking better care of her, then return to the sitting room, retrieve her mug and dump its revolting contents down the kitchen sink. As tired as I am, I lie awake in bed for at least an hour, unable to sleep.

In the morning, Mother is up before I am, puttering about the kitchen in her patched housecoat and slippers, her eyes bleary but focused.

"How do you feel this morning?" I ask. "You seemed almost ill last night when I got home."

"What are you talking about?" she says. "I'm fine."

"I'm glad." I give her a little hug. "I'll be here all day if you need anything."

I have a piece of toast and a cup of tea and retreat into my bedroom. As I close my door, I see her staring after me, as if she's wondering who I am and how I got into her flat.

I don't think any more of it until the next week, when it happens again. Damn that Bärenfang! I wonder how many lonely women get drunk on it day after day after day. I should talk to Anni, if I can ever catch her at home. There must be some way we can take better care of our mother. It's not her fault she's stuck in the life she's ended up with—no husband, no interests, no opportunities. I do know one thing, though. I don't ever want to be stuck in that life myself. Even if all I ever do is teach unwilling children their scales, it will be better than that.

✦　✦　✦

I was nervous before recital last year, but this recital is a different order of magnitude. The Wolff expects a professional performance and we promised we'd give one. But all the tricky passages that could go wrong are the least of my worries. Will people be so shocked they don't hear us? Will they walk out? Will someone try to stop us? Have we really endangered the Conservatory? Was this whole radical experiment a giant mistake?

But what's even so radical about it? Men and women have played music together in their homes forever. Men and women opera singers perform together all the time and have for centuries. Why not us? This is the modern world. Even Herr Kurtz said so.

We're good. We're ready. We're going to be professional. I'm even going to *look* professional. Schubert would be proud, and possibly not even all that surprised.

I argue through this internal debate several times a day for the last two weeks of the term.

✦ ✦ ✦

"I require a word before you leave."

We're packing up after our final coaching session before recital week, after the Wolff has allowed us to play *Rosamunde* through without interruption and then given us another barrage of microscopically finicky corrections.

We stop packing.

"A parent has complained to the provost regarding the unconventional membership of your ensemble," she says.

"Someone complained because Marthe's in it?" Felix says.

"Very perceptive, Herr Apfelbaum. Yes, in fact, that was the core of his complaint," she says.

"Do you mean we won't be able to perform?" Arnold says.

"I did not say that, Herr Blum. This individual heard from his son that we are allowing Fraülein Adler to perform with a male ensemble. He was indignant, perhaps I should say incensed, at the Conservatory's departure from tradition."

"Why does he care?" Franz demands.

"Also a perceptive question, Herr Herzberg. As it happened, the provost called me into the meeting with this parent, because I am your ensemble coach and Fraülein Adler's teacher. I explained that, while the division of ensemble by sex is traditional, it is not part of the Conservatory by-laws. Moreover, while it reflects the composition of professional ensembles, it in no way reflects the composition of the ensembles for which most chamber music was originally composed, that is, for families and friends to play together in their homes, as many families and friends still do.

"I then explained that we allowed this temporary arrangement, with the consent of the three of you—"

"We begged her, more like," Franz says.

"—and your families. They don't object, do they, by the way?"

"No," Franz says.

"No," Arnold says.

"Mine's been chaperoning all term," Felix says. "If my parents had any objection, I'm sure they'd have mentioned it by now. Besides, they want to adopt her."

"Yours, Fräulein?"

I think of my mother, drunk in her armchair. "No," I say.

"I further explained that the administration wished to meet Fraülein Adler's sponsor's requirement that she be denied no essential element of her musical training, with the understanding that it does not represent a change in Conservatory policy."

"This individual could hardly object to something so reasonable," Franz says.

The Wolff's eyebrows suggest otherwise.

"In fact, he made rather a lot more objections, I'm sorry to say. And a threat or two. They are of no importance. I only mention this unfortunate episode to you because you all need to be aware that not every person in the student body feels benignly toward your departure from tradition. Do not allow yourselves to become the objects of petty harassment. Look out for each other. Do you understand me?"

"Yes," we say.

There's no need to ask whose father complained.

"Good," she says. "And you have no knowledge of any private administration business, I hope that is clear. Just concentrate on that list of corrections and I will see you on Tuesday next. I expect a professional presentation."

"You'll get one," Felix says with an uncharacteristic edge to his voice. She smiles a tight smile at him.

"Excellent," she says. "I look forward to it. Fraülein, a moment, if you please?"

When the others have left, she turns back to me.

"Please tell me you will be dressed professionally this time," she says.

"Yes, Professorin," I say. "I have a proper gown now. And shoes. I didn't like the last one, either."

"I regret even having to mention it," she says. "It is not a cross male artists bear nearly to the same degree. It is just how the world is. I'm relieved to hear you have arrived at a solution. That is all."

"Thank you, Professorin. And—thank you for defending us. I'm sorry he made threats."

She waves that off.

"He threatened to remove his son from the Conservatory and put him in a more proper academy," she says. "I think the Conservatory can bear the strain. As to the tradition, it is deeply entrenched. And, frankly, an archaic holdover in our modern age. Truthfully, I would have liked to explain this to Herr—to this individual—along with several more such points, but it seemed unwise to overburden him. As I say, just be aware. Don't leave your possessions lying around."

"I won't, Professorin," I say, wondering at her change of opinion.

"You may go," she says. "Rehearse, won't you, before next week?"

"Yes, Professorin." I pick up my coat, bag and case and open the door. I look both ways before stepping out into the corridor.

"That's the spirit," she says as I close the door softly behind me.

✦ ✦ ✦

"Even if we didn't know who it was, he'll be easy to spot at the recital," Franz says. "Just look for a pompous ass who's about five centimeters tall. I wish I could have seen her tearing him to pieces."

"Me, too," Arnold says.

By unspoken agreement, we're walking in a tight little group on our way to Ear Training. Felix's eyes are roving over the crowds of students in the corridors.

"And just let Moron von Mar—"

142

"Hush!" Felix snaps. "We don't know anything about it, remember? Keep your eyes open and save the rest for when we're at home, all right?"

"Sure," Franz says. "But just let someone or other mind his own damn business, that's all. Nobody specific."

"That's more like it," Felix says.

✦ ✦ ✦

In the foyer on the morning of our recital, I encounter the Wolff. She commands me to follow her upstairs, where she shuts her studio door behind me.

"It is probably an overabundance of caution on my part, Fräulein, but leave your belongings in my studio today. They will be safe here. If I leave, I always lock my door," she says.

"You don't think my locker is safe, Professorin?"

"Let us say, your gown might get wrinkled in it. You may hang it on the hook behind the door. Leave your violin, too. Bring the others here for a run-through later."

I hang up my dress bag and set my case on the floor by the wall.

"I'm not sure if we're better off rehearsing again or just getting our minds off it for an hour or two," I say.

"Under the circumstances, I would say rehearsing," she says. "Come at three."

"Yes, Professorin," I say. I leave her opening mail at her desk and slip quietly out into the empty corridor.

After our Theory exam, we head downstairs to the crowded common room. Felix stops so suddenly, the rest of us run into him. He turns to me, a sharp, anxious look on his face.

"Did you leave your locker open, Marthe?" he says.

"No, I—" I look over at the wall of lockers. Mine is standing wide open and is, of course, empty.

I dodge past milling clusters of students, all discussing the exam. The lock has been forced. It won't stay closed even when I try to latch it.

"It was closed this morning," Franz says. "I'd have noticed one left open."

"Marthe—your things!" Arnold's voice sounds faint under the general rumble of conversation.

"They weren't here," I say. "They're—never mind. I need to report this."

I nearly knock over one or two people in my rush to the nearest staircase up to the Wolff's studio on the third floor, the other three close behind me. I tell her what happened, still panting for breath.

"I am disappointed," she says at last, "although, I regret to say, less than surprised. Report the damage to maintenance. In the meantime, your bag and case are still quite safe."

"But, vandalism!" Felix is indignant. "Surely there must be a report of vandalism. And discipline! We know who it has to be. Surely the school will punish him?"

"That will be for the provost to decide, Herr Apfelbaum. I will see that he is informed. For the moment, if I'm not mistaken, you have an exam in approximately an hour. Go eat lunch and focus your minds on it. Come back at three for a run-through."

"Yes, Professorin," we say.

"As much as anything, he was trying to rattle us," Felix says as we sit on our usual bench with our bread and cheese. "He figured he'd put us off just enough to throw us tonight."

"Well, I'm rattled," Arnold says.

"I'm not rattled. I'm going to kill him," Franz says. "Little bastard."

I feel heat rising under my collar, my heart pounding with anger, even as the absurdity of the whole thing almost makes me laugh. I imagine Marburg, dressed as usual in Madame Kurtz's light blue morning dress, forcing the lock and swinging the door open to see . . . nothing. His look of consternation. His disappointment. His hasty retreat up to the exam, for which I now remember he was slightly late. The way he trips on the morning dress, which is too long for him, as he runs up the stairs.

"Listen, all of you." To my surprise, the voice is mine. "Yes, we know it was Marburg. Yes, he was hoping to damage my clothes, or worse. And no, no one is going to catch him or get him thrown out. A pity, but that's how the world is. Yes, he was trying to wreck our performance. But he's not going to succeed. And why not? Because we are *better* than that. We've trained like professionals for months. We're going to play *Rosamunde* at three with the Wolff. We're going to put this nonsense behind us and tonight we're going to make Schubert proud. No one is going to waste time or energy killing Marburg, however much he might deserve it, because we have a quartet to play. Any extra energy we get from thinking about my locker we are going to channel into a performance people will be talking about years from now. Because we are *that good*. Do I make myself clear?"

The three of them look like fish, staring at me with their mouths open.

Felix recovers first. "Fraülein Generalin is correct, as usual," he says. "We're going to learn today what it means to be disciplined. And tonight, we will play the pants off Marburg."

"Dress," I say without thinking.

"What?" Arnold says.

"Nothing."

"All right, the bastard can live another day," Franz says.

"Ignore his existence," Felix says. "Got it? Excellent. All right, exam time. Good luck, everyone."

I might have to keep Marburg with me forever. I always play so much better when he's just driven me to the edge of my senses with fury.

But not immediately. The run-through starts badly. Everyone's concentration is in pieces and our playing is ragged. The Wolff lets us struggle through the first movement before she stops us.

"Close your eyes," she orders. "Now. Take five deep breaths. Picture yourselves walking onto the stage tonight. Acknowledge your audience. Take your seats. Picture the music on the first page. Check your tuning. Take your time. Three more deep breaths. Place your instruments at the ready. Eyes on your first violinist. Do you understand?"

We nod.

"Good," she says. "Again."

This time it's better.

"Once more," she says.

This time we play it straight through. It sounds like it's supposed to.

"Not bad," she says. "Add an audience's energy and you may approach decent. Leave your things here. Go have dinner. Come back for them at six."

"Yes, Professorin," we say.

The hour passes, somehow.

"And remember," the Wolff says as we collect our bags and cases at six o'clock, "you are *professionals*."

"Just what we've been telling ourselves all term," Felix says.

"See you in the waiting lounge," I say as I head for the women's toilet. "If you get there first, persuade someone to guard our things while we're on, all right?"

"Is von Moron even on tonight?" Franz asks.

"Naturally," Felix says.

"What luck," Arnold says. "Just who we'd like to wait with. And leave with our gear."

"We'll take care of it, don't worry," Felix says.

✦ ✦ ✦

Ros is impressed when I tell her about the days' events.

"You do know how to stir things up," she says, brandishing my hairbrush before the mirror in the women's toilet. "But you're all right, your gear's all right, and you look absolutely stunning. One of these days I'll teach you how to do your own hair and then I won't have to follow you to all your concerts."

Under her skillful hands, I transform from a student wearing a gown that looks like it should belong to someone else into a young professional violinist, albeit one who ate caterpillars for dinner. I shake my head in disbelief.

"If you can teach me to do that," I say, "you're a regular miracle worker."

"It's not as hard as it looks," she says. "When you solo, we'll get you some jewelry. It seems silly that it matters, but it does. It's showmanship. Show-womanship, if you like."

"If I played behind a curtain, people would just listen to the music," I say.

"But you'd lose their energy," she says. "And half the fun. You look fantastic. Go, my child, make some history!"

"Right," I say.

Jaws drop when I walk into the waiting lounge. I smile coolly at everyone, including Marburg, who is oddly early. His eyes narrow as they follow me across the room.

"It's the strangest thing," I say, slightly louder than necessary. "Someone tried to break into my locker this morning. Can you believe it?"

146

"That's terrible!" Franz says, catching on. "Was anything damaged?"

"Just the lock," I say.

"Any idea who it was?" he says.

"No," I say. "Nor why. Probably just a prank."

We settle into our corner for the wait. Marburg's quartet is after the intermission; we're last.

The provost makes his introduction and gives the usual announcements. The first two groups are both capable. We tune and warm up. Intermission arrives.

"Number three and number four to stage right." The imperturbable Herr Schädler pokes his head in the door and disappears again.

Felix nods to his friends from the second group who are guarding our gear and we carry our instruments, bows, and parts to the stage right wing, where we listen to Marburg's group perform Haydn. They're not bad, I admit grudgingly to myself. Marburg has applied himself more this term and, though he hasn't Felix's ability or flair, he acquits himself competently at the first violin part of the quartet.

"I heard the other three threatened to dump him if he didn't buckle down," Felix whispers. "Honestly, he's not bad when he puts in the work."

"Focus," I whisper back.

The others salute.

What will happen when we walk onstage, three men and a woman? Our names are in the program; still, I imagine scandalized murmurs, little ripples of surprise, as if a Martian walked out to play the violin for them. My caterpillars stampede. I think I might throw up.

The heat of my fire, stoked white hot by the events of the day, burns in my throat, on my cheeks, in my fingers. It spreads all the way to my toes, tucked into their beautiful black satin slippers. Gradually, as the Haydn progresses, my nausea gives way to excitement. We're professionals. We're ready.

We're going to show them how it's done.

Herr Schädler beckons. We line up: me, Franz, Arnold, and then Felix. The Haydn rises to its spirited finish. Under the applause, Felix says, "Remember, we're going to make Schubert proud. And more importantly, the Wolff."

"Right!" we say.

The day's anxieties and the ragged first run-through are behind us. Now all that matters is our music and the audience who will give us the energy to make *Rosamunde* soar.

"Sounded great!" Felix says to Marburg and his fellows as they exit.

"Thanks!" three of them say. Marburg glances at us and looks away.

The applause quiets. Herr Schädler waits for an inscrutable interval and then says, "Go."

We stride onto the stage, into the footlights, a thrill of excitement coursing through us. We take our places. Bow to our audience. The applause seems as loud as for any of the other ensembles; a good sign. Is there a murmur of surprise under the applause? A rustle of paper? Well, we can't help it if they didn't read their programs.

We sit. Set up our parts. Bend back the first corner for easier turning. Adjust our chairs. Check our sight lines. Check our tuning. Take our time. Instruments in position. Bows in position. Three deep breaths. All eyes on Felix. Three beats. And then Felix nods and we begin.

The energy of the audience works its magic. *Rosamunde* takes off and flies of its own accord, carrying us with it. We focus, we communicate, we listen. We are four equal voices, conversing. We recover from the occasional slip and keep going. I've never given a performance like it.

I've never felt so happy making music.

A half hour later, when we stand for our bow and applause fills our ears, I can see in the others' faces the same things I feel: exhilaration, triumph, and pure, golden happiness.

✦ ✦ ✦

The Wolff is waiting for us in the lounge, along with Felix's two friends, who report no problems while we were away.

"Bring your instruments to my studio," she says. "You can leave them until tomorrow's notes if you like."

"The audience didn't seem to mind our unconventional membership," I say.

"Was it . . . was it decent, Professorin?" Arnold asks, a little breathless from hauling his cello case up the stairs.

She turns to look down at us from the third floor landing, the corner of her lip twitching.

"Reasonably." She sweeps majestically down the hall to unlock her studio door.

"I will be in the foyer," she adds as we deposit our cases and bags. "I dislike receptions, as a rule, but I want a word with Professor Nodelmann."

She steps out after us, locking the door behind her.

The reception is in full swing by the time we arrive. Our families, all friends by now even though this is the only place they ever meet, are deep in several conversations. We help ourselves to cookies and survey the crowd.

"Oooh, Marthe, I *wondered* what you'd be wearing!" Katerina practically fizzes with excitement. "You were fantastic! What a *beautiful* gown! You *must* tell me the name of your dressmaker! I'm going to be her best customer. And please introduce me to your quartet!"

In short order, she's chattering to them about what a marvelous teacher I am, while Herr Kurtz approaches with far more dignity and kisses my hand, which makes me blush to my ears.

"Congratulations, Fraülein. The Schubert was beautifully done. I trust we will hear the four of you again."

"I'd like nothing better, sir," I say. "Next fall, maybe. I hope."

"Very good," he says. "Katerina, by the way, is eager to entertain our guests again this holiday season. She reflects well upon her teacher."

"She's an excellent student," I say.

"Your modesty becomes you," he says. "I hope being a dedicated amateur will bring her pleasure in her life."

Considering that Katerina's life seems to be devoted to nothing but pleasure . . . I dismiss the thought as ungenerous. And I need the money.

"I hope so, too," I say.

"I trust you've had no more difficulties with your fellow student?"

My voice catches. He doesn't know about this morning and now is certainly not the time to tell him.

"Er, no," I lie.

"Speaking of whom . . ." Herr Kurtz glances past me and gives what might or might not be a small sigh. "I suppose we should say hello to his family. Katerina, my dear, I believe I see Otto von Marburg."

Katerina disengages herself from my quartet-mates and takes her father's arm. As they turn to leave, Herr Kurtz catches my eye and chuckles.

"That girl is a walking glass of champagne," Felix says to no one in particular. "Effervescent, golden, and she'll go right to your head."

"There you are!" Ros appears with Johanna and Anni. Johanna clasps the hand of a little girl of about eight. "We were looking all over for you."

"We were keeping Franz from eating all the cookies," Arnold says, biting into his fifth.

"I beg your pardon, sir, I've been a model of restraint!" Franz says, his mouth full of his eighth, at least.

"The dress worked!" Johanna says.

"Absolutely perfect," I say. "And I need some of your cards. My student just declared her intention to become your best customer."

"Excellent," Johanna says. "And this is my sister, Heidi."

"Johanna says you play violin," I say as Heidi nods and edges closer to Johanna. "I'd love to hear you play sometime."

"Johanna says she'll make my recital dress," Heidi says.

"Lucky you," I say. "I had to wait until now for her to make one for me."

"Cards," Johanna says, handing me several. Then, to Heidi, "Come on, I promised you cookies!"

"A mark a month," I say, putting the cards in the hidden pocket of my gown.

"I didn't know you could look like that!" Anni says.

"I didn't either, I promise you," I say. "Did you like the music?"

"Oh, sure, the music was terrific. Always is," Anni says. "But you looked like an *adult*. I couldn't get over it."

"I'm pretty shocked, myself," I say.

"Well, come and let everyone make a fuss over you," Ros says and we start back toward our families. At a tap on my shoulder, I turn to see Herr Dietrich and Gerda.

"I'm sure you know you were fantastic!" Gerda says, hugging me. "And you look every inch a virtuoso."

"I'm beginning to think that's more than half the battle," I say.

"The other half went well also," Herr Dietrich says. "I could see the Wolff's paw-prints all over you."

"Tomorrow's notes may tell a different story," I say.

"I expect you'll survive," he says. "I heard her talking to Professor Nodelmann a few minutes ago. I couldn't catch the details, but she seemed quite smug. And the audience survived your being female, once they got over their shock. At the Sinfonia it would be different, but, luckily, we're here."

"Some of the students are handling it better than others," I say. "Tell you later. But I can't wait to do it again."

"I predict you will," he says.

"Come see us this holiday!" Gerda says.

"I will!" I say, and wave as they depart.

I spot Marburg at the refreshment table, helping himself to punch. On impulse I square my shoulders, concentrate on standing up very straight, and walk over to face him.

"I just wanted to say, I thought you played beautifully tonight," I say.

He looks up, surprised, sees it's me, and his expression retreats.

"Thanks," he mutters after an awkward pause.

"And I also wanted to say," I continue before I have a chance to change my mind, "I'm here for the same reason you are: to become a musician. I've earned my place, but I've no wish to be your enemy. I respect you as a colleague and hope you will consider me a colleague also."

I'm stretching things here, obviously, since I've spent most of the last several months veering between terror that he would get me thrown out and a furious desire to have him trip down a flight of stairs while wearing Madame Kurtz's morning dress. This very day, in fact. But, still concentrating on standing as tall as possible, I look him pleasantly in the eye, daring him to look away.

It's one thing, apparently, to pick on a girl of modest means who wears ordinary clothes with a few discreet bits of darning here and there and another thing to be confronted in public by a woman in a formal gown, elegant shoes, and a sophisticated hairstyle. Marburg shifts uneasily from one foot to the other. As his eyes begin to falter, I smile my most winning smile and hold out my hand.

Grudgingly, he takes it for the briefest second, then turns red, grabs his cup of punch, and hurries away to rejoin his family.

I smile to myself. Score one for me.

"Did I just see what I thought I saw?" Felix asks when I return. "How on earth did you manage that?"

"It just seemed like a good opportunity to rise above his level," I say. "He was a bit surprised, I think."

"He's over there dying of shock right now," Franz says. "Maybe you've dealt him a fatally civilizing blow. My offer stands, though."

"I hope I won't need it," I say.

Suddenly, the provost himself appears. He looks around at everyone, as if he's never seen a crowd of parents at a reception before, and clears his throat.

"Well done!" he says. "I can't remember when a second-year quartet shone at such a level. Perhaps not since Herr Morgenthaler was a student." He nods politely at Berit. "I commend you for making the unfortunate circumstances work in your favor. Your performance should help allay fears of such unconventional ensembles among the parents and community. And the press."

"Thank you, sir," Felix says.

"Thank you," I echo, trying to work out what he actually meant. "I trust my locker will be repaired by the start of next term?"

"Oh. That. Yes." He sighs. "Most unfortunate. Yes, of course. Have a good holiday, everyone." And he vanishes into the crowd.

I thank Oma Judith again for the shoes.

"You've got good aim, my dear," she says. "You just keep kicking."

Mother tells me it was lovely and kisses my cheek, but she keeps looking at me as if she doesn't quite recognize me. She says little until we're rattling our way back to Ehrenfeld on the streetcar.

"You really are growing up," she says, shaking her head. "I hadn't realized it."

"It's just the dress," I say. "And the hair. Ros is going to teach me how to put it up for myself. Really, I'm no different."

"You are, though," she says. "I can't put my finger on it, but you are."

I retreat into awkward silence. One moment, I think she might be right. In the next, I'm quite sure she's not.

✦   ✦   ✦

To no one's surprise the next morning, the Wolff makes us play through *Rosamunde* two full times, stopping every few measures. I want nothing more than to go home and sleep some more and a little voice tempts me to skip checking out next term's orchestra parts. But, of course, I must squash that little voice flat. So, I tell the others they can hibernate all December if they want to, but if I want the chance of being allowed in Orchestra again, I need to start working now. Everyone groans, but they follow me down the stairs to the basement.

"You show us up badly enough, anyway," Felix says. "I'm not giving you that much of a head start."

Arnold searches the bulletin board for the program.

"Here we are," he says. "Mendelssohn, *A Midsummer Night's Dream* Overture. Mozart, Symphony No. 30. Brahms, Symphony No. 1. Nice mix. And guess who's concertmaster!"

"Marburg? That's it, I'm definitely going to put him out of our misery," Franz says.

"No! Our very own Felix Apfelbaum! Congratulations, Felix!"

"Excellent choice!" I say. "I'll be glad to have a friend in the first chair."

"It's good we checked," Felix says. "That's a lot of extra notes. The sooner I get started, the better. All right, let's find the parts. I'm taking tomorrow off, though."

"Agreed," Franz says. "I'm taking the day after that, too."

"At your own risk," Felix says.

I'm with Franz. But I bag the parts, sign the register "M. Adler," not that anyone won't know right off who that is, and head back up the stairs with the others.

10

WINTER, DECEMBER 1907–APRIL 1908

December 1907

The highlight of Katerina's next lesson comes when I give her Johanna's card. Her squeal of delight attracts the unwanted attention of Frau Schmidt, whom Katerina dismisses with a fib so polished I stand in awe of her skill at duplicity.

Saturday afternoon, I take Mother to see Anni fence.

I had no idea there were so many school fencing clubs in Köln, nor so many girls who fenced. In their identical quilted white jackets, black skirts, and masks, the only way we can tell Anni from the rest is when the announcer keeps repeating her name as she wins each bout and moves to the next. Even though I know nothing about fencing, I can see how skilled she is. Her touches are fast and accurate, her salutes proud, her posture beautifully erect.

"She couldn't put this much energy into her schoolwork," Mother grumbles.

"I'm glad she's found something she loves," I say, although I was thinking the same thing myself.

We cheer louder than anyone when Anni wins the seventeen-year-old division, her face, freed of its mask, flushed with sweat and pride, her hair pulling out of its plait. I've never seen her this much at home in herself, this happy.

After that, I sleep for the better part of two days, during which I don't touch the violin.

✦　✦　✦

My plan for the holiday is simple: to be a better daughter and a better sister. Also, to practice Mendelssohn, Mozart and Brahms, not to mention the Wolff's holiday assignments. The unnerving prospect of being the orchestra's lone female tempts me to abandon the whole undertaking, except my quartet-mates, who have sworn to look out for me, made me swear in turn to persevere.

The Wolff, on the other hand, will be waiting to pounce with my solo recital piece. She'll consider this far more important than my continued infiltration of the orchestra and she won't hesitate to say so.

On the third hand, she'll be right. But nobody says that to the men.

The Saturday evening before Christmas, I imagine Katerina playing her Christmas carols with the divine Otto at the party in the Kurtz fairy-forest mansion, while the other Marburgs lurk in the audience, feeling superior. I wonder idly if my attempt to make peace with the youngest Marburg will persuade him to stop tormenting me.

I decide it's too much to hope for, but at least I'm free of him until after the New Year.

Felix says he and the others are going to a concert at the cathedral on Christmas Eve, but I'm not interested. I spend enough time away from Mother and Anni; this is my chance to make it up to them.

And so, December passes.

✦ ✦ ✦

January 1908

Monday afternoon.

The new year arrives hard and cold, with high winds and snowdrifts that have to be plowed off the streetcar tracks before the city can function. Even indoors, the corridors and classrooms are far from warm and I'm not the only orchestra student wearing fingerless gloves. The departed third-years have been replaced by first-years, who all look terribly young.

I add my seat to the rear of the second violins, as before. This time my stand-mate is a dark-haired first-year with a wary expression in his dark eyes.

"Christian Königsmann, viola," he says when I introduce myself. "But for once there were too many violas and I had bad luck, so here I am."

I sympathize.

"I heard your quartet," he says. "You were terrific."

"Er, thanks," I say. Something in his direct, serious manner suggests an intensity I find slightly unsettling.

"About time they integrated the orchestra," he says.

"Well, *they* didn't exactly," I say. "I just sat down last year and stayed."

"Nicely done," he says. "The modern world storms the fortress of the medieval."

"Something like that," I say.

Felix makes his way up and down the aisles, introducing himself to all the first-years and welcoming them. One by one they jump to their feet and shake his hand. I watch him circulate with almost as much pride as if he were my own brother. When he gets over to our end, he shakes hands with Christian, who stands up, looks him in the eye and repeats his compliment about *Rosamunde*. Then Felix turns to me.

"Felix Apfelbaum, concertmaster," he says, grinning.

"Marthe Adler, infiltrator," I say, standing up to shake his hand and grinning back.

"Have we met?" he says.

"Possibly," I say.

He moves on.

"He's good," Christian says.

"Very good. And a great quartet-mate." I like the sound of the word: quartet-mates. More than friends, more even than a partnership.

My allies.

Marburg saunters in at the last minute, as usual. He sees me and looks away as if I were the evil eye. But he doesn't complain to Herr Zeidler, so that feels like a victory. Christian doesn't notice my sigh of relief.

Herr Zeidler spots me right away.

"Fräulein, I see you are back," he says. "You have prepared?"

"Yes, sir," I say.

"The whole program?"

"As much as possible, sir," I say.

"Who else practiced over the holidays?" he asks.

Some people shift uneasily in their seats, but several others raise their hands—more, I think, than last year—including my quartet-mates and Christian.

"Let me hear the opening of the Mendelssohn," he says.

I sigh. Yes, it's not fair, but he's handed me an invitation to show the men up. So, I play the opening's first four lingering notes, then continue into the first rapid, whirling theme. When it resolves, I stop.

"Shall I keep going, sir?" I ask.

"That will do, thank you," he says. "I expected no less of you. Very professional."

He continues on to the podium and begins his introductory speech. I settle back into my chair. That was easier than last year.

Christian leans over and whispers, "He did that because you're a woman, didn't he?"

I nod.

"Shit," he says under his breath.

"Always be over-prepared," I whisper back and put my finger to my lips.

The rehearsal is rough, but that's only to be expected.

✦ ✦ ✦

Wednesday morning.

The Wolff is resigned to, if not pleased by, my continued presence in the orchestra.

"It will distract you from your solo preparation," she says.

I remind her that every male student will be doing the same and no one seems to think they're not equal to it. Also, Ros managed both last year without damage to either.

The Wolff shrugs. "The burden is yours," she says.

"I don't consider it a burden," I say. "I consider it an essential—"

"—part of your training. I know. Enough."

She next informs me that my solo recital piece will be Bach's Violin Partita No. 3, my chance to match Berit's turn with No. 2. No. 3 will be twenty minutes of the most difficult music I've ever attempted: six short dance forms full of double-stops, tricky fingering, and unforgiving phrasing. I spend the rest of my lesson looking over the score, sight-reading the opening Preludio, noting potential trouble spots (all of it) with a mix of excitement and trepidation.

Later, I remember that Berit declined the orchestra-crashing adventure in order to concentrate on her partita for five months. For an hour after my lesson, I wonder if I'm making a terrible mistake, but what I told the Wolff is true: every male student in this place is doing both. If they can, I can.

✦ ✦ ✦

From my vantage point in the back row of the second violins, I watch the orchestra slowly begin to transform itself under Herr Zeidler's experienced hand from a ragged group of first and second-years into a disciplined and responsive unit. Somehow, the process is clearer to me this year. I also see how Felix, as concertmaster, sets an example for everyone by his own personality and serious attitude, which makes his section fall all over itself to please him.

Marburg, on the other hand, is now principal second violin, which makes him my section leader. Franz, who knows all the eddying currents of gossip to which I'm oblivious, says both Marburg and his father pestered Herr Zeidler all last term for the concertmaster position. While there was little danger that Herr Zeidler would capitulate and thereby turn the orchestra into a waking nightmare for everyone, I suspect he finally tired of Marburg's perpetual presence in his office and offered him the second violin chair just to get rid of him.

But a section leader is supposed to lead and Marburg is not a leader. I'm sure he dislikes most of all having me in his section, although at least he's in front and doesn't have to look at me. His sullen presence in the first chair is a little black cloud two seats over from Felix's bright sunshine. From my spot in the rear, I enjoy watching the petty dramas unfold, especially as they generally have nothing to do with me.

Christian's opinion is quick to form and unequivocal.

"What an ass," he mutters as Marburg voices yet another complaint about something irrelevant.

"Mmhmm," I say.

"You have stories?" he says.

"Mmhmm."

"I'd love to hear them sometime."

He is, most uncharacteristically, blushing.

One of the oldest fossils had a heart attack over the holidays and a

Sinfonia violinist, Herr Grimmelshausen, has stepped in to take his place. Franz reports with a mixture of contempt and glee that Marburg lost no time transferring to Herr Grimmelshausen from his previous teacher, Herr Klein, who was doubtless happy to unload him.

I begin to notice the tall, blond figure of Herr Grimmelshausen in the corridors, usually with Marburg following him like a puppy. His studio is around the corner from the Wolff's and I become accustomed to seeing Marburg in it, listening raptly to whatever wisdom Herr Grimmelshausen may be dispensing.

Inevitably Marburg's confrontations with Herr Zeidler begin to show Herr Grimmelshausen's influence.

"Herr Grimmelshausen says . . ."

"It is Herr Grimmelshausen's opinion that in this passage . . ."

"In Sinfonia practice, Herr Grimmelshausen informs me . . ."

"When Herr Grimmelshausen and I were discussing this phrasing the other day . . ."

"What a toady!" Christian whispers.

"Agreed," I whisper back.

At last Herr Zeidler has had enough.

"Herr Marburg," he says on the third Monday after one too many revelations of Herr Grimmelshausen's profound wisdom, "doubtless Herr Grimmelshausen has instructed you in the difference between memorizing what he says and actually studying the music. If you wish to keep your position, I suggest you do more of the latter and reserve the former for the edification of your friends. Do I make myself clear? Excellent. Attention, everyone. We will now repeat from measure 126."

And he raises his baton to continue.

Next to me, I hear Christian very quietly snickering.

Not much distracts Christian, however. The violin may not be his preferred instrument, but he's far better at it than I was at the viola. Whenever I glance over at him, he's attacking the music with furious concentration. I begin to sense an inward, controlled personality at work, a driving energy held in check by strict discipline. The more we rehearse, the more impressed I become.

Besides managing Marburg's insubordination and the natural chaos of fifty first and second-year students, one of Herr Zeidler's great skills lies in choosing programs of connection and contrast. As much as mastering their notes, our task in the orchestra is to understand them.

Like the story it opens, Mendelssohn's *A Midsummer Night's Dream* Overture is lighthearted and magical, the doorway into a dream world of quarreling fairies, foolish lovers and a weaver with a donkey's head. Mozart's mature Symphony No. 30 sparkles with clarity and grace. "Like the finest crystal!" Herr Zeidler says, but it also resonates with depth and power.

Brahms, by contrast, struggled under the self-imposed weight of Beethoven's legacy. He took twenty-one years to compose this First Symphony, heavy with tension between its traditional structure and the Romantic period ideas that burst out of it. It's a magnificent work to lose oneself in, which we do constantly those first few weeks, and have to be stopped in order to find our places and start over.

✦　✦　✦

February 1908

"You need to think about your recital gown," Berit says.

So *that's* why they suggested lunch at the Café Max Bruch.

"I have a recital gown," I say. "And shoes, thanks to Oma Judith."

"Black is for ensembles," Ros says. "But you'll be solo in May and you didn't see us in black last year, did you?"

"You mean I have to buy another gown just to have a different *color*? That's absurd!"

"Look," Berit says with a patient sigh. "Trust me, will you? I grew up in this world. I know what I'm talking about. I loved what Johanna did for you last fall, truly. But when you're the soloist, you need to be more flamboyant—not too much more, but just enough more. It's part of performing in front of an audience, dressing the part. Men have their formal uniform, but women have more freedom to express their individual taste, which also makes it harder. That's just the way the world works."

"I don't have any individual taste," I say. "Or any money."

"And," Ros adds, "you need jewelry."

"I *definitely* don't have any money for that."

"This is why you have us," Berit says. "No one is born knowing these details. So, you're going to go back to Johanna and she's going to make you a gown. You can check the second-hand shops and pawn shops for jewelry—"

"I'll go with you," Ros says. "I trust you, but I enjoy the hunt for hidden treasure."

"And if I don't find anything?"

"You will," Ros says.

I hate the very thought of wasting even one more afternoon scouring Köln's second-hand shops for jewelry under the bored eyes of supercilious clerks. And as for pawn shops . . .

"Let's go see Johanna this Sunday," Ros says. "Give her more time for this one. Spring's a busy season for gowns. I'll tell her we're coming."

"I haven't even finished paying off the last one yet," I say.

"Welcome to the musician's world!" Berit says.

"Still, I'm lucky you're looking out for me," I say. "Clothes are not my area of strength."

"It's not a gift, it's a skill," Ros says. "They just don't teach it at Conservatory. So, each class of women teaches the next."

"You mean I'll have to teach the next women, if there are any? They're doomed."

"You *are* something of a special case," Berit says. "A *tabula rasa* for us to create in our own image."

"Wonderful," I say. "But don't think I'm not grateful. It's not like I *want* to stand up in front of everyone and look stupid."

"Sunday at Johanna's shop," Ros says.

I sigh. "Oh, all right," I say. "See you there."

✦ ✦ ✦

Johanna suggests a royal blue silk for this new project and has sketches already drawn: a long, slim silhouette, similar to the last one, but the neck and sleeves are more open, so my forearms would be bare when I play. Lace of the same color cascades down the front and back.

"Bare arms?" The thought makes me nervous.

"And you'll need a cloth to protect your violin from your skin," Ros says.

"I do, anyway," I say. "I'll have to get a nicer-looking cloth. This dress looks more expensive than the other one."

"Good," Johanna says. "It's supposed to. It isn't, but it's a little more flamboyant. It will billow a little behind you when you walk."

"I don't want to buy new shoes," I say.

"Black shoes will be fine," Johanna says.

I sigh. The sketch is really beautiful and the bolts of fabric and lace she has on the table are wonderfully sensuous to the touch.

"How much?" I say.

"Same, plus about five marks for the extra fabric and lace," Johanna says.

"I can't believe it isn't more than that."

"Heidi was very impressed with your recital last fall," Johanna says. "I'm bringing her to your solo turn also. So, practice, all right?"

"Oh, I will," I say.

"On to look at jewelry!" Ros says.

"I. Have. No. Money. I told you that."

"We can look, anyway."

"There's no point. And I hate shopping."

"Just a little bit."

I groan. "Oh, all right. If it will pacify you."

In fact, a tour of three secondhand shops and two pawnshops yields nothing except a headache (me) and a craving for coffee (Ros).

"Did I mention I deeply and profoundly hate shopping?" I say, rubbing my temples.

"Maybe once or twice." Ros laughs. "I think of it as more of a sport. But if you stick with classics, once you're set you'll be set for years."

"Preferably forever," I say, finishing my coffee. "I suppose I should go home and practice. Now, besides the Wolff, I have Heidi to please."

"So you do," Ros says.

We pay our bill and head back out into the cold, rapidly darkening afternoon.

✦ ✦ ✦

The partita requires every bit of Mozart's clarity and expressive phrasing without Mozart's reliance on tuneful melody. Without expression, the partita will be dry and mechanical—the Bach I thought I knew before—

but it must never be overdone. Here, even *vibrato* is an ornament to be used with judicious care. The Wolff says Bach's music is like architecture: its beauty lies in its structure. Once I understand the structure, I can express and ornament it however I think best. Also, it contains an enormous quantity of double stops and ties my fingers into knots.

I'm glad I have two terms to try to master its six parts: a Preludio of racing sixteenth notes, then the dances: a slow Loure, a lively Gavotte, two stately and seamlessly connected Menuets, a fast Bourée, and a faster Gigue. When I have them, they'll be as exhilarating as if I were dancing the steps myself, instead of only playing them.

While I'm struggling with the partita, the end of winter term approaches like an oncoming train. Orchestra rehearsals extend by a half hour, starting in the eighth week, as Herr Zeidler isn't satisfied with our progress. Felix has his concertmaster responsibilities: solos to master, maintaining discipline among the sections, and taking a personal interest in the progress of every student, so we seldom see him outside of rehearsal. No one has time to socialize, or to make mischief.

I beg Ros to teach me how to put my hair in something other than a bun. It takes more sessions than I expect, but at last she pronounces my French roll acceptable and suggests extra hairpins for insurance.

"If I go outside with that many hairpins, I might get hit by lightning," I say.

"Wear a hat," she says. "Here, stick a few more on this side. Did you ever find jewelry?"

"That's Spring. I'm not thinking about it."

"Spring will be here before you know it," she says.

"Thanks for the reminder," I say. "Do you think this will hold?"

She pokes it. "Shake your head," she says.

I shake it.

"Yes, it will hold. Now we take it out and do it again."

I groan. "You and the Wolff."

"No one said music was easy," Ros says.

✦ ✦ ✦

The last rehearsal is terrible, of course, but Herr Zeidler is undaunted.

"This is why we rehearse," he says. "Now you know what you need to practice before Friday."

163

So, we keep practicing. At last, the evening of our performance arrives.

My caterpillars begin crawling around in my stomach by late afternoon. My gown transformation goes smoothly, but my hair refuses to behave as it did for Ros. I run out of time and have to put it back in its ordinary bun. It doesn't do the gown justice, but there's nothing I can do about it.

I take my seat along with everyone else. Do I imagine a little murmur rippling through the audience? The lights dim. The house quiets. Next, the ritual: Felix enters, supervises tuning, sits. Last, Herr Zeidler enters. We stand. He bows to the audience, gestures to us to sit, raises his baton, and the four magical opening chords of the overture to *A Midsummer Night's Dream* rise into the air.

Like last year, I marvel at what we've accomplished in less than three months. We're not perfect, but we're remarkably good. The places we kept stumbling over in rehearsal are smoother; a few easy places slip a little. No matter. For two hours, there's nothing but us and the music. Our audience projects its considerable energy to us. We double it and send it back. Mozart flies by after Mendelssohn, then the intermission, then Brahms, in which now losing myself doesn't mean getting lost; it means being immersed in the music, unaware of anything else.

Two hours pass between one breath and the next.

Afterward, I join Felix, Franz and Arnold in accepting compliments. No one says, "What were you doing there?" As a bonus, Marburg ignores me.

"Congratulations!" Herr Zeidler himself approaches to shake hands with us. "Nicely done, all of you. Ah, these must be your families. Delightful to meet you all." He makes the rounds of introductions and finally turns to me.

"Fraülein, I must ask you: do you plan to join the upper level orchestra next year?"

"Yes, sir," I say.

"Excellent. In that case, I shall be sure to include you in the seating chart and place you where you may perhaps do more good than in the very back."

He gives me a courtly little bow and turns to Ros.

"And I'm sure I need not ask if you, too, will return next year?"

"I'll be there," she says.

"Also excellent," he says. "There are so many very fine women musicians; this bias against them in the orchestra is completely outdated and unprofessional, in my opinion. It is my hope, now that we are in the modern age, that we will see an end to all such archaic practices." He smiles confidently at us and takes his leave.

"No backing out now!" Felix grins at us.

"The modern age," I say. "Can the Sinfonia be far behind?"

"Yes," Franz says.

"The hair didn't work out, eh?" Ros says.

"I tried four times," I say. "It just *wouldn't*."

"It looked fine. You saved well, my child," she says. "A little more practice, that's all you need. Come over tomorrow and we'll keep working. About three o'clock, stay for dinner."

"I should say so," a gravelly voice says over my shoulder. "We haven't seen you in an age."

"I'll be there," I say. "Hopeless hair and all."

"Hardest part of the job," Oma Judith says, nodding wisely and rapping her cane on the marble floor.

11

SPRING, APRIL–JUNE 1908

April 1908

One afternoon proves insufficient. Over the spring holiday, I spend a ridiculous number of hours in Ros's bedroom, glaring at myself in her mirror while brandishing my hairbrush and pins. My hands apparently do only one thing well, but Ros seems to enjoy making a project out of me. By the end of the third afternoon, I can produce a reasonable French roll, plus a more elegant and secure bun than before.

"Call it a *chignon* and it already looks better," she says. "Wear it down to dinner and see what the others think."

The others approve. It's just family tonight, except for Franz, who is as skinny as ever, but looks healthier than he used to, and somehow happier, too. He's certainly much more relaxed.

Oma Judith demands to know why I hid at the back of the section, rather than making a statement by sitting up front.

"I made a statement at the back," I say. "Sitting up front would be making a death wish."

"You should have been first chair," she says. "Felix told us about the idiot who had it. Sounds like a complete ass."

"Mother!"

"Funny, that's what my stand-mate called him," I say.

"Christian impressed me," Felix says. "Watch out, Franz, he's really a violist. He'll be after your job next."

"Must be decent if he thinks Marburg's an ass," Franz says. "But thanks for the warning."

"What's next?" Oma Judith says.

"Solo recitals," I say.

"I'm glad to have orchestra finished so I can concentrate on mine," Felix says.

"What are you talking about?" I say. "I've been concentrating on mine since January."

"That's the Wolff for you," Ros says. "And look for more new drills and exercises at the start of next week. They'll make your Bach even better, at the mere cost of your sanity."

"I can always rely on the Wolff," I say.

"Strudel, anyone?" Frau Apfelbaum asks, though it's not really a question.

"Yes, please," Franz says.

✦ ✦ ✦

Sure enough, when I leave the Wolff's studio on the first Wednesday morning of spring term, I have three new books of drills in my bag, plus two new sonatas, a Mozart and a Schumann.

"You need balance," she says. "Working in different centuries simultaneously will teach you to distinguish the techniques needed to do justice to them. And you need enough work to keep you out of trouble this term—unless you've signed up for something I don't know about."

"No, Professorin."

"Good," she says. "For next week, prepare the first movements of each sonata and the first five drills in each book."

"Yes, Professorin." The spring holiday suddenly seems a long time ago.

"Close the door on your way out," she says.

I do indeed manage to keep out of trouble. Days become weeks; weeks expand into the most uneventful Conservatory term so far. I learn the new drills. I learn the new sonatas. I practice the partita. I go to class, study, do assignments in Theory and History (minor composers of the early nineteenth century). I practice the partita some more. I have balance, all right, and so does the whole second-year class, even Marburg. No one has the time or energy to get into mischief.

As I delve deeper into the partita, I begin to understand why the

Wolff compared it to architecture. I begin to understand Bach's vision, his sense of awe before the structure and power of an infinite universe, and his genius, translating that awe into exquisitely complex sound through the transparency of a single instrument.

For Bach, even the smallest fugue contains within it a kind of vastness.

I love every note of it. I love its intricacy, its range of moods. Even when practice goes badly, I catch myself whistling its passages afterward. I imagine Papa Bach whistling them to himself. The partita feels like a direct connection between the master of the eighteenth century and me, a student in the twentieth; a glimpse into his mind, a chance to feel the emotions he felt, as if he's trusting me, personally, to bring his innermost thoughts to life.

I can't believe I ever thought he was boring.

To rescue me from the sublime, Ros drags me out twice more to hunt for jewelry. The secondhand shops offer cases of oversized brooches and garish necklaces bristling with glass. Pawnshops are worse: when women need money, the first things they sell are necklaces bearing hearts, kissing doves, and initials. I finally tell her I can't take any more; my bare neck will have to do.

"My hair will be so elegant, no one will notice," I say. I can tell my bad luck is spurring her on to a larger quest. I'm having none of it.

"I'll lend you a necklace," she says.

"Honestly, you've done so much for me," I say. "I would never ask to borrow something so personal and I don't want the responsibility, anyway."

"Ask Katerina."

"*Definitely* not! Can you imagine the explosion if Madame found out? No, thank you, there's nothing wrong with my neck and I'd like to keep it in one piece."

Ros sighs.

"No, really. It's fine," I say. "You're a wonderful friend. Stop worrying. Let's have coffee and go home. My treat."

"I'll find something," she says.

Thankfully, she doesn't.

✦ ✦ ✦

May 1908

Two weeks before my recital, Mother and I attend Anni's graduation from secondary school, where she's conspicuously absent from the honors category, but at least she squeaks through. Mother said she wouldn't believe it until she saw it with her own eyes. I confess I felt the same.

In her final year Anni amassed an impressive collection of mediocre marks, though she distinguished herself by starting a fire in the chemistry laboratory through her carelessness in leaving a burner on. At least she persuaded several girls to join the fencing club, so she apparently sets a more inspiring example than I do.

She has neither prospects for, nor interest in, marriage, as far as I can tell. In any case, what foolhardy man would marry her?

But without marriage, how will she survive? As Gerda said: teacher, nurse, clerk—all honorable professions, but I can't imagine Anni thriving in any of them. She would make a magnificent warrior princess, if only we still had need of one in our humdrum modern age, and there was my original dream of her becoming a pirate. But the papers are still woefully short of employment opportunities for either.

Anni brings home her large, ornate certificate of graduation and stuffs it, still rolled up, into her bottom drawer, where, as far as I know, it remains forever after.

✦　✦　✦

A week later we attend Anni's fencing championship, a tournament of all the school clubs in Köln. Again, Anni is clearly in her element, her foil a blur of speed, an extension of her body. She wins one match, another, a third, gaining energy, speed, and power as she advances. I'm not surprised at her ferocity, having been on the receiving end of it since childhood. But when she removes her mask after her sixth match to accept her division's gold medal, her face flushed and triumphant, her eyes bright, her hair messy, her fierce, aggressive pride on display for all to see, I feel the way Ros must feel watching Felix play: a rush of tremendous pride, and also the realization that Anni is so much more than my sister. She is her own person. She belongs, more than anywhere else, in this world of foils, helmets, rituals, ferocious competition, and sweat.

How she'll make her way in it, I can't imagine. But watching her, I begin to think it's possible she might succeed.

On the way home, Mother seems tired. I'm tired myself, and all I did was watch. At last, she takes a deep breath. "That was good, Anni," she says. "You did a good job. You showed them who you are. That you're not afraid of anyone. You *keep* doing it. Keep showing them."

We stare open-mouthed at her, and then at each other.

"I will," Anni says, hugging her. "Somehow."

Mother doesn't say any more. The moment passes, but we both remember it.

✦   ✦   ✦

The last time I walked out on this stage all alone, I was auditioning for admission to the Conservatory, nervous beyond imagining. This time, most of my classmates will have their teachers as accompanists for their recitals. But I, once again, am entirely, completely alone.

My violin has new strings, my bow, new horsehair. I'm wearing my new royal blue gown and my beautiful shoes. I've put up my own hair. I have a square of leftover blue silk to protect the violin from my skin. My caterpillars are dancing a vigorous bourée in my stomach.

I have the partita in my mind, to understand its difficulty and structure, and in my heart, to feel its depth, beauty, and energy. My father's violin feels eager in my hand. I heard his voice earlier today, when I was practicing. I feel him beside me now, invisible but solid, silent but encouraging.

I'm ready.

I watch the first half from the stage left wing, where I'll be out of the way. A horn player leads off. Franz follows with a transcription of Brahms, whose customary weight favors the darker color of the viola. He plays with fierce skill and a deep intensity he usually keeps well concealed. After Franz comes a flutist, followed by Marburg with an unusually polished Haydn sonata. Clearly, even Marburg isn't taking any chances with his third year.

At intermission I cross behind the stage to wait. My caterpillars begin an enthusiastic gavotte. The second half begins with an oboist, followed by Arnold, whose earnest sweetness inflects all the moods of his Schubert transcription, even the melancholy ones. Next, Felix, with his teacher, plays Beethoven. I don't hear much of it. At the start of the final movement, Herr

Schädler beckons. I take my place in the wing. My caterpillars have given up dancing for relay races now and my heart is pounding, but my breathing is even and deep and my hands are steady.

Felix finishes with a flourish and takes a bow to the applause.

"Fantastic!" I say as he and his teacher pass me.

"Good luck!" he says.

Herr Schädler signals. I walk out into the lights, the back of my blue gown floating behind me, to a wave of applause, not just polite but enthusiastic, as if they're with me and want me to succeed. I stop in the center, all alone under the lights. Face the darkened hall. Bow to my audience. Raise my violin, place the protective blue silk cloth. Pause. Take a deep breath, raise my bow. Feel the stillness, as if I'm entering an altered state of consciousness, and in the stillness, I feel my father standing beside me. And then I draw his bow across the strings of his violin and there's no one in the universe except Bach and me, Marthe Adler, bringing him to life.

✦ ✦ ✦

"I have an idea," Felix says, but is immediately cut off by a wave of people congratulating us on having survived our ordeal. Katerina is the most excited, but the most adorable is Johanna's sister, Heidi, who brings me a little bouquet of flowers she's clearly been clutching all evening. I'm enjoying the attention, wondering if anyone other than the Wolff noticed that I recovered from a miss early in the Preludio that could have been disastrous.

"I really enjoyed that Beethoven sonata," Felix continues when the crowd clears. "And you liked yours last year, right?"

"I did."

"And we all liked our early Beethoven quartet last year. So, let's tackle a Beethoven quartet for fall. The three Razumovsky quartets turned a hundred years old last year. We should celebrate."

"Do you think we can pull it off?" I ask. "I've heard they're very tough."

"You doubt us?" Franz says. "We can do *anything*."

"With the Wolff on our side? Absolutely," Felix says. "If we start now and work on it all summer, like we did with *Rosamunde*."

"Someone call me?" Ros says, strolling up.

Everyone laughs. I can't remember the last time I felt so light.

"You looked gorgeous," she says to me. "All you needed was some sparkly jewelry."

"I'll have a rich count fall in love with me. That should take care of my jewelry problem."

"Aren't you going to tell me I looked gorgeous, too?" Franz demands.

"You *all* looked gorgeous," Ros says, kissing his cheek and causing him to blush an extraordinary shade of pink. "*Especially* you, Franz. I can tell a new suit when I see one."

The Wolff approaches. I brace myself.

"Quite decent, Fraülein," she says. "The Preludio—"

"I slipped," I say. It wasn't even one of the usual trouble spots.

"You *saved*," she says. "Saving is an essential element of musicianship. Notes, tomorrow, nine o'clock."

"Yes, Professorin."

She nods to all of us and departs.

"Was she *smiling*?" Arnold says.

"Looked more like a dangerous structural crack to me," Franz says.

I take a deep breath. My happiness is complete. Even though I made a slip, the Wolff thought it was quite decent. In my world, it doesn't get any better than that.

"So, are we on for a Razumovsky?" Felix says.

"Sure," I say. "We can do *anything*. Saturday afternoon, your house."

And we raise our cups of punch to each other—a toast, to us, halfway through.

Year Three:
Dangerous Ideas
1908–1909

12

SUMMER, JUNE–SEPTEMBER 1908

June 1908

I continue to feel euphoric the rest of the week. Saturday morning begins with a salutary correction.

"Good morning, Frau Schmidt," I say.

The housekeeper stands back in expressionless silence to let me in. I hold myself very straight as I cross the entry hall with her cold little eyes on my back, past the table with my envelope on it, and into the rear sitting room where Katerina is waiting for me.

"Good morning, Fraülein Katerina," I say in my best teacher voice.

"Good morning, Fraülein Adler," she says in a demure tone that reeks of mischief.

Frau Schmidt's footsteps recede up the stairs. Somewhere in the upper hall a door closes. Katerina leaps up and throws her arms around me.

"You were *wonderful*!" she whispers. "I was so inspired! I'll never be that good, but it was just . . . wonderful!"

She actually has tears in her eyes.

"You'll be famous one day!" she says, holding me at arm's length. "You'll be Marthe Adler, the great violinist. You won't forget me, will you, when you're famous? You'll be a great soloist and play Bach and all the rest and take the world by storm! Was that another gown by Johanna?"

"Er—yes," I say.

"You must have her make all your gowns," Katerina says. "She's making some for me, too, did I tell you? I'll come see you play, wherever you are!"

"As long as I'm wearing one of Johanna's gowns?"

She giggles. "I'm serious, though. You'll have the most marvelous career."

"I hope so."

"I know so."

"Well, if I'm to afford a closet full of gowns by Johanna, I suppose we should get started," I say. "Lovely as it is just to be praised."

"You deserve it," she says, suddenly serious. "I wish—I wish I were as brave as you."

"Er . . . well, I'm sure . . ." I feel my face growing warm. "Ah, are you ready, then?"

"Fairly," she says and hugs me again.

The lesson itself is unexceptional; the spring social season has, as usual, eroded Katerina's practice. But the hour glows with her warmth. By the time we finish, I've forgotten all about the haughty Frau Schmidt and her cold, beady, bottomless eyes.

That afternoon at the Apfelbaums, after an expedition to Karol's for scores, we begin to take apart Beethoven's Quartet No. 7, Opus 59 No. 1. Clearly, we've bitten off a large chunk of joy and pain. It's longer than *Rosamunde*, in four movements: fast, faster, not so fast, and fast again. Though it begins with a simple opening in which Arnold is happy to have the first word for once, it doesn't stay simple for very long. We try sight-reading. It's chaos.

"We might actually have to practice this one," Franz says after about an hour.

"Possibly," I say. "But I like how he breaks themes into bits and tosses them around between voices."

"I love it," Arnold says. "We're all equal voices, like with *Rosamunde*."

"And remember," Franz says, "if Felix complains, even once, about all the extra work he has and how much time he's spending at the very top of his range trying not to squeak, this whole thing was his idea."

"When have I ever complained?" Felix says. "I think this will knock the Wolff right off her chair."

"Worth doing for that reason alone," Franz says. "Although it might be easier just to push her."

"Let's see if we can put the first movement together for next week," I say. "Just take the hard parts and easier parts in order. No sidestepping. One movement a week, right?"

"Right, Fraülein Generalin!" Felix says.

"Nothing to it," Arnold says.

"Is it dinnertime yet?" Franz says.

"Manners!" Arnold swats him.

"What about them?" Franz says.

✦　✦　✦

Something occurs to me at dinner.

"Ros, I didn't think of it till just now," I say, "but am I creating a problem for you if I keep playing with Felix and the others? It leaves you and Berit short a player."

"No," Ros says. "We suspected you four would stay together. First, because you obviously really liked it, and second, having once stormed the fortress of oppressive tradition, why would you retreat? So, we snagged a couple of fellows whose quartet-mates graduated. We're going to have our own mixed four this fall."

"Really! That's terrific!"

"They had to agree to have the Wolff as our coach. They're suitably terrified."

"Don't tell me you tried to scare them!"

"Heavens, no!" Ros says. "Well, maybe just a little."

"Will you practice here over the summer?"

"Starting next month. Unlike you, we thought we'd try learning our parts first."

"A novel idea," I say. "We might try it sometime. What are you playing?"

"Dear old reliable Mozart. No. 17, *The Hunt*," she says. "We didn't want to tempt fate with anything too radical."

"Does the Wolff know?"

Ros smiles a sly smile. "She might have an inkling. But we'll go see her on the first day of term. If she balks, we'll say, well, you let Adler do it, you can't say 'no' to us."

"I'm such a troublemaker," I say.

"And then some!" Oma Judith shakes her fork at me. "You keep that up, you hear?"

177

✦ ✦ ✦

Anni goes to fencing camp again. Mother drinks her Bärenfang and does little else. I practice Beethoven and the load of summer assignments the Wolff handed me on my way out the door after my notes.

On Saturday mornings, I teach Katerina. Saturday afternoons at the Apfelbaums', we rehearse. Slowly, the Beethoven begins to sound less like chaos and more like . . . something.

In July, Berit and Ros start rehearsing with their new quartet-mates, whom I recognize by sight: violist Matthias Grüneberg and first violinist Jan van der Doort from Amsterdam. Both seem delighted at the arrangement. It doesn't take long to see why.

"Lots more interesting," Jan says, glancing at Ros, who has the decency to blush.

Ros reports that Berit was ready to duel Jan over the first violin spot, but they finally concluded that a woman in the first chair might be more than the old fossils could tolerate. Berit, being Berit, drove a hard bargain: in rehearsals, they're trading off, so both of them are learning both parts.

In August, the Kurtz family leaves for Gstaad. Katerina says the Marburgs might be there, too, perfect for long, romantic walks with Otto. I try not to roll my eyes in her presence.

In this way, summer passes.

13

FALL, SEPTEMBER–DECEMBER 1908

September 1908

Monday morning.

The new first-years look terribly young and so pale they must all be child prodigies who have never gone outdoors even once in their lives. Six are girls. I fume at the unfairness of this for about ten seconds, then consider if I would trade Felix, Franz, and Arnold for an ensemble of girl children with ribbons in their plaited hair. The answer is no. Ros, Berit, and I introduce ourselves, offering them the benefit of our wisdom and experience. They seem baffled.

Maybe they already know how to dress and do their hair. Maybe they won't have a Reinhold von Marburg in their class.

The third-years look the same, except for Franz, who's grown at least ten centimeters since this time last year. He must have gained at least ten kilos at the Apfelbaums' table so as not to be even skinnier than before. A few familiar faces are missing; a few new students have taken their places. One of these, a young man with red-blond hair and blue eyes, is American. Felix, being Felix, is the first to welcome him. He introduces himself in moderately fluent German as Robert MacInness, piano, from New York.

"Oh, sure, we have conservatories in America," he says when we ask at lunchtime, pausing occasionally to figure out how to say something. "Chicago and Philadelphia. A few others. But I wanted to train in Europe, just for the adventure. I spent my first year at the Moscow Conservatory. I was too naive to know how crazy that was. The training was solid, mostly

Russian music, but the language—impossible. And the winter! New York winters have nothing on Moscow. So last year I transferred to Paris. French music is fine, but the professors were arrogant snobs. At least the Russians were respectful. Paris was a nightmare. I couldn't stand it."

"You must be good if you got into Moscow *and* Paris," Felix says. "But I can't promise you there's no arrogance here."

"I guess Europeans think all Americans are pretty dumb," Robert says. "But the Parisians were in a class by themselves. So, I came to Cologne—sorry, Köln—because I have family here, sort of. I should have come here in the first place—at least I might get treated like a human being."

"Around here you work your way up to that," I say.

Robert laughs, a big, uninhibited laugh. "So, I have a chance," he says. "Say, don't we have a class about now?"

We do. We lost track of time, talking.

"Where are the practice rooms?" Robert asks as we hurry off to Orchestration.

"In the basement," Arnold says.

"So you can stay cold both summer and winter," Franz adds.

"Perfect," Robert says. "It'll remind me of Moscow."

We may have been the first to welcome him, but Robert has no difficulty making friends. He has a certain exotic appeal and he's not shy. Marburg is rude to him, which we explain is a compliment; Robert assures us Germans have nothing on Parisians in the rudeness department.

The air of the Swiss Alps, if he got any, hasn't improved Marburg's personality in any way. I try my best to avoid him.

✦　✦　✦

Wednesday morning.
Robert's story reminds me how much my education is missing. I always liked the foreign music Herr Dietrich assigned me. But at Conservatory, it's been Austrian and German music only, at least so far.

So, I ask the Wolff if I can branch out. I expect her to say no, but she doesn't.

"The music of Germany and Austria is the greatest achievement in our art since the Baroque," she says, sounding like an extremely biased textbook. "The young artist must have a solid foundation of this superior repertoire and technique, hence the Conservatory's exclusive focus for the first two years. After this, it is safe to expand one's study to the contributions of other national traditions, such as they are. As in language, once you learn your own, you may study others without danger."

I imagine myself tumbling into a life of iniquity and squalor under French or Italian influence.

"So, this year and next, we can learn foreign music?"

"That is the Conservatory's policy." The hint of a growl in her voice suggests she might prefer the Conservatory's policy to be less liberal.

"I want to be the best," I say. I'm surprised to hear myself say it, but in this moment, I believe it. "I want to play it all."

The Wolff's eyebrows press tightly together. "Somehow," she says, "I'm not surprised. You have done your summer assignments?"

"Yes, Professorin."

"We will start with those. The rest of the world's music will have to wait."

But as I'm leaving, in grudging accordance with Conservatory policy, the Wolff hands me two books of French solos: Baroque dances by Jean-Philippe Rameau and some fiendishly difficult Kreutzer études. They *are* different, yet even as I practice and study them, it's still hard for me to say just how.

✦　✦　✦

Wednesday afternoon.

Perhaps because Ros and Berit and their two new co-conspirators got to her first, the Wolff doesn't give us as much trouble as last year about our performing together. After a few half-hearted objections and warnings, she merely sighs and furrows her ever-expressive eyebrows at us.

"I assume you have chosen something in advance of my advice?" she says, sounding resigned.

"Yes, Professorin," Felix says. "We wanted to be prepared to work."

"Which is . . . ?"

"Beethoven. Opus 59, No. 1," Felix says.

She stares at us in frank disbelief.

"The first of the Razumovskys?"

"Yes, Professorin."

"You have an elevated idea of your abilities."

"I hope not, Professorin. We feel we're getting the basics and have been looking forward to your coaching." Felix is *so* smooth.

The Wolff sighs another deep sigh.

"Well, Beethoven has survived a great deal over the years," she says. "I suppose he will survive you, too. Play."

She lets us plow through the first movement. It's not too bad, considering the ferocity of her expression.

"Again," she says.

We get as far as the cello's opening passage.

"Stop! Wrong dynamics! Wrong phrasing! The cello must float above the *ostinato*, even though the notes are lower. Start over!"

That's more like it. We exchange glances. Everyone is grinning.

It's good to be back.

✦ ✦ ✦

Robert MacInness turns out to be the rare sort of person that virtually everyone likes. Perhaps because he's American, he's immune to the cliques and sub-cliques that attract and repel most of the other students. He soon knows the name of everyone in our class, which I barely do after two years, even though nearly every time I pass by his favorite practice room I hear him at work inside. But he often has lunch with us, where we pepper him with questions about America, New York, Moscow, and Paris.

The ease with which he seems to travel between worlds makes me feel provincial, like girls on postcards dressed in dirndls with their hair in plaits. An idea begins to form in my mind that I, too, would one day like to travel between worlds, though how this might happen I have no idea. I suppose if I led Katerina's fantasy life of the famous soloist, that would be one of the rewards. I had thought mainly of its loneliness, living out of a trunk, having no proper home. But I could see the world. It bears thinking about.

✦ ✦ ✦

Even though he failed last fall in his moral crusade to have me ejected in disgrace, even though he's ignored me ever since, even though he has several more women to be upset about now if he wants to, I fully expect Marburg to try again.

I'm almost disappointed in his lack of imagination when Franz reports that his new campaign is the same as the old one. Marburg claims to know, somehow, that I'm sleeping with Robert MacInness.

Oh, damn, not again, I think. But the curdling fear of last year is missing; in its place I feel only resignation and weariness. What a stupid, unnecessary headache, as if Conservatory life weren't difficult enough.

Robert, of course, doesn't care. His family lives an ocean away and gossip won't reach his relatives here if he doesn't carry it. Also, besides being well-liked, everyone can see he's serious, shutting himself in a practice room almost any time he's not in class. And I never see him outside it without plenty of other people around. For whatever reason, the rumors don't cause the excitement they did last time. After a week, the smear seems to run its course and fade away for lack of energy.

So, I'm caught off guard one early October day when I emerge from the women's toilet to encounter Marburg, who has absolutely no business being here and has plainly been lying in wait for me. I nod curtly, without speaking, and start to walk past him, back toward the stairs.

"Well, what a surprise!" he says, stepping into my path. "The celebrated prodigy and lover of American pianists!"

My heart begins to race under a little cold prickle of sweat.

"Excuse me, I have a composition class to get to, as do you," I say. I try to step around him.

"No, you don't. You have an assignation with the American pianist. Perhaps the American pianist *and* your intimates of the quartet. I expect you crave variety. I hear women musicians are insatiable for variety. Is that true?"

I'm determined to keep walking, even if I have to push him aside. But I have no hands free; I hold my case in one and some notebooks in the other. My bag, which if anything is heavier than last year, is slung over my shoulder.

"You're very amusing." I keep walking.

"Is he good?" Marburg leans in so close I can smell his cologne, which is revolting. He speaks low in my ear and edges me toward a wall, which I do not under any circumstances want to be trapped against. "I'll bet Americans know all sorts of tricks. And he'll know Russian and French ones, too. We poor old Germans might learn something from him, what do you think? You've had enough to compare, haven't you?"

I can feel my color rising in spite of myself. I mustn't let him know he's getting to me and I mustn't let him corner me. Anni showed me one or two ways to defend myself in a hard place, but she admitted, reluctantly, I think, that the important thing is to avoid getting into a hard place at all. I walk faster. I want to shout at him, *Go away, you bastard! Leave me alone!* But I don't.

He slides his arm around my waist and pulls me toward him. He's leaning his face toward mine, to try to kiss me. In a panic, I jab my elbow into his ribs and twist away from him. My bag swings around and hits him, not hard, but enough to startle him. I hear myself give way then, louder than I intend, and as much in fear as anger.

"*Go away, you bastard! Leave me alone!*"

I speed up, almost running now, and burst around a corner into a larger corridor, where I collide with someone who is deeply engrossed in studying a score and not paying attention to anything else. Marburg, flushed and visibly angry, steps away just in time and walks on, smoothly pretending he hasn't even seen me.

"Oh, I'm so sorry!" I say.

Herr Zeidler looks over his score at me. "Ah, Fräulein Adler. I was just reading a little Haydn. What did you say? I didn't quite catch it."

Out of the corner of my eye I see Marburg round a corner and disappear. I pause to catch my breath and try to read Herr Zeidler's face. He's been fair to me in the past. I don't want to alienate him and I don't want to drag him into my personal headaches.

"I just had a—an unwanted advance from—a certain student," I finally manage to stammer. Herr Zeidler's eyes, the only part of his face I can see, assume a look of mild concern. "He's paying entirely too much attention to me. I want him to leave me alone."

"Very wise," Herr Zeidler says. "Conservatory is no place for romance. It is a concern, having women in our midst. Fortunately, you are serious-minded and understand this." He nods approvingly and walks on.

I stare after him, wondering if he understood me at all. Should I follow him to his office and explain that I've been attacked every year by this same certain person and now he's lying in wait for me by the toilet? I can't even imagine this conversation. At least, I can't imagine it will do any good. Maybe Felix can think of something, short of my having bodyguards everywhere I go.

I collect myself for a moment, trying to get my breathing back to normal, and then, casting a careful eye around for Marburg or one of his cronies, I continue down the corridor to Composition with my heart still pounding.

"What's up? You look like the Wolff chewed you up and spat you out," Franz says, sliding into the chair next to mine.

"Marburg," I say under my breath. Across the room, I see Marburg sitting with his friends, laughing at some private joke. I suspect I know what it is. "Scared me half to death."

"Jackass," Franz says, throwing him a look of open contempt. "You want me to rough him up for you?"

"Thanks, don't," I say. "But I'm afraid he'll just keep trying, any time he thinks he can get away with it. I don't know what to do to make him leave me alone."

Whatever is being taught in Composition that day, I don't hear much of it.

✦ ✦ ✦

That night after Mother has gone to bed, Anni calls Marburg a variety of colorful names that put Franz's to shame. She has plenty of advice, but following most of it would land me in prison for a nice long time, even if I could prove self-defense. I hate the thought of having to scurry around the Conservatory like a mouse trying to hide from the cat. But I can't imagine Marburg giving up the fun of tormenting me. Probably I shouldn't have shouted at him.

Well, it's done now.

"Report him, then," she says, her tone suggesting she finds bureaucratic solutions highly unsatisfying. "Go explain to the provost that the son of a bitch is a serious menace and it's not just you, it's all the new children you're worried about."

"I guess I should," I say, and the next day, I do. The provost is very sympathetic. And absolutely nothing happens.

✦ ✦ ✦

On Saturday morning in the rear sitting room with Katerina, the high-backed chair sits mercifully empty.

"I have to talk to you," I say in my lowest voice. Crisp footsteps sound on the parquet floor outside. "Let's hear a C-sharp scale today," I say in my slightly-louder-than-normal teacher's voice.

"Certainly, Fraülein. C-sharp Major or C-sharp Minor?" Katerina says, winking at me. "Oh, hello, Mamá. Are you going to join us today?"

"I have an important appointment," Madame says, pulling on her gloves. "I will be back shortly. Stick to your lesson, please. No silly gossiping."

"Yes, Mamá."

"Naturally, Madame."

Madame's footsteps recede. The front door opens and shuts.

"What about?" Katerina says.

I take a steadying breath. "I need to warn you about Reinhold."

"Again?"

"Again. Not just spreading stupid rumors. Worse. He attacked me. I'm not asking for sympathy." Katerina looks dangerously close to embracing me. "I just need you to understand what he is, so you'll be careful. Because he didn't invent his attitude; he must have learned it somewhere. I don't know anything about Otto. But I know Reinhold entirely too well and I'm sure I haven't seen the end of him. I think he's dangerous. I couldn't stand the thought that he might do something to you and I hadn't warned you. So, I'm warning you. Do you understand?"

Katerina nods slowly, sadly, not taking her eyes off me.

I feel like an old witch out of the Brothers Grimm. In Katerina's fantasy world, she's a princess and Otto is her prince. She forgets that in fairy tales there is always evil to be overcome. Always struggle. Their notion of struggle is waiting until she's of age to marry and she actually believes living happily ever after is real.

Just now she looks so shocked that I wonder if I've done the right thing. Rumors are one thing; she can understand defending my reputation. But physical attack ... she's not competing with Marburg for anything except possibly the admiration of his older brother. She's his social equal, or very nearly. Will that keep her safe? I don't know.

I take another deep breath.

"That's all. We should get on with your lesson before Frau Schmidt turns up. Are you ready to go on? Perhaps we should start with that C-sharp scale. Er, major. Then the relative minor. And then the arpeggios."

Katerina gives me one last sad look, then looks away with a little shake of her head, as if to shake the ugly pictures out of it. She raises her violin, picks up her bow.

"I'm so sorry," she whispers. "I'm just so sorry."

✦ ✦ ✦

But in the following days, Marburg confines himself to leering at me whenever our paths cross, which is as seldom as I can manage. If he gets close enough, he hisses, "Whore!" But in general, he avoids me. Only later do I find out why.

Felix, after hearing about my altercation in the corridor, with a few choice words regarding Herr Zeidler's reaction and the provost's lack of one, started a little rumor of his own. Marburg, he mentioned casually to a few key people, appears to be passionately in love with me, as he tried to kiss me in one of the corridors after waiting for me to come out of the women's toilet so he could plead with me to pay attention to him.

It works. At least, it works well enough to keep Marburg out of my way so I can finish the term. At this point, I'm not asking for anything else.

✦ ✦ ✦

"Which is the most important instrument in the quartet?" the Wolff demands one Wednesday afternoon.

Trick questions aren't the Wolff's usual style.

"All of them?" Felix says.

"By definition, yes," she says. "But the first violin's job is to sound beautiful and play many extra notes and the cello's job is to provide richness and depth. The job of the inner voices is to connect them. And of these two, while the viola more frequently partners with the cello, the second violin must be able to partner with everyone. If a strong second violin is lacking, the glue of a quartet will not hold. And the second violinist must always know in any given moment which voice is the partner. Is that clear?"

"I think so, Professorin." I thought that's what I was doing, but she makes the job sound completely impossible.

"That makes sense," Arnold says.

"I'm so glad you agree, Herr Blum," the Wolff says. "You have chosen to embrace a great masterwork. You must elevate your understanding in order to reach its heart. And you must also understand—"

We brace for another impossible technical hurdle.

"You will play this work reasonably well for where you are in your training. At least, you had *better,* or you risk my extreme disappointment. But return to it ten years from now, or twenty, and you will find it very different. Not because you played it badly now, but because now you're very young. Music rewards age and experience, as long as you have the courage to keep up the struggle. The great musicians aren't the little prodigies one sees from time to time, however fast their fingers move. The great musicians are those who have persevered, devoted their lives to the struggle."

We absorb this rare bit of philosophizing as best we can.

"If you have no questions," she says, "do it again."

✦ ✦ ✦

"What would happen if all four of your instruments were made from the same tree?"

The following Wednesday, the Wolff discourses on resonance.

"They'd be perfect together, wouldn't they?" Arnold says. "All the overtones would line up. All the resonances would agree."

"Wrong," the Wolf says. "For exactly the reason you state, Herr Blum. All the overtones would align and the resonances would be identical. The resulting sound would be anemic. Two-dimensional. It has been proven. All of your instruments are different—different periods, different countries, different trees. Therefore, their resonances also differ and the way they combine is unique. You are fortunate that your instruments complement each other well—no doubt one reason you find playing together so satisfying that you're willing to flout Conservatory policy in order to do it. Your unique resonances spin themselves around the core of your sound and enrich it."

I try to picture this in my mind.

"If you ever buy an instrument for use in an ensemble, you must test it with the other instruments first. How it sounds in a luthier's shop may differ from how it sounds on a stage with other instruments, no matter who made it. Remember this."

Not that I ever expect to buy another violin, but it's worth filing away, nonetheless.

✦ ✦ ✦

"Think of any passage as occupying a particular space," the Wolff says the Wednesday after that. "And think of that space as the sum of your instruments' resonances. The closer the pitches and volumes align, the smaller space the resonances occupy. The space varies from moment to moment. It is the job of the inner voices to be aware of this space at all times and play in response to it. You may even need to play a passage in some way you would prefer not to, because it is what the space requires. Do you understand?"

"I think so, Professorin," I say, feeling baffled.

"Yes," Franz says.

Fine. I'll ask him later.

"Excellent," she says. "Again."

✦ ✦ ✦

By the next Wednesday, the Razumovsky begins to feel like music. Of course, it needs an enormous amount of polishing, but we're making progress on the tricky parts, of which there are dozens, and our understanding is growing deeper.

"I think our recital's going to be the best of anyone's," Felix says, unfortunately within the Wolff's hearing.

"Herr Apfelbaum, you surely understand," she says, fixing him with her most intimidating stare, "that in choosing this quartet, one of the towering works for string ensemble, you are not being measured in comparison with other student ensembles. Do you not?"

"Er—"

"You are being measured against every ensemble which has played this quartet in the century since it was composed. You are setting yourselves against professionals and virtuosos. You are young, but I expect an interpretation of maturity, understanding, and nuance. Do I make myself clear?"

"Quite, Professorin," I say. "That is our goal."

"Good," she says. "From the beginning, then . . ."

✦ ✦ ✦

I look forward to our rehearsals with almost indecent pleasure. We make mistakes, play through stubborn trouble spots over and over again. We think about who's in charge, who's partnering with whom. We think about resonances and space. We try to feel mature and nuanced. We face our chairs outward and afterward always feel our hearing has improved. Sometimes we get frustrated and sometimes we have a breakthrough.

It feels good. It feels right. It feels like I'm doing what I was meant to do, being what I was meant to be.

✦　✦　✦

October 1908

"My neighborhood in Brooklyn was a real mix," Robert explains one day over lunch. "Dad's a Scot, my mother was English. She died when I was little and our neighbors stepped in. Aunt Hedy's German, Uncle Teo's Polish. A lot of American families are like that. Aunt Hedy cared for me every day after school and taught me German. They had a piano. I went for it. They talked my dad into paying for lessons. I practiced at their house. I even stayed there when he traveled on business.

"Dad and I are close and he's footing my bill here—one reason I work my tail end off—but Aunt Hedy and Uncle Teo are as much my family as he is. Aunt Hedy's a regular steamroller when she gets an idea. So, when Moscow and Paris flopped, she insisted I transfer here and live with her sister and brother-in-law. So here I am, with a new aunt and uncle. And a new cousin. And they want you all to come for dinner."

"They sound wonderful," I say, wishing I had relatives like that.

"Tante Hanne thinks I won't make any friends if she doesn't feed them," Robert says.

"I'll be your friend if she feeds me," Franz says.

"You're already his friend!" Arnold says.

"That's very kind of her," Felix says.

"Not that you're having any trouble making friends," I say.

"You can meet my new cousin, Joseph. He's an architect, but he likes to sing. I accompany him sometimes, when we have time."

"I'll bet my father knows him," Felix says. "I'll ask."

"Come this Friday. Maybe we can manage a little concert after dinner."

"Excellent!" we all say, and so the arrangements are made.

Friday turns cold and dark early. On the streetcar to Neuehrenfeld, north of my neighborhood, our breath fogs the windows and our coats stay buttoned to our necks. From Robert's stop, we walk two blocks down Droste-Hülshoff-Strasse through drifts of fallen leaves, climb the stairs to a broad covered porch, and stop mid-sentence at the sound of a piano.

It's a most un-German minor-key carpet of notes that builds into a torrent of arpeggios and then becomes a song. Even the piano is singing, as if the hammers are caressing the strings instead of hitting them. The effect is mesmerizing. We would hear it to the end if we perished of exposure, but a voice interrupts the music and it breaks off mid-phrase. Footsteps grow louder and the door opens.

"Sorry, I didn't hear you," Robert says, shooing us inside and helping us out of our coats. "You should have rung the bell, it's an icebox out there."

"We didn't want to interrupt," Arnold says. "What was that?"

"Chopin," Robert says.

"French?" I ask. Even the Wolff, it seems, doesn't know everything.

"Polish," Robert says. "Uncle Teo's very firm about that. But he lived mostly in Paris. I learned a lot of Chopin last year at the Paris Conservatory."

"Lucky," Franz says. "You won't get much of it around here."

"We do concentrate on Germans and Austrians here, don't we?" Robert laughs. "Which is fine. I just like to review what I learned last year on my own sometimes."

"I'd like to play Chopin," I say.

"Thinking of taking up piano in your spare time?" Robert says.

"What? He didn't write for violin?"

"No. Other French composers did, though. Go to Paris and visit a music store. You'll have plenty of choices."

"No doubt. All I need is, let me see, time and money."

"You won't be a starving student forever. Speaking of which, I think dinner's nearly ready."

Go to Paris to buy scores? I try to imagine being Robert, to whom everything looks easy.

In her brightly lit kitchen, from which all sorts of delicious smells are drifting, tiny, round Frau Walter only stops racing around long enough to greet us.

"Welcome, welcome!" she says and takes off again, flitting from stove to sink to cooler to worktable like a large bumblebee. "I'm so happy to have Robert's friends here at last! You were all so kind to make him welcome when he arrived. Poor dear, his German's getting better every day, but it must still be *very* hard work. Your brain gets tired trying to think in a foreign language all the time. Could you hand me that oven mitt, please? Thank you, dear, and the music we get here at home now! It's *such* a joy to hear him practice! And he's been accompanying our Joseph when he sings, something Joseph doesn't do at a professional level, you understand, just for fun. They enjoy it so! Joseph should be home soon. I think Papa's in his study with the evening paper, so Robert, dear, go call him, would you, please? And my goodness, how hard they work you all over there at the music school! Poor dear hardly has a moment's rest and even less recreation. Well, I promised my sister Hedy I'd take good care of her boy and that's what we're doing. And you, my dear, how brave you are, to be one of so few girls! Probably the best, too, I should think, eh?"

I have no idea what to say, but she doesn't pause for an answer. In fact, she doesn't stop until Herr Walter appears.

"Where is Joseph?" Herr Walter asks, looking around.

"Not home yet," Frau Walter says. "But on his way, I hope. They work him much too hard. It's Friday night, he should be able to come home and have dinner with us, or take a girl out if he has one. Not that he has one. But if he did, he'd lose her because he never has time to take her out! Dear, could you please take these potatoes to the table? Thank you. And you, dear—" In five seconds she's put us all to work, carrying serving dishes, plates, and silverware into the dining room and setting the table.

"Just like Aunt Hedy," Robert whispers, handing me glasses to carry in on my second trip. "They could be twins."

We've just finished setting the table when the front door opens to a blast of cold air and slams again.

"Be right there," a muffled voice calls, followed by footsteps up the stairs and then back down again. A young man joins us in the dining room.

"I'm Joseph," he says, shaking hands with the others. He stops at me.

"Marthe Adler," I say.

"Er, yes," he says. "Robert told me about you. I'm, er, glad to meet you, finally."

"Likewise," I say, glancing at Robert for explanation, but Robert is studying something on the ceiling. At this moment Frau Walter buzzes through, in one motion pulling off her apron and propelling the people nearest her, who happen to be Felix and Arnold, toward the table.

"Everything's ready, don't let it cool off!" she says.

In short order we wish each other a good appetite and start passing platters of sausage, potatoes, roasted cabbage, and salad. Conversation flows as people share the day's gossip, which is how I learn Herr Walter is an assistant to the mayor of Köln. I don't learn much else about him; he seems content to let other people do the talking.

Joseph, next to me, is quiet, too, until I ask him about his singing.

"I like to, but I don't sing in front of real musicians," he says.

"But Robert promised us a concert after dinner!"

"I'm sure he meant you and your friends," Joseph says.

"Maybe," Robert says from my other side. "But we've been having fun with those Schubert *Lieder*. I'm game if you are."

"Er, I know I said . . . but . . ." He gives Robert a pleading look, which Robert ignores.

"Oh, all right," Joseph sighs. "I'll just embarrass myself, though."

Robert winks at me.

"I doubt it," I say.

At last, the apple strudel has disappeared. Herr Walter retires to the sitting room, while the rest of us help clean up, frequently asking, "Where does this go?" and getting in each other's way. Frau Walter provides a steady stream of instructions and commentary and soon we reassemble in the sitting room on comfortable chairs around the piano.

"Are you *sure*?" Joseph says. "I'm really not—"

"You're too humble," Robert says. "If you miss a note, blame it on too much strudel. Come on, let's warm up."

Joseph does, indeed, have a fine singing voice, a lovely light baritone.

"He could have been a great singer, you know," Frau Walter whispers, "if he hadn't been so fascinated with architecture. Even when he was a little boy, always with the building blocks—"

"Ready?" Robert asks.

Joseph gives a resigned nod and closes his eyes, probably so he can pretend we're not here, a feeling I know well.

He underestimated himself. His voice is natural and expressive, the characters of the *Lieder* believable—a real pilgrim, a real lover, a real seeker. His rapport with Robert shows; clearly, they're having a lot of fun.

When he finishes the third one, we let the final longing notes hang in the air for a moment before we break into applause. For six people, we make a lot of noise.

"See?" Robert says. "I told you you could do it."

"That was beautiful," I say as Joseph holds the door open for us to depart.

"Er—," he says, suddenly awkward again. "Ah—thanks."

After the warmth of the Walter house, the October air outside feels colder than ever.

✦ ✦ ✦

November 1908

Sometimes the Beethoven flows and sometimes we sound like we've never met each other before. Still, week to week, it improves. It's magnificent and we're all pushing ourselves as hard as we can to be worthy of it.

"Stop! Check your tempo. Again."

"Stop! I can't hear the inner voices at all. Again."

"Stop! Who's in charge here? You must always know which voice is in charge. Again."

"Stop! This modulation must be as smooth as the finest silk. Again."

"Stop! How many times must I remind you to decide who is in charge? Again!"

The coaching is going well, I think.

Then one Wednesday afternoon in early November, the Wolff says, "Leave it."

"*What?*" All that work! And we thought it was coming so well!

"If you would be so kind as to not interrupt," she snaps. "Leave it. For one week. Do not look at the music or practice it. You all have plenty of other work to occupy your time, I believe. You may not always have the opportunity to leave a work you have mastered technically and then return to it, but you have it with this one and you will take it. No practice of the Beethoven. Not a peek at the score. Do I make myself clear?"

"Yes—Professorin, why?" I say.

We look like four baby birds, our mouths hanging open.

"You will see," she says.

"Won't we forget?" Arnold says.

"If you do, you will have to learn it again," she says. "Until next week, then. You may go."

"Well, *that's* terrifying," Franz says as we head down the stairs.

"I trust her," I say. "She's got some plan."

"I hope so," Felix says.

"No cheating, all right?" I say.

"You're joking, Fraülein Generalin," he says. "Run afoul of the Wolff *and* you? Never."

"Even if we have to start over," Arnold says. He sounds glum.

"If we have to start over, I'm leaving," Franz says.

"I'm pretty sure one week won't mean starting over," I say.

"It damn well better not," Franz says.

Even though we trust the Wolff, it's a long week. We work on our other assignments and try not to worry about the Razmovsky melting out of our fingers.

✦　✦　✦

"Play it."

We play it. It's rough at the edges, but there's something else: a sense of space, as if the work is breathing more easily, as if we'd been squeezing it too hard before.

"Better," she says when we reach the final flourish. "Do you perceive it?"

We nod. It's hard to put into words, but it's there.

"You cannot force music to live," she says. "You can only allow it to live. When you step away from it briefly—not too long—it grows. Especially in a quartet, where everything is transparent. Do you understand?"

"I think so," I say. The others look dubious.

"Understanding will come," she says. "Do it again."

We do it again. The space is there. The raggedness diminishes.

The third time through, we play eight measures before she stops us.

"Very well," she says at the end. "Take the third movement apart this week. *Slow* does not mean *loose*. The meter must be pliable, but smooth.

Turn your chairs around at least once."

"Yes, Professorin," we say.

The next Saturday afternoon, Oma Judith, listening from the corner of the Apfelbaums' sitting room, notices.

"It's getting there," she says over dinner. "That smart professor of yours did you a favor."

"I think so, too," I say. "I don't really understand why, but I think we're better on this side of it."

"Keep it in mind," she says. "You won't always have someone to tell you what you need to do to master something. You'll have to figure it out for yourself. What's working, what's not. When you're failing, when to let go and step back, when to try again. You'll have to be your own biggest advocate and at the same time your own worst critic."

"That sounds impossible," I say. "You seem to know a lot about it."

"Welcome to being an artist," she says. "Pass the potatoes, will you?"

✦ ✦ ✦

December 1908

We perform the Razumovsky No. 1 in two weeks and we still have a problem. The fourth movement is based on a Russian folk tune, Beethoven's tribute to his Russian patron. We have it technically, but the Wolff isn't satisfied.

"It must sound *Russian*," she says at our Wednesday afternoon dismemberment.

"Professorin, what does *Russian* sound like?" I say, deciding not to belabor the obvious point.

"You have not heard of Balakirev? Mussorgsky? Borodin? The Russian Nationalist School?"

"Where would we—er, no, Professorin. At least, I haven't." The other three shake their heads.

"Well. If you can find someone to play you some Russian music before the recital, you will learn. If not," she shrugs, "you'll have a German-sounding Russian folk tune. You will have to play it extra-perfectly, in that case. Once more from the beginning."

We play five measures before she stops us.

✦ ✦ ✦

"Robert, do you know any Russian folk tunes?"

"Have you ever heard of Mussorgsky? Borodin? And what was that other fellow's name?"

"Balakirev," Felix says. "And the Russian Nationalist School?"

"I was up to my neck in Russian Nationalists in Moscow," he says. "Why?"

We explain our difficulty.

"A Russian tune filtered through German sensibility," he says. "Are you sure the Wolff isn't just pulling your leg?"

"Doing what?" Franz says.

"Sorry—messing with you?"

"Possibly," I say. "But if we come back next week and it sounds more Russian to her—"

"She'll realize we really are amazing," Franz says.

"I'm sure she already knows that," Arnold says. "But we want to keep her proud of us."

"I'll bring one of my Russian books tomorrow," Robert says. "We'll hole up in a practice room and you play me your Russian bit and I'll play you some Russian tunes. Will that work?"

"Yes! Please!" we chorus.

"Anything to keep you out of the Wolff's jaws." Robert laughs his big American laugh, picks up his bag and saunters off to get in a little practice before our next class.

The next day, in a large practice room that manages to be both cold and stuffy, we play the fourth movement for Robert. He thinks a bit, then pulls a book out of his bag, thumbs through it, and sets it on the rack.

"How about this?" He plays a student piece by Mussorgsky, then a couple of dances by Balakirev and a folk tune arranged by Borodin. Even though they're rough, having been put away for two years, we can hear that they're different—a little wilder? A little less regular in the beat? More minor, less major?

"The thing you have to understand," Robert says, "is that in Russia, everything is related to winter. Everything. The year I spent there, winter started in October and lasted until May. It was dark, much darker than here, because it's so far north. And *so* cold. It gets plenty cold in New York, but honestly, in Moscow I thought I would die of the cold. When it got to be February, I couldn't remember it hadn't always been winter. It's bad enough in the cities, but it's even worse in the country. Russian country life is just so awfully hard. Spring and summer are an explosion of life and high spirits. Relief, and the energy to do things. Everything! But you have to do them fast, because there isn't much time. So, a tune like yours is a summer tune, happy and exuberant and picnics and folk dancing and love. But it's also aware, because every aspect of life in Russia is aware, that before long, winter will come roaring back down from the Arctic. That's why everything has an undercurrent of melancholy. The people, too. It makes for great music, but I couldn't stand it in person."

"I can see why," I say.

"I hope that helps," he says.

"An extra edge of passion," Felix says, "to celebrate the brevity of decent weather, plus an undertone of sadness for the rest of the year."

"That's it," Robert says. "That's it, exactly."

✦ ✦ ✦

"Better," the Wolff says when we play our winter-aware summer folk tune-inspired fourth movement for her the following Wednesday. "Do it again."

On recital day we do a run-through in the afternoon, then leave our instruments in the Wolff's studio and go for a walk, followed by a light meal of food we've brought from home. My caterpillars dance frenetically about my stomach as if winter is just around the corner. When it's time at last, I change my clothes in the women's toilet, put up my hair, check everything twice in the mirror, retreat to the waiting lounge, and sit quietly with my quartet-mates, mentally rehearsing. We're last. Marburg's not on the program, for once, but I don't need him. Not tonight.

At the end of intermission, we move to the stage right wing and then, when the group ahead of us begins its finale, we line up. Despite Mozart pouring off the stage not ten paces away from us, our deep concentration persists.

I think of my father.

At their final flourish, applause fills the hall.

"Lady and gentlemen, the Octopus Quartet is ON," Franz says.

The performers take their bows and file offstage. "Well done!" we say. "Fantastic!"

"Good luck!" they answer. And at Herr Schädler's signal, we walk onstage, bow to polite applause and a possible murmur of surprise, and take our seats.

There is no doubt in our minds and we leave no doubt in anyone else's. The mountain of work has been worth it. The energy of our audience feeds our own, crackling like electricity, making our bright passages brighter, our dark ones darker. Our solos rise to new heights. Our fingers feel invincible. Nothing matters except the music and our audience. And each other, our one brain hard at work as our voices take turns leading and following. Our exhilaration, like the music itself, has no words, but it's real and all-consuming.

In the final movement our Russian folk tune celebrates brief summer as winter begins to loom. And when at last, after a half hour of sweating intensity, we play the final notes and hear their reverberation in the hall, the echoes hang in the silence for perhaps three seconds before we lower our bows. The hall erupts. Applause rolls over us as we stand and take our bows. Even our classmates in the wings are applauding. We want the moment to last forever, but a few short minutes later we're back in the lounge, packing up.

On the way upstairs the Wolff's praise reaches new heights of eloquence.

"Intelligent," she says, her eyebrows arched as if she can't quite believe it. "The fourth movement was much improved. Notes tomorrow, nine o'clock."

"'Intelligent!'" Franz says once she's out of hearing. "She's going soft."

"She'll shred it tomorrow," Felix says.

"I don't care," I say. "We were on fire. Didn't you feel it?"

"Absolutely," Arnold says. "You could really hear how the inner voices hold everything together."

Our families find us and we bask in their praise as everyone talks at once. Robert brings over the Walters, congratulating everyone along the way.

"Oh, my dears!" Frau Walter says. "That was simply magnificent! Just *think*! Learning all that and being able to keep your mind on what you're doing! Gracious, such complicated music! Isn't it the most exciting thing in the world, playing in a group like that? So much concentration! You must come and see us over the holidays, my dears. It won't do to have

Robert practicing all the time with no friends around. You must all come! Promise! And Joseph should have some time off. You can't build anything in the winter anyway, it's too cold and too wet. And too much snow. You promised, now, do remember!"

Herr Walter shakes my hand. "Fine ensemble," he says. "A thoroughly professional performance."

"People around me were whispering when you came on with the others," Joseph says. "But afterward, they applauded as hard as anyone. When they heard you play, it didn't matter anymore. You're making history!"

"We'll see if history stays made, or if I have to keep making it over again," I say.

"I hope you—I mean, all of you—will visit during the holiday," he says, turning slightly pink.

"I hope so, too," I say.

"I'll look forward to it," he says.

The Dietrichs. Johanna and Heidi. Herr Kurtz. Katerina, who practically swoons. Parents of other students marvel at my bravery, as if my quartet-mates have fangs. The whirl continues for an hour, after which I'm completely exhausted.

Two nights later, we hear Berit, Ros, Jan and Matthias. All around me, little gasps of surprise accompany their entrance. So *that's* what making history sounds like.

When they finish, I applaud harder than anyone.

14

DECEMBER 1908

December 1908

But the others leave Köln to spend the holiday with relatives and, with one eye on my scholarship, I decide there's probably something improper in making a purely social call to a daughterless house. So, except for Katerina's last pre-Christmas lesson, during which I marvel at the annual transformation of the Kurtz mansion into an enchanted forest and Katerina into a bundle of lovesick nerves, I'm nearly as alone as if I'd landed on the moon.

I look perversely forward to winter term, when I'll be consumed by study, practice, and rehearsal. I even look forward to the Wolff ripping me to pieces every week. Because I've come to understand a truth about the Wolff that Ros and Berit told me long ago: she's trying, not to break me, but to temper me, like steel.

Gerda rescues me from my isolation with an invitation for Christmas Eve. A celebration of family, she says, not dogma, and this year their mothers are away. My mother doesn't care. I accept, feeling guiltily, indecently happy.

I know I must bring gifts; unfortunately, gifts cost money. I bake Frau Apfelbaum's ginger cookies, hardly up to her standard but at least edible. I also find books for Thomas: a big one about trains and a tiny one in English for Gerda to read to him, about the misadventures of a rabbit in a garden.

On Christmas Eve, night falls early. In Johann-Christoph-Strasse, fresh snow dusts every surface. Pools of light glitter under the streetlamps and candles flicker in every window. A reflective, thoughtful stillness permeates the cold air. I pause to breathe in the quiet magic of midwinter.

The Dietrichs' third floor window flies open.

"Come up, silly. It's freezing out there!"

"Coming!"

Upstairs, the flat smells wonderfully of the forest. I trade my coat and muffler for a cup of mulled wine and an excited toddler.

"Mewwy Christmas! Saint Nich'las! Kwampus! Twee!" Thomas squeals, pointing to the ancient wooden pair standing knee deep in fir boughs and a small tree decorated with tiny animals and musical instruments.

"Last year, he didn't care," Gerda laughs. "This year he's been wound up for two weeks."

Thomas wiggles down and runs for the tree. Gerda grabs him and rescues a carved bear.

"I hung these on my grandmother's tree when I was small," she says, showing it to me. "They're at least a hundred years old, probably older."

"How wonderful you still have them," I say, thinking of all the treasures we sold.

"Pwesents!" Thomas insists, grabbing the nearest one and nearly flattening the tree.

"We'll have no peace until we open gifts," Herr Dietrich says, grabbing Thomas. "And at this rate we'll likely have no tree or ornaments, either."

So, we top off our mulled wine and hand around gifts. Thomas loves his books. Herr Dietrich helps himself to a ginger cookie.

"Delicious!" he says. "A good thing I have to squeeze into my suit later, or I'd eat them all."

"Your suit? Why?"

"For the Bach Christmas Oratorio at the Dom. The first three sections, anyway. The hour and the temperature will put you off religion altogether, but it's a grand hall to play in. Music sounds fantastic in cathedrals, even if you're playing in your sleep. Which I might be."

"That sounds amazing, and also terrible," I say.

"Correct on both. For you," he says, handing me a package.

"Me? You didn't—"

I tear off the wrapping to reveal two scores for Camille Saint-Saëns's Sonata No. 1 for Violin and Piano.

"I was feeling subversive," Herr Dietrich says. "All that myopic

German-only nonsense for your first two years!"

"This is fantastic! Where did you find it?"

"You can buy foreign scores in Köln, you know. We're not so provincial as all that. You'll hear the Sinfonia play foreign work, too—if you're attending as you're supposed to."

"Sometimes," I say. "Even the student price is expensive."

French music! I want to throw my arms around him, as if that could thank him for all his years of patient encouragement. But I can't hug a teacher; it would be disrespectful.

"You've done—so much." My voice is suddenly rather hoarse.

"It's you who've done so much," he says. "A teacher's job is just to keep pushing. My advice with Saint-Saëns is, don't rush him. Take the time to get him into your blood."

"I'm sure Robert could play this—he spent a year at the Paris Conservatory. Maybe the Wolff would let us play it for spring recital. That's enough time, isn't it?"

"I should think so," he says. "Not that I had that exact possibility in mind, of course."

"I'll ask him," I say.

"Book him early," he says. "I think you'll love it."

"I already love it and I haven't even heard it yet."

"Merry Christmas!" he says, raising his cup of mulled wine. "Ugh, gone cold."

Everyone laughs, even Thomas. And in our shared laughter, I suddenly feel as if, on this one midwinter night, surrounded by old family heirlooms, new gifts, and the smell of the forest, the Dietrichs and I have become a family.

As if there's only one family in the world, and it is ours.

✦ ✦ ✦

"So, how's your pupil doing?" Herr Dietrich asks over a supper of fish, potato salad, and cabbage.

"Still enthusiastic," I say. "Especially since she started playing Christmas duets with Otto von Marburg."

"That rather confirms the Sinfonia gossip," he says.

"What gossip?"

"Well, their families, you know, come from different social classes—"

"What? There's more than one class of rich people in Köln?"

"Certainly," Herr Dietrich says. "The Marburgs are petty aristocracy. Hereditary wealth, a moldering castle somewhere. Kurtz fought his way to the top at the bank. Altogether different. Traditionally, aristocrats only married other aristocrats, so, besides becoming progressively more inbred, like the Hapsburgs, each generation is more strapped for cash than the one before. As a result, in our enlightened times you'll often see purity quietly ignored in favor of marriages that provide transfusions of money. So, Otto and Katerina may be madly in love, but if Marburg the Elder is allowing his first-born to court a commoner, you can bet it has more to do with her money than her sparkling personality or, with all respect, her ability on the violin. In fact, there are rumors, which you didn't hear from me, that Marburg borrows freely from Kurtz's bank and considers the terms of his loans to be little more than unpleasant formalities."

"Now, Wil, should you be spreading gossip like that?" Gerda says.

"What's the good of knowing it if I can't spread it somewhere?" he says. "Anyway, it's hardly a secret. All the little barons do it. Let's just hope Otto is a better man than the rest of them. It's not Katerina's fault she's filthy rich. She doesn't deserve to be married to an arrogant boor."

"Or a family of them," I say.

"On more pleasant topics," he says, "your quartet interests me. Most student ensembles don't last. People scramble around from term to term, looking for more congenial partners. But you've stayed together. Will you continue next fall?"

"I hope so," I say. "The Wolff said we were starting to think like a quartet. Four instruments—"

"Eight arms and one brain," Herr Dietrich laughs.

"Franz thinks we should call ourselves the Octopus Quartet."

"I like it, personally," Herr Dietrich says. "But you'd spend a lot of time explaining it. He's right, though. You mostly agree and, when you disagree, you can work it out. Ensembles fall apart all the time because people fight over tempo and phrasing. It sounds ridiculous, but it happens."

"The Wolff has definite ideas. We follow them."

"If you stay together, eventually you'll have your own ideas. But you'll always hear her voice in your heads."

"That'll explain the headaches," I say. "But I doubt we'll continue after Conservatory. They'll all get jobs somewhere and I won't."

I really don't want to talk about what comes after Conservatory, not tonight.

"There are professional quartets, you know, even all-women quartets," Herr Dietrich says. "They make a good living, with no boards and conductors telling them what they can and can't do. An appealing thought, at times, I can tell you."

"I've never heard of a mixed one."

"That's because yours isn't out there yet."

That stops me for a moment. "I don't think—that would—I mean, theoretically, but—"

"Wil, enough," Gerda says. "Tonight isn't for solving the future. It's for celebrating present blessings. Marthe, more potatoes?"

"Sorry," he says, though he doesn't look it. "Which reminds me, don't miss the Vienna Quartet at Sinfonia Hall in February. Bring your quartet with you. I dare you to imagine yourselves doing that."

"But a *mixed* quartet—"

"Time for dessert," Gerda says, standing up. "Or Wil will be late, Thomas will be impossible, and everyone will be grumpy tomorrow."

She hands around delicate china plates with slices of braided stollen, sugar-glazed and studded with candied fruit.

"My great-grandmother's recipe. And her plates," she says.

"The best kind of connection to the past," I say. "It's absolutely delicious."

Too soon, Herr Dietrich disappears to dress and Gerda puts Thomas to bed. I clear the table and wash dishes. I've mostly finished by the time she returns, looking suddenly tired, and he reappears in his formal suit, case in hand.

"Would you like to come, now that you're a Bach convert?" he says, putting on his coat, muffler, and gloves. "It'll run from ten to midnight. I could see you back to your flat afterward."

"Oh!" I hadn't considered it, though the poster was up in the Conservatory foyer for a month. "I'd love to . . . but my mother expects me home."

"We could stop by your flat on the way to let her know. I've got time, really."

Suddenly I want to. The crowds, the cold night air, the giant cathedral.

Bach. Massed voices reverberating down the stone walls and up to the vaulted ceiling. So what if it's Christian? I'm not religious, it doesn't matter. It's music—great music, that's all.

"I really would love to," I hear myself saying. "But . . . my mother . . . I leave her alone so much during the term. I really should go home."

Maybe I'm hoping he'll try to persuade me.

"I understand," he says. "I'll be off, then. Are you staying, or shall I see you to the streetcar?"

"I'll go with you," I say, glancing at Gerda's tired face. I pull on my own layers of woolen armor and give Gerda the hug I would give both of them if it were proper. I want to hold her tight, hold on to the love and acceptance I find here in this little flat with its candles and fir tree smell and its warmth.

"See you later, my love," Herr Dietrich says, giving Gerda a kiss. "Don't wait up."

"My plan exactly," she says.

Out in the sharp air, flickering, golden light sparkles on all the little snowdrifts and through the clouds of our breath. The street has come to life with people making their way to the city's churches for Christmas services. Everyone we pass says, "Merry Christmas!" and looks happy. Midwinter's magic has indeed enchanted Köln, just for tonight, sweeping away its everyday pettiness and dirt, revealing the beauty of what the city could be, what human beings could be.

If the world were really like this, the way it feels at this moment, I would try to be a better person, in order to deserve to live in it.

The crowds build as we make our way to the main road, where the streetlamps glow like little moons as far as we can see. Whole families wait for streetcars—couples arm in arm, grandparents gripping children firmly by the hand, everyone bundled shapeless in layers of wool. I wish I were going to the Altstadt, but my sense of duty—no, guilt—has won.

For now.

The Altstadt streetcar clangs up. The crowd surges toward it.

"Goodbye, then. Merry Christmas!" Herr Dietrich says.

I struggle to find the right words, and fail. I seize his free hand in both of mine. A hot tear freezes on my cheek. I hope he doesn't see, or if he does, that he understands.

Alone on the Ehrenfeld streetcar, I think about hearing, or rather not hearing, Bach in the cathedral. Next year, I tell myself. Next year.

No one else gets off at my stop. I trudge up Hildegardstrasse and climb the steps to my front door. Before I unlock it, I look back down the street. Yes, the enchantment is here, too: candles in windows, golden light pooling and flickering on the sidewalk. A few pedestrians pass in and out of the shadows on their way to catch their own streetcars to wherever they're going. The occasional "Merry Christmas!" filters back to me.

Enchantment, indeed. I try to memorize every detail against Köln's inevitable return to its normal, hurried, noisy, self-absorbed, grubby self. At last, the cold seeps through my coat. I turn away, unlock the front door, slip into the entry, and close it quietly behind me.

Mother is snoring on the sofa, her mug beside her on the table. I leave her there. Anni is either asleep or out. The colors of our flat seem unusually drab in the yellow gaslight. I imagine the crowds filling the cathedral. As I finally turn out my own light and crawl under my eiderdown, our clock strikes ten. I imagine an opening fanfare shattering the cold cathedral air, the orchestra stirring to life, the choristers raising their voices to the rafters, the soloists' voices soaring above all, and the audience, believers or not, immersed in an ocean of sound.

✦ ✦ ✦

For the rest of the holiday, I do little besides practice my assignments and the new orchestra repertoire. But I also study the Saint-Saëns and try a few passages. It's very beautiful, and definitely not German.

I can't wait to get started.

The first bitterly cold Monday morning of the New Year, warmed by a sense of anticipation, I board the streetcar so heavily dressed I can barely sit down. Twenty minutes later I step down into a pile of dirty snow and tramp down the block into the relative warmth of the Conservatory.

"Happy New Year!" Robert grins when he spots me in the foyer. "Say, we were looking all over for you at the Dom on Christmas Eve. I was sure you'd be there."

"I couldn't go."

"The music was incredible," he says. "Long, but so worth it." He lowers his voice to a whisper. "Joseph was pretty disappointed. He was hoping you'd be there."

"Oh . . . ah, I mean, really? I mean, well, I'll definitely go next time."
I feel my face turn pink.

"Definitely," Robert says. He looks like he's trying not to laugh.

"By the way," I say. "I need to talk to you about a project I have in mind . . ."

15

WINTER, JANUARY–APRIL 1909

January 1909

Monday morning.

"Where did you get this?" the Wolff asks, eyeing me suspiciously over the top of the Saint-Saëns score.

"Herr Dietrich gave it to me," I say. "I'd like to do it for my spring solo recital. Robert MacInness says he'll play it with me."

She furrows her eyebrows even more tightly together.

"You have already asked him?"

"I didn't want to ask your permission if I didn't have a pianist," I say.

"I have laid out a great deal of other repertoire for you to master this term," she says.

"But this fits Conservatory policy—"

"I am aware of Conservatory policy, Fraülein."

"I love our German repertoire. You know that. But to build a career, I need to learn other musical languages. As Berit is learning."

This, at least, is true. I asked her.

"I see."

There follows a long pause while I keep my expression earnest and neutral.

She thumbs through the score, frowning occasionally, humming little passages to herself. Finally, she looks up at me again. "You wish to become a soloist, then?"

"Mmm . . . maybe. I want to see the world beyond Köln. That's one way to do it."

"A hard way," she says.

"Yes, Professorin. I have no illusions."

"Well, you have Rameau and Kreutzer, you might as well add Saint-Saëns. Bring Herr MacInness in with you on Wednesday afternoon. Have you already learned half of it, as usual?"

"I only got it a week and a half ago," I say. "And I worked on the new orchestra repertoire over the holiday. But I have six months."

"You will be busy," she says. Distant thunder rumbles in her voice, but now is not the time to waver.

"I can do it, Professorin. I'm sure of it."

"Wednesday afternoon, then. And your regular lesson Wednesday morning. Which I hope you have prepared."

"Yes, Professorin, of course."

She holds the score out to me.

"The first movement. Do what you can before then. And tell Herr MacInness."

"Yes, Professorin." I leave her studio, my heart thumping with elation.

✦ ✦ ✦

Monday afternoon.

I'm dragging a chair from the stack to my usual spot at the rear of the second violins when Ros appears behind me with her cello case.

"What are you doing, you silly thing?" she says. "Haven't you checked the seating chart?"

"No, why?"

"Have you forgotten? Z asked you specifically last year if you were crashing again. Go, have a look."

I put the chair down and go study the chart. At first, I think Ros is teasing me, for my name isn't in the spot I've been occupying for the last two years.

"You're looking in the wrong place," she hisses over my shoulder, jabbing her finger at the chart. "There!"

I turn back to her in astonishment.

"Third row!" I say.

I check the chart again. Marburg is two rows behind me.

"I'm not sure I like Marburg being where I can't see him."

210

"At least you don't have to look at him. Welcome to upper level orchestra!"

"Did you make first chair?" I ask.

"Heavens, no! I didn't audition. He wouldn't give it to me and if he did it would be too much work. Come on, let's get ready." She unpacks her cello and carries it carefully across the stage to her seat. Other people are filtering in, checking the chart, greeting each other. I stare at my name a bit longer before I come to my senses and hurry off to my new seat, leaving the extra chair behind.

Marburg isn't happy about being with the second violins again, of course, even though lots of people have been switched between sections from what I remember two years ago. He seems to think it's inferior, which, as everyone else knows, it's not. Doubtless he's also furious about sitting behind me. I set up my parts and tune, facing resolutely to the front.

Herr Zeidler starts off with a few introductory remarks about our program: Papa Haydn's Symphony No. 50 and Beethoven's great Symphony No. 5, followed after intermission by our first Wagner, his brief *Polonia* concert overture from 1836, followed by—I didn't believe it when I saw the program—the Czech Antonin Dvořák's Symphony No. 9, *From the New World*, composed in 1893 while he lived in America.

Finally, the Conservatory orchestra plays non-German music!

One thing all but the Haydn have in common is that our upper level orchestra isn't big enough to play them, especially in the percussion and brass. I wondered how we would do without them. The answer is, members of the Köln Sinfonia will fill out our ranks, starting the last week of rehearsals.

This announcement sends a thrill of excitement through the third-years, who will share a stage with professionals for the first time, while the fourth-years, who did the same last year, try their best to look blasé. Real professionals! So, we mustn't be alarmed, Herr Zeidler says, if we don't sound complete; everything will be all right in the end.

Ros and I do our annual bit of theatre and then the rehearsal begins.

✦ ✦ ✦

Wednesday afternoon.

"Herr Becker speaks well of you," the Wolff says.

"I'm honored, Professorin," Robert says.

"Play. You first, Fraülein," she says.

She lets me hack my way through the first movement. It's rough, of course, on barely more than a day of real practice, not counting my nosing through it over the holiday, but I manage to get to the end at last.

"You next, Herr MacInness."

Robert sits down at the piano and plays a scale and arpeggios to get the feel of the instrument. She watches him minutely, her expression unrevealing.

The piano part is just as challenging as the violin's, an equal voice, at least. He's had one day to study it, on top of his other work. He must be sight-reading, but his year in Paris shows. He understands the French character of the sound in a way I don't yet: he makes the piano sing, even though the sound still comes from hammers hitting strings inside it. He, too, is rough, but I can tell by listening that he understands the music, even on such short acquaintance.

"How long have you been practicing this?" the Wolff asks him when he finishes.

"Marthe gave it to me on Monday after she talked to you," he says. "I started Monday evening when I got home."

"At least she allowed you to enjoy your holiday," the Wolff says. "Bring the first movement back next week. We will proceed from there. You may go."

"Well, that wasn't half bad!" Robert says as we head back downstairs.

"She can't rip apart something you haven't learned," I say. "Just wait."

"I like her already, though."

"Franz says her special gift is crushing the souls of music students, but other than that, she's an excellent teacher."

Robert laughs. "Remind me to tell you about Professor Meunier someday," he says. "In Paris. A notorious soul-crusher. The Wolff is a martinet, but she's not a monster. I think this is going to be fun!"

"Likewise."

"Guess I'd better get started, then," he says. "I'll be in my practice hole, if anyone wants me."

"Good idea," I say.

At the landing, Marburg and Herr Grimmelshausen, deep in conversation as usual, pass us going up.

"Afternoon, Marburg," Robert says. As we start down the next flight, he says in a carrying voice, "That poor guy. Is he still in love with you? I pity anyone who thinks he's going to get between you and your work!"

When we reach the basement corridor, I realize I've been holding my breath.

"I hope he doesn't decide to start on me again," I say. "I've really had about enough of that."

"He might," Robert says. "Though he could certainly put his time to better use. My guess is he won't want to jeopardize his standing with his precious Herr Grimmelshausen. No point worrying, anyway. Here's my door. See you!"

I never come down here without thinking that the basement is a perfect symbol of the hard, gritty work required to create the music we play on the stage above it. The only natural light comes from small windows that open into light wells and an ugly service alley and the paint is probably original. It's as different from the elegant foyer as the moon, and just about as welcoming.

I claim an empty practice room, open the Saint-Saëns score, kick Marburg's backside out of my mind and get to work learning the first movement.

✦ ✦ ✦

February 1909

A poster appears in the foyer for the Vienna Quartet at Sinfonia Hall, playing a program of Mozart, Schumann, and Tchaikovsky. I tell the others Herr Dietrich said we must go. But I keep his thought experiment to myself. It's impossible, anyway; men and women can't play together in public. Civilization would collapse. Why would the others commit professional suicide by trying?

Anyhow, life after Conservatory seems impossibly far away, even now, when I'm over halfway there. So, I do the only thing I can imagine doing right now.

I push it out of my mind.

None of us attends concerts as often as we should, or would like to. We all agree that if our teachers really want us to go, they shouldn't overload us the way they do, and also some of us should have more money. So, the Vienna Quartet is a very special treat.

Sinfonia Hall personifies the grand tradition of nineteenth century theatres: four levels of boxes, every surface decorated, a great chandelier hanging from the ceiling. We head for the cheap seats in the top balcony, where (we tell ourselves) the sound is better. The elegance of our fellow concertgoers declines as we climb the many staircases to the highest tier, along with the elegance of the staircases themselves. As usual, we encounter several classmates on our long trek upward.

Marburg, with minimal standards for his own playing and lots of money, doubtless attends far more often than we do. Sure enough, we spot him tonight, sitting with his parents and his brother in their private box in the second tier, where they can be seen and admired, should anyone want to admire them. The inferior sound there doesn't concern them; for denizens of the boxes, hearing the concert is hardly the point of attending the Sinfonia.

No matter. They can have their boxes. For me, it's exciting just to be here.

When they enter and bow, the four men of the Vienna Quartet look rather small on the Sinfonia stage, but applause fills the hall as if they were a whole orchestra. After all, their accolades from fifteen years of touring throughout Europe, England, and America fill an entire page of the program.

They begin with Mozart, Quartet No. 22, the second of the Prussian Quartets. Our faces soon wear identical expressions of amazement: this is quartet music at a whole different level. Mozart shimmers under their bows, as bright and precise as fine crystal, as warm as a summer day. Melodies leap from voice to voice as they carry on their conversation, the pace seemingly effortless, but thoroughly under control. These four have clearly played together so long they can read each other's minds. The showy final flourish leaves us breathless.

"Wow!" Arnold says under cover of the applause. "Just, wow."

Next, Tchaikovsky, the most European of the Russians, according to the program, but still definitely Russian. In this quartet, as in our Razumovsky, I hear a Russian folk melody with a melancholy edge. Brief summer, endless winter. What a terribly exotic place Russia must be. Harsh, but also mysterious and enticing. I wonder, before my mind snaps back to the music, if I'll ever have the chance to go there and what it would be like to live a life of such possibilities.

At intermission, we spot the Dietrichs through the crowd at the bar. We elbow our way through to them and introduce Robert.

"What do you think?" Herr Dietrich says.

We pour out our opinions, all talking at once.

"That's you in twenty years, isn't it?"

The torrent stops in mid-phrase. So much for my secret thought experiment.

"Well, it *is* a possibility, you know. Would you like to meet them?"

"Yes!" we all say at once.

"You *know* them?" I ask.

"Slightly. I was on the welcome committee yesterday."

"Is there anything he *doesn't* do around here?" I ask Gerda.

"He'd sweep the floor, if need be," she says.

Herr Dietrich ignores her. "You can be my guests at the reception afterward," he says. "Meet me here afterward and we'll go in together."

"Fantastic!" Robert says.

"Wow," Arnold says.

"But first, a little Schumann," Herr Dietrich says. "Pay close attention. Since you've adopted a pianist, you might want to try it sometime."

"I've thought all along a quintet would be fun," Robert says. "You think we could handle this one?"

"You decide," Herr Dietrich says. He and Gerda wave as they melt into the crowd.

The Schumann Quintet nearly blows us out of the hall with its energy and drive. From its first crashing chord, it races along, enveloping us, spinning us around, practically knocking us into each other. I forget to breathe. Voices chase each other, contrasting themes interrupt, major becomes minor and returns to major, but the energy never flags, no matter the tempo. The pianist, sitting behind the four string players, keeps his eyes on them, only rarely looking at the keys. The finale winds up into a great final burst and the house erupts into a frenzy of applause. This time it's Robert, down at the end of the row, who shakes his head and says, "Wow. Just, wow."

"Yeah," he says, more to himself than to us as we make our way back to the bar to meet the Dietrichs. "Yeah, I'll do that one of these days. I could do that. Yeah."

Herr Dietrich leads the way backstage to an ornate salon featuring three chandeliers, miniatures of the one in the hall. On one side stands a table loaded with desserts; on the other, a long, crowded bar.

"Good evening, Herr Lübeck," Herr Dietrich says to the doorman. "You know my wife, of course. And these are my guests."

Herr Lübeck bows, ignoring with professional politeness how scruffy we look compared to the tuxedoed men and glittering women already milling about, sipping glasses of schnapps or champagne.

I spot the Kurtz family at the bar, talking to the Marburgs. I decide not to intrude. Madame would hardly be pleased to see me and, anyway, I'll see Katerina Saturday morning.

"May we—?" Franz is eyeing the dessert table.

"Help yourself," Herr Dietrich says. "Champagne, anyone? Gerda, my love?"

"I'd better see he doesn't make a pig of himself," Arnold says and hurries after Franz.

Herr Dietrich signals a passing waiter and hands us glasses of champagne, which I've only ever had once before in my life, at a wedding.

"A toast to the art of the string quartet," he says. "And quintets, of course," he adds, nodding to Robert. "And to string quartet ensembles, present and future."

I raise my glass and take a sip of champagne. It feels like little fireworks going off in my mouth, the perfect reflection of my mood at this moment.

"I feel like such a beginner, hearing them play," Felix says.

"You are," Herr Dietrich says. "Not that you aren't already very accomplished, believe me. But music like this you never truly master. Play it when you're twenty and you'll do it well. Play it when you're thirty, or forty, or fifty and you'll pour your life experience into it, not just your technical expertise, although that keeps growing also. Works I thought I understood ten years ago I find deeper meaning in now. It's one of the great rewards of studying music. You never run out of room to grow."

"Hey, where did you get champagne?" Franz says as he reappears holding a plate crowded with two kinds of torte.

"Turn your back, take your chances," Felix says.

"Ah," Gerda says, looking over my shoulder. "Here they come!"

The instant the members of the Vienna Quartet and their pianist appear, patrons flutter around them like moths around a light. The musicians, to whom this must be a regular obligation, shake hands with the men and kiss the gloved hands of the women. A few people, notably the Marburgs, continue their conversations without a glance at the guests of honor.

"Come on, I'll introduce you," Herr Dietrich says, beckoning us over to the edge of the crowd, where we wait for the handshaking and handkissing to reach us. At last, the glittering knot unravels as people drift back to the dessert table and their own conversations.

"Gentlemen, may I present five of the Köln Conservatory's finest third-year students?" Herr Dietrich says, bowing as the four musicians approach for a rather involved round of handshaking. The violist, a short, stocky man with a full beard and an extravagantly waxed mustache, kisses my hand just as if I were an aristocrat with a fine gown and opera gloves instead of a down-at-heel student in a dark blue woolen dress. "These four are a very fine quartet themselves and, with their pianist colleague here, will be tackling the Schumann Quintet in the next year or so."

"You don't say," says the Vienna's pianist, who also sports a luxuriant, if unwaxed, mustache. In half a breath he and Robert are deep in conversation, presumably about the intricacies of the piano part.

"You are a quartet?" the first violinist says. "Most curious. I would not have thought such an arrangement would work. But these are modern times, I suppose, and the young people are more adaptable. With whom do you study?"

"Professorin Maria Wolff," I say. "She's our quartet coach and my teacher."

"Ah," he says. "Professorin Wolff. That explains a great deal."

"You know her?" I knew the music world was small, but I didn't know it was *that* small.

"From the Vienna Conservatory," he says. "And what is she teaching you?"

"We just finished Beethoven's first Razumovsky," Felix says.

"Most ambitious for a student ensemble," he says.

"We'd love to play the repertoire you played tonight," Felix says.

"Especially the Schumann. It sounds like Robert's getting instructions right now."

"It is possible," the violinist says, "for very talented students to approach the work, though only with the level of rigor Professorin Wolff would provide. But it requires a seamlessness of thought. A mixed group . . . that is doubtful. Very doubtful."

"Nonsense!" the violist says. "Have you forgotten, Adolphus, the piano part was *written* for Clara Schumann? It is difficult," he continues to us, "undeniably so. But the fingers of a man or a woman, what's the difference? By all means, learn it. It will reward you many times over. My card." He hands us each a calling card, which we take in stunned disbelief. "If you have any questions about the work, please feel free to write to me and ask. I'll be happy to guide you if I can, although under Professorin Wolff, you're unlikely to need an outside consultant. And should you find yourselves in Vienna, please do come and see us."

And with another handshake (the violist kisses my hand again), the men move on. We stare at each other and then at the calling cards in our hands. *Johann Lorenz, Vienna Quartet*, it reads in flamboyant black script, and an address in Vienna.

"Well then," Felix says after a long pause in which our minds don't seem to want to work at all. "So, it looks like we're doing the Schumann Quintet next fall, eh, Robert?"

"Looks like," Robert says. "Any time, as far as I'm concerned. That is one incredible piece of music!"

"It will take time," Herr Dietrich says. "Do it right, don't rush it."

"They don't seem to be of one mind about mixed quartets," I say.

Herr Dietrich laughs. "There's only one way to change minds," he says. "Which is?"

"Just go be one, I know. Easy enough to say. But—"

"One step at a time," he says. "And I believe the first step—ah, I see Franz has already taken it—again. The first step is to try some of the torte before it's all gone."

✦ ✦ ✦

Saturday morning, promptly at ten, I present myself at the Kurtz residence, now back to its florid, Art Nouveau self. Every Saturday so far this year,

Katerina has talked about little besides Otto von Marburg, how wonderful their duets were at the Christmas party, and how in love she is. I have to let her bubble a little at the beginning of every lesson before we can do anything serious. Today, Madame is mercifully absent and Frau Schmidt disappears once she's let me in. It's no wonder Katerina is so excited about parties, considering how much time she spends at home by herself.

"You know, I was thinking," she says as we unpack our instruments.

"And?" I wait for some new tidbit about the fabulous Otto or something about someone's dress.

"That was such a wonderful concert last night, wasn't it? You could do that! You really could. Because you told me you weren't sure about being a soloist, you know. In a quartet, you'd always have your friends. You could travel, but not be all alone. And inspire young artists, and play all the great quartets, and add other people when you needed them, like the pianist last night. It would be so marvelous! I'd be completely envious, I know I would!"

"I appreciate your confidence in me," I say, marveling at how easy she must think it is.

"I can see it!" she says. "You'll be the next famous quartet and play all over Europe, even America! You'll make history! Three men in tuxedos and a woman in an evening gown, glittering with diamonds, playing together in a group as equals. Don't tell me you wouldn't like that!"

Ah, the world according to Katerina. The sheen of silk and the flash of diamonds! I should show her the practice rooms sometime.

"Your mind runs the same direction as Herr Dietrich's. Minus the gowns and diamonds, he didn't mention those. But the future's a long way off yet, too far away to worry about."

This isn't true. I find I worry about it quite often these days, possibly because people keep insisting on bringing it up.

"Perhaps we should begin before Frau Schmidt comes back. You're stuck with me for at least another couple of years. Best to let your parents think I'm teaching you something. How about that Haydn?"

Katerina is undeterred. "All right," she says as she opens her book. "But I still say you could be the next famous quartet. The Köln Quartet, how's that?"

✦ ✦ ✦

At Herr Dietrich's suggestion, we all write to thank Johann Lorenz for the concert and for his encouragement. To our complete astonishment, we receive personal answers in return, brief, but encouraging, and not a word anywhere about the impossibility of mixed quartets. The term is roaring down by then, so we have no time to discuss the future, or even the Schumann, but I carry Herr Lorenz's letter around with me until it's worn at the edges, and his card I keep safe in my bottom bureau drawer at home.

✦ ✦ ✦

March 1909

Haydn's Symphony No. 50 is a pleasure, as any Haydn is. But even in rehearsal I always get a chill from the ominous opening phrases of Beethoven's Symphony No. 5, like an announcement of impending doom out of a clear blue sky. The rest of the Fifth is, in Anni's phrase, like riding a tiger. Beethoven tears his themes apart, hurls the fragments back and forth between sections, and reassembles them, over and over again in his titanic struggle from darkness toward light. It's even more exhilarating to play than it is to hear, over half an hour of tumultuous, relentless drama.

Wagner, on the other hand, even early on, abandoned melodic structure, while Dvořák filtered the American tunes he heard through his Czech sensibilities and came up with something neither entirely Czech nor entirely American, but certainly not German.

I wanted to learn about music beyond Germany. I'm getting my wish and working hard for it. If Orchestra were always like this, I might not be looking forward to our next quartet quite so much.

Occasionally, out of the corner of my eye, I catch Marburg staring at me with a stony, sullen face. Early on I hear whispers from a few other students in our section and notice a few strange looks. No one challenges the seating chart, however, and it's not as though I stole the seat out from under someone else. Besides, as rehearsals progress, everyone behind me can see I know what I'm doing. I always arrive early, I have the music under my fingers, I ask intelligent questions, and I'm polite to everyone, even Marburg. After a few weeks, the novelty of my presence at the front of the section wears off and, much to my relief, other topics of gossip take my place.

The second violins' first chair, a thin fourth-year named Vogel, doesn't have the burden of the concertmaster, but he instructs us in bowing, so we all bow the same, and if someone has a technical question, he's supposed to answer it. I begin to think Ros is right. Even if invited, I shouldn't audition for first chair next year. I can too easily imagine the section refusing to follow me and Marburg lying in wait some evening to take revenge. I'd be better off putting my foot into a nest of stinging ants.

I keep my head down and concentrate on getting the phrasing and mood of the Wagner *Polonia* Overture.

✦　✦　✦

Saint-Saëns, too, is proving a different sort of challenge. The Wolff knows more than she let on about French style and essence and she approves of Robert. Still, he inevitably comes in for his share of the Wolff's special treatment.

"Herr MacInness, I will blindfold you!" she snaps during our second rehearsal. "You are too fond of looking at your hands. Keep your eyes on the violinist! Your fingers must know where they belong without your eyes for help."

I, on the other hand, endure a large dose of remedial instruction in French essence.

"The bow must always caress the strings, even at volume," she says. "The French attack must be as authoritative as the German, but the passion is different. The French are always singing. They are always in love. It is the chief reason they lost the Franco-Prussian War."

Robert loses his place as he tries to keep from laughing.

"You didn't tell me she had a sense of humor," he says afterward as we head down the stairs.

"I didn't know," I say.

I can't worry about our slow progress at this point. Orchestra, plus the Wolff's other assignments, take first priority. After our orchestra concert in April, that will be the time to devote myself to Saint-Saëns.

Still, by the middle of term we have the skeleton of the sonata down. The Wolff makes us take it apart measure by measure and reassemble it, refining, searching for meaning, seeking deeper nuance. I begin to understand the singing attack. I wonder idly if I'd grasp it more easily if I'd ever been in love. Since I haven't, and since that's unlikely to change before June, I'll have to get it through extra practice instead.

One night, I'm working over the slow second movement at home in my bedroom. It has deep emotional resonance, but mostly I'm wrestling with the trouble spots, repeating them over and over, then starting from the beginning and trying to play it all the way through. I happen to glance up at the photograph of my father I kept for myself after he died. In those first awful months, I held this photograph by the hour, memorizing his features, which mine resemble, his expression of gentle, amused earnestness, the way he combed his hair, the weave of his necktie. Since I began at the Conservatory, I haven't looked at it as much, but now I pick it up and study it again.

We contemplate each other for a long time, my father and I. It's not that I don't think of him anymore; he's present for me, always, in his violin, if I'm aware enough to feel him. I sense him here with me now, through his photograph. I think of the happiness he would have felt in my progress, the encouragement he would have given me when I needed courage, how, when I've felt overwhelmed, he would have said, *Of course, you can do it. Just keep working. It will come.*

I think of how much he loved me. How much I loved him. How much I still love him, though his easy smile and even temper are frozen in this picture, where I can't reach them. My eyes sting, not with the raw grief that consumed me in the beginning, but because of the bond we share now between us, a bond that no one, and no amount of time, can break.

I look at the little photograph a while longer, then dust it off with my sleeve and put it back on the bureau. When I pick up his violin again and take the second movement from the beginning, I find it no longer matters that I have never been in love.

I have loved. I do love. I will always love.

✦ ✦ ✦

April 1909

In the last week of term, twenty Sinfonia musicians crowd the stage at our Monday orchestra rehearsal, Herr Dietrich among them. Our anemic sound suddenly multiplies tenfold. Beethoven's Fifth deafens us under its full power. Likewise, the Wagner comes into its own and Dvořák's *New World* swells into the Late Romantic fullness its composer intended.

The professionals are all business. They're not here to teach, after all; that's Herr Zeidler's job. And they're definitely not here to socialize, although Herr Dietrich always stops to say hello. They arrive, play, wait patiently as Herr Zeidler stops to correct us. When we're finished, they pack up and leave.

Herr Zeidler, on the other hand, they treat with fond respect, like the old mentor he is, for he taught at least half of them when they were students here and greets them jovially by name. They keep their opinions about the rest of us to themselves, though Ros and I get some very strange looks, which I attempt to ignore. Their looks might be even stranger, but they all know I was Herr Dietrich's student, so they let me be.

After four such rehearsals and a weekend, the afternoon of our performance arrives—a change from the usual, but the Sinfonia people have a concert in the evening. The timing throws me off; I have plenty of time to get ready while it's still morning, but suddenly I'm late getting to the women's toilet to change and put up my hair and nearly collide with a few early patrons on my way out. Ros, always so much more organized, came and went long before.

I warm up backstage, stretch my fingers, tune, practice tricky passages, tune a bit more while my caterpillars dance enthusiastically to a vaguely American folk melody out of the Dvořák. People wander past, intent on their own pre-concert warmups and nerves. Felix and Franz come in together and wish me well on their way to their seats.

"At last, we perform in the same orchestra!"

Herr Dietrich walks past, wearing his formal performance clothes, his expression merry, his violin tucked casually under his arm.

"So we will!" I say.

His mood is infectious and I feel my nerves lighten a little. "Do you still get nervous beforehand?" I ask.

"Always!" he says. "It's more reliable than checking for a pulse. It's going to be a fine concert, you'll see. You're very fortunate to have Z, you know. He's every bit as good as our conductor, Reinecke. Better, maybe; Reinecke hasn't the patience for training students, never mind getting such good results. Well, carry on! See you under the lights." He strolls off to his seat.

I take a few last runs at a particularly unreliable passage of the Dvořák and follow him onto the stage, where I settle into my chair and keep working on it.

Before long the orchestra seats have filled, the house has filled, the house lights dim, and everything is still. The concertmaster enters. The first oboe gives the A. We tune. Repeat. The ritual is important for sound, but even more important to center our minds. A pause. Herr Zeidler enters to applause. We stand. He motions us to sit. He raises his baton. We begin.

We are, if I may say so, excellent. Not perfect, but excellent. Our mental and physical concentration pours into our music. We have no sense of time passing, no stray thoughts. Our universe becomes our instruments, our parts, Herr Zeidler, and our total trust in his baton.

Afterward, the professionals melt away as soon as the applause ends. Herr Dietrich barely breaks stride as he says goodbye on his way to the Sinfonia's evening performance. But the students are ecstatic at pulling off this massive program. Even the fourth-years don't succeed in looking like this is an everyday occurrence. We flood out into the foyer and work our way through the larger than usual crowd toward the refreshment table.

"Everything all right on your side?" I ask Ros over a cup of punch.

"Fine," she says. "One of the Sinfonia cellists was a little forward, but nothing I couldn't handle."

"My goodness! What did you have to do?"

Ros shrugs. "I asked if he'd like to talk to my big brother over there on the other side of the stage. Maybe not the most elegant solution, but he backed right off without making a fuss."

"But Felix isn't your big brother, he's younger than you!"

"Have you seen us side by side? Honestly, Marthe. You do what you have to do to let other people reason to your conclusion. In your case, a fictional boyfriend would serve you well. You should invent one and keep him handy, just in case. Which reminds me, I have to find Jan. See you in a bit!" She plunges into the crowd and disappears.

I love Ros, but sometimes she makes me feel like I have no idea what's going on.

Our families are enjoying their quarterly conversations perfectly well without me, so I raid the cookie table. I couldn't eat beforehand, but now that the pressure is off, I feel as ravenous as Franz.

Katerina drags her father up to congratulate me and just as quickly drags him off again, probably to find Otto. A few other people stop to talk while I fill my plate.

"How did you get that seat?" a familiar voice says behind me. I whip around to see Marburg standing a little too close to me.

"It was assigned to me at the beginning of term, if you recall the seating chart," I say, taking a smooth step to one side and standing up very straight. "It was a good program, though, wasn't it? I thought we did well."

"You know you had no business being there," he says. "Nor in the orchestra at all, you and your cellist friend."

"If you're worried about me competing with you, don't bother," I say. "I'm quite aware no orchestra will hire a woman, no matter how good she is. You're very talented and you played well today. As I told you before, I consider you a colleague, not a rival. I hope I made that plain."

"You don't even belong here," he says.

"So you've said. And yet here I am. There's enough space for all of us. My plan is just to keep practicing and studying. That's all."

Marburg slouches off, his hands in his pockets, Madame Kurtz's light blue morning dress swishing about his ankles. I watch him go, my pride in our program and a perverse satisfaction at having once again annoyed him tempered by the infuriating reminder that, as long as I'm here, he simply will not leave me alone.

16

SPRING, APRIL–JUNE 1909

April 1909

I've barely gone home when I'm back in the large hall, listening to a long list of post-performance notes. After that I have several exams. Only after they're finished do I begin my short spring holiday, which I spend, as usual, at home, trying to atone for my absence during the term.

But what I see at home worries me. Mother isn't doing anything, as far as I can tell, except possibly drinking herself to death. She rarely leaves the flat except to buy groceries. She has almost no friends. She's driven away most of the people she and my father used to know with her harridan's temper and her Bärenfang breath. Her teeth are in terrible shape and doubtless the rest of her is, too. She says there's no money for a dentist, even though I know there certainly is. She walks with a kind of shuffling step I'm sure is new. I feel I'm somehow responsible for her condition, as if I'm the neglectful parent and she the wayward child, even though I know I'm not, even though I have no idea what on earth I can possibly do to change it.

Her nagging, at least, is nothing new.

"I worry about you," she says, starting the day after the performance and repeating at least once daily for the whole week. "What are you going to *do*? When are you going to get *married*?"

It doesn't help that I have no answers for her.

After two days of this, still feeling fatigued from last term, I begin counting the days until I start the next one.

To escape Mother's relentless lecturing, I yield to the temptations of the outdoors and walk for hours through the Ehrenfeld and beyond, where I can revel in everything just awakening: spring's delicate colors and eager restlessness, the smell of earth warming under a beckoning sun. Pale leaves fur the branches of elm and linden trees that line the streets and arch over gravel paths in the parks. In the public gardens, where the clang of streetcars and the roar of engines sound muffled and far away, thousands of rosebuds hint at the colors waiting to burst from their identical green coats.

I entice Anni out to walk with me one day. I learn a few things, but not as much as I hoped. She holds her inner world close, even from me. Maybe especially from me. Nothing she says suggests that her road in life will be anything but difficult. Where is there a place in this world for an intelligent, rebellious woman, a magnificent athlete with a temper like a hornet? Nearly a year out of school, she's still working at the bakery; she has no young man, nor any evident interest in young men, nor the security one might provide.

On the positive side, her tournament victory last year earned her membership in the Köln Fencing Club. She didn't even have to challenge the officers to duels, though she said she might, anyway, just for fun. Its female members are few, so far. More, she says, are joining all the time.

Along with haranguing me, Mother harangues Anni about her future daily, so I try not to. What would be the point? I can't tell her anything she doesn't know. I just want her to trust me.

We have the roof over our heads, thanks to our little investments, but beyond that, both my future and Anni's appear woefully uncertain.

Maybe something good will happen. That's not much of a plan, but it seems to be all we have.

The week passes. I run errands for Mother, cook dinner, and spend the time I'm not helping her or walking practicing Saint-Saëns. Because my prediction was correct: on this side of the winter term, my spring recital looks significantly closer than it did last week.

✦ ✦ ✦

Naturally, the Wolff isn't going to let me spend spring term focusing only on my recital. Before the holiday she assigned more Bach, more Kreutzer études ("In order to play French music properly, you must master French études") and Ludwig Spohr's single movement Concerto No. 8, the orchestra part arranged for piano. But Saint-Saëns is the main challenge. We need more rehearsal time than we're getting; the second, final section, in particular, is very difficult. Our practice room sessions and Wednesday afternoons in the Wolff's studio are clearly insufficient.

"Do you have a piano at home?" Robert asks on the first Monday back.

"No," I say. I don't mention we had to sell ours when my father died.

"Come to our house to rehearse," Robert says.

This proposal makes me nervous. I stayed away over the winter holiday, much as I would have liked to visit, because it felt somehow riskier than Ros inviting me to her house. It still does.

"Stay for dinner," Robert says. "You'd thrill Tante Hanne beyond words. Joseph or I can see you home afterward. We have to do something. We need the hours."

"Your aunt beyond words for any reason is something I can't even imagine," I say.

But Robert is right. We need the hours and we have no practical alternative. So, starting the next day after classes, I ride the streetcar with Robert to the Walters' house in Neuehrenfeld, where Frau Walter makes a terrific fuss over me, hovering for a voluble fifteen minutes before setting a plate of spice cookies down on a small table by the piano and bustling back to the kitchen. We play the Saint-Saëns through from the beginning, then go back and work on individual passages. I wonder if we'll ever get that fourth movement up to tempo. We practice watching each other out of the very outermost corners of our eyes. I decide musicians must have the best peripheral vision of any profession.

We're still working at five o'clock when I look up to see Joseph, who has settled into an overstuffed armchair. Neither of us heard him come in.

"I'll go if I'm disturbing you," he says, starting to get up.

"Hi! You're fine, stay put," Robert says, turning back to his score.

Joseph sits back down and watches so quietly we forget he's there.

We run through the passages over and over again. Slow, slower, note by note. Fingering, phrasing. Bowing. At least Robert doesn't have that problem, although playing up to ten notes at a time looks at least as difficult. We begin to improve. Then, as we tire, we start backsliding.

"I need a break," I say.

"Should be dinnertime, anyway," Robert says, glancing at Joseph, who nods.

"Saved, then! Can I help?"

Joseph escorts us both into the dining room, where, unlike last time, everything is already set out and waiting.

"I didn't want to interrupt you," Frau Walter beams. "You sounded so *professional* in there! It's so very complicated, your music, isn't it? I expect you've already worked hours and hours and hours on it. I know it will be wonderful when you have it all perfect and polished! Sit there, dear, won't you, between our two young men?"

Joseph pulls my chair out for me. There's no reason to blush, but I do.

"You must tell me all the latest from the Conservatory, dear! Our Robert mostly brings home piano stories. We don't hear many violin stories, do we, Joseph, dear? Now everything is steaming hot, so you must pass me your plates and I'll dish you up some stew, and there were lovely fresh spring greens in the market today, so we know it really is spring and not just pretending! Is your family enjoying the warmer weather, Marthe, dear? I'm so glad it was pleasant during that terribly short break you had . . ."

Eventually she winds down enough for me to tell her that everyone at Conservatory is so focused on their recitals they lack the energy to make trouble; my family is well enough, with Anni more focused on fencing than anything else; and, yes, everything she's heard about Professorin Wolff is true.

Joseph spent his day drawing plans for a new school out on the west edge of Köln. Herr Walter says little about his work at the mayor's office, though when he does speak, he's incisive and to the point. The serving dishes go around again, strawberries with biscuits and cream appear, and afterward I help clear the table and wash up. After that, another hour of rehearsing and then it's time for me to go.

"We'll see you again before too long, I'm sure!" Frau Walter says.

"Day after tomorrow," Robert says. "We need all the time we can get."

"If that's all right with you, Frau Walter," I say. "Robert's right, we definitely need the time."

"Tomorrow, if you like!" she says. "I love having more people around my table, so much more interesting that way, and call me Tante Hanne, everyone does. All of the boys Joseph grew up with, even now they're all grown up. And which of you is seeing our Marthe home?"

"I am," they both say at once.

"Two falls out of three for it," Joseph says.

"I'll be fine, really," I say. "I take the streetcar all the time. It's not that far."

"Nonsense, dear," Tante Hanne says. "It's dark out. You can trade off. Joseph, dear, you go tonight. Don't let anything happen to our Marthe!"

"Right then. You can have it by decision," Robert says, punching Joseph in the arm.

"Before you go—"

Herr Walter appears from his study with a book in his hands.

"Take this with you," he says. "Robert gave it to us. It may help you."

I take the book and open it in the dim light of the entry. It's titled, simply, *Paris* and it's full of pictures: broad avenues, narrow side streets, shops, parks, churches, the Eiffel Tower, the Louvre, people on bicycles and in streetcars, young couples, old men with berets, old women carrying bags with skinny loaves of bread sticking out. Drawings, too, of nightclub posters, advertisements, theatre bills.

"Get a feel for the place," he says. "No rush to return it."

"I—"

"Best get going. Everyone has an early day tomorrow. Good night!" Herr Walter turns back into his study and shuts the door.

"Ready?" Joseph says. "Here, let me get your coat."

"I can't wait to look at it," I say, slipping the book carefully into my already heavy bag.

He helps me with my coat, which is hardly necessary as I do it all the time by myself, usually with my arms full. He opens the door for me, too, a level of chivalry completely beyond my experience. He even offers to carry my case and bag, but I decline and he doesn't argue.

"Please thank your father for me," I say. "Pictures will be a tremendous help, I'm sure of it."

"I'm glad," Joseph says.

A long pause.

"She can be a bit overwhelming—my mother, I mean," Joseph ventures.

"She's so warm and energetic," I say.

"That she is," he says. "Nicely put. My father and I, we're just used to it."

"I notice he's on the quiet side," I say.

"So am I," Joseph says.

Another long pause.

"Your practice sounded great," he says.

"This sonata is tough, I don't deny it. But I begged the Wolff to let me do it, so I can't back down."

"I heard it improve in less than an hour," he says.

"I just hope there will be enough hours before June," I say.

"You'll get it," he says. "I know you will."

"I appreciate your confidence," I say. "Not that I have a choice."

The streetcar comes and we climb on. It occurs to me to ask Joseph more about his job and he seems more relaxed on familiar ground: his firm's clients, how he learned to draw, how the pens always blot at the end of a line, what it's like to walk into a real place you've created from your imagination.

From my stop he walks beside me up Hildegardstrasse to the front door of my building. He studies it by the light of the streetlamps while I unlock the door.

"Well . . ." His awkwardness returns in full force. "Good night, then. Day after tomorrow, right?"

"Yes," I say.

"I'll look forward to it," he says, then abruptly turns to walk back down the street toward the streetcar stop.

"Likewise," I call after him.

He turns, flashes me a quick smile, and continues on his way.

✦　✦　✦

My visits to the Walters become a pattern, every other day. The Saint-Saëns slowly grows tighter and more polished. Tante Hanne relaxes a little as my presence becomes less unusual, but I notice it's usually Joseph who escorts me home. Truly, I think it's not necessary, but I enjoy the company and talking about something besides music for a change, and he gradually begins to seem more at ease. Two more brothers, I think. I'll have quite a crowd of brothers by the time I finish Conservatory. It's a good feeling. I like it.

On the in-between days, I practice all my other assignments, do class homework, try to exchange a few words with Mother and Anni, and go to bed early.

✦ ✦ ✦

May 1909

A few weeks into the term, I arrive home from the Walters' one evening to find Anni pacing in our sitting room like a caged bear. Mother is in bed, she says. She sounds angry, but her eyes have a wild look to them. As she paces and talks, I begin to understand how afraid she's been, how afraid she still is.

"She was yelling at me. Drunk. On and on and on. Then her voice slurred even more. I thought—I hoped—she'd pass out and shut up. Her face began to sag. She had to sit down, said she felt weak. Dizzy. She didn't pass out, but just sat there for the longest time. 'I can't see!' she said, over and over. 'Anni, help me!' I didn't know what to do. I just tried to get her to lie down. Or call the doctor, in case it wasn't just the Bärenfang talking. You know she's been adding schnapps to it lately? It's absolutely disgusting. But she wouldn't move. Maybe she couldn't. Just sat there for at least an hour and then she said she felt better.

"I said we should call Dr. Goldmann, but she refused. Too much money. I tried for another hour. She finally hauled herself off to bed and went to sleep. I'm sure she wasn't just drunk. There's something wrong. I thought you'd know what to do but you weren't here." She fights back tears, but they come spilling down her face, making her look suddenly very young. Her tough exterior shell is no match for her fear.

"I don't know what it could be," I say. "Some kind of a seizure, maybe? But then she felt better? Let's see how she is in the morning. I'll stop at Dr. Goldmann's before I go to school; maybe he can come by. He'll know what it is. Maybe there's something he can give her."

Anni allows me to hold her while she gives in to her emotions. We talk a little longer and then go off to bed ourselves. I lie there, wide awake in the dark, hearing her accusing words over and over.

"You weren't here. You weren't here. You weren't here . . ."

Dr. Goldmann, who attended our father after his accident and has treated every illness Anni and I have ever had, thinks Mother had a stroke. A small one, since in the morning she seems like herself again, except for her ashen color. He prescribes aspirin, which he says will thin the blood, but he warns us she may have more and to come get him under any circumstances if it happens again. We promise, wondering what will happen if she's here by herself, as she so often is. What we might find someday when we come home.

✦ ✦ ✦

Mother complains of fatigue and weakness for two weeks after this episode. Dr. Goldmann looks in from time to time and encourages her to get up off the sofa, get out in the fine weather and go for a walk. Anni and I take turns dragging her out into the sunshine and around the block. The stairs back to our flat are almost more than she can cope with. She stops every few steps to rest and complain some more. It doesn't help that she's taken so little exercise since our father died, and so little care of her health generally. She's grown heavy and flaccid, so that even on flat ground walking is slow and difficult. Still, I suspect (and Anni is quite sure) she's malingering, both for the pleasure of having something new and interesting to complain about and for the attention she's getting because of it. I really don't have time to be her taskmaster, but neither does Anni, and there isn't anyone else.

The scare shakes my concentration for several days. The quality of my work plummets. I explain to the Wolff what happened; I don't mean it as an excuse, though it sounds like one under her stern gaze. I have to force myself to shut off the part of my mind that's scared to death for my mother while I'm practicing or rehearsing. *Later,* I tell myself, every time I close the door of our flat behind me. *Not now!*

It's even harder to concentrate at home, where Mother sits at the kitchen table for hours at a time, looking gray and forlorn, which makes my evenings at home exercises in mental discipline more than music.

Along with my fear comes a slow ache of guilt I have to try to suppress every time I go to rehearse at the Walters'. *Not now!* I say to myself. *We need to master this!*

Tante Hanne insists on sending food home with me so Mother won't have to cook, which I accept with gratitude and more guilt. I'm the one who should be cooking for my own mother, but I just don't have enough hours in the day, even if I had the skill.

At least my time at the Walters' is beginning to yield real progress. The work is tightening up, beginning to sound more lyrical and confident. Aside from the many rough spots, which we're gradually smoothing down, Robert and I are feeling positively excited about performing the sonata now, as the recital date draws nearer. It sounds good, it feels good, it feels *French*. After all our hard work, it's beginning to feel like we're nearly there.

✦ ✦ ✦

By mid-May, the Wolff feels that the Saint-Saëns has reached a plateau and, as she did last fall, she orders us to drop it for a week. I'm not as nervous about it this time, but it's a new technique for Robert. Nevertheless, neither of us would dream of going against the Wolff's orders and we both have plenty of other pressing work to fill the time.

Robert has to perform his own solo, a Beethoven sonata, which he's somehow been finding time to work on—maybe at two or three in the morning. And I have Bach, Spohr, and the Kreutzer études, so we go our separate ways and attack those. When we come back to the Wolff's studio the following Wednesday, sure enough, while less precise than before, the Saint-Saëns breathes with a new kind of life.

"No more breaks," the Wolff says. Not that we expected to take any from here on, of any kind, for any reason.

✦ ✦ ✦

Mother recovers enough for me to take her to Anni's spring fencing championships, where Anni demonstrates her usual ferocity. She doesn't win this time; she's at the bottom of a higher, steeper ladder as a young, very junior member of the Köln Fencing Club, pitted against fencing clubs from the whole region instead of schools. But she acquits herself well against women far older and more experienced than she and her energy and aggressiveness are second to no one's. Mother nods from time to time, as if remembering that she herself told Anni to stick with it. Good. If this is how Anni can win our mother's respect, how fortunate it's something she loves.

✦ ✦ ✦

After Anni's tournament, time gathers speed, as it always does toward the end of a term. The recital schedule appears the first week in June. Robert's solo turn with his Beethoven sonata is on Friday, when he'll be joined by Arnold, playing a Baroque cello sonata by Luigi Boccherini, and Felix, tackling a Russian violin sonata by Anton Rubinstein.

On Saturday, Robert and I will perform our Saint-Saëns, along with Franz, also playing something French. And, because this is apparently my destiny, Marburg will play the same Spohr single-movement Concerto No. 8 I've been working on, with Herr Grimmelshausen at the piano. At least he's in the first half of the program and we're on after intermission. I note that I'm evidently not the only one eager to branch out from German orthodoxy, whatever the Wolffs of the world might think about it.

But before all that I have exams in Theory and History to think about, and practice, practice, practice. As my reward, the fourth-year solo recitals will take place next week, so I'll finally see Ros and Berit, who have been practically invisible this term as they, too, practice, practice, practice.

As for our Saint-Saëns, we finally have it. I've more or less got the hang of the attack and state of mind needed to achieve a lyrical singing tone. In our rehearsals the music flows and the technical fireworks of the last movement explode around us in showers of bright sound. It's only been the last couple of weeks, after our break, that it has really felt right. But it does. It very much does.

Friday evening, in a welcome change, I let the nerves bother other people. Arnold and Felix, who were very quiet all day, are both in the second half of the program, along with Robert, who sequestered himself in a practice room early in the afternoon and only came out briefly at five for a light dinner.

Arnold, with his teacher at the piano, leads off after intermission with his Boccherini. It's a treat to hear Arnold as a soloist. He has the gift of treating every phrase with love, as if Boccherini were his personal friend and sitting in the front row.

Robert, feeling more need perhaps to prove himself in German repertoire, gives us Beethoven's Sonata No. 8, *Pathétique,* with fire and

delicacy in equal measure, as if he had been playing Beethoven all his life—
as perhaps he has, minus his years in Moscow and Paris. Even when he plays
fast, he never seems rushed. Every note has the space it needs to shine. He
almost—*almost*—makes me wish I played the piano.

Felix has persuaded a third-year pianist I barely know to accompany
him in the Rubinstein Sonata No. 1, a full-throated Romantic adventure
and a long one, too, a most un-German half hour of summer, winter, and
virtuosity with a very showy finish.

"So did you have trouble convincing your teacher to let you do
something Russian?" I ask Felix afterward in the foyer.

"He gave it to me," he says. "I said I was interested after that Russian
tune in our Razumovsky. Why?"

"The Wolff seems to think foreign music is subversive," I say.

"Somehow that doesn't surprise me," he says.

"And yet she understands it. At least, she understands the French."

"That's probably why she thinks it's subversive."

"You know, you might have something there. Ah—here come the
pianists."

Robert makes his way over, his plate laden with cookies, stopping
every few steps to talk to someone.

"Robert, dear, here you are at last!" Tante Hanne exclaims, and proceeds
to express her admiration for his performance at some length.

"Save some for tomorrow!" I say when she pauses for breath.

"Oh, my *dear*, I can't *wait*!" she says and plows on.

Joseph catches my eye and winks. Herr Walter waits patiently, arms
folded, surveying the crowd.

Since Franz and I are playing tomorrow and Robert is playing again,
the plan is to celebrate at Robert's house after tomorrow's concert. So,
Arnold gets to spend a rare evening with his family and his sweetheart,
while I go home to practice a little more. The big end-of-year party will
come next week at the Apfelbaums' after Ros and Berit give their final
recitals. Just now, next week seems to me a very far-off time indeed.

✦　✦　✦

Saturday drags on for hours, even with Katerina's lesson occupying the
morning.

236

"You'll be fantastic!" she says. "I can't wait! I'm so excited for you, I can hardly concentrate!"

"Try," I say with perhaps less than my usual indulgence. In truth, I'm having the same problem, more focused on Saint-Saëns than her Spohr drills and folk songs.

I pack and repack my bag with my sonata part (but at least I can take out everything else), my blue solo gown from last spring (still no jewelry), my good shoes from Oma Judith, and my hair tools. I arrive at the Conservatory in good time for a last run-through with Robert, and then head for the women's toilet to get ready. I wonder if they'll get a women's dressing room in this place in my lifetime. My caterpillars wake up, as they always do right about now, and crawl around my stomach, hunting for mischief.

Franz already occupies one corner of the waiting lounge with his teacher. Robert shows up a few minutes later, back in the formal suit he wore last night. He has in tow a plump first year named Oskar, whom he's been training to be his page turner, since he, unlike me, will not be playing from memory. Tonight's other recitalists filter in, several with their teachers to accompany them. Marburg, of course, arrives well after his beloved Herr Grimmelshausen, whom I notice once or twice looking surreptitiously at his pocket watch. He plants himself before me.

"You're playing a French piece, then," he says. "Did your Paris Conservatory star talk you into that?"

Heads turn. Herr Grimmelshausen raises one eyebrow but says nothing. Possibly psychological warfare is a subject they discuss at lessons. How to rattle your fellow performers, as if there were any point to that.

Robert, seated where Marburg can't see him, wears a look of something between pity and disgust, but doesn't interfere. Franz, in the opposite corner, glares at Marburg, his lip curled, and leans in to whisper something in the ear of his teacher, who nods agreement.

"No." I turn away to say something to Robert.

"French music is insipid," Marburg says. "I wouldn't bother with it, myself. Some of the Russian's not bad, but French music is almost as bad as English, in our opinion."

"*Our* opinion?"

"My opinion."

"Music is music," I say. "I'm sure you'll do well tonight."

The flutist in the opposite corner catches my eye and gives me a thumbs up.

Marburg stares at me with a belligerent expression for another moment and then turns his back and saunters off to sit beside Herr Grimmelshausen. Madame Kurtz's light blue morning dress swishes back and forth as he walks. I suppress a giggle. I wonder why Herr Grimmelshausen didn't call him off. They're probably cut from the same cloth, those two.

Our opinion, indeed.

"Is he always like that?" Robert asks in a low voice.

"Usually worse," I say.

"Pathetic."

"Agreed."

The tension drops noticeably when Marburg and Herr Grimmelshausen leave with the others playing in the first half. Everyone's mind is preoccupied, but there's a collective deep breath when the door shuts behind them. Robert and I review our own parts, obsessing over minute details, while Oskar looks over Robert's shoulder and hangs on every word.

Marburg's Spohr Concerto No. 8 isn't nearly as difficult as the Saint-Saëns, but it has some tricky passages, which he's obviously practiced.

"Guess he'll make fourth-year," Robert says in a casual tone that others in the room choose to interpret as regretful. A low ripple of laughter echoes around the remaining groups.

At the end of intermission, Herr Schädler calls the rest of us to the stage right wing, Robert and I are next to last, after Franz and before the flutist. The flutist, too, is playing a French work. Odd how Marburg didn't bother him. Never mind. Robert and I retreat into our parts again. I, at least, don't really register what's on the page. It's just a way of being alone in a crowd. My caterpillars are out in force now, dancing a can-can in my stomach. There's a lot of jumping and kicking and swishing of little skirts going on down there, that's for sure.

Franz, as always, takes on a different personality when he plays. Neither shy, nor, as among his friends, scrappy and sarcastic, he becomes intensely focused, as I imagine a marksman to be: driven, even fiery, in his interpretations. Listening to the deep, throaty tones of his viola against the piano, I hear him bring a passion to his Brahms that he seems unable to express any other way.

It's always when Franz solos that I remember his mother is dead.

As they begin their last movement, Herr Schädler beckons us forward, me first, then Robert, and Oskar in the rear. The Brahms builds to an enormous finish. The applause for Franz almost seems to embarrass him. He nearly forgets to take his bow as his teacher stands back to let him receive the attention. "Fantastic!" we say when they exit past us.

"Good luck, Frenchies!" Franz says.

It's perfect. Herr Schädler says "Go!" and we walk onstage still chuckling at the joke. The audience murmurs, but applauds politely as Robert sets up his part. We make eye contact. I nod and, precisely together, we begin.

I looked at Herr Walter's book until I had the pictures by memory as much as the music. In passage after passage as we rehearsed images popped into my mind: a bridge over the river Seine, tall, thin stained-glass windows, a circus, a family strolling in a park, a parade. Someday, I always thought, I'll visit this city, really not so far from Köln, though for me it might as well be on the other side of the moon. Perhaps when I see it, I'll hear in my mind the singing, virtuosic, very French passages of this sonata. Not that the sonata itself is programmatic, but pictures and music together allow me to imagine in some mysterious way what it might be like to *be* French— to try to understand, as Saint-Saëns understood, the music now swirling out of my violin.

We pause between the two sections, the only break in the four movements. I make a microscopic adjustment in my tuning. Robert waits. When I'm satisfied, we exchange a look, I nod, and we're off again. The last movement contains the real virtuosic test. The images of Paris vanish as all my concentration focuses on the finger work and bowing of its frenzied passages. The music builds and builds to its spectacular end and the last notes hang in the air for a second or two, while I leave my bow raised to enjoy the silence.

When I've lowered it—not before—the applause begins. Judging by the volume, it seems our audience quite likes French music. Robert stands and steps forward beside me while Oskar practices the page-turner art of being invisible. We bow, then bow again.

It turns out there were, in fact, enough hours between April and June, barely.

The flutist and his teacher say, "Well done!" as we pass and we wish them good luck. Oskar is waiting at the back of the wing and hands Robert's part back to him.

"Fantastic!" Oskar says. "I can't wait to try that myself. But I don't know if my year has anyone who could handle the violin part."

"Give them time," I say. "I couldn't have done it two years ago, either."

We settle ourselves in the hard wooden chairs along the back wall to hear the flutist, where we discover Franz has been tucked into a shadowy corner listening to us.

"Good job, Frenchies!" he says.

Our pulses slow gradually to normal while the flutist and his teacher launch into a lovely French flute sonata. It has the same singing quality as the Saint-Saëns, plenty of virtuosity and a rousing finish, followed by enthusiastic applause.

"All right, food!" Robert says after we've congratulated the flutist. "Go ahead, Oskar, you've earned it. We still need to lock our stuff up."

Oskar doesn't need much persuasion.

"Nice kid," Robert observes at his departing back. "Always hungry. Reminds me of you, Franz."

"Speaking of food," Franz says and leads the way back to the lounge to pack up.

✦ ✦ ✦

"You might have been raised in Paris, both of you!" Herr Dietrich says, shaking our hands.

Gerda kisses each of us on our cheeks. "The French way!" she says with a wink.

"And the Wolff gave me such a bad time, when other students had foreign work, too!" I say.

"She's Viennese, you know," Herr Dietrich says. "You must forgive her little biases."

"And yet she *knew* how different the character of the music should be and how to pull it out of us," I say.

"And a thing or two about the French," Robert adds.

"Never, *never* underestimate Professorin Wolff," Herr Dietrich says in a slightly raised voice, looking over my shoulder. "Why, hello, Professorin, we were just congratulating two of your best students."

"You embroider my reputation, Herr Dietrich," she says. "I concur, it was decent. I will see you both Monday morning at nine o'clock for notes." And she nods to us, picks up a glass of punch and strides away.

Robert laughs. "Underestimate the Wolff? Never!"

"Don't stop," Herr Dietrich says. "There's a world of repertoire out there for you to devour. Get as broad a taste as you can while you're here. You, Robert, have a head start, I hear."

"A painful head start, but worth it," Robert says. "I like knowing the countries the music comes from, the sounds of the language, the national character. But nobody knows everything. You just do your best. And practice more than anyone else."

"That's it precisely," Herr Dietrich says. "Keep pushing, Marthe. The Wolff may surprise you. But I'm sure you have some massive project planned for summer?"

"The Schumann Piano Quintet," Robert says.

I look at him in surprise. "Had we decided—"

"Oh! Yes," he says. "Definitely."

"Excellent choice," Herr Dietrich says. "If you start tomorrow."

"And with that we're off to relieve my mother of Thomas," Gerda says. "See you between rehearsals this summer?"

"Yes!"

"We can get the scores and parts from the library Monday after notes," Robert says as we fill plates with cookies and head over to our families.

"Oh, dear," I say. "Look!"

Tante Hanne has buttonholed my mother.

". . . so glad you are feeling better and so pleased to meet you properly at last! How incredibly proud you must be of Marthe! My goodness, she is so unbelievably talented and she works *so* very hard! What a joy! I've been so eager to meet you, to tell you how much we like her and how we hope she and the others will come to our home to play music with our Robert— well, he's not really ours, of course, but we certainly think of him as ours! Don't we, Joseph dear? Joseph? Where did you get to? Oh, there you are.

Never mind, dear, sorry to interrupt you. At any rate, my dear, dear Frau Adler, I can only say again how proud you must be of your daughter. She is truly a credit to you!"

Mother looks as if she's suddenly found herself standing too near a moving train. I sympathize, but I'm not inclined to interrupt someone saying nice things about me. So, I just stand back.

"Nicely done," Herr Walter says under the torrent of words. "The Saint-Saëns was delightful. Very French."

"The book you lent me was a huge help," I say. "I loved the pictures. I'll get it back to you the next time I visit."

"No rush," he says. "I understand from Robert your quartet will be rehearsing with us this summer."

"So I've just heard," I say, casting a sideways look in Robert's direction. But he's deep in conversation with Felix, probably about that very thing.

"We'll count on it," Herr Walter says.

Katerina is effusive as usual, her father, as usual, quietly complimentary. Both leave me with a warm glow. Knowing my benefactor is pleased is, in its own way, as fantastic as having pleased the Wolff.

I spot Anni and Franz laughing about something. I'm surprised at first; they've seen each other at these events for three years now and barely spoken. I always thought Franz would curl up in a ball like a garden bug under the social attention of a girl, but he seems to be holding his own. Now that I think about it, they have a similar world view, not to mention a similar sense of humor, which may make Anni less frightening to him. It also makes me think perhaps I don't want to know what they're laughing about.

Having no wish to spoil a perfectly good time, my instinct is to avoid Marburg altogether. But I see him momentarily separated from his family and Herr Grimmelshausen as he saunters over to the refreshment table to pick up a glass of punch. On impulse, I push instinct aside and stroll over to stand across the table from him.

"You were very good this evening," I say.

He looks up with a start. His eyes narrow. "Fishing for praise?" he says.

"No," I say evenly. "Giving it where it's due. We'll be colleagues again next year, I'm sure."

"I suppose so," he says, giving me a curt, resentful nod before he hurries back to his family. I don't know what I think this boldness on my part will accomplish, but the reception is one place I don't have to be afraid of him and it seems important to take advantage of it.

The Apfelbaums offer to take Mother home so Anni can come with me to the Walters'. Mother is clearly exhausted. She seems dazed by her encounter with Tante Hanne, but Anni is sparkling like I've rarely seen her. When the reception begins to wind down, Robert, Felix, and I leave to change into our street clothes and collect our instruments and bags. We're a noisy group on the streetcar to Neuehrenfeld, where the Walters' house is soon full of food, drinks, songs at the piano, and more conversations, it seems, than there are people.

Whenever I overhear Robert and Felix, they're discussing Schumann. Arnold and Herr Walter find a common interest in the stock market. Anni and Franz continue their plotting, whatever it is, and Tante Hanne presides over all, replenishing food, filling glasses, and talking without pausing for breath to everyone she encounters. Joseph and I sit quietly in a couple of armchairs and watch the swirling hubbub.

"You're done now?" Joseph says.

"More or less," I say. "We have notes Monday morning. We'll play it through twice before the Wolff is done with us. Then Ros and Berit's recitals on Tuesday evening. I expect Robert will be eager to get busy on the Schumann Piano Quintet, but I could use a rest, to be honest."

"Er—I was wondering, speaking of taking a rest, if perhaps you might permit me to, ah, invite you for a walk next Saturday afternoon in the Botanical Garden in Riehl? It's very beautiful just now. I would call for you, of course." He leans back in his chair, as if he thinks I might slap him.

The light isn't very bright, but I'd swear he's turning red.

"I teach in the morning." I immediately see from his face that he's expecting me to turn him down. "But I'm free in the afternoon. A walk in the Botanical Garden sounds lovely. Everything is in bloom now and the days have been so warm, it's been hard to spend them indoors."

"Oh! Oh, that's terrific! Ah, would twelve o'clock be convenient? We could have lunch at the little beer garden there, if you like. I promise I'll have you home before dark."

He sounds and looks enormously relieved, perhaps not so much because I said yes, but because he finally got up the nerve to ask.

"Twelve is perfect. And considering the hours I've been keeping—as you well know—home before dark is quite conservative. But I suppose it would make my mother happy. Or, less unhappy, at least."

"Thank you," he says. "I'll look forward to it."

"So will I," I say. "I haven't been there since Anni and I were small."

A sudden awkwardness fills the space between us. I must be feeling Joseph's nerves, which are obvious. Silly, I think. We're friends. Friends do things together all the time.

We settle deeper into our chairs and turn our attention back to the social whirl around us. It's nearly midnight when Joseph accompanies Anni and me home.

"You really were terrific, you know," Anni says as we climb the stairs to our flat. "It was nice to hear you out from under the others, for a change. I'm sure I saw smoke coming out of Papa's violin."

"I wish he could have heard it," I say. It's my ritual thought after every performance. Usually, I keep it to myself.

"Of course, it's really your violin now," she says.

"I suppose so," I say. "But it brings him back a little to think of it as his."

"Sure," she says. "Too bad he didn't fence."

I catch a glimpse of her face in a beam of moonlight on the landing.

"Oh, Anni," I say, reaching out to hug her.

At our door I fumble with the lock. The flat is dark; Mother's gone to bed.

I feel I should say something comforting, but I can't think of anything that seems right. Anni doesn't offer anything more.

"Well, good night, then," I say.

"Good night," she says.

We retreat into our rooms, taking our different memories with us.

Year Four:

A Tempering Fire

1909–1910

17

SUMMER, JUNE–SEPTEMBER 1909

June 1909

On Sunday, I sleep without moving until nearly noon. Mother comes in and pokes me a few times, but eventually decides I'm still breathing and leaves me alone. Anni, too, is late to rise.

"Would it be impertinent to ask what you and Franz were plotting last night?" I ask when we finally drag ourselves out for some toast and tea.

"Oh, very," she says.

"Well, then," I say, "I guess I won't."

I wonder if I should worry.

That night, during a quiet dinner at the kitchen table, Mother clears her throat.

"You know something," she says. She studies my face, as if she hasn't really looked at me in a long time. "I've been thinking about your recital last night. With that young man. I'd heard you practice it, but I didn't know it would sound like that when you played it together. It made me think of your father . . . I don't know what all this is ever going to lead to, but he was right. Music is where you belong. He told me so, I remember, so many times. I still don't know how you'll live if you don't get married soon. But you did a good job last night. A professional job. He'd have approved."

"I—I'm glad you think so," I stammer. "That means a lot to me. And I hope it would make him happy."

Her eyes look past me to something that isn't there.

"Of course, it would," she says.

✦　✦　✦

After two hours of grueling notes on Monday, the Wolff hands me a thick stack of summer assignments and dismisses us. I slide the assignments into my bag; we wish her a good summer and leave her at her desk.

We decided to wait until fall to mention the Schumann to her, so she won't have all summer to think of objections.

Tuesday evening, Ros, in a flowing midnight blue gown, sweeps through Bach and Paganini before playing her major work, a Rachmaninoff sonata for cello and piano, with the Wolff. She closes her hour with Dvořák: *Silent Woods*, a lyrical, expressive and very non-German song, at the end of which Oma Judith jabs me in the ribs with her elbow, whispers, "I told her if she didn't play something Czech, I'd write her out of my will!" and then laughs her cackling laugh.

Berit, dressed in ruby-colored satin, also starts with Bach, then contrasts with Brahms's only violin concerto, a virtuoso powerhouse from the very first notes, with the Wolff playing the piano reduction. Finally, out of chronological order but a perfect, fiery finish, she makes the fiendishly difficult Paganini Caprice No. 24 look easy.

Those trios the three of us played together seem a lifetime ago.

"Inspired?" Oma Judith whispers as Berit takes her bows.

"Inspired and intimidated," I say. "An hour is a long time. And they're both just *so* good."

"Ros has been working since fall," Oma says. "That's why you haven't seen much of her. Neither have we."

"Right," I say. "So, I should start tomorrow, then."

"If not sooner," Oma says and winks. "You're going to outdo them all."

"Er—"

"If you outwork them."

She pushes herself to her feet and leans heavily on her cane. "Damn," she says. "Sitting, now *that's* hard work."

Afterward in the foyer, Ros and Berit have their hands full with well-wishers. I hang back with Felix and the others.

"I'm definitely going to choose a Paganini Caprice," Felix says.

248

"And how about that Rachmaninoff?" Arnold says.

"Glinka for me," Franz says. "My teacher already assigned it. What about you, Marthe?"

"I have no idea," I say.

"First things first." Robert strolls up behind us. "How about starting the Schumann on Saturday? We'll trade off houses to spread the joy. Mine first."

"I'm busy Saturday," I say, blushing and annoyed with myself for it.

"Oh, right!" Robert says. "Sunday, then?"

"Could I just have a week to try to learn a little bit of it?" Arnold says.

"A week from Sunday," Robert says. "My final offer."

"Sure," Felix says. "Our house tonight, remember—Ros and Berit's celebration."

"Did someone say food?" Franz says, a stack of cookies in one hand.

"Don't fill up," Felix says. "Oma made enough strudel for fifty people."

"Since when have a few cookies ever been a problem?" Franz says.

"Since never. Everyone ready? If we leave now, Franz can test the strudel to be sure it's not poisonous."

We head for the streetcar, feeling abnormally light without our bags and cases while the reception is still at its peak and the musicians of the hour are still raking in the compliments.

✦   ✦   ✦

"So, what will you do now?"

The celebration at the Apfelbaums' house begins to wind down. Plates full of crumbs are piling up in the kitchen faster than Dora can wash them. The strudel is gone. Ros and Berit both radiate happiness, but they look tired, too.

"I'm going on a concert tour with my father," Berit says. "He's been talking about it for two years. Six cities, mostly smaller ones, a program for two violins plus a few solos, and several summer assignments in preparation. He's almost as tough a coach as the Wolff."

"Not surprising," I say.

"I'm going to Amsterdam," Ros says. "Jan's aunt plays in a women's orchestra and he talked her into arranging an audition for me."

"It must be nice to know people," I say. I don't mean it to sound petty, but it does anyway. "I hope you get in. I'll miss you, though."

"You know lots of people," Ros says. "More than you think. You'll be fine, just keep yourself open and think about where you want to go. If I have one regret, it's that we never found you a necklace. Once you have that, you'll be ready to soar."

"I'm so glad to know you're joking," I say.

"Anyway," Ros says, "I'm not leaving for several weeks. Until then I'll see you here when you rehearse your Schumann."

"Oh, you heard about that? I only heard about it last week."

Ros laughs. "I've been hearing about little else since you all went to hear the Vienna Quartet."

I hadn't thought about endings, but Ros's departure will certainly be one. The first, certainly not the last. I'll feel lost without my guide to the world, and lonely.

"We might find you that necklace yet," she says.

"As long as I don't have to help look for it," I say.

✦ ✦ ✦

Friday night I remember to mention that Joseph is calling for me the next day at noon. I have to remind Mother who he is, but she just shrugs. Anni nods wisely.

"About time," she says. "He's mad about you, anyone can see that. I wonder what took him so long."

"What on earth do you mean?"

"Are you really that dense, or are you toying with me? Why do you think he ties up into a pretzel every time he tries to talk to you?"

"I don't know," I say. "I thought he was just reserved."

"So, you really *are* that dense. It's a good sign, actually. The smooth ones are mostly interested in themselves."

"What do you know about men? You spend all your time threatening to stab them with foils."

"I keep my eyes and ears open. Like you should."

"The Conservatory's not a hotbed of romance," I say. "Harassment, now I could tell you about that. Although thankfully it seems to have eased off."

"You wouldn't want romance there, anyway," she says. "Your life looks complicated enough. Joseph, now, he's ideal. Out of school, good job, musical, but not a musician—"

"How do you even know all that?" I demand.

She smiles a sweet, sisterly, infuriating smile.

"He's not afraid to talk to *me*," she says.

Saturday morning, Katerina notices I seem a little fidgety and demands to know why. When I confess I'm having an outing to the Botanical Gardens with a friend, the sort-of-but-not-really cousin of our American classmate, she squeals as if I'd just given her a puppy. Then she rattles off a long list of what I should and shouldn't say and what I may and may not let him do, all of which strikes me as absurd.

"Really, Katerina," I say when she pauses for breath, "be sensible. It's a *walk*. In the *park*. In the *daytime*. He's a *friend*. We might have lunch. Honestly, that's *all*."

"Will you see him again if he asks?" she says.

"Well, I presume so, since we'll be rehearsing at his house this summer."

"No, silly!" she says. "I mean *see* him. For romantic outings. Oh, I hope so! You deserve a nice young man to pay attention to you. Life isn't all work, you know!"

There are so many leaps in this remark, I don't even know where to begin. Such as how Katerina would know about hard work, for example, but there I go, being uncharitable again. She does work at the violin, after all. But a sudden step on the stairs stops the conversation short. With a wink, she launches into a B flat minor scale.

I've barely been home long enough to check my hair and grab my sun hat off the shelf when the doorbell rings. Anni's door bangs open and she practically knocks me over to get there first.

"What the—"

"Hi, Joseph!" she says. "Come on in! She's almost ready."

"What do you mean, 'almost ready?' I *am* ready. Hello!" I say, suddenly feeling as awkward as he looks.

He hesitates on the threshold, as if there might be snakes hiding under the furniture.

"Good morning! It's a perfect day for an outing." He glances about our sitting room, taking in all the worn edges and threadbare spots I never notice any more, probably because no one I know ever comes to see me.

A chair scrapes in the kitchen. Mother lumbers out, wearing the ancient, mended blouse and skirt she lives in every day.

"How nice to see you again, Frau Adler," he says. "I'll have Marthe back by dinnertime."

"Fine," she says.

"Off with you, children," Anni says. "And behave!" She smiles her sweet, dangerous smile at Joseph.

I think I'll just die of embarrassment right now, to save time.

Joseph smiles back.

"I saw your name in the paper," he says. "You did very well for your first year in the Köln Fencing Club."

Now, it's her turn to be surprised.

"Er, thanks!" she says.

As she shuts the door behind us, I glimpse a thoughtful, quizzical expression on Anni's face.

✦ ✦ ✦

Later, I promise myself I'll remember as if it were etched in crystal every detail of this afternoon in the beautiful Botanical Gardens of Köln and not let it blur into a few fleeting memories, pressed and faded like dried flowers. The streetcar, jammed with people seeking the warm, early summer sun and fresh air. Joseph, insisting I sit down while he stands. In the Gardens themselves, wide gravel paths meandering among enormous lawns dotted with families enjoying picnics. Huge trees—beech, spruce, oak—casting cool shade we can step into if we tire of the sun. Everywhere, the sound of water, burbling along stone channels and splashing in fountains of all sizes. Most of all, countless flowerbeds celebrating all the colors of the flower world: whites and yellows, pinks and reds, lavenders and purples. My favorite, a rose of pale apricot tinged with pink and yellow so delicate the colors seem to shift in the light, with an elusive, haunting scent. The lure and danger of roses, with their rich beauty, heady fragrance, and hidden thorns.

On and on we walk, through garden after garden and the majestic iron and glass Flora Palace that presides over them. Joseph's reserve melts as he expounds on the genius of its iron structure, waving his hands to show me how forces are transferred from roof to earth and how it resists winter storms without walls of stone or brick.

"You must think I'm a complete bore," he says, suddenly self-conscious.

"I think you're passionate about your work," I say. "Which makes you very fortunate."

"But you're passionate about your work, too," he says. "You make it look easy. It shows how hard you work. I've watched Robert. He always looks like he's just having a good time when he performs, but he practices like a demon at home, sometimes until midnight."

"I think this last recital even convinced my mother I'm serious," I say.

"She didn't think—?"

"She just worries. I can't blame her. I have no idea what will happen to me after Conservatory."

"Surely, you'll begin a performing career? It's what you're training for."

"You must have noticed there are no women in orchestras," I say for what seems like the fiftieth time.

"But you could be a soloist, or part of an ensemble, like your quartet! You won't just stop, surely?"

I seem to be having this impossible conversation everywhere I go. "I don't know," I say. "I just don't know."

We have lunch at an outdoor beer garden by one of the great, curving flower beds and then walk some more. Eventually we settle on a bench near a huge fountain in which jets of water arc skyward, splinter into thousands of tiny sparkling diamonds, then cascade down into a rippling pool. I try to follow single droplets on their journey, but I always lose them in a cloud of their fellows somewhere as they fall.

As we rest here, hands firmly in our own laps, neither saying much, but not out of awkwardness as in the beginning, I notice something about Joseph: a sense of solidity, of warmth, an inner quiet not easily disturbed.

I like it. I like it very much.

We sit, watching the fountain until the light shifts and nearby trees begin to cast their shadows across the path. Joseph checks his pocket watch.

"Oh, no! Look at the time! Your mother will never trust you in my company again," he says. "We should go—you'll be late as it is."

"I wouldn't worry about Mother," I say. "I just hope she hasn't fallen asleep on the sofa by the time we get back. Anni, on the other hand . . ."

"She's a little terrifying," Joseph says.

"I don't think she's as dangerous as she pretends," I say. "Although I've seen her fence and I wouldn't want to test her. I suppose we should go."

The streetcar homeward is nearly empty; people are loath to give up a moment of precious fine weather on these longest days of the year. Joseph sees me to my door, but he declines to come in.

"I'll only be intruding," he says. "I hope you'll allow me to see you again. Perhaps the Dom next time? Or the Rheinpark?"

"Either sounds lovely," I say.

"And"—he's taken a step away when he remembers—"you're rehearsing at our house this summer, aren't you?"

"Starting a week from tomorrow."

"I'll look forward to it," he says.

In a quick motion, which I suspect he's been steeling himself for all afternoon, he takes my hand in both of his. Before I can say anything, a smile flashes across his face as he lets go, rounds the corner, and disappears down the stairs.

✦ ✦ ✦

Since her stroke, Mother seems a little softened, somehow. Her conversation, though hardly animated, seems less bitter, less angry. She smiles once in a while, and in her smile, I catch a glimpse of the woman she used to be, who, though always frugal and often prickly, loved us, loved our father, and cared for us all. At such moments, a shard of the raw grief I thought had faded threatens to pierce the battlements I've built around myself in order to survive. Yet I hope this change means she's beginning to lower her own defenses, walls built of hostility and Bärenfang to shield her from a grief greater even than ours.

If she's allowing us to see in, even a little, maybe she herself is beginning to be able to see out.

✦ ✦ ✦

I work on my summer assignments: drills, études, a mountain of small, difficult things, and I practice the Schumann Quintet. If I'd been feeling at all cocky, with polished bits of the Saint-Saëns still running through my head, the Schumann Quintet wastes no time in sending me back to my usual anxious starting point.

The following Sunday, as we set up in the Walters' sitting room to begin, it turns out we're all a little cowed, even Robert.

"I thought you were never intimidated by anything," I say.

"Wrong," he says.

"It's a beast," Franz says.

"You already knew that," Felix says. "You're not having second thoughts, are you?"

"No, just complaining."

"Let's just take it slow," I say. "We can play it half speed all summer if we need to. We have six months. Plenty of time to get it right."

"Fräulein Generalin is correct," Felix says. "And that's three months to practice making our own decisions. No Wolff to tell us what to do."

"Just hearing her voice constantly in our heads," I say.

"No fighting," Arnold says.

"Agreed," Robert says. "Tante Hanne won't be happy if we start knocking over her table lamps."

"We've never had to resort to violence yet," I say. "I think the table lamps are safe enough."

"Well, then?" Robert says.

We begin.

We make almost no progress this first Sunday as we try to sort out the basics of the Quintet, including the inordinately difficult problem of how to arrange our chairs. Adding the piano complicates things more than we expected. Robert, sitting behind us, can't see us very well and we can't see him at all. So, we must learn to communicate with our backs to him. We adjust, then adjust again. Our best configuration still seems far from perfect. Clearly, Robert won't be spending a lot of time looking at his hands.

"The Vienna's pianist warned me about that," Robert says. "I'll miss a lot of notes for a while, but it'll come together eventually. In time, I hope."

The evening's dinner conversation shifts between Tante Hanne's chatter about this and that—the slave-driving character of Joseph's employer figures prominently—and our discussions about the Quintet. Herr Walter and Joseph say next to nothing. When we've helped clean up, Joseph and

Robert see us out. Unlike our first visit, the evening is balmy and twilight lingers in the western sky.

"Saturday at my house," Felix says.

"And then back here, same time next Sunday," Robert says.

"Absolutely!" we chorus.

"Eventually we'll need more, but as long as we're just learning our parts, that should do," Robert says. "Practice hard this week!"

"You, too!" we say.

June becomes July. Not that we're surprised, but our progress is slow. Partly it's due to the lack of a deadline, partly to the weight of our summer assignments, and partly just that the Quintet's a monster. Our rehearsals are notable mainly for their raggedness, during which our conversation consists mostly of, "Oh, sorry, can we try that again?"

"Patience," Felix says midway through the third Sunday. "Patience."

"No fighting," Franz says, giving Arnold a poke with his bow.

"Children," Felix says. "Attend. From the beginning. Ready?" And we try it again.

Still, Saturday afternoons at the Apfelbaums' and Sundays at the Walters' are an excellent way to spend the summer. Tante Hanne knows as many cookie recipes as Frau Apfelbaum and doesn't seem to mind baking in the hot weather. We bring bags of produce from the greengrocer as a hostess gift, which always seems to surprise her.

"Oh, my dears, you shouldn't have! My goodness, look at the size of that cabbage! Where on earth did you find it? We'll have some lovely cabbage salad for dinner, never fear! And do tell me if you want coffee or tea with the ginger snaps, won't you? It's the easiest thing in the world to make!" And so on.

Little by little, fueled by cookies and coffee, bits and pieces of the Quintet begin to coalesce.

✦ ✦ ✦

Joseph takes a Friday afternoon off for an excursion to the Rheinpark and another to show me the Dom, where he makes Gothic arches, groin vaults, and flying buttresses seem very exciting, indeed. I like his enthusiasm and I also learn how buildings stand up, something I'd never thought about before. He seems more relaxed in his role as teacher and we even share some laughter together. In all, they are exceedingly pleasant outings.

✦ ✦ ✦

In the process of cleaning a year's accumulation of debris out of my bedroom at the beginning of summer, I reach the sorry conclusion that I desperately need new dresses for school. My three old ones have served me well, but they've been mended several times too many and the cloth is wearing through, especially in the shoulders from the strap of my bag. At the Apfelbaums' table the first Saturday evening, I mention my reluctant plan to check the secondhand shops in the coming weeks.

"Have I taught you nothing, my child?" Ros exclaims. "Go see Johanna, for heaven's sake!"

"I don't need gowns," I say.

"She makes day dresses, too," Ros says. "You've seen them on her mannequins. Better quality, better fitting, and not much more expensive than anything from a secondhand shop. Go on Monday."

"I can't afford—"

"Silly. Go!"

So, of course, because it's impossible to out-argue an Apfelbaum and there's no point trying, that is what I do.

"Almost no change!" Johanna says when she finishes measuring. She reaches for a pile of sketches and bolts of fabric. "Not bad for three years on a diet of Ros's mother's cooking. All right, then. You need three everyday dresses, correct? Very basic. You like dark blue, for one. How about maroon? A little daring but not so faddish you'll feel silly in it by next year. And a nice blue-gray. Very sophisticated. If you watch your weight, these will last you for ten years. The fabric should come to about ten marks apiece. Good wool is cheap compared to the silk we used for your gown. And speaking of gowns—"

"No!" I say.

"Not now," Johanna says, very soothing. "But you have your solo recital next spring, don't you? You'll need a new gown for that. Your other two are in good condition, of course. But your recital will be special. Then, you'll have two to alternate for solo performances and the black one for ensembles."

I give up arguing. Next spring is too far off to think about.

"Fitting in two weeks," Johanna says. "You'll love them."

"I'll be paying you a mark a week forever," I say.

"I'm not worried," Johanna says. "I know where to find you. Remember all those little girls you're going to inspire."

"One of these days," I say. "Apparently none yet."

"One thing at a time," she says.

I stare out the streetcar window all the way home. So many people have invested so much in my success. I don't want to let them down, but I don't know how to go about creating the future they all seem to think will somehow fall into my lap. One thing at a time, Johanna said. Right. Now, and for the next several months, Conservatory is going to be that thing.

+ + +

At the end of July, Ros leaves for her audition with the Amsterdam Women's Orchestra. Frau Apfelbaum goes with her to chaperone and when, to no one's surprise, Ros earns a place in the cello section, to help her settle in with the family of one of the musicians. In August, the Kurtzes depart for Gstaad. I wonder for about five minutes if the Marburgs will be there, too, then put society's upper crust out of my mind.

After that, the time whisks by until suddenly I'm sitting in the recital hall, wearing one of my new dresses and listening to the provost's long-winded welcome back. My last year at Conservatory is about to begin.

18

FALL, SEPTEMBER–DECEMBER 1909

September 1909

Monday morning.

After the welcome, which I could give myself by this time, I encounter the Wolff in the corridor. On impulse, I mention that our quartet has adopted Robert to work on a piano quintet.

"Hmph. You are aware, perhaps, that it is traditional for the professor to assist in the selection of student repertoire?" she says.

"We got very excited about this one," I say.

"Wednesday afternoon," she says. I can't tell whether she's surprised, annoyed, or just resigned.

"Yes, Professorin," I say, and hurry off to Musicology.

✦ ✦ ✦

Wednesday morning.

My first lesson of the term unfortunately reveals that I spent less time than I should have on my summer assignments. I did work on them, but they were difficult and dull, while the Schumann Quintet, which is also difficult, was far more interesting.

"Did you spend the summer eating chocolates and reading novels?" the Wolff snaps, pacing. "You are not up to your own standards, never mind *my* standards! Did you use your metronome at all? Did you not see the modulation to B flat?" And so on.

I wait for her to run out of ammunition. Finally, she stops pacing, folds her arms, and glares, breathing heavily from her exertion.

"I did work on them," I say. "I didn't get as far as I wanted to, though. We were working hard on the Quintet."

The Wolff's expression is really *very* intimidating.

"Ah. Yes." Her voice carries an ominous edge.

"Yes, Professorin."

"Is one allowed to ask what manner of quintet might conceivably take precedence over your assigned repertoire?" she asks.

I take a deep breath.

"The Schumann Piano Quintet, Professorin. With Robert. We heard the Vienna Quartet do it last winter and thought—"

"You've taken on the Schumann Quintet?"

"Yes, Professorin."

"For this fall term recital?"

"Yes, Professorin."

Her eyes grow beadier and beadier as her eyebrows contract into a solid line across her forehead. She seems to be coiling, like a snake, to bite my head off. I wonder if the storage closet in her studio is filled with the heads of students she's bitten off over the years. Slowly, she sits down at her desk, absent-mindedly picks up a pencil and starts tapping it.

"The Schumann Quintet."

"Yes, Professorin."

"And what made you think you could master the Schumann Quintet?"

"We fell in love with it when we heard the Vienna Quartet," I say, trying to sound matter-of-fact. "We met them afterward. They were very encouraging. They also said you would be the right person to coach us."

"Hmph," she says.

There's a long pause while she studies me. I try not to fidget.

"It is a common fourth-year conceit to take on more than you can do well," she says finally. "You surely realize you will have considerable individual repertoire in preparation for your solo recital and you still have classes. Composition, Musicology and Orchestration, if I'm not mistaken. And if you are determined to participate in the orchestra again—"

"Yes, Professorin."

"You will also be expected to start learning your winter orchestra program, as it is substantial."

"Yes, Professorin."

"You have attended the final recitals. You surely understand what will be required of you."

"I do, Professorin."

"There are many more manageable quintets if you are so determined to learn one."

"We can do it, Professorin. It needs a lot more work, of course, but considering we haven't had the benefit of your coaching yet, it's coming along decently well, I think."

I try to sound very objective in my opinion of our progress.

She continues to glare, tapping her pencil. I wonder if I'll just stand here for the rest of the day until she decides to go home. Eventually her head begins to nod slightly in time with her fingers. I suddenly realize she's tapping out the rhythm of the Quintet's first movement.

"*Allegro brillante*," I say.

She stops tapping.

"I will hear it this afternoon," she says. "The first movement. Or as much as you have. I shall determine whether you may continue. But if so, I warn you: no slacking on your other assignments, just because you've got something you like better!"

"Yes, Professorin."

I wonder if the Wolff will think the Schumann is something we can handle, perhaps with her own particular brand of loving care, or if she'll hear what we've done and tell us to abandon it. Perhaps the lure of yet another opportunity to needle Professor Nodelmann . . . I pack up to leave, but turn back at the studio door.

"Thank you, Professorin," I say.

"No more novels!" she snaps. "And no more chocolates! Is that clear?"

"Yes, Professorin." But I risk a small smile as I turn back to the door and out of the corner of my eye I see a look of—what? Something complicated—on the stern, unreadable countenance of Professorin Wolff.

✦ ✦ ✦

Wednesday afternoon.

"Come in!" the Wolff says in answer to my knock.

"Ready?" I say.

The others nod.

"Piece of cake," Robert says.

"What?" Franz says.

"Figure of speech. Not a real cake."

I open the door.

Somehow adding an extra person to the Wolff's studio makes it seem far more crowded, even though Robert is sitting at the piano, which is always there. We arrange our chairs as well as we can and take our places.

"Begin," the Wolff says.

We begin. She lets us play through the first movement.

"Again," she says.

We know we won't get far this time.

"Stop!" she says. "The first chord must be one large explosion. Everyone exactly together. Who is in charge in this moment?"

"Me, I guess," Felix says.

"Then you must signal. Again."

We do it again. We go through it measure by measure. By the end of the first hour, we've made it through the first movement.

"Next," she says.

We play the second movement.

"Again," she says.

We begin again.

"Stop!" she says.

And that's how the second hour goes, too.

But she doesn't make us drop it.

✦　✦　✦

Daily life assumes its pattern: classes, lessons, practice, rehearsals in the basement, coaching. We check out the orchestra parts from the library. The Wolff wasn't exaggerating. I wonder if there's enough time between now and April to learn them. The second Wednesday morning, the Wolff declares my summer assignments acceptable, then hands me a pile of scores to consider for my spring recital.

On Saturdays, I spend my hour teaching Katerina, come home for a quick lunch, then head to the Apfelbaums' to rehearse. On Sundays, I take the streetcar to the Walters' to rehearse some more. In between I start to learn the winter program: Berlioz, Tchaikovsky, Bruckner, and Strauss—all monumental, but the Bruckner's going to be a nightmare, I can tell already.

By the third week I settle on my spring program. It seems politic to defer to the Wolff's judgment for once, so I take her recommendations without argument.

"You must demonstrate an understanding of and facility with Bach," she says. "You have played a partita; take one of the solo violin sonatas. Let us say, No. 3. It will demonstrate your ability with double stops. For lyricism, try the early Dvořák *Romance* for piano and violin. I get equal billing there, you see." She seems to be in an unusually good mood, giving me assignments for once instead of being confronted with my choices.

"In between, as an aspiring soloist, you must play a concerto."

"Which one do you recommend?"

"You must demonstrate mastery of something well-known. You've heard the Brahms. There are also the concerti of Beethoven and Mendelssohn. But I think it would be appropriate for you to pay homage to Köln's native son, Max Bruch. His Violin Concerto No. 1 is not that many years older than you are. A significant challenge, but you are up to it, if you can manage the time to learn it."

"Bruch, then," I say. I don't know anything about the Bruch, but if the Wolff thinks I'm up to it, I had better be up to it. I decline to take the bait about managing my time.

"Here," she says, handing me a score. It's quite old, with some pages turned down, and I see as I thumb through it, its pages contain many notations in a familiar hand.

"Take good care of it," she says. "It is a loan, not a gift."

I turn back to the title page, inscribed in the same old-fashioned hand: "Property of Maria Anna Wolff, 1870." It is, I also note, a full orchestra score such as the conductor might have, not just the solo part.

"Your own score?" I say. "Are you sure? I can easily get it from the library downstairs."

"The school's copy lacks the proper notations," she says. "And you will gain a better understanding if you can see what the orchestra is doing behind you. I will not pretend the piano reduction does the orchestra part full justice. Don't let your dog chew on it."

"I haven't got a dog."

"Good. Finally, although not in chronological order, I think a Paganini Caprice, such as Fraülein Morgenthaler chose. Here are all twenty-four. Look them over and choose one by next week."

"Yes, Professorin."

"While no one expects you to have these mastered by Christmas, it is important that you become familiar with them as early as possible. They will take time to memorize, mature, and settle confidently under your fingers. It may seem like a great deal to master by spring, but I believe you to be capable of it. There must be no slacking on *any* of your assignments," she says.

"Of course not, Professorin," I say.

The Wolff believes me capable. I hope she's right. If I stop wasting time eating and sleeping, I might—*might*—be able to learn everything in time.

Still, I have no choice but to live up to her expectations. I've never let her get the best of me yet and I don't intend to start now.

Schumann Quintet. Orchestra. Solo recital. Bruch. Taken altogether, it's a ridiculously impossible amount of work, but I feel immersed in it with a breathless sense of something like joy. It's not just my work but my whole self and it feels good, and pure, and right.

+ + +

October 1909

The Wolff's weekly coaching doesn't lead the Schumann Quintet to any kind of immediate breakthrough.

One of the biggest hurdles is that very first note, when all five instruments explode into the first chord precisely together. It plagued us all summer, to the point where we had to leave it ragged and move on, just to make some progress. The rest of the piece is improving steadily, but that opening—occasionally it's perfect and more often it's not. It's been so stubborn that we've developed a block about it, no matter how we tinker with the adjustment of our seats.

In our Wednesday sessions, Felix gives the signal over and over while the Wolff paces and snaps, "Stop! Again!" It's not until one chilly after-noon in mid-October that it suddenly clicks into place and, just like that, feels crisp and sure. We do it perfectly ten times in a row and feel like cheering. The Wolff stops her pacing to listen.

"About time!" she says. "Well, don't stop, there's more, you know."

Week by week it improves steadily, but slowly, despite our daily work. We begin to wonder if we'll have it mastered well enough by the end of term to perform it. Or if, much as we hate to consider it, we should give it up.

"Give it up?" The Wolff actually leans across her desk when we muster the courage to voice our doubts. "After all this time and work? Don't be stupid! You think everything was easy for Mozart? For Beethoven? You think they never struggled? You are just learning how to struggle. That is the musician's life. It's any artist's life. It is the *nature* of life. There is no such thing as a life without struggle. Since you ask my opinion, of course, you must continue. It has the potential to be decent by December, maybe, but only if you persevere."

This vote of confidence is reassuring, but we feel like we've been per-severing since July. Nothing has even been this stubbornly rough for this long.

For just a moment, so subtly we almost miss it, her voice softens.

"If you give up, you have nothing. You'll have wasted your work and your time, and mine. But there is no middle ground here, no room for superficiality. This Quintet must be played with your whole heart or not at all. All that magnificent running water. It is the music of mountain streams in the spring melt."

A pause.

"Well? What are you waiting for? Again!"

Marveling at this unprecedented revelation of the Wolff's inner emotional life, we arrange ourselves and start from the beginning, which we flub.

✦ ✦ ✦

Through it and through it, again and again. The Wolff is relentless.

"Too slow! Too stiff! The modulation in the *Scherzo* must be smooth, like flowing water! The snow is melting in the Alps! You must keep in your minds an image of early spring!" And so on. It's a good thing we're working on something we like so much, or we'd be sick of it by now. But it is coming together, bit by laborious bit. Once we have it, we'll have something monumental. Robert is particularly excited about its potential.

"I can make a name with this!" he says.

"If we get it in time," Franz says.

"We'll get it," Robert says. "We *are* getting it. We just have to stick with it."

When I look at his photograph on my bureau, my father says the same thing.

Robert has his own lessons, of course, on top of the ones he shares with us, in which he's learning solo repertoire and concerti that may well take him farther than the Quintet. When he's not with us, he seems to live in the practice room. He pushes us almost as hard as the Wolff does, though thankfully without the temper. One Wolff, in my view, is enough.

+ + +

November 1909

Somehow, in early November, the Schumann finally clicks. Another five hundred times through those exuberant opening chords, further microscopic adjustments to our seating arrangements, drilling our way through the multiple themes of the four movements, and it's starting to sound like music. The Wolff doesn't let up. Every coaching session involves ripping some part of it into bits and putting it back together again.

It's exhausting work, but we feel like we're on the track of something extraordinary, something that inhabits us like a physical presence, a living waterfall of sound and emotion. We begin rehearsing at Robert's house on weekdays, too, because the Walters' sitting room is larger and more comfortable than the school practice rooms, the piano is better, and Tante Hanne takes such pleasure in feeding us.

Joseph's frequent absences at dinner due to overwork are among Tante Hanne's favorite topics of conversation.

+ + +

By mid-November, cold wind whips down the streets and buffets the streetcars. It tears the last of the dead leaves off the elms along Hildegard-strasse and eddies them into shifting piles on the sidewalk. Each morning I push open the heavy Conservatory front doors feeling disheveled and irritated, relieved to be indoors at last.

One Wednesday morning, acutely conscious of having too many things to do and too little time to do them, my lesson is, at best, workman-like as I struggle to pull my concentration into the moment and follow the Wolff's corrections. At last, she folds her arms and frowns, her eyebrows furrowed in a dark line across her forehead.

"I did warn you," she says.

"Yes, Professorin. It will be all right. I'll get there. Just more practice."

"You must take care of your health," she says. "And your hands."

"I try, Professorin."

"And you must learn your limits. It is harder for very gifted students. They think they have none. But everyone has limits. It is a fine line between achieving your utmost and falling into chaos. I trust you're not thinking of auditioning for first chair next term?"

The audition notice went up at the beginning of the week. The Wolff's perception, as usual, is uncanny.

"I had been thinking of it, Professorin."

"There is no point," she says. "Not because you are incapable of filling the first chair role, and not only because it is more work than you should undertake when you are practicing for your solo recital."

"Why, then?"

"It's one thing to hold your own in a mixed field of support and resentment. Herr Zeidler is a fair man who speaks highly of you. But he will never elevate you to a position of authority over male students. If he did, I promise you, they would mutiny."

I frown. "Surely—"

"It is the truth," she snaps. "I have seen it."

When? I wonder. Thirty years ago? This is the modern world. But there's no point in arguing with her. And, if I'm honest with myself, I suspect she's right. Would Marburg follow instructions from me? Would Herr Zeidler back me up?

"I understand, Professorin."

"Spend your energy practicing, instead," she says.

"I will," I say. "See you this afternoon."

She answers with a curt nod and I step into the corridor, shutting the door behind me.

After lunch, on my way back upstairs to the Wolff's studio, I hear voices approaching.

"You think the Adler bitch will go for it?"

I stop short.

"Let her try. Insinuating her way into the orchestra was bad enough. She doesn't belong there."

"Wonder if she slept with Zeidler, too."

Laughter. Some low muttering.

"They'd never throw her out. She's got too many gullible faculty right in the palm of her hand."

"At least the other bitch is gone. The cellist."

"Nothing ladylike about a cellist."

More laughter.

My cheeks are burning. But I need to get upstairs. I take a deep breath and keep climbing.

Sure enough, it's Marburg and three of his friends, all rich blonds with solid builds and expensive clothes, blocking the stair. One of them, a horn player named Georg, has the decency to blush.

"Excuse me, I need to get upstairs," I say.

"Why, Fraülein Adler, we were just talking about you," Marburg says.

"I know," I say. "Could you move, please?"

"Maybe you can satisfy our curiosity." The others titter. "Are you going to go for first chair? Your ambition knows no bounds, after all."

"I haven't decided. Is there a problem? You think my directions might be too complicated for you to follow?"

I immediately regret this. The stairs are not completely deserted at this moment, but I don't see anyone I know and I'd promised myself I wouldn't goad him. It would only make things worse.

"Why, you—"

Before I have time to react, he raises his hand to slap me. Georg must have anticipated this, because his hand flies up in the same instant and grabs Marburg's wrist.

"You idiot! You'll get yourself thrown out, and us, too!" he hisses.

I seize my small advantage.

"It is only a matter of practice," I say. "Now, if you don't mind, you're blocking the stairs."

Several other students round the corner at this moment. Marburg wrenches his arm out of Georg's grip and pushes past me. Georg turns to me as he passes.

"Be careful, Fraülein," he says and hurries after them.

My heart is still pounding when I arrive at the Wolff's door. The others are already there. I unpack without a word and we take our places.

"When you are ready," the Wolff says.

I take a couple of deep breaths and keep my eyes on Felix, who gives me a questioning look. I nod. He makes eye contact with everyone and then gives the signal.

We begin. The Wolff listens to our run-through without comment, which is unusual. When we're finished, she says, "If the rest of you could begin to approach the level of intensity of your second violin, I would say you were making excellent progress."

I know the others heard it, too. I keep my face expressionless.

"I'm feeling a little extra fire today, that's all," I say.

"Well, keep it burning," the Wolff says. "The rest of you, light yours. Whatever it is, whatever it takes. *Passion!*" she barks, making us jump. "This is a work of utmost passion! You have the notes, now you must find the source for your passion and apply it to create the music. Fräulein Adler's level next time. Do you understand?"

"Yes, Professorin," we say.

"Again," she says.

We play it again, trying for more passion.

After that, we take the last movement apart for an hour. We leave the Wolff tapping out the rhythms of the last movement with her fingers on her desk.

"What was that all about?" Robert says as we head downstairs for a much-needed break. "Marthe's on fire and everyone exchanges knowing looks? Not that the Wolff isn't right—you really gave the outfit some class today. Sorry, ah, you raised expectations. Made the rest of us look like we were loafing. But in a good way, of course."

"Marburg?" Felix says.

I nod.

"That son of a—" Franz says.

"What did he do now?" Arnold says. "Whatever it was, I'm sorry we weren't there to prevent it."

"Don't be," I say, "if it improves the Quintet. I appreciate the thought, though. He was just being his usual self. Him and his friends. It had to do with the first chair business."

"Are you auditioning?" Felix says.

"I wasn't going to," I say. "The Wolff strongly advised against it. This very morning, in fact. Said the section would mutiny if a woman were first chair."

"Why?" Arnold demands. "That's silly."

"That's what I like about you," Franz says. "Your extreme naiveté. Too pure for this world, you are. It's more than silly, it's stupid and wrong. But I can see it. Especially any section that has that ass Marburg in it."

"A fair point," Felix says. "And by 'I wasn't going to,' do you mean to say that Marburg's special brand of diplomacy is making you change your mind?"

"He made me angry," I say. "He insulted Ros, too."

"Really good reason to stick your neck out," Felix says. "Ros will survive insults from Marburg. She's not here, remember?"

"He's just jealous. I saw a lot of that in Paris," Robert says. "We had several women in my year there. Hugely talented, intelligent women. Some of the men just couldn't stand it. Resorted to all kinds of stupid things."

"Well," I say, trying to make light of it, "I guess our homework is to go find Marburg before our next rehearsal and let him work his magic on us. When we take the city by storm at the recital, we can go thank him. I've got my dose, though. I'll be sufficiently passionate for life if I never see him again."

This is not my destiny, however, as I begin to see Marburg even more frequently in the corridors. He doesn't usually try to talk to me. He just stares. His expression is hard to read: not overtly malevolent, not openly sneering, just intent, frowning, as if he's studying me. I look the other way, but try not to alter my stride.

On the positive side, my old angry fire seems to be stoked for the duration and I need all the fire I can get.

✦ ✦ ✦

Herr Zeidler, in my first chair audition, asks for the repertoire from the upcoming orchestra program. Quite honestly, this is some of the most difficult music I've ever tackled, and not just because the first half of the program is French and Russian. I haven't mastered it yet, what with the daily distraction of the Schumann Quintet and everything else, but I do my best.

He leans back in his chair and conducts with his eyes closed as I play the main themes of four radically different works: Hector Berlioz's *Symphonie Fantastique*, an opium-induced capital-R Romantic symphonic poem; Pyotr Tchaikovsky's Fantasy Overture *Romeo and Juliet*; Anton Bruckner's hour-long Symphony No. 7; and for a light finish to this massive pile of music, a short early work of Richard Strauss, *Till Eulenspiegel's Merry Pranks*.

"What do you think, Fraülein Adler?" Herr Zeidler says when I've finished.

This is not a question I expect to be asked at an audition.

"It's an ambitious program," I say, choosing understatement. "Interesting, two such different views on the subject of love as the Berlioz and Tchaikovsky. And the Bruckner is, er, rather difficult." Hellish, more like.

"Ah! Yes. That is why I've programmed *Till Eulenspiegel*. To give our audience a sense of perspective. Perhaps our musicians, too. I will tell you, Fraülein, I can't remember when I've had an orchestra that I thought could handle work of this magnitude. And I do believe that is, in large part, a credit to you."

"To me, sir?"

Herr Zeidler leans forward across his desk. "Perhaps you didn't see the looks on the other students' faces when you and Fraülein Apfelbaum first appeared unannounced in the orchestra. The two of you were better prepared than anyone. I could read in their faces that they suddenly realized this was going to be more serious business than they thought. You forced them to work harder. And so they did better. Because that is the secret, isn't it? Working harder. You've continued to make them work harder ever since, just by your presence. They don't want—forgive me, Fraülein—they don't want to be out-performed by a woman. It is what I thought would happen when I let you stay.

"Now, three years later, we have the best student orchestra in all my years of teaching here. One that can handle the opium fumes of Berlioz, the recklessness of Tchaikovsky, the mountain range of Bruckner, and still have the energy for the anarchy of *Till Eulenspiegel*. I'm quite eager for the term to get underway."

"Well," I say. "I'm happy to have had such a stirring effect. I guess."

"I hope you will realize two things, Fraülein," he says, suddenly serious. "The first is, you absolutely deserve to be first chair. No other second violinist has come in here as well-prepared as you. Nor are any likely to. And the second is that there is no possibility of you becoming first chair. None whatsoever."

I suppose I know where this is going, but I'm not eager to hear it.

"You must believe what Professorin Wolff has told you. No section of men will follow a woman. Not even a qualified and intelligent woman who has proven herself over and over, not in any orchestra that I know of. Most orchestras refuse women members entirely, as you know. It would be an abuse to give you that assignment. Someday this will change. But an orchestra is a traditional organization. Slow to adapt. If I did break with convention and give you the chair, I would be depriving some promising young man of the additional training he will need in his career. I hope you also understand that this seeming unfairness will protect you from a great deal of unnecessary trouble and disrespect."

"Yes, sir." I know he's right, but it's infuriating. I feel my face grow hot. "But then, why did you audition me? If you had no intention—"

"I wanted to hear you," he says. "Fraülein, I personally respect you enormously, based on your discipline, skill and, yes, courage, since the first day you appeared in my orchestra. I predict you will have an illustrious career. Just—not in an orchestra."

"I did know that," I say more curtly than I intend.

"It will be the orchestra's loss, believe me."

"I appreciate your frankness," I say.

Maybe I do and maybe I don't. On the other hand, if I were first chair and there was a mutiny . . . where would I be then?

✦ ✦ ✦

December 1909

We take a few days off from the Schumann at the end of November, then come back to it refreshed the first week of December. The recital schedule is posted the next week. We're to perform last on Thursday—naturally the same night as Marburg, this time playing Beethoven in a trio.

"His reputation preceded him," Franz says. "He couldn't find another violinist in our class who who could stand to work with him."

Robert has the audacity to write to Herr Lorenz, the violist of the Vienna Quartet, and invite all of them, including their pianist, to come and hear us perform. To my very great surprise Herr Lorenz answers, though with regrets, because the Vienna Quartet is engaged in performances in Italy all that week. But the tone of the letter is kind and encouraging and he says he will hope to hear us on some other occasion.

"Never hurts to try," Robert says. "I'm keeping this letter."

✦　✦　✦

We take our Orchestration and Composition exams and practice obsessively. We attend our classmates' recitals, but leave immediately afterward. We try hard to eat decently and get some proper sleep.

Performance day follows its familiar routine: I obsessively pack and repack my black gown, shoes, hairbrush, hairpins, and part; check and recheck my list; glance compulsively at the hands of the clock that crawl in the morning but speed up so by noon that I have to watch them constantly for fear of being late for our last run-through with the Wolff.

Marthe, go," Anni says after lunch. "Get out of here. Be early. Be really, really early. You aren't doing anyone any good pacing around here. Don't worry about us, we'll be there in plenty of time. We have this down to a science."

"We do?" Mother says.

"Of course, we do. We've done it dozens of times. You can relax a while longer. Put your feet up, rest yourself for tonight. Marthe, just *go*."

Anni is really trying hard with Mother, I think as I climb the stairs to the Wolff's studio. I feel like I've barely seen either of them all term. When did the wild child turn out to be the good daughter and I the guilty, neglectful one?

I push the thought aside. Now is not the time. They believe in me. That means I have to do whatever is necessary to succeed here, and if that means not being home much, well, so be it. Right now, the most important

273

thing—the only thing—is this evening's performance of the Schumann Quintet, the culmination of six months of hard work.

The run-through is good. We're as ready as we can be.

I pull on my gown and shoes in the toilet stall. My hair is soon up and pinned. My neck is still bare. It doesn't matter, just one less thing to worry about. My caterpillars begin their ritual gallop around my stomach— *allegro brillante*, if I'm not mistaken.

"We're going to be fantastic," a voice says. It startles me until I realize it's my own.

The waiting lounge is crowded and quiet. Felix, Arnold, and Franz are already here. Robert shows up a few minutes later with Oskar, back on page turner duty. Marburg drifts in fashionably late, as usual. He glances my way and smirks, as if he's about to say something about my harem, but thinks better of it.

Whatever our individual level of nerves might be, we're all experienced enough by now not to show them. Some people study their parts. No one really needs to—by this point they'd better not need to—but looking at the notes occupies the mind. A few quiet conversations between ensemble-mates about technical minutiae murmur in the corners. Marburg is mercifully quiet. Robert and Oskar flip through the piano part, pointing at things. My caterpillars practice calisthenics in my stomach.

We wait.

Herr Schädler calls the groups for the first half. Three sets of people stand up and leave, including Marburg's trio. After the provost gives his usual welcome, the first group, a wind quintet, goes. They're very good. Next, a piano trio. They're also very good. After them, Marburg's trio. They're good, too.

"I always said he could do well if he only practiced," Felix says. "Maybe even he finally figured that out."

"I heard he wants to audition for the Berlin Philharmonic," Arnold says. "You can't name-drop your way in there."

"Knowing him, he'll drop it anyway," Franz says. "The Berlin Phil will be consumed in awe at the mention of . . . Herr Grimmelshausen."

A ripple of laughter goes around the room.

I say nothing. I don't want the distraction, not even a pleasant one of imagining life in Köln without Marburg anywhere in it. I imagine instead that first explosive chord, all of us hitting it perfectly together and racing on from it for a perfect performance. Well, no performance is ever perfect. A brilliant performance, one people will talk about here for years to come. I imagine it again, and again, and again.

Marburg's group finishes. Enthusiastic applause. Intermission seems very short. Herr Schädler beckons. Three ensembles stand up in unison, gripping instruments, bows, parts. We follow him to the stage right wing.

The first ensemble, a quartet, pulls off a tricky late Dvořák. The second, another trio, waits while Herr Schädler rearranges the chairs. He returns, signals, and out they go. At the beginning of their final movement, Herr Schädler beckons. We line up. When the trio has taken its bows, Herr Schädler goes out and rearranges the chairs again for us.

"Check the chairs before we start," Felix hisses in our ears. "Take your time. There's no rush."

"Right!" we hiss back. The thought of starting and then realizing we can't see each other sets my caterpillars to a sudden tug of war. One of them, with very cold feet, crawls up the back of my neck.

When Herr Schädler returns to his post, he waits a full ten seconds before he nods to us to go.

At his signal we head onto the stage for what I suddenly realize is our last performance as an ensemble. Why I hadn't realized it until this moment, I don't know, but the thought hits me with a wave of some emotion I can't name, as blinding as the footlights.

Put it into the music, I tell myself. *This is your moment. Uncertainty is for tomorrow.* I stand alongside my friends, bow to our audience, and sit. Sure enough, the chairs and stands require adjustment, but only slightly. Herr Schädler has arranged chairs for so many ensembles for so long, he could probably do it in his sleep. Felix waits a long five seconds, looks around at all of us. We nod. Three deep breaths. He gives the signal. The first chord explodes, crisp and precise, and the race is on.

The first movement tumbles out of us; through it flows the lyrical second theme, with conversations between piano and cello, piano and violin. The slow second movement weaves its subtle theme, by turns tiptoeing, elegiac, fiery, delicate. After its quiet end we correct our tuning, then plunge into the short *Scherzo*, in which scales chase each other up and down like the first great musical romp of springtime.

The Wolff was right: it does feel like coursing snowmelt. Without pause the third becomes the fourth, playful and introspective by turns as it tears the themes into fragments, then disciplines them into a fugue, until finally they reunite for a building, crashing finish: six months of hard work poured into a half hour of being fully, extravagantly alive.

The applause is wonderful. We take two bows and exit. Herr Schädler points us back on for another bow. I imagine Clara Schumann, for whom her husband wrote the Quintet, standing beside us.

What a fabulous woman she must have been: to be the first to play this music, to *inspire* it.

✦　✦　✦

"I forgot to mention, there's food at my house," Robert says as we make our way out to the foyer. "And Tante Hanne said you must all come and eat it."

"I'll be there," Franz says.

"We'll all be there, right?" Felix says.

"Right," we say.

"But we need to be gracious about allowing our public to congratulate us," I say.

"Absolutely," Robert grins. "First rule of stardom. And here we are."

The foyer hums with conversations and laughter among the other five ensembles, families, friends, faculty, bargain-minded music lovers. Heidi hands me her tiny bouquet of flowers and curtsies adorably. The Dietrichs don't seem surprised that we pulled it off.

"If I'd thought you weren't ready, I'd have done my best to dissuade you," he says. "And if the Wolff had been in doubt, she'd have put her foot down, hard. You can always trust her judgment."

"You do me too much credit, Herr Dietrich," the Wolff's voice says behind me. "I confess I was uncertain at first. But there is only one way to find out. I've pulled ensembles out of performances up to the last minute if they weren't ready. Though one can usually tell much earlier."

"May I ask when you decided we were ready?" I ask.

"You may," she says. "Notes, tomorrow, nine o'clock."

She strides away.

"Smooth, isn't she?" Herr Dietrich says. "Well, Gerda, my love, shall we?"

"Come see us this holiday," Gerda says. "And promise you'll come to the Dom on Christmas Eve for the Bach Christmas Oratorio. Thomas wants to hear Papa play, but it's a long time for a three-year-old to sit in the cold. I'll be glad of a little help."

"I promise," I say, and wave goodbye.

Our families all look happy. Even my mother, talking to Arnold's mother, looks happy. Tante Hanne is in fine form.

"And oh, my dear, you all were leagues above everyone else! Our Robert was up practicing every night after you all left, just practicing and practicing, until the small hours, and every day you weren't there, too. Hours and hours and hours! I've been humming the piano part while I work. I heard it so often—just bits of it will pop into my head, in and out all day. Your part must pop into yours, too, I should think? I'm sure you must all have worn yourselves to pieces, but, oh, my! Robert says he can make his name with this and so can all of you, I'm sure! What magnificent music! What energy! You must be exhausted! You're all coming over to our house, aren't you? I'm sure Robert must have told you—"

"Yes, indeed," I say, not mentioning that he did it five minutes ago.

"If I didn't know better, I'd say you were becoming an artist," Oma Judith says, taking advantage of the momentary lull.

"Tonight, it almost feels like it," I say.

"Just a simple matter of working harder than everybody else," she says. "Anyone can tell that's what you did. Felix was at it every night, too, until all hours. Long after I went to bed. I was hearing it in my sleep."

"Me, too," I say.

She laughs her gravelly laugh. "There's no substitute for being young," she says. "None at all."

Tante Hanne agrees with her at some length and doesn't seem to need me for the conversation, so I edge away to where Joseph is talking to Anni.

"Did I hear a little slip somewhere?" Anni teases. "Something sounded microscopically different from the eight hundred times I heard it at home."

"No, there wasn't—" Joseph begins indignantly.

"If you only heard one, you weren't paying attention," I say. "The important thing is that you heard our brilliant recovery."

"Definitely!" she says. "I'm only joking. It sounded perfect as far as I could tell."

"That's better," Joseph says. "It sounded perfect to me, too."

"Can I come with you to the Walters' tonight?" Anni says.

I glance at Joseph. "Of course," he says.

"Of course," I say.

"I'll tell the Apfelbaums." Anni disappears into the crowd.

"That's very kind of you," I say.

"The more, the better," Joseph says. "You really were amazing, you know. All of you."

"Thank you. It hit me tonight, this is our last performance together. Which made it a little sad, too."

"Why?" Joseph frowns.

"Next term's orchestra, then in spring we have our recitals. Then, poof, everyone vanishes to wherever and that will be that."

"You don't know what the future holds," he says. "You four have something special. It would be a shame to let it go. Something will work out, if you keep in touch, keep playing together for fun."

"Maybe," I say.

"Adding to your collection of men?" a bored voice behind me says. I whip around to see Marburg saunter by with a cup of punch in his hand and a sly smile on his face. I resist the impulse to slap him. I hear Joseph's sharp breath behind me.

"You played well tonight. The Beethoven was really good," I say as coolly as I can.

Marburg says nothing.

I press the advantage. "Have a good holiday," I say, and turn away.

Joseph's eyes follow Marburg as he saunters away. "Shall I knock him down for you?" he says. He sounds as though his teeth are clenched.

"That would only cause more trouble than it's worth," I say. "Just paying him a compliment when his playing deserves it, like tonight, seems to be the best approach."

"What an ass," Joseph mutters under his breath.

"Little dogs in fancy clothes, that's what Oma Judith says."

"I like Oma Judith."

"Two more terms and I'll never see him again."

Mother has sagged into one of the foyer chairs with Frau Apfelbaum beside her. I sit down on her other side and give her a hug.

"I'm so glad you came tonight," I say. "I know it was a long evening."

"You had to go last," she says.

"We didn't choose the order," I say. "I hope it was worth waiting for."

"You did well," she says. "And I always like seeing your father's violin in action. He loved it so much."

"It was stupendous, dear," Frau Apfelbaum says.

"We're lucky we had Robert," I say. "Not many pianists here could have pulled it off."

"Indeed," Frau Apfelbaum says. "I predict he's headed for a stellar career. I believe we're taking your mother home again?"

"Any time," Mother says. "I'm very tired."

"We can go now if you like, Sarah. We've congratulated everyone, I think."

"I appreciate it so much," I say.

"It's our pleasure," Frau Apfelbaum says. "You deserve to celebrate with your friends."

"I won't be late," I say. "We have notes tomorrow morning, as usual."

Mother grunts a bit as I help her to her feet. I hear my name echoing off the walls and look up in time to see Katerina hurtling toward me while Herr Kurtz follows at a more dignified pace.

"Oh, darling, you were fabulous!" Calling people "darling" is one of her new fads. "You were *all* fabulous. You *must* introduce me to Robert. I've met everyone else. Oh, now, please! Before he gets away."

Smitten. Like every other girl who sees him, I suppose, even from a distance. Well, it's not often I have access to the currency she trades in, so I introduce her. She makes a charming fuss over him and then I take her back to her father.

"It's a pleasure watching you grow, Fraülein," Herr Kurtz says when we return. "And astonishing to think you're nearly done."

"There's a mountain of work between now and then," I say. "Orchestra and recital. But I'll see Katerina Saturday morning."

"We will expect you," Herr Kurtz says, bowing slightly. "Ready, my dear?" Katerina blows kisses over her shoulder as they walk away.

"Shall we, then?" Robert has at last finished holding court for his admirers. "Off to our house for a little food and maybe a beer!"

At the streetcar stop, Robert, Felix and Arnold begin dissecting our performance, Anni and Franz chortle about something subversive, and Joseph continues praising me. We're a merry crew indeed as we board the streetcar for Neuehrenfeld.

The party is short because of our early notes, so we decide to go to Café Max Bruch tomorrow after the Wolff finishes dismembering our performance and relax over coffee. This annoys Joseph, as he has to work. He insists on seeing Anni and me home. I protest at keeping him up so late on a work night, but Anni says sweetly, "Thank you, Joseph, that will be lovely," causing me to wonder, not for the first time, who this girl is and what she's done with my sister. When he goes to get our coats, she kicks me in the shin.

"For being *so* dense," she hisses.

"You're coming to the Dom concert this Christmas Eve, aren't you?" Joseph says when we're settled on the streetcar.

"I promised Gerda just tonight," I say.

"Will you come, Anni?"

"Too much, too cold, too late for me," she says.

"I'd have agreed before last year," Joseph says. "Robert dragged me, but it was terrific. The acoustics in the Dom are incredible and of course it's a magnificent building, under any circumstances. We'll make arrangements ahead of time, won't we?"

"Yes, indeed," I say.

Nobody says much for the rest of the ride. I feel myself sagging against Joseph. I try to sit up straight, but it's a lot of work and in a minute I'm sagging again. When we reach our stop, he insists on walking us to the door of our building.

"See you soon," he says when my key turns in the lock. We wave and step inside, shutting the door behind us.

"He's wild about you," Anni says as we climb the stairs.

"He is not. He's a friend. I keep telling you that."

"You are the densest woman alive and I'll keep telling *you* that until you stop saying such stupid things."

Now, *that's* my Anni.

"Have it your way," I say. "I'm too tired to argue."

"That's better," she says.

19

DECEMBER 1909

December 1909

The Wolff's notes on Friday morning are as exhaustive and exhausting as ever. We play through the Schumann twice before she's satisfied.

"You are becoming artists," she says in an uncanny echo of Oma Judith. "It is the goal of every student who enters Conservatory, but they are all mistaken: it is not a goal one attains but a lifelong struggle. Gift plus discipline, technique plus perseverance, enlightened by the joy and pain of life. I have said this before: when you return to this music in five, or ten, or twenty years, you will experience it very differently."

"*If* we can return to it," I say. The end of our ensemble feels acute today, replacing last night's euphoria with a kind of melancholy.

"Of course, you will return to it," she says. "You haven't put in all this work to let it drift into the past, a pleasant memory only. Or so I trust."

"It's only that the future is uncertain," I say. I shouldn't have said anything. It's only my future that seems so uncertain.

"That is part of the struggle," she says. "You are an artist. You will persevere."

There follows a silence in which no one knows what to say.

"You all have your holiday assignments, I believe?"

Everyone nods.

"Very well. I advise you not to leave them until New Year's Eve. The orchestra program in particular is substantial. As I suspect you are already aware."

"Yes, Professorin," we say. Except Robert, who has a different pile of challenges to keep him occupied over the holidays.

"Then I will see you, Fraülein, in January. Prepared, this time, I hope."

"Yes, Professorin. No novels, no chocolates."

"Precisely."

We pack up and leave the Wolff at her desk, looking out the window and tapping her pencil in the rhythm of the Quintet's finale.

Such a curious woman, our Wolff, the terror of the Conservatory. Robert was right about her: a martinet, but not a monster. A teacher I would, after all, work my fingers to the bone to please. I feel a sudden wave of affection for that forbidding exterior, the occasional glimpse of a human being underneath it. Her love of Schumann. Her love of music, even after so many years of teaching. I wonder if she ever loved a person as much. I wonder if she has a completely different personality that she allows out only at home. I wonder if she's lonely. An arresting thought, one that follows me around for the entire holiday, and for some time after.

✦ ✦ ✦

Café Max Bruch is end-of-term quiet.

"To our last performance together," I say, raising my mug when our coffees arrive. "We did well."

"What are you talking about?" Franz says. "Are we all going to be guillotined tomorrow, only nobody told us?"

"It's our last performance together as students," Felix says, "but I don't want to stop, do you?"

"No," I say. "It's been the best part of Conservatory for me. Like— well, just the best part."

Like gaining three brothers. Like finding a family.

"Me, too," Arnold says.

"I'm glad I had a chance to horn in," Robert says. "Or piano in, I guess. I tell you, I saw a lot of student quartets in Paris and Moscow and you four really do have something special. Most people just want to play the big stuff, or flashy solos. You four almost make me wish I were a string player."

"But you'll all be doing that before long," I say. "Playing in orchestras, or being soloists and traveling all the time. You must have plans."

"My plan is to survive winter term," Franz says. "Compared to that orchestra program, my recital will be a piece of cake."

"You all have fun with that," Robert says.

"Are you going back to America, Robert?" Felix asks.

"Eventually," Robert says. "I'd prefer to debut here. Any European debut carries a lot more weight in America. We feel provincial by comparison to you."

"How do you make a debut?" I ask.

Robert shrugs. "Get a manager. Audition. Conductors and managers attend Conservatory recitals sometimes, looking for new talent. Provosts might invite them if they have very promising students."

"I wonder how well that works if you're a woman," I say.

"That I don't know," Robert says. "It's a different problem, clearly."

An awkward pause follows.

"I'm with Franz," Arnold says. "If we don't survive Orchestra, it won't matter. I'm doing a lot of practicing this holiday."

"But you're all coming to the Dom concert on Christmas Eve," Robert says.

We all are.

"Tell you what. Come to our house for dinner and we'll go together. Tante Hanne will be over the moon to have you all there."

"Where?" Franz says.

"Figure of speech," Robert says. "American for 'happy.'"

"Oh," Franz says.

"I promised Gerda I'd help her with Thomas if he gets restless," I say, "but I can meet her there."

"Settled, then," Robert says. "Come early, bring your instruments. We can have some fun in the afternoon."

"Excellent plan," Felix says.

The familiar thought weighs on me for the rest of the day: how easy the world looks to a man.

✦ ✦ ✦

"We'd love to have you visit again for Christmas Eve," Gerda says when I drop by to tell her. "But I'm glad you're going with friends. We'll go with Wil and I'll find you there."

"I want to introduce you to Joseph," I say. "He's really been most kind to me."

"Kind? It sounds to me more like he's madly in love with you."

"Oh, no!" Why does everyone harp on this ridiculous idea? "Not at all. We're just friends."

"Oh," Gerda says. "Friends. Of *course*. Silly me."

Unfortunately, the memory of this conversation makes me blush when Joseph opens the front door for us on Christmas Eve.

To our surprise, a small, decorated fir tree stands in a corner of the Walters' sitting room by a small pile of wrapped packages.

"Isn't it adorable?!" Tante Hanne exclaims. "We never had one before last year, of course, why would we? But when Robert came, we decided of course we must have one and he showed us how to decorate it. Joseph won't let us use candles, though. Too dangerous, he says. So, no lights, such a shame, but not worth setting the house on fire, is it? He says not to worry, we'll have electricity before long, which I can't *imagine*, and Robert taught us a few of the old songs. I quite like them. They're so very *German*! And, of course, you can't have a proper Christmas without gifts, can you? Nothing fancy, just small things. Robert taught me some American recipes, too, and Scottish ones, from his father's people. Cock-a-leekie soup!" She sounds the syllables out. "Cootie pudding!"

"*Clootie* pudding," Robert says, stifling a laugh.

"Clootie, cootie," Tante Hanne giggles. "Such odd words! Whichever, I've been steaming test batches on the stove all week with all sorts of dried fruits and spices. Christmas Eve is no time to experiment! Anyway, Robert's been the education of us. And we've taught him about Hanukkah, too, haven't we, dear? We let him light the last candle. It was *quite* special! I've made hot chocolate and gingerbread men, so do fortify yourselves before you begin!"

These vanish in short order.

"Well, I mustn't keep you. Would anyone like more gingerbread?"

"Yes, please!" Franz says.

"Well, yes, dear, obviously."

She swoops back to the kitchen and returns with more cookies and another cup of hot chocolate for Franz.

"Do you *ever* get full?" I ask him.

"No," he says.

Robert chuckles as he pulls out the piano bench.

"'Cootie pudding,'" he says, mostly to himself, and chuckles some more.

Dinner follows our afternoon of improvisation and songs, and the clootie pudding, studded with candied fruit and spices, follows dinner. Washing up takes no time at all; by now we make a smooth and efficient team. As we assemble at the door to set out, Herr Walter appears with an armload of blankets and cushions.

"We must hope for the sake of our Christian friends," Herr Walter says, handing them around, "that their heaven is warmer than their church at mid-winter."

As we tramp down Droste-Hülshoff-Strasse two and three abreast toward the streetcar stop, I compliment Tante Hanne on the clootie pudding.

"Oh, lovely, dearie! That's Scots, too, 'dearie' is, I mean. I'm learning all sorts of new words from Robert, that's part of the fun of having him here, isn't it? It was easy, really, the pudding, I mean. I was a little disappointed not to open our wee gifts tonight—more Scots, isn't it *fun*! But Robert says in America they open gifts Christmas morning. So, of course we will, too. I think Ernst is giving me a scarf. I wish I had it tonight! It's as cold as the Alps, don't you think? I found him a nice pin for his tie. The boys helped, of course. I'd have only thought of something practical, like socks, and how silly that would be! I can buy him socks any time, can't I? Gifts are special, not something you get just because the old ones have holes in the toes too big to be darned. Just like birthdays, or anything else. And, of course, I might not get another chance, because who knows where our Robert will be next winter. You're all graduating and off to the four winds and we'll be back to just our quiet little household. We've grown so used to all of you coming and going and Robert playing at all hours! The house will seem terribly lonely, won't it, dear?"

"Now, Tante Hanne, one year at a time," Robert says. "I have no idea what I'll be doing a year from now and neither does anyone else. Besides, I could always drop in for the holidays."

"Ah, that would be grand, dearie, wonderful! Promise you will! We'll have the wee little Tannenbaum for you and everything. And the cootie pudding. And—"

"*Clootie* pudding!" Robert laughs.

"I know it now, of course!" she whispers to me. "But it's so much fun to tease him!"

Crowds pack the streetcar tighter at every stop as we rattle toward the Altstadt. It's a relief to step off into the main square in front of the Dom and breathe freely again, though the cold river air fills our lungs like splinters of ice. People stream toward the cathedral's huge western doors, past dozens of carriages drawn by horses whose breath steams upward in great clouds.

If anything, the still air inside the Dom feels colder than outside, even as the pews fill with people. Robert and Felix decide on a row near the back, where we lay out our cushions, wrap ourselves in our blankets and settle in to watch the parade of arrivals. Under the blankets, Joseph quietly takes my gloved hand in his. I feel my face warm by several degrees, but I feel no desire to pull away.

Among the crowd of strangers and some of our classmates, we spot the Kurtz family heading for the reserved pews at the front, doubtless equipped with braziers and foot warmers. Katerina sports a fur-trimmed velvet cloak in royal blue and a matching hat with feathers; Madame's identical outfit is the color of red wine. Between them, Herr Kurtz wears a sober black overcoat and carries a top hat.

"Extravagantly impressive, aren't they?" I say.

"No, just extravagant," Joseph says.

"Look who's with them," Felix says from my other side.

I have to crane my neck to see. Sure enough, Otto von Marburg has Katerina's arm tucked firmly into his. Reinhold, close behind with his parents, has a young woman on his arm outfitted, as far as I can tell, entirely in fur. I start to point them out to the others when Marburg happens to turn in our direction. His normal expression of bored superiority gives way to surprise, and then to a sneer. He whispers something in his young lady's ear. I can't see her reaction.

"Aristocrats!" Joseph snorts. "Nowadays, it just means you wear expensive clothes, treat other people like servants, and don't pay your bills. We've had plenty like them through our office. They always want to modernize castles with no plumbing and century-old mildew everywhere and they never pay without a fight. I'd guess the son got his manners from his parents."

"Probably," I say. "Luckily, we'll be done in six months and then he'll join some prestigious orchestra and get famous on his family connections. Arnold says he wants to go to Berlin."

"You can't cheat in music," Joseph says. "I've seen how hard you all work. Family connections may get you in, but if you don't work, you'll get booted right back out."

Gerda and Thomas emerge from the crowd and inch down the row toward us.

"Come on, there's room!" I call. "Everyone, this is Gerda and Thomas. Thomas's Papa is in the orchestra."

"I'm not sure how long he'll last," Gerda says. "But he wanted so much to see his Papa play. He brought Bear with him, so he might just go to sleep. I hope, anyway." Thomas produces a small and exceedingly well-loved stuffed bear for our inspection and, before I quite know how it happens, he's snuggling on Tante Hanne's lap.

"How does she *do* that?" I ask Joseph.

"Happens every time she meets a child," he says. "When they're too big for her lap, she settles for feeding them. As you've discovered."

I'm still marveling at this gift of Hanne's when the musicians take their seats on the dais. The chorus files onto risers behind them, at least eighty men in black suits and women in dark blue robes. Performing together, I can't help noticing, and yet the world is not ending. Next, the soloists: two men in tuxedos and two women in long-sleeved velvet gowns, the mezzo in dark green and the soprano in brilliant red, each with a long matching scarf about her neck. An uncommon accessory, but then, the Dom is an uncommonly cold concert hall. The orchestra tunes. At last, the conductor enters, bows, raises his baton, and Bach's great opening fanfare of drums and trumpets rings down the stone walls, just as I imagined it would.

Herr Dietrich wasn't joking about the Christmas Oratorio's length: the three parts last two whole hours. Bach never rushes: his long, majestic phrases build and repeat in the best Baroque style. Even though it isn't my story, even though, despite my pillow, I begin to ache by the second intermission, I feel like I'm flying on the music, soaring around the massive fluted columns and up past the high stained-glass windows, into the great vaults of the roof on billows of sound.

Herr Walter has his eyes closed, whether for better hearing or better sleeping I can't tell. The others study the orchestra, whispering occasionally. Gerda watches her husband. Tante Hanne gazes down at Thomas, sleeping curled up under a blanket on her lap, with an expression of exquisite tenderness. I catch Joseph watching me watch them, his expression thoughtful, private. I glance away, feeling as if I have somehow intruded.

At last, the final ringing chords reverberate up and down the nave while the conductor keeps his arms raised high to let the echoes diminish into profound silence. Only then does thunderous applause echo off the walls. The crowd rises to its feet. Robert says under the noise, "Don't you just want to yell, 'One more time!'?"

"Honestly, no," Joseph says.

Tante Hanne reluctantly hands Thomas back to his mother.

"What a sweet child!" she says. "He slept beautifully."

"I hope he wasn't too heavy," Gerda says. "He's almost too much for me. But Wil should be out soon and I'll trade him his violin case for a sleeping boy."

"Oh, yes, we want to see him!" I say.

"We're meeting by the western doors," Gerda says. "Come on, we'll wait together."

We gather our pillows and blankets and edge our way out to a spot by one of the pillars away from the crowd to wait. The square teems with people, talking, laughing, embracing, heading for home.

"Ooh! You're here! Wasn't it grand?!" Katerina appears, dragging Otto by the hand while her parents follow behind. "Papá! Mamá! Look who's here!"

Herr Kurtz shakes my hand while Madame looks pointedly the other way.

"I've been dying to introduce you! Otto, this is my amazing violin teacher, Marthe Adler."

"A pleasure to meet you at last, Fraülein," Otto says and kisses my hand. He bears a slight resemblance to his brother about the cheekbones, but their manners couldn't be more different. "Katerina sings your praises. And I admired your Schumann Quintet very much."

His voice is silky and deep and he's undeniably handsome. I can see why Katerina finds him irresistible. Her puppy eyes are almost embarrassing.

"She's too kind," I say. "And I understand you are a considerable pianist."

Otto laughs. "Christmas carols are my specialty," he says. "I rely on the violinist to carry the tunes."

I decide this isn't the moment to ask him why his brother keeps harassing me. Instead, I make all the other introductions, which takes some time and involves a lot of shaking hands and bowing. At this moment the younger Marburg and his parents walk out the cathedral door. Again, Reinhold happens to look in my direction and the sneer returns to his face. I brace myself.

"Thinking of converting, then?" he says.

"To Bach-ism, perhaps," I say.

"I can't think why you'd be here otherwise," he says.

His young lady giggles. Katerina looks shocked. Herr Kurtz frowns. Joseph's hand tightens on my arm. The elder Marburgs appear not to have heard.

"Shut up, you idiot," Otto snarls in a low tone. "Go on, get out of here. Go be a fool somewhere else."

"We *all* have better things to do," Reinhold says. He smirks and saunters off, his fur-clad companion's arm tucked into his.

"Fräulein," Otto bows again, "please allow me to apologize for my brother. He's a disgrace. I hope he will learn better. And"—he throws a dagger look over his shoulder at the younger Marburg's retreating form—"soon."

What should I say? That I'm used to it? That this is nothing, you should see what he does at school?

"We're all here for the music. It transcends religion, though it was written for one," Otto continues. "At least, that's my belief."

"And ours," I say.

"Come, Katerina, Otto, our carriage is here," Herr Kurtz says. "My dear, allow me. Fräulein Adler, a pleasure to see you and your friends."

"Goodbye till Saturday, then," Katerina says with a quick hug.

"What did I tell you?" I say quietly in her ear. Then, louder, "Merry Christmas!" as they climb into their carriage and rattle away on the cobbles of the square.

✦　✦　✦

"*Why* didn't I think to have you all stay here?" Tante Hanne laments when we return to the house. "It's *so* late and *so* cold and here you are going out on the streetcars again! We could have had a lovely slumber party with hot chocolate and more cookies and then you'd have been here for Christmas morning! It's almost here, after all! Well, next time, then! Now, Marthe, dear, Joseph is taking you home and no arguing. You simply must let him, it isn't safe for a woman out at this hour, even if it is Christmas Eve."

"I wouldn't dream of arguing, Tante Hanne. Joseph is very kind."

"We'd best be going," Joseph says.

The others murmur agreement, though Franz looks disappointed about the slumber party. We exchange farewells, collect our instruments and head back out into the cold.

The Ehrenfeld car arrives first. Felix, Joseph and I climb on board, leaving Franz and Arnold dissecting the performance.

"What a night!" I say. "I'm exhausted, but I'll remember it, always."

"The Dom was built for music," Joseph says. "That Marburg brat, though . . ."

"It almost wouldn't have been as special without him," I say.

"What did he say?" Felix asks. "I was doing my best to ignore him." We tell him.

"Idiot!" Felix snorts.

"Funny, that's what his brother called him," I say.

"Just try to avoid him," Joseph says.

"I do my best. You see how well it works. Six months, that's all."

I'm too tired to say any more. At my stop we say goodbye to Felix and walk up Hildegardstrasse under a black web of bare trees. Our steps fall into a slow, easy rhythm on the icy sidewalk. Joseph tucks my hand into his. I find I'm not eager for this night to end, to climb the dark stairs to our flat, only to lie awake and worry about the future.

Joseph stops under a tree. I stop, too.

He lifts my chin gently with his free hand. His eyes look directly into mine with an expression of anxiety, even worry, but also warmth—and longing. No one has ever looked at me with such complex eyes. It suddenly dawns on me that Anni and Gerda might have been right about him and I—I might have been wrong.

290

"May I—" he whispers.

I nod, barely moving. I feel myself falling into his eyes. I see every detail about them, how they crinkle at the corners, the little gold flecks in the irises that reflect the moonlight. He bends his face down to mine and kisses me, very softly, on the lips.

He pulls away, studies me, questioning. For answer, giving in to the moment, I let go of his hand and slide my arm around him. He pulls me to him and kisses me again, longer and more purposefully. I don't know how long we stand there, heedless of the cold. Minutes, maybe, or hours. Through all our layers of coats and mufflers we feel our hearts race, and the world is ours alone.

20

WINTER, DECEMBER 1909–APRIL 1910

December 1909

"You won't despise me if I confess I got a little bored?" Katerina says the following Saturday.

"There's no denying it was a long night," I say. "So, no, I won't."

"Thank goodness for the foot warmers, though! And Otto kept his arm around me the entire time, so I didn't get cold. And your young man—how handsome he is! I can tell he's mad about you."

Foot warmers. I thought so. As for my "young man," I've decided to stop being quite so dismissive of comments of that sort.

"Um, well . . . and Otto seems quite the gentleman."

"Always." Katerina frowns. "I was so embarrassed, though. Reinhold should never have spoken to you like that. I'm sure Otto reprimanded him *very* firmly about it later."

"Not that it's any of my business, but which of them takes after the rest of the family?"

Katerina bites her lip. "Otto's mother is very nice to me," she says. "A little distant, but they're nobility, you know, and we're not. His father is the old-fashioned stern type. He and Papá both sit on the Sinfonia board. He's always very respectful to Papá."

Because Papá's his main creditor, I think. But I don't say it.

"You remember I warned you about Reinhold," I say.

She nods. I don't belabor the point.

"Then let's begin," I say in my carrying teacher voice, and we do.

✦　✦　✦

292

Herr Zeidler must be pacing his sitting room like a caged and hungry lion, impatient for the winter holidays to end. We may be the best student orchestra he's ever had, but his mammoth program will take every available second of the term to shape into some semblance of proficiency.

I, by contrast, wish the holiday were longer, so I could have more of the music under my fingers before I submit to the annual ritual of having to demonstrate bits of it for the inspiration of my male counterparts. I make sure the first few pages of each work are reasonably competent before digging deeper into any of them—and so much digging lies ahead.

The Berlioz borders on bizarre. The Tchaikovsky favors a great deal of very rapid finger work. The Bruckner is enormous and intimidating. The Strauss, a light dessert after three heavy courses, at least demonstrates that Herr Zeidler, as well as being a sadist, has a sense of humor. I hope, without much optimism, that the Wolff will have some mercy regarding my recital work, to give me a chance to master this mountain of music before April—*Wolff* and *mercy* not being words I would normally pair in the same sentence.

The quartet meets a few more times over the holiday at Felix's house to rehearse the orchestra parts. It's almost funny, turning these huge symphonic pieces into rather incomplete quartets and it's a good excuse to be together and play. We joke about sleeping on cots in the practice rooms, but really, I'm not the only one who would far rather rehearse here.

Otherwise, I spend my days practicing in my bedroom and trying to be a good daughter and a good sister. I try not to think about the unfairness of the first chair business, or what will happen to me after June. I have enough music to learn that I need to put both out of my mind, but they intrude nonetheless with unwelcome frequency.

I think about Joseph, about how he kissed me, and about being kissed. He was kind, polite, shy, gentle, but he *kissed* me. No one ever kissed me before, not like *that*. Maybe Gerda and Anni were right. Maybe he really does love me. How did they know and I didn't? Do I love him? How am I supposed to tell? What should I do?

I never find any answers.

I try to put Joseph out of my mind, too. I can't afford to be distracted, now or in the foreseeable future, however agreeable the distraction might be.

The new year dawns cold under a fresh layer of snow that blankets the whole city. Every black tree branch wears its white coat. Every garden is filled with white mounds, as if the earth itself were bubbling up under the snow. The streets and sidewalks are soon cleared, but still icy. The walk to my streetcar stop on the first day of class, loaded as I am with my case and bag, requires my complete concentration so as not to slip. Even on the streetcar, my breath is a visible, frosty cloud.

✦ ✦ ✦

Monday afternoon.

The first thing I notice on the orchestra seating chart is that Herr Zeidler has seated me directly behind the first chair of the second violin section, one up from last year. So I can have a good view of where I belong, I suppose, or perhaps he expects me to tap the first chair on the shoulder if he's missed something and whisper corrections. At least it isn't Marburg; Herr Zeidler has selected a fellow with the improbable name of Adelhard Schroop. Marburg is behind me, which will require watchfulness. But Felix has, once again, made concertmaster and Franz is first viola. Arnold is in my position behind the first cello.

"I didn't audition." I hadn't noticed Arnold coming up behind me, apparently reading my mind. "I have enough work without being first chair. And I don't really like telling people what to do."

"At least if you told them what to do, they'd do it."

"Maybe," he says.

"Hello!" A familiar voice behind me makes me jump. Christian carries a viola this time. "Sorry to say I won't be your stand-mate in the miniature instrument section this time."

"I'm glad you're playing your preferred instrument," I say. "Oversized though it is."

"Good thing," he says. "This program is oversized, too."

"You'll be in good hands with Franz. It won't be dull, I expect."

"I know him. We have the same teacher," he says. "And I expect you're right."

"Herr Zeidler thinks this will be the strongest orchestra he's ever had," I say.

"Where'd you hear that?" he asks.

"Ah—the usual rumor factory," I say. It would hardly do to reveal the

294

secret of this orchestra's extraordinary potential.

"It's manageable, if people put the work in," he says, glancing over his shoulder at the sound of Marburg's voice.

"Schroop!" Marburg's voice drips with contempt. "At least he didn't make the mistake of picking *you*," he says over his shoulder as he heads toward his seat.

"So, the idiot's back," Christian says. "Pity. I so enjoyed last year without him."

"You know, you're the third person in a month I've heard call him that," I say. "Including his own brother."

"It's a useful euphemism," he says. "Well, off to my spot. See you later."

I settle into my seat and start tuning. Schroop, like Felix, greets everyone in the section and introduces himself to the third-years. Marburg just glares at him.

"Might have a little trouble with that idiot Marburg," he says when he takes his seat again.

"Entirely possible," I say.

"Good afternoon, everyone!"

Herr Zeidler strides across the stage and onto his podium, practically bouncing up and down with eagerness to get started. He taps his baton for attention and the murmur of chatter dies down.

"This will be a spectacular program!" he says. "I've waited years to have an ensemble that could perform work on this level. Just a few words of introduction . . ."

Not that everyone doesn't know the rules by now, though the prospect of adding members of the Sinfonia to our ranks is exciting news to the third-years.

"You are all prepared, I trust?" Heads nod.

"Fraülein Adler? You are prepared also?"

Time for my annual bit of theatre.

"Yes, sir."

"May I please hear the second violin opening of the Berlioz?"

I raise my violin and play it. He knows perfectly well I can play it; I played it at my audition.

"Thank you, Fraülein," he says when I reach the end of the first theme. "I presume you have the rest of the program in hand, as well?"

"Still a few rough spots in the Bruckner," I say with a straight face.

"We shall smooth them out, never fear. Now then. You have all studied the origin and program of Berlioz's *Symphonie Fantastique*? The French express themselves differently from the Germans, as you know. Herr Berlioz is telling us a fanciful version of his own story. His dreams, his passion, his restoration in the natural world. A torrid, unrequited infatuation with an actress. In despair, opium. But opium is a fickle muse, as he is fated to learn. In the end, his downfall. A witches' sabbath—and his beloved among them! It is all on the outside, this emotion. There must be no holding back. No rational German understatement. Are you ready? Then let us begin."

He raises his baton.

The notes are there, more or less, ragged, but not hopeless. But there is a good deal of rational German understatement to be overcome. Clearly, most of us are used to ruling our emotions with a firm Teutonic hand. But Herr Zeidler is delighted.

"A good start! It will come, through steady practice and a close reading of dynamics. I trust no one is considering the use of opium in order to understand it? It is neither necessary nor helpful, believe me. Do not attempt it."

He doesn't crack a smile. Surely, he's joking? But there's no time to think about it; he's on to the Tchaikovsky.

". . . a different sort of love altogether. Not the obsession of a grown man but youthful, impetuous passion. A *first* passion, the very most intense. Rash eagerness. Reckless haste! And, finally, the inevitable tragic consequences. Consider, too, the international provenance of this work: an Italian tale of two unfortunate young lovers made into an English play in the sixteenth century. From the play, this Russian symphonic poem by the great Romantic Tchaikovsky, who was still living when you all were born. Youthful madness is universal, it seems. Perhaps some of you have known this feeling yourselves. To a better end, I trust. Ready?"

He raises his baton again.

After three hours of this, I'm exhausted.

The two works do make a fine pair, though. I'm still hearing them in my head on the streetcar on the way home. Still, I wonder if I would find them more accessible if I had ever felt the intense passions they express.

Because I haven't, and I'm more likely to experience the weather on Mars. I'll have to pay extra attention to those dynamic markings. Maybe that will spare me the need to feel passions firsthand at all. Which might be a good thing, judging by how badly they seem to turn out.

My thoughts drift back to Christmas Eve. And what about Joseph? What about me, for that matter?

I've never felt safer with anyone. Never more enveloped in kindness. I'm happy every minute I'm with him, and comfortable, and a little less shy every time I see him. Is this love? Is it passion? How am I supposed to know? It doesn't feel like *Romeo and Juliet* and definitely not at all like the *Symphonie Fantastique*.

Still no answers. Eventually I give up wondering and just listen to the music in my head.

✦　✦　✦

Tuesday morning.

I'm hurrying down a corridor to Musicology, minding my own business, when I hear a familiar raised voice. I look around for a way to get out of sight and then realize the voice is coming from behind the closed door of Herr Zeidler's office. The voice is Marburg's and, who'd have guessed, he's complaining.

"...should have been mine! Herr Grimmelshausen says so, too. Schroop is a hack! Always turning around to whisper something to Adler—I know I had the best audition. I deserved that chair!"

Herr Zeidler's response is unintelligible. Doubtless Marburg isn't the first disgruntled student he's had in his office complaining about the results of first chair auditions. I should be somewhere far away when that door opens, I really, really should, but my curiosity gets the better of my common sense. I edge closer.

"You are correct in one regard, Herr Marburg," Herr Zeidler says. "Herr Schroop did, in fact, have the second-best audition."

I should go. *Now.*

"Well, then!" Marburg snaps. "He shouldn't have it."

"Is it your opinion, Herr Marburg, that the first-place audition should have the chair?"

"*I* had it. *I* should have the chair."

"It was not you, in fact, Herr Marburg. You placed, if I recall—" A pause; Herr Zeidler must be consulting his notes. "—yes. Fifth. No, in fact, the first-place audition was Fraülein Adler."

Silence. I start walking. The door bursts open.

"You! Listening at the door like a little rat, you—"

"I don't know what you're talking about. I'm on my way to class. Leave me alone."

"There's no way you won that audition. He's making it up. Or you slept with him, or something."

"That certainly is your answer to everything, isn't it?"

I should walk away, but his red face with its contorted expression is too good to pass up, and besides, I don't want to turn my back to him.

"It's so much simpler than that. I keep telling you, I just practice. That's all."

"You—"

Herr Zeidler's door pops open.

"Is there a problem?" he says mildly.

"No, sir," I say. "Herr Marburg is just telling me what he thinks of me. But, of course, I already knew." And I walk away as calmly as I can toward Musicology. As I round the corner, I hear Herr Zeidler say, "There is nothing wrong with your musicianship, you know. It is merely a matter of discipline."

I walk as fast as I can without actually running, which would attract far too much attention, and fall into step with the first friend I encounter, who happens to be Franz.

"You have your Marburg face on," he says.

"Very perceptive," I say, breathing hard.

"It's only the second day. What did that idiot do now?"

"He didn't like the results of the first chair audition. And he didn't like hearing who actually won it. I guess he thinks being several rows back might hurt his chances for the Berlin Phil. I happened to be in the neighborhood."

"Shithead," Franz says.

"Funny thing, that's what Anni calls him."

"I'm keeping it clean for your benefit," he says.

"Very chivalrous," I say. "But not necessary."

We continue in silence to Musicology.

"Six months and I'll be rid of him forever," I say.

"You need to watch out for him," Franz says. "And you need the rest of us to help."

"I'd like to say that's absurd," I say. "But, since it's not . . . thanks."

✦ ✦ ✦

At the next orchestra rehearsal we tackle Bruckner's Symphony No. 7. It sounds thin without the extra musicians we'll have at the end, especially in the brass. I don't know if there are enough brass players in all of Köln; we may have to import some from Bonn. And yet it has a comforting sort of Germanness to it after the Berlioz and the Tchaikovsky: a traditional structure, a language I understand. But we'll be doing well to have the notes by the end of term, never mind the polish, or the brass.

The last hour of rehearsal we devote to Strauss's *Till Eulenspiegel's Merry Pranks*, which is fun and not too terribly difficult, being among the composer's earlier works. We all grew up with stories about the trickster Eulenspiegel, always wriggling out of trouble and off to his next prank.

Perhaps Strauss felt Till needed to be taught a lesson, for the work ends with his execution. Except—at the very end his theme returns, like a secretive wink to say that a fellow like Till can never really be destroyed. The trickster will always stroll among us, mocking with crafty impudence and scorn for puffery. It's hardly a charitable view of human nature, but it provides a robust antidote to the rest of this emotionally wringing program.

Throughout, I keep half an eye on Marburg. He ignores me.

The Wolff expands my lesson to two hours. In Musicology we're studying acoustics, which includes large doses of physics and math, and in Orchestration we're to compose a short symphonic poem.

My Saturday lessons with Katerina begin to feel like a vacation.

✦ ✦ ✦

February 1910

On a cold, wet evening at the end of February when Anni is out somewhere, Mother and I are washing dishes after dinner when I hear a crash behind me. Mother stands in the middle of the kitchen, swaying slightly, a towel in one hand and a broken plate at her feet.

"Wha' happened?" she says. She sounds drunk, but she wasn't at dinner—we only had water with our stew.

"No matter, I'll sweep it up," I say.

"I can't feel it," she says, still swaying. "I can't feel my hand."

I look up at her in alarm. Her eyes look unfocused. Was she drinking all afternoon while I was at school? But I've seen her drunk entirely too often, and she wasn't drunk a half hour ago. This is different.

Her swaying increases. She tries to take a step and stumbles. I drop the broom and take her arm to steady her. This looks like what Anni described last year. She must be having another stroke, or something like it. Panic rises in my chest. What to do? My mind feels paralyzed. Think, I tell myself. *Think*.

"You have to lie down," I say, trying to sound calm. "I'll take you to the sofa. Come on, lean on me. Can you walk a little? That's it. I won't let you fall. Just a little farther. There, lie back on the pillows and I'll put your feet up." I step back and look at her. Her face is slack, her eyes dull. What next?

"I'm going for the doctor," I say, reaching for my coat on the stand by the door.

"Don't need a doctor," she slurs. "Just a little . . . I'll be fine in a . . ." She closes her eyes.

"Stay there!" I order, which seems ridiculous even as I say it. "I'll be back as quick as I can."

I grab my coat, pull my hat over my ears and race out the door, almost forgetting to lock it behind me.

Dr. Goldmann doesn't live far from us, only about four blocks, and he's most fortunately at home, though I interrupt his dinner. He snatches up his medical bag and an umbrella on his way out the front door and walks back with me, his strides so long I practically have to run to keep up.

"I'm sorry to drag you out on an awful night like this," I pant as we round the corner into Hildegardstrasse.

"The weather's not your fault," he says. "I was out during that storm on New Year's Eve, delivering a baby. Wasn't the baby's fault, either. You did right to come. I've been expecting her to have another one of these episodes, and it's easier to diagnose during than after. This is your building, isn't it?"

We race up the stairs. Our door is unlocked, which frightens me, until I realize Anni's come home. She's staring down at Mother, lying exactly where I left her on the sofa with her eyes closed, her breathing irregular.

"There you are! I was hoping you'd gone for the doctor," she says. "I just walked in and found her like this and a broken plate in the kitchen. I thought you'd been fighting."

"Same as you described last time," I say, pulling her out of the way so Doctor Goldmann can examine Mother. "Anyway, throwing plates is your style, not mine."

She doesn't laugh. We subside into anxious silence while the doctor takes her pulse and listens through his stethoscope to her breathing. He shines a small flashlight into her eyes ("Great invention, these things," he says) and presses her hands and feet.

"Can you feel this? Can you feel this?" he asks.

She nods her head. "'S only my hand," she says, her words slurring. "'S better now."

He studies her intently, frowning. "Have you aspirin?" he asks us.

Anni nods and goes to get it. I run for a cup of water from the kitchen.

Doctor Goldmann takes both and deftly gets Mother to swallow a tablet and a drink of water without spilling too much.

"Can you help her into bed?" he says.

Between us, we manage to help Mother into her room and onto her bed. She lies still, her breathing a little less ragged now, her face still limp. Anni's face reflects my own fright. I can only imagine how terrified she was, dealing with this same situation last year by herself.

When we return, the doctor is sitting at the kitchen table, next to the pieces of broken plate on the floor.

"More aspirin in the morning," he says. "It's almost certainly another small stroke. She's had one already, that you know of; she may have had others you don't know about and will quite likely have more. The next could be more severe. If it's severe enough, I'm sorry to say it, but we have no really satisfactory treatment. Yet. Perhaps someday that will change. Then, too, if you'll pardon my bluntness, it's far from the unkindest way to die. The patient suffers relatively little compared to many diseases."

He contemplates us both before continuing. "The most humane course of action in the case of a massive stroke is to do nothing. Really, there is, as I say, nothing to be done. Loosen a collar, or a belt. Hold a hand. It's the body's way of saying it is time. I'm sorry if I sound callous, but it's the truth. Do you understand?"

We glance at each other and nod. Anni's jaw seems very tightly clenched.

"I'll look in on her in the morning," Dr. Goldmann says.

"I leave early," we both say at the same time.

"I'll stop in around seven on my way to the hospital," he says. "And I'll send you my bill." He stands up with a sigh. "I'll let myself out. Please don't trouble yourselves," he says.

We see him to the door and he disappears down the stairs.

"Well," Anni says. "Here we are again."

"I wonder how long we have to go through this," I say.

"It's not up to us."

I think of all the music I should be practicing tonight. I know better than to try.

"Have you eaten?" I say.

"I knew there was something I forgot," she says.

"We had stew. There's some left in the icebox."

"I'll take care of that for you," she says.

I sweep up the forlorn remains of the plate. It was one of our old set, from before.

"Did you think she was just drunk at first?" Anni asks over the clinking of broken china.

I sit back on my heels. "I couldn't figure it out," I say. "It came on so suddenly. And it wasn't like the usual effect of too much Bärenfang. It was . . . odd."

"That's what I thought. Odd."

"I hope she recovers as well this time," I say. "We can't be nurses, we don't have time. And we haven't the money to hire one."

"I could quit my job—"

"You will not! You deserve to have your own income."

"I like that part, to be honest, if not much of the rest of it. And you'd better not be thinking of taking time off from Conservatory."

"Ugh, no. I'm nearly done. That would be terrible."

"Agreed," she says. "So, she'd better recover. We'll tell her in the morning. No lasting effects allowed."

"Maybe she'll listen to *you*," I say.

"That's when we *know* she's not right in the head," she says.

Mother is better enough the next morning to be upset about the expense of calling Dr. Goldmann, who looks in as promised and advises her to keep taking aspirin, rest for a day or two and then get up and take some exercise.

With low expectations, I head out the door to school.

✦ ✦ ✦

The Wolff comments on my distraction and the pallor of my face. I tell her the truth. It sounds as if I'm making excuses, even though I'm not. She assures me a leave of absence, if I need one, will do my record no harm, but I'll have to repeat any class I don't complete. I refuse even to consider it, at least until I absolutely have to. Fortunately, we are far enough along in mastering the orchestra program that my lackluster efforts don't attract undue attention. My quartet-mates greet me with, "You look awful," and offer sympathy. Arnold even pats me gingerly on the shoulder, but there's nothing they can do.

The uncertainty hurts, like a tight band around my chest. If Dr. Goldmann is correct, it is not a matter of if, but when, Mother will have another such stroke, or a larger one. It could happen at any moment. Or maybe months from now, or maybe years.

I have to push away my worry and fear, or I won't be able to do what I have to do. *Not now,* I tell myself as I did before, whenever I lock the front door behind me. At school, I throw myself into the work. Practice, grapple with the physics of sound, practice, belabor my symphonic poem (a sophomoric hash which luckily will never be played anywhere by anyone), practice. The more I'm completely immersed in the work, the better I can keep my fear at bay.

When I go home, fear greets me at the door. But Mother seems to return more or less to herself in a week or so, though she has good days and bad days. Anni and I take turns trying to get her outside for short walks. The weather is treacherous, so up to the streetcar stop and back is about all we can manage. I bring home groceries, I cook, I clean up, I practice and study, study and practice. The days pass into March. The orchestra concert begins to loom ominously closer.

✦   ✦   ✦

March 1910

Orchestra rehearsals increase to four times a week. The sprawling program comes together slowly, particularly the Bruckner. But the unflappable Herr Zeidler hasn't been leading student orchestras for thirty years for nothing. He repeats and repeats, measure by measure, until he gets what he wants and he gets it without shouting, without berating, without undue humiliation. Even Marburg starts doing better.

Still, we never walk out of rehearsal without wondering if our fingers will fall off before we're done. I consider that, if I never play Bruckner again, I'll live a life of perfect contentment. Arnold and Felix feel the same.

Franz, however, is a convert. The stranger and more unconventional Bruckner's harmonies and structures, the better he likes them.

"He's trying something new," he says. "Messing with the old forms and rules. If you don't do that, at some point you just stagnate. Bruckner's not the only one. Strauss is pushing, too, not just playing new tunes to old rules. Some composers now are pushing way past him, even. Schoenberg, in Vienna. He's writing music without any key signatures at all."

"I've heard of him," I say, "but you won't be hearing that stuff around here any time soon."

"You wait," Franz says. "Someday the old fossils will be gone and the world will move on."

"You revolutionary, you," Arnold says.

"Thank you, sir," Franz says with a wide grin.

The last week of the term I finish my ridiculous miniature symphonic poem and decide I know as much about physics as I'm ever going to. The Sinfonia musicians arrive for our final rehearsals. A dozen brass players have been recruited from somewhere and, along with extra percussion, winds and strings, turn our student orchestra into a full Romantic powerhouse. As before, they're pleasant, if businesslike; for many, their own Conservatory days aren't long behind them. They remember what it was like to be in our place. The third-years are wide-eyed. We fourth-years try to act unimpressed, although we're as excited as before to mingle with the professionals.

Whether because of the goading presence of a woman in the orchestra, or because of the arrival of the Sinfonians, or because we've finally beaten it into submission, our mammoth program is coalescing, just in time.

✦ ✦ ✦

Performance day turns out to be one of Mother's bad days. She has no symptoms, but wakes up grouchy, complaining of old aches and new pains. I was hoping she would come hear us and I'm disappointed when she declines.

"I'd like to hear you play your father's violin," she says. "Not that you can pick it out of the crowd. But it's too cold and I haven't the strength. I might fall."

"It's best she's not coming," Anni says as we walk briskly toward the streetcar stop. The trees along the street are just beginning to leaf out; their branches arch against the gray April sky like painted lines. "She'd be exhausted before you start, even though it's in the afternoon. And then she'd just complain the whole time. At least now I can enjoy it."

"It is a brutally long program," I say. "I'm glad you're coming."

"Is there a party after?"

"Not that I know of. Just the reception."

"I'll have to make do."

"I'm glad you like my friends."

"The cookies are better than the ones at fencing matches."

"So *that's* what you and Franz have in common. I wondered what you two had taken to talking about."

"Oh, just plotting world domination and general mayhem," she says.

"Well, that was my first thought," I say.

I leave Anni at Café Max Bruch and head for the women's toilet to slip into my beloved black gown. *Maybe the last time,* I think. Because next term I have to wear the other one and after Conservatory, who knows when I'll have a chance to perform again. When I arrive backstage several people are already there, doing some last-minute practicing, mostly troublesome bits of Bruckner. I can think of several troublesome bits of Bruckner I should practice, too. So, I unpack, find a corner and practice them.

"What are you practicing for? You know your parts better than anyone here."

I turn to see Christian unpacking his viola.

"You can't be too well-prepared," I say.

"You're not afraid it'll get stale?"

"Not very."

"Good luck," he says, starting to tune. "Not that you need it."

Marburg saunters by and ignores us. Christian's eyes follow him across the room.

"Has the idiot given you any more trouble?" he says in a low voice.

I shake my head.

"He'd be wise not to," he says. "But he's not wise. He's not even very bright."

"Three more months," I say in the same low voice.

The room fills. It seems almost no time before Herr Schädler sticks his head in the door and says, "Places!"

The last time I'll sit in an orchestra. I try not to think about it.

We're good. We're actually *very* good. The professionals inspire us. The electrifying effect of having enough brass inspires us. Our unusually large audience inspires us; we absorb their energy and respond to it. The Berlioz builds to its frenzied witches' sabbath. The rash young lovers of *Romeo and Juliet* don't stand a chance against their passion.

The Bruckner is still a mountain, but a mountain we've climbed enough times that we finally know the way. The rough patches go reasonably well and I save my inevitable slips without choking anyone around me. After that I breathe better, experience the wonderful feeling of teamwork, of being an essential part of the art we're creating, which will never be created exactly the same, ever again.

Till Eulenspiegel sparkles with playfulness and irreverence. Everyone is tired and sweating, but our exhilaration from having survived Bruckner and the audience's energy both carry us along. When Till's theme recurs at the very end, it feels like a triumph, not only of the trickster's resilience, but of the orchestra's hard work, my own hard work, and Herr Zeidler's confidence in us. *It is in large part because of you,* he said. I smile to myself as we attack the final flourish and hold our bows aloft in the ringing silence until he gives the signal to drop them. We've done it. *I've* done it. If I never get a chance to play in an orchestra again, I will always have this concert.

Applause reverberates through the hall. Herr Zeidler motions to us to stand. I feel like more than a lone woman on a stage with a great many men.

I feel like an artist.

✦ ✦ ✦

In the foyer afterward, people I don't know tell me I was wonderful. Of course, I know it's impossible to distinguish one player from another in an orchestra this size. But I do stand out in a crowd. A few people stare (where have they been the last three years?), but fortunately no one seems inclined to lecture me on my impropriety.

Out of the corner of my eye I notice a vaguely familiar, important-looking man elbowing his way through the crowd, speaking to the fourth-years and handing them cards. Felix, Franz, and Arnold take them with a look of surprise and a nod of thanks. The man glances in my direction and turns away.

Joseph and Robert stroll up with cups of punch. "That was stupendous!" Joseph says.

"I thought I worked hard," Robert says. "You people make me feel like I've been on vacation all term."

"Piece of cake," I say, giggling.

Robert laughs and vanishes into the crowd to find more people to congratulate. Joseph and I start over to where our families have picked up their conversations where they left off last term.

"I—" he begins.

"Darling!" Katerina flutters up, kisses me on both cheeks and gushes excitedly for a while, then turns to exclaim over Felix, Arnold and Franz (who takes a step back) before rushing off to Otto's side. Herr Kurtz shakes my hand solemnly and follows her. Joseph clears his throat as the Wolff appears out of nowhere.

"Now you will be able to concentrate on the important work," she says.

"I may give my fingers a day off," I say.

"Not more than two," she says with no change of expression.

"Four, maximum," I say.

"Three. Not a day more." She nods and walks away.

"I was wondering—" Joseph says.

"I hope you know you have an appointment with me at my shop at ten on Sunday morning. We need to measure you for the new spring recital gown I designed for you."

Johanna and Heidi have appeared from nowhere.

"I was going to wear the blue one," I say. "I surely don't need *three* gowns?"

"My dear, we talked about this already. Solo recital is important," she says. "Ros and Berit both had new gowns for theirs. You should, too."

"Ros and Berit have money, too," I say.

She waves that off. "You'll love what I came up with," she says. "And then you'll be equipped for years of professional engagements. You haven't found a necklace yet, I suppose? Never mind, there's time. Sunday morning at ten. See you there!" And they wave and depart.

"A necklace?" Joseph says.

"Johanna and Ros are obsessed with my having some metal object around my neck. Ros dragged me to secondhand shops all over town. It was awful. I saw some of the ugliest jewelry ever made, you wouldn't believe it. I told her I didn't care. I'm fine with a bare neck, believe me."

"Would you wear one if you had it?" he says. "If it weren't ugly, I mean."

"I suppose, as long as it wouldn't scratch the violin. But it doesn't matter."

"Ah," he says. "By the way, I was wondering—"

"I'm so sorry your mother is ill." Frau Apfelbaum bustles up, looking very concerned. Everyone else echoes their best wishes for her speedy recovery. I promise to tell her when I get home.

Oma Judith marches over with her cane tapping the marble floor of the foyer. "So, you finally did something modern!" she says. "About time."

"Franz definitely agrees with you," I say.

"And you?" There's something hawk-like about Oma Judith.

"It's been interesting," I say. "Of the two, I prefer the Strauss."

She laughs a barking sort of laugh. "Diplomatic!" she says, raising her glass of punch to me. She leans in on her cane. "The hardest trick in life is to look back and forward at the same time." She raps her cane on the floor for emphasis. "Keep the past with you and keep pushing ahead. Hardest thing in the world."

"You mean in music?" I ask.

"In anything! Everything! Life! Music, certainly. It's even harder when you're old, but you have to keep pushing. Remember that. Remember I told you."

"I'll try, Oma Judith," I say. "Along with everything else you've told me."

"Good," she says. "You do that."

"Where's Anni?" I suddenly realize I don't see her.

"She left right afterward," Oma Judith says. "Told me to tell you she thought you did all right. But she wanted to get back to your mother. She didn't feel right leaving her alone so long."

"She's been alone nearly every day for over a month," I say. It's childish of me, but I feel a little hurt. I was looking forward to Anni's teasing.

"She wanted you to have a chance to enjoy yourself without worrying. No, she actually said that. So go enjoy yourself. And don't worry. She's a most interesting young woman, your sister."

"Yes," I say. "Yes, she is."

"Anyway, you held your own," Oma Judith says.

"For the last time," I say.

"Talk to Ros," Oma says. "She's having a grand time in her orchestra in Amsterdam and all women means a lot fewer big heads to get in the way. She plays plenty of duets with her young man, too."

"Her young man?"

"You remember Jan, the Dutch fellow whose aunt got her the audition."

"Oh. Right."

Oma Judith winks and limps off, tapping her cane heavily on the stone floor.

"Speaking of interesting people," Joseph says. "By the way, I was wondering if you have—"

Felix arrives at that moment.

"Who was that man who talked to you when we came out?" I ask him.

"Oh. Er—that was Reinecke, from the Sinfonia," he says. "Just congratulating everyone. He mentioned you, too, but you were somewhere else."

I wasn't, of course. I was right here.

"He's inviting fourth years to audition, isn't he?" The cards. Of course. Scouting talent for a growing orchestra. Getting reports from the musicians who worked with us. That explains why he turned away from me.

"Well, yes," Felix says, looking both awkward and sheepish. "But you know he'll be asking you someday. Soon. We're in the modern world now. All kinds of stupid rules will wither up and die. You wait. It won't be long. You've shown the way right here."

"Absolutely," Joseph says.

"And in the meantime, he'll be begging you to solo."

"No doubt," I say.

The crowd begins to break up. Felix wanders off to talk to Franz.

"I was wondering—do you have some place to go this evening?" Joseph says.

"Just home."

"Come home with me for dinner," he says. "Mama would be thrilled. I'll take you home afterward. Like old times."

"I should get back and help Anni," I say.

"Help Anni do what?" he says.

"Look after Mother."

"Anni wanted you to be free to celebrate. You can let her go play tomorrow."

I look up at his hopeful smile and remember Christmas Eve under the bare trees on Hildegardstrasse.

"All right," I say. "I'm convinced."

I didn't take much convincing.

By the time I return home it's quite late. Mother has gone to sleep. Anni is reading on the sofa.

"Have fun?" she says.

"I did, thanks to you," I say.

"My pleasure," she says. "You earned it. By the way, I'm out all day tomorrow and back late. So, you'll be on duty."

"I'll be here. All I want to do for the next couple of days is sleep."

"I guessed as much."

"How's Mother?" I ask.

"Asleep," Anni says. "She was glad your concert went well. I thought you did all right, by the way."

"Oma Judith told me," I say. "Thanks."

"She's a very interesting person," Anni says.

"Funny, that's what she said about you."

"We're fellow subversives." She grins her dangerous little grin at me and goes back to her book.

Not for the first time, I wonder if I should worry.

21

April 1910

On Sunday morning I arrive at Johanna's shop, resolved to tell her *No*, I can't afford another gown, I don't need another gown, my beautiful blue gown will be perfect for my solo recital, and I'm very grateful, thank you a hundred times over, but *No*.

"Here are the sketches," Johanna says.

Several drawings are spread out on the cutting table in the back room. A far more sophisticated version of me looks up from the loose pages, holding her violin and bow. Her dress is a slim, sleeveless sheath with a high waist. A knee-length over-layer of some light, lacy fabric covers the shoulders and creates elbow-length sleeves with long flowing backs. Her hair is styled in a French roll and a filigree necklace of gold and pearls graces her neck. It does look beautiful, I have to admit.

"It's gorgeous," I say. "But I can't—"

"This style should be good for the next five to ten years. And a professional musician definitely needs more than one gown. You might have two performances in one place. You might have one being repaired. Every couple of years you get a new one and eventually retire the oldest or most worn."

"Yes, but I don't have—"

Johanna plants her hands on her hips and looks at me sternly. "You want a career, yes?"

"Yes," I say, "but right now—"

"Then listen to me. I don't know about the violin, but I do know about presenting yourself. Especially a woman in a man's world. You're almost there, almost ready to start breaking the doors down. You need to look the part you *want* to play, not the part you've been playing. You need to look like you *know* how good you are. You need to look assured, confident, up-to-date, like you're already successful, not like a student on a threadbare budget, begging. You're not *asking* the men in charge of the music world for permission to enter. You're *telling* them to make room for you. Because you're *that good*. Every part of you needs to send that message and that includes your clothes, your hair, your jewelry."

I begin to object.

"I agree, it isn't fair. Men buy a couple of formal suits and they're set for life. A woman's presentation is more subtle and complex. Maybe because women are subtle and complex, I don't know. But that's how the world is. I dress all kinds of women for all kinds of purposes. I'm not telling you this just to sell you a gown or put my name on something. I'm telling you this because it's true."

She waits. The silence stretches out.

"I believe you," I say, finally. "I believe everything you say. The truth is, I don't have the first notion of how to break into that world. I don't know if I can, or if I'm good enough. And even if I am good enough, even if I manage to do it, I don't know if I can survive in it."

"You ask the people who can help you," Johanna says. "You know people in that world already. Teachers. Friends. Ask them for introductions. Find a manager. Nobody in any profession succeeds without help from a lot of other people. When you're established, you help younger people who are trying to do the same thing. It's not complicated. Not nearly as complicated as dressing yourself. As for surviving in it, there's only one way to answer that question and that's to break the doors down and find out. If you want my very amateur opinion, I'd say, yes, you most certainly can. And not because I want to make every gown you'll ever own, although I do."

I can't meet her eyes. "Thanks," I say in a very small voice.

"Any questions?"

I shake my head.

"All right then. Let's get back to the sketches, shall we?"

I nod and try very hard not to think about the expense.

"I recommend a blue-green satin. Like your blue gown, it will work all year. When you have dozens, we'll branch out to seasonal colors like red."

"Dozens. Right," I say.

"The overlayer is a darker version of the same color in a silk lace chiffon. Here, feel it."

The lace feels soft and flowing, like water pouring through my fingers.

"It will move with you, every motion. Your bow arm's best friend," she says.

"How do I walk in this skinny dress?"

"Ah, I'm glad you asked," she says. "The sheath is the new silhouette for the new century. But in order to maintain the slim shape and yet allow you to walk onto a stage like a normal human being, this sheath has—inverted pleats! Look here, on each side."

She pulls out another sketch. "Here, starting at the hip. When you're standing still you can hardly see it. But when you walk, it will give you enough room to take a normal stride. It leaves the front and back smooth under the lace. What do you think?"

"You're a genius," I say.

"When you're famous, I'll make all your gowns," she says, smiling. "Remember that."

"Agreed," I say.

"Fitting in two weeks," she says and ushers me out the front door of the shop.

✦ ✦ ✦

"Dr. Goldmann stopped in today while you were out," Mother says at dinner that night. Anni is out somewhere.

"I'm sorry I missed him. What did he say?"

"Nothing I didn't expect," she says.

I look up from my potatoes. "What do you mean?" I ask.

"What do you think I mean?" she snaps. "I have as much strength as that sack of potatoes you brought home today and Dr. Goldmann says my heart isn't strong. You think I'll live forever at this rate? Puh. I don't. 'Not too long,' he said. I'm glad he said it. I'm not a child, I don't need to be lied to. I've lost a husband; I know something about losing things. It made me think, though."

"What about?" I try to keep my voice casual. She's not saying anything I don't know, but hearing her say the words gives me chills.

She chews a bite of potato. Chews some more. Swallows. Reaches for her water glass. Drinks, sets it down. Looks out the window and back. I wait.

"Things I'm glad of," she says finally. "I'm glad I've lived long enough to see you and Anni get along. You two, like ice and fire. I thought you'd end up hating each other. Somehow, you didn't. Maybe we did a better job than we thought. You must always be good to each other, you and Anni. Though God knows what will become of you, you're both so determined not to play by the rules."

"The rules are changing. We can at least try to live on our own terms, as men do."

She shakes her head. "I wish you'd both get married," she says. "You'd be secure then. That would make me happy."

"Maybe someday. If the right person comes along."

Mother looks at the ceiling, then back to me. "The right person," she says. "Well, let's hope."

✦   ✦   ✦

The Saturday before spring term begins, Joseph picks me up for an afternoon walk in the Rheinpark across the river. Spring is hesitant after our cold, cold winter and the earth in the flowerbeds is still dark and bare. Beech and birch trees are just beginning to soften their dark branches with pale green edges. We walk and walk, saying little, my arm tucked into his, gravel crunching under our feet, our breath visible in the chilly air.

It feels good to get out of the flat, good to be walking. Good to adjust my eyes to the vast expanse of the park after months of closed-in walls and crowded, slushy streets. Good to be next to someone who appreciates quiet.

The future looks a lot closer now that winter term is over. Nothing but the last few classes and my recital and then I'm done. And if Mother's right, soon Anni and I will be on our own, the last of our family. I've pushed this thought away, walled it off, ever since Mother's stroke in

February. Maybe it's good Mother said it, forcing me to confront reality, so I can prepare. So we can both prepare. But how?

And what then?

"You're very pensive," Joseph says.

"Sorry," I say. "It's so good to be outdoors, moving, breathing fresh air. I feel like someone's lifted a rock off all the things I couldn't think about during the term."

"Such as?" he says. "If you want to talk about them, I mean. It's not my place to pry."

I look up at him, searching his warm eyes with the gold flecks, the same ones I fell into on Christmas Eve. My own eyes sting, not only from the cold.

I tell him everything. My mother. My future, or lack of it. The Wolff, who talks as if orchestra conductors will be lining up to engage me when they hear me play the Bruch, and yet Reinecke, the Sinfonia's conductor, handed his cards to the men, looked right through me and turned away. Not that I didn't know it would happen, but how badly it stung me. The loss of my quartet. Because I will lose them, I feel sure of it. They're good, they'll get work, maybe not even in Köln. What Johanna said. Anni, so young, and what good is it to be a superb fencer but indifferent to the needs of everyday life? She needs parents, not an older sister with problems of her own.

As for marriage, if there's a man alive who will marry her, I'll eat my violin.

All the while, we walk. Joseph doesn't interrupt, not even once.

"I shouldn't burden you with all this," I say finally. "You must be sorry you asked."

"Not at all," he says. "I'm sorry your mother is so ill, though. I didn't realize it was that bad."

"We can't do anything but wait for another stroke," I say. "And if it's big, wait some more. Do nothing, because there's nothing to be done. That's what the doctor said."

"You'd still have the flat, wouldn't you?"

"I suppose," I say.

"That's good," he says. "You'll have a safe place to plan."

"I can't imagine it with just Anni and me," I say. "Mostly just me.

Between work and the fencing club and wherever else, she's almost never home. Maybe she belongs to a secret society. A clandestine organization of warrior princesses."

"That wouldn't surprise me in the least. All the better for your practicing," he says. "And teaching. When you're not playing concerts, I mean."

"Don't mock me, Joseph!"

"I'd never mock you. I have every confidence in your future, even if you don't. But I know all musicians teach."

"I suppose they do."

"What do your teachers say?"

"About teaching?"

"About your solo career."

"The Wolff said being a soloist is a hard life. We haven't talked about it since last fall."

"And Herr Dietrich?"

"He said to think about it. That was over a year ago."

"Well, you've thought about it. Johanna's right. They're the people who can help you get started. Make introductions, help you arrange auditions."

He makes it sound so simple. It doesn't seem simple to me, but he's right; at least they're a starting point.

"What do you think?"

"I don't know any orchestra conductors, but if I did, I'd tell them to hear you," he says.

"I mean about my being a soloist. Traveling all over, living out of a trunk, not having a real home—"

"And playing the greatest music in the greatest cities in the world? I think it sounds amazing. Well worth the difficulties."

"Would you still be my friend?" It just pops out. Immediately, I feel foolish, like a child.

The gravel stops crunching under our feet. A cloud pushed along by the April wind crosses the sun and briefly erases all the highlights and shadows, then just as quickly continues on its path across the sky. The branches above us with their new leaves wave their long, twiggy fingers. A few loose strands of hair blow across my face as I look up into his. I should apologize for being so ridiculous, but he doesn't seem offended. I can't read his expression at all.

"Marthe," he says. He shakes his head a little, as if to clear his thoughts.

"Marthe. I will always love you. No matter where you go or what you do. I will always love you."

A long pause.

"You—you will?"

"I will."

"I didn't—I didn't know."

"You know now," he says. And he leans down and kisses me again, there in crisp April daylight in the middle of the Rheinpark, where anyone can see us.

He doesn't ask me if I love him, too. Right now, right this minute, I think maybe I do.

✦ ✦ ✦

The day before classes start, I put new strings on my violin, tune them, and apply some serious practice to my recital pieces. After being far off for months, my recital looms closer even than last week, like an oncoming train. I've practiced the music since last fall, of course, and I have much of it memorized, but I need to be able to start or stop at any measure, get it up to tempo, shape it, polish it until it gleams, and the Wolff will know just by listening precisely how many days I spent over the break not doing that. A few days away from the material at some point may be beneficial, but too many and I'll have lost a dangerous amount of ground.

Of the Bach sonata's four movements—a short Adagio, a long Fugue, a slow Largo, and a final Allegro—the Fugue is in a class by itself: twelve minutes of double stops and weaving lines, each demanding precision in pitch, volume, tone, and coherence, with no margin for error. The whole must fit together, like the pieces of a puzzle arranged, not in space, but in time.

Yet every time I play it, I find more depth in it. When Bach composes for a single voice, as in this sonata or the partita I played two years ago, he is, I still believe, setting the universe to music.

Next, the Bruch. The Wolff says it's one of the great German violin concerti and I believe it: a half hour of Romantic intensity that reaches both outward and inward.

After the Bruch, a contrast: the early Dvořák *Romance* for piano and violin. It's pretty, not flashy and not technically difficult, intended to demonstrate that I can play with proper lyrical feeling. When I practice it on this Sunday before term, I keep thinking of Joseph. Well, then, I'll think of Joseph and maybe I'll play it better. I wonder if the Wolff will notice.

Last, the Paganini Caprice. I chose No. 1, after which I'll never need further training in ricochet bowing. The Wolff approved, so that was easy. Nothing else about the Caprice is easy, however. It's only two minutes long, but it took me most of Fall term just to bounce my bow all the way through it.

All in all, the program is in decent shape after eight months of sporadic work. But now, it's time to focus.

I play it through, reviewing old trouble spots and finding new ones. Anni sticks her head in my door on her way between somewhere and somewhere else, says it sounds good, then vanishes for the rest of the day. The recital seems closer on Sunday evening than it did Sunday morning. I try not to think about it. One thing at a time. Just do the work. It will come. It always has.

✦　✦　✦

Wednesday morning.

"Not as bad as it might be, considering you took at least four days off," the Wolff says after I play the Bach. "It needs considerable work, of course. Fortunately, you will have fewer distractions this term. Bruch next."

My lessons will be two and a half hours twice a week from now on, during which I'll stand, as during the performance. I play all four pieces. The Wolff stops me every few measures. The Bruch and the Paganini are still about half speed. The risk with the Dvořák will be if I neglect it and render it sentimental rather than subtle. I wonder if twice a week will be enough.

When it's time to pack up, I summon my nerve to ask the question that's been plaguing me for what seems like years.

"How does one begin a solo career?" I say, wishing I didn't sound so hesitant.

She studies me intently, one eyebrow raised.

"You are still set on following this path?" she says.

"Yes, Professorin. I understand I'll teach and I like teaching. But my quartet-mates are bound to find stable work in orchestras and I don't blame them for taking it. I would myself if it were open to me."

"Artistic directors and conductors—often the same person—may attend solo recitals. Even yours, especially if the provost or I invite them. You may certainly inform them of your intentions. Eventually, you must learn all the great concerti and be ready to perform them at any time; after this you must learn both lesser-known works and new ones. It is a path without end."

"That means I'll have to continue to have a teacher myself," I say.

"A coach. You know how to learn music. You need a second pair of ears to help you shape it. Every artist does. And you must have someone to travel with you. It is inadvisable for a woman to travel without a chaperone. Your mother would be the obvious choice, but if she's unable, you must find someone else."

I try to imagine my mother traveling with me even as far as Bonn, even if she were well enough.

"Maybe Ros and Felix's grandmother would go with me."

"Judith Čápová? She might, indeed. Although you might get into more mischief with her than without her."

"You know Oma Judith?"

"The poetry of Judith Čápová exists in German translation," the Wolff says. "If you have the opportunity, look it up. At any rate, the larger obstacle will be the mastery of new repertoire on short notice."

"Do you teach—coach, I mean—outside of Conservatory?"

"Occasionally," she says. "And you are still on decent terms with Wil Dietrich. I think if you are determined, it is possible. But, of course, your recital must be as close to flawless as you can make it. You need not plan on having spare time this term."

"No novels, no chocolates," I say.

"Precisely," she says with the barest hint of a smile.

✦　✦　✦

The only punctuation to the weeks of this term is Katerina's lesson in the small sitting room every Saturday at 10:00 a.m. Madame is seldom even at home now and Frau Schmidt has not thawed even one degree. Katerina remains miraculously unspoiled, if still naive. And she works at least as hard at the violin as she works at anything else. Harder, probably, because of Otto, and because she genuinely likes it. Little drama seems to be coming from that quarter at the moment—fortunately, as I have absolutely no room in my head for any more drama of any kind.

At home, Mother's appetite gradually improves and she begins to regain a bit of strength. But she dislikes the idea of exercise even more than she did before, though the weather is cool and fine. It takes both of us to drag her out for even a short walk. The stairs are a time-consuming challenge in both directions and she complains nonstop through all four flights. I try to be gentle and encouraging. Anni tells her if she has the energy to complain, she has the energy to climb the damned stairs.

✦ ✦ ✦

June 1910

With two weeks to go before recitals, the fourth-years seem lost in their own private worlds. We hurry through the corridors, humming passages from our programs. We're often inattentive in class, but our professors haven't given up stuffing more information into our heads or demanding papers on Hungarian folk music or comparisons of French and German style. Still, a kind of clarity pervades the atmosphere. We all know the stakes. The third-years stay out of our way and we barely notice the existence of the younger students.

In this oblivious state, I climb onto the streetcar one Friday evening in early June and drop into a seat across from the driver with my case and bag on my lap. I dig around to find one of my scores to study on the way home and pay no attention when someone sits down beside me.

"Well, what a coincidence!"

That voice. The back of my neck prickles. I look up to see Reinhold von Marburg sitting beside me, his leg pressed up next to mine. At least his hands are in his lap, for now. He laughs at my startled expression. It's not a particularly nice laugh.

"You look like you need an escort home," he says.

"I'm fine, thanks," I say. I slide over as far as I can away from him on the seat, but I can't get away.

"You can't be too careful," he says, putting his arm around my shoulders.

I stiffen. "Don't touch me." I can't think of anything else to say through my clenched teeth.

It's the hour when the streetcar is full of men riding home from work, tired from long days in offices, their faces buried in the evening papers. I know many of them by sight; we're on the same schedule. I know this driver, Herr Goslach: I bid him good evening several times a week when I get on and off and I always sit at the front.

Marburg chuckles, as if he's indulging a child and puts his hand back in his lap. I can smell his cologne; I remember it from the last time he got too close. It's musky, expensive. Nauseating.

"Oh, all right, then. I'll save that for later."

"What do you want? Why are you following me? You don't live in this direction."

"I can go wherever I like," he says. "I want to see that you get home safely." His voice carries a soft kind of menace. I think about getting off and walking up Hildegardstrasse to my building with him following me. I decide in that moment I will not go home.

"You're too kind," I say, my teeth still clenched. "It's thoroughly unnecessary. I've been doing this for four years. I don't need any help. Get off. Go home."

"Keep your voice down. People are starting to stare." As indeed a few people are, peering over their newspapers at us. Herr Goslach, the driver, glances over.

I could get off now and go into a shop, if I could find one that's still open. But, of course, he would follow me. And that won't help me get home.

"How's your recital coming? Mine's going to be brilliant. Father's taking me to Berlin in July to audition for the Philharmonic."

"Congratulations."

I could get off and start walking anywhere, as long as there are people and streetlights. I could walk back to the Conservatory. It's only been a couple of stops.

"I suppose you're going to show us all up again."

"I doubt it."

I could go to the Apfelbaums. It's two stops further out than mine, so there will be fewer people left on the car by then. But their house is less than a block from the stop, the streetlights are better than on my street, and there will be several people at home. It seems the least bad of my few options. If I tell him now, will he get off?

"I'm not going home," I say. "I'm expected at a friend's house. For dinner."

"Ah. Anyone I know?"

"Why do you care?" A few more heads turn. The man behind us rattles his newspaper, shaking it out so he can peer over the top.

"Just making polite conversation," he says.

What will happen when we reach my usual stop? The driver will expect me to get off. He'll look around. Can I signal him in some way? Marburg's arm is starting to creep around my waist.

"I said, don't touch me."

"Funny you of all people should play hard to get," he says. "A woman who runs around all over town at all hours without a chaperone. And attends a man's institution. And plays in a men's quartet."

"I told you, don't touch me. I'll scream if you touch me. Here's a stop. Get off, go home. Practice for your audition."

"I told you, I'm seeing you home."

"I told you, I'm going to a friend's."

"Well, as I am a gentleman, I must see that you get there safely."

I inhale sharply, as if I'm going to scream, as I might be, I'm not sure. But he pulls his arm away.

"Fraülein?"

The driver looks across at me. I shake my head, make eye contact, and try to telegraph my thoughts.

"Thank you, Herr Goslach, Josephine-Lang-Strasse tonight." I see his eyebrows furrow in the mirror as he takes in the fact that I'm shrinking away from a man he doesn't recognize. My face feels bloodless. Maybe he can see it. He touches his cap to let me know he's heard.

"So, this is your regular stop, is it?" Marburg says, looking around.

"None of your business."

"You're not very polite, did you know that?"

Two stops more. The crowd thins considerably. I'll have to get up with my case and bag and cross in front of him. Will he grab me? I got him with the bag once before. I can keep it between us. But I can't risk dropping the case. I pick it up and get a firm grip on it. When we leave the stop before Josephine-Lang-Strasse, I stand up.

"Let me by."

"But of course, Fraülein." Marburg stands up and steps back to let me out.

I step on his foot. He growls angrily.

"Oh, sorry," I say.

The driver slows as we approach the stop.

"Thank you, Herr Goslach." I jerk my head toward Marburg. "This fellow student of mine isn't getting off here."

Herr Goslach studies me quizzically, then nods. He pulls up at the corner, stops, opens the door, and I practically leap out. I hear the door close behind me. The streetcar clatters away and above the noise, Marburg yells, "Hey, you, open the door! You old fool! Damn you, I want to get off here!"

I run. With my case and bag hitting my legs, I reach the Apfelbaums' garden gate, throw it open, race up to the door, and bang the knocker while looking over my shoulder to see if Marburg has managed to get Herr Goslach to let him out. I don't see him, but he could be behind a tree somewhere.

Quick footsteps inside. The door opens. Felix stands there with his hand on the knob and an astonished look on his face. I push past him, breathing hard, and he shuts the door.

I'm safe.

"Hi! What's up? We didn't expect you tonight, but there's plenty of—what's the matter?"

"Marburg," I say, leaning against the wall and panting. I tell him what happened.

"Good God. Your instinct was right not to go home. What a wretched ass. He's trying to rattle you before your recital. Come in, have something to eat. I'll take you home afterward."

"Could I maybe just move in?" I say. "No, no, I'm joking. But what do I do now?"

"Eat dinner," he says. "One thing at a time."

I set my things down and take my coat off. The family is still sitting around the table, talking, as usual. Felix explains the nature of my visit while Frau Apfelbaum fixes me a plate of chicken.

"Little dog!" Oma Judith says. Her eyes flash dangerously. "Going to Berlin, is he? I pity Berlin. You should carry a revolver."

"Anni would say I should carry a sword. A dagger, at least," I say. Now that I'm safe among friends, a little of my fear ebbs away, to be replaced by a sense of the absurdity of it all, and a bit of nagging doubt. Did I overreact? Did he really intend to harm me?

Oma Judith shakes her head. "Quieter, true. But harder to hide. And very messy. Here, have some potatoes."

"Did I make too much out of it?" I look around the table. No one seems to think so. "I can hardly imagine he really meant to hurt me. But I don't know. It was so frightening, to have him sitting right by me like that, trying to touch me. I have two weeks left. What should I do?"

"I'll stop by and pick you up on my way in and I can see you home," Felix says. "That seems obvious enough. I'll bet you could talk Joseph into bodyguard duty, too."

"But that's so much trouble for everyone! I don't want to be—"

"Marthe, dear," Herr Apfelbaum says. "You would do the same for any friend, I'm sure. You mustn't argue. This individual may or may not be physically dangerous, but there's no real point finding out, is there? You have a recital to prepare for and perform. You have to make sure nothing— and no one—interferes."

"Maybe I'm crazy to think of being a soloist," I say, "if I can't even ride on a streetcar in my own city without being accosted. The Wolff says I need a chaperone who can travel with me if I get any engagements. My mother can't, obviously. Anni's too young and has her own life to figure out. Anyway, I'd be pulling her out of trouble, not the other way around."

"You get the engagements, and I'll come with you," Oma Judith says.

"That'll be interesting," Felix says to no one in particular.

"Would you, Oma Judith? I was thinking of asking you. But I don't have any prospects yet, of course. I may never have any."

"Play a great recital," she says. "That's the first thing. The engagements will follow. I'll bring my revolver."

The mental picture of Oma Judith leaning on her cane with one hand and shooting a revolver at some luckless criminal with the other makes me laugh. Laughing loosens something inside me and, before I can stop them, tears start running down my face, which everyone is kind enough to ignore.

"Cherry tart," Frau Apfelbaum says, setting a dish in front of me. "And then we need to get you home. Your mother will worry."

The cherry tart tastes delicious. I hardly tasted the chicken at all, though I'm sure it was excellent. When I've cleaned my plate and thanked everyone for giving me refuge, Felix and I put on our coats, I gather my bag and case, and we walk back to the streetcar stop.

"I hope he's not on this one. Or waiting for me," I say.

"I doubt it," Felix says. "I know his kind. He's a coward and an opportunist, like all bullies. He's done what he wanted: he scared you. He might have followed through if he could have done it without risking much himself. It's a pity he really does have some talent; he could have just joined the army and bullied people there."

Marburg is not waiting in the shadows at the streetcar stop. The streetcars don't run as often at this hour, so we have a while to wait.

"You pretty much ready for recital?" Felix asks.

"Mostly," I say. "I'm polishing now. You know how the Wolff is about polishing."

"That I do," he says. "I'm in the same spot."

"An hour's a long time."

"You'll be fantastic. Practice tells and no one practices more than you."

"Still, I'll be glad when it's done," I say.

"You and everyone else," he says. He falls silent for a bit.

"One thing Marburg's likely to do between now and then is just turn up unexpectedly, to leer at you, or make a pass at you if he thinks no one's looking. He's just trying to rattle you, I think, so you'll be just enough off to make a difference in your playing. He really is dense—he's never figured out that his antics actually make you play better. I predict your recital will be your best performance yet."

"I hope that's all he'll do," I say.

"Don't let him catch you alone," he says. "I'll put the word out to my friends. They know what he is. You'll find yourself quite popular between now and recital."

"He's always got the women's toilet," I say. "Pity there weren't a few more women in our year. We could have traveled in a pack."

"True," he says. "But the pack's loss was our gain."

I sigh. "I'm really going to miss the quartet. More than anything else about Conservatory,"

"Agreed," he says. "We should try to continue."

"I don't see how, but count me in," I say. "Oh, finally. Here comes the streetcar. And it looks like—yes! It is Marburg-free."

"Excellent," Felix says.

We chat about the recitals for the two stops. He looks around curiously when we get off at my corner.

"You know, I've never been to your house," he says.

"It's not really worth visiting. We had to move to the flat after my father died."

"Oh. Right, of course."

We walk the long blocks in silence. I stop at my building.

"Thanks for seeing me home."

"Be here at seven-thirty Monday morning and I'll ride in with you," he says.

"Honestly, do you think that's necessary? Maybe I really did overreact."

"Were you scared?" he says. "Be honest."

"No," I say with more bravado than I feel. "He took me by surprise, that's all."

"I said, be honest," he says, his normally smooth voice sharp at the edges.

"Y-yes," I say.

"Seven-thirty," he says. "Exactly."

"Yes, sir," I say.

"That's better." He sees me in the front door of the building, waves goodbye, and turns to walk briskly back toward the streetcar stop. He has a lightness to his step and even from here I think I can hear him humming.

Felix is waiting outside at seven-thirty Monday morning and escorts me home that evening. Throughout the day, I find myself in conversation with one or another young man of my year every time I step outside a classroom. I manage to follow younger women to and from the toilet. I see Marburg several times, but thankfully only at a distance. Felix is waiting for me again Tuesday morning and every morning after that. To my surprise, on Tuesday evening Joseph is waiting in the foyer.

"My turn," he says with a grin.

"I'm going this way, too, you know," Felix says. "But I won't crowd the seat."

"This way you don't have to get off," Joseph says.

"If you insist," Felix says. "After you."

"And we're agreed, if we encounter any trouble from certain over-privileged spoiled brats—"

"Let's hope for his sake there won't be any," Felix says.

After this, Joseph waits for me every evening. The three of us talk about all sorts of things on the ride back to Ehrenfeld and Joseph sees me to my front door, where he bids me goodbye with a little kiss, if people are passing by, and a longer one if the street is empty.

Later, I find out he often goes back to his office to continue working well into the evening.

✦ ✦ ✦

Wednesday morning.

"What is the matter with you?" the Wolff snaps. "You weren't shaky on the Fugue last week."

It's been five days and my concentration is still in tatters. I take a deep breath and explain. Her face hardens.

"You were sensible," she says. "You must continue to be sensible and make use of it. You know how to transform adversity into musical passion. You must do so again, like alchemy. You will never lack for adversity to transmute into gold, because that is the nature of life as an artist. Did he frighten you?"

I nod. I remember his arm sneaking around my waist on the streetcar and feel the fear again.

"Did he make you angry?"

As if I were watching it happen to someone else, I see Marburg press himself against a young woman in my clothes, riding home from school, tired and preoccupied, with too much to carry. I see him speak low in her ear, see his ugly smile. I see her shrink from him.

I want to slap him across the face and yell, "Leave her alone, you bastard!" I want to slap him so hard I fracture his cheekbone, break his teeth and his nose. I feel the familiar heat in my face.

"Yes," I say. It sounds like a hiss.

"That is what you need to feel in order to play your recital to the level of which you are capable. Once again, he has done you a favor in his own particularly obnoxious way, which fortunately did you no physical harm and will strengthen you in the end. You do not need more such favors, however. I trust you are not wandering the school alone or staying late by yourself. You are in a uniquely vulnerable position."

"My friends are looking out for me," I say.

"Very good," she says. "Take a moment to collect yourself and give me the Bach again."

"Yes, Professorin."

The Bach goes better. The ragged places aren't ragged this time because of the drum of anxiety banging in my head. They're ragged because they're hard and because anger in its raw form is an uncontrolled fire. It will take more work to harness it so it flows out of my fingertips instead of scorching me.

Later, it occurs to me that she never suggested reporting the incident to the provost, or anyone else. I suppose she thought, as I did, that, as we're nearly finished, there's no point. And also that, since the only witness was a streetcar driver, no one would believe me.

✦　✦　✦

The cacophony emerging from behind the closed doors of the basement practice rooms fills the corridors with a kind of frenzied energy. I never see Marburg down here. I suppose he practices in a lavishly appointed studio in his palatial home rather than mingle with the sweating multitude. I spend several hours a day in one or another of these cubbyholes, drilling one passage after another, concentrating on trouble spots, fine-tuning phrasing, fingering, and bowing, drilling the passages again.

When my energy flags I think of Marburg's creeping fingers, his smirking face close to mine, the smell of his expensive, rank cologne, and I gain a second wind. Eventually, the raw fire begins to turn into fiery playing. The process has worked before, it's working now. My confidence grows.

Sometimes, just for balance, I call to mind the trusty image of Marburg tripping on the hem of Madame Kurtz's light blue morning dress.

In the after-dinner quiet of our flat, with Mother occupying her favorite chair in the sitting room and Anni, when she's home, doing whatever she does in her bedroom, I play the program through every night from start to finish, from memory, for the photograph of my father on my bureau. I feel him standing beside me, saying, as he used to say to me when he was first teaching me where to put my fingers on the strings, *That's it, sweetheart. Patience, you're getting there. Feel that calmness inside you? That means you can do it. Just feel it. It will come. It will come.*

I begin to look forward to my recital.

✦ ✦ ✦

The schedule is posted Friday afternoon before recital week. Franz and Felix will play on Tuesday, Arnold and Robert on Friday. I'm playing after intermission on Thursday. And the person playing before intermission is Reinhold von Marburg.

There's no way it's a coincidence. It's a diabolical plot, though who would do that to me I can't imagine. Spend half an hour or more alone in the waiting lounge with someone who wishes me nothing but ill? I'd rather lock myself in the women's toilet and give my recital to the mirror. I'll wait in the stage right wing under the watchful eye of Herr Schädler. I'll handcuff my case to my wrist. I'll change at home if I have to and wear my gown on the streetcar under my coat. Felix and Franz will be finished; I'll beg them to wait with me.

I'm still staring at the schedule, numb with shock, when I hear the Wolff's voice behind me.

"I predict you will play with a fire you've never felt before." She's looking over my shoulder with an expression of satisfaction on her face.

"This is—deliberate?"

She shrugs. "I should say it is fate," she says. "You must remember the feeling; you don't want to have to take him on concert tours with you."

"Ugh, no," I say. "I'll ask Felix to guard my case while I play."

"It will be quite safe with Herr Schädler," she says. "During recitals he has nothing else to do but guard students' possessions. You are ready?"

"Yes, Professorin," I say.

"Come see me Thursday morning," she says. "We will apply the final polish. You may leave your things in my studio and change there. Good evening."

"Yes, Professorin," I say as she pushes open the front door and disappears outside.

I look back at the schedule, hoping it's changed in the last ten seconds. It hasn't. I sigh, hitch my bag further up my shoulder, and turn to go.

"Who've you got?" Felix says, coming up to have a look. "No. *Really?* That has to be some kind of practical joke."

"The Wolff says it will make me more fiery," I say. "Let's go. I'm beginning to think I might not miss this place so much after all."

We enlighten Joseph as we wait for the streetcar. He says he'll guard me and my possessions backstage. I explain about Herr Schädler.

"Besides, you have to hear it."

"I can hear it fine from the wing."

I explain again about Herr Schädler.

"He might be called away."

"Let's talk about something else."

"What else is there?" Felix says. "Oh. Ros is coming home for the week. I just found out."

"That's good news," I say. "And I hope someone's planning parties."

Felix and Joseph both burst out laughing.

"We planned those ages ago," Felix says. "Our house on Tuesday, Walters' on Friday. Didn't you know?"

"I've been busy, in case you hadn't noticed."

"Then it's a good thing we told you," Joseph says.

"And a good thing I don't practice as much as you do," Felix says.

Joseph and I get off at my stop and stroll up Hildegardstrasse toward my building. He stops under a tree, the same one he stopped under last Christmas Eve.

"I have something for you," he says. "An early graduation gift."

"What? You didn't have to—"

"I know I don't have to. I want to. No fussing, promise?"

"I'm in your debt already."

"You are the most maddening woman." He reaches into his coat pocket and produces a small box.

"For a brilliant recital, a happy graduation, and a shining future," he says and puts the box in my hand.

I look from him to the little blue velvet box and back in wonder and astonishment.

"You're supposed to open it," he says.

Inside on a white satin lining lies a delicate filigree necklace of gold and tiny pearls with a shape like the letter Y. A scattering of tiny crystals sparkles in the soft twilight. It looks uncannily like the necklace in Johanna's sketches.

"It's the most beautiful thing I've ever seen!" I say when I can speak again. "I couldn't possibly—"

"You promised no fussing," he says. "I went to Franz's father, the goldsmith. I figured he'd know how to make a necklace for a violinist. I told him to be sure none of the stones would scratch your violin. They won't. He promises."

"It's the most beautiful—I can't believe you're giving this to me. Franz's father *made* this? I can't *believe*—"

"Just don't forget to wear it for your recital," Joseph says. "I'll be looking for it specially. Now go home and practice some more. I'll see you next week."

He gives me a tiny kiss—several people are approaching from the corner—and sees me in the front door.

I climb the stairs in a daze, clutching the little box in my hand. When I get to my own door, I put it in my bag. Mother is napping in her chair. I check to be sure she's breathing. Anni isn't home. Safe in my own room, I take out the box and open it again. The necklace shines even brighter against my faded wallpaper. I hold it up next to the blue-green gown waiting in my wardrobe on its wooden hanger. The effect is electric, as if they bring each other to life.

"Papa, can you believe it?" I say to the photograph. "That he would give me this?"

My father looks contentedly out of the little frame.

I replace the necklace carefully and put the box on top of my bureau next to the photograph. I unload my bag, lay the scores on my bed and open my case. Just a little run-through before dinner . . . but my mind keeps wandering back to the blue velvet box on the bureau-top.

✦ ✦ ✦

Like a stream approaching a waterfall, time speeds up. Every hour that disappears over the edge carries with it the last of something. On Monday,

I take my last Conservatory exams, in Composition and Musicology. In between, I retreat to my usual practice cubbyhole in the basement, where I become acutely aware of the cracks in the plaster and the pattern of tiles on the floor and where my violin sounds unusually loud. The old piano, which has probably lived in this room since the Conservatory was built, undoubtedly remembers the fingerprints of every student who has sweated over its keys. They are still in some way present; I feel them.

I wonder if some essence of myself will remain here after I've gone. Perhaps the walls have absorbed my struggle, my concentration, my frustration, my moments of revelation. There are a few passages in the slow movement of the Bruch that seem to say, *Yes, they have. The students who follow you will feel your presence, too.*

It's too complex a feeling for words, but the music expresses it very well, I think.

On Tuesday Franz plays first, wearing his intensity like a suit of armor. He has grown taller and looks more like a man now, albeit still quite a skinny one, but there is something of great age in the deep, rich timbre of his instrument and in his expressiveness, a hint of inner life hidden beneath his pugnacious exterior.

After him Felix, brilliant, showy, and tender by turns. His self-assurance is complete, his technique impeccable. Everything is clean: double-stops, *pizzicato*, phrasing, bowing. He, too, plays expressively, although he's chosen work more for virtuosic showmanship than lyricism. His time races by; his final flourish is greeted with cheers as well as applause.

Afterward, in the foyer, both are besieged by well-wishers: classmates and younger students, parents who have watched us all perform over these last four years, and several men I don't recognize. They must be the mysterious artistic directors and orchestra conductors. I try to memorize their faces in case any should be present on Thursday.

Ros, just arrived from Amsterdam, bubbles over with sisterly pride and later, when I finally get a chance to talk to her at the Apfelbaums' house, with the excitement of her life in the Amsterdam Women's Orchestra. The walls of the sitting room where we've rehearsed so often quiver with triumphant merriment. The revelry continues on, I'm sure, long after Joseph and I leave.

On Friday, Arnold pulls riveting emotional and technical depth out of his natural sweetness, and after him, Robert's apparent effortlessness belies the hundreds of hours I know he has dedicated to Rachmaninoff, Liszt, and Brahms. Afterward, the revelry at the Walters' house goes on for hours. But by then, of course, I, too, have played; my work at the Conservatory is complete and I've acquired a great deal to think about since yesterday morning.

22

THE SOLO RECITAL, JUNE 1910

June 1910

Thursday begins like and unlike any other day. I wake before the sun rises with snippets of my program racing through my head and getting tangled up with each other. They race on during breakfast, while I pack my scores, gown, and shoes, while I dress to go to school.

First, Joseph's necklace. I can't resist studying it in my hand mirror, its tiny pearls, bright crystals, and delicate gold cool and elegant against my bare skin. I'm going to wear it all day under my dress, where I know it will be safe. It feels magical hidden there, like a secret talisman. I imagine playing tonight, the power of his necklace flowing down through my arms to my fingertips, into my bow and my violin, and emerging as sound.

It makes me feel invincible.

"I'll see you tonight," I say to Mother and Anni as I collect my case and bags.

"Practicing all day?" Anni says.

"The Wolff said I could work and change in her studio," I say. "Just a few last-minute adjustments. I'll be an asylum case here, anyway."

Mother looks up from her soft-boiled egg. "Nearly over," she says.

"Yes," I say. "Nearly over."

The foyer is mostly empty when I arrive. The few students in evidence hurry along, staring at the floor, deep in concentration. My footsteps echo off the marble floors and columns. *The last time.* At least, the last time as a student. The last time with a recital to play. Perhaps I'll return as a member of the audience. Perhaps I'll have students playing here one day.

I glance at the recital schedule as I pass. It hasn't changed. Never mind. Whatever cutting thing Marburg might say, I doubt he'll dare do anything to me today, with the Wolff so close at hand.

Up the staircase, then, to the third floor.

"You're early," the Wolff says. "Good."

Maybe today won't be my very last time in this room—I'll have notes tomorrow, after all—but after that I won't belong here. I've tried to memorize it: the piano, the artwork on the walls, the ornate certificate from the Vienna Conservatory. The formidable desk with the equally formidable Wolff sitting behind it. The decades-old photograph of the mysterious young woman.

"Warm up for ten minutes and let me hear the Bach."

"Good morning to you, too, Professorin," I say.

We work through the morning. We go through the whole program. She spends an inordinate amount of time on the Bruch. Not correcting, but examining interpretation: which phrasing I think is more expressive, whether a passage has too much overt emotion, not enough, or a perfect level—details that only someone who has played the concerto, or the composer himself, would notice.

"There is nothing technically wrong with your playing at this point," she says. "Interpretation lies in the realm of nuanced personal choice and your choices must come from your heart. You must try different approaches, as we have done and are doing now, in order to find the one that feels right to you. The score is the skeleton, but you must flesh it out with your own truest self. You know this, of course, we have discussed it before."

"Yes, Professorin," I say.

"What does it mean to play music?" she asks.

"Er, well, I suppose . . ."

The Wolff looks amused, which is at least better than looking impatient.

"It means, I guess, to bring to life what's written on the page. Because that's how a composer makes people feel things. And feeling things is important, isn't it? Isn't that why there's always been music? Since the first people?"

The Wolff allows herself a small smile.

"That is not nearly as inadequate an answer as you might assume," she says. "You are correct, in fact. There has always been music. Music existed before language. It is fundamental to all human beings from before birth, when the first sound they hear is their mother's heartbeat. It is essential to every human culture. It is the most abstract of the arts, precisely because of how deeply it can make us feel—deeper than words can reach. Not that I wish to overburden you tonight, but remember that, whenever you play music, you are touching the core of what it means to be human."

"Yes, Professorin." I suddenly feel very small.

"And remember that you play, ultimately, because you love music and feel it in the core of your own being. Sometimes that truth becomes obscured under layers of technique and practice."

"Yes, Professorin," I say.

"The Dvořák, then," she says.

When we're done, there are still a few hours before I need to get ready. I leave my bags and case in the Wolff's studio and wander the corridors, looking hard at everything. *The last time.* After tonight this place won't belong to me anymore. It's a complex feeling: thrilling, anxious, and sad. I end up in the common room without really intending to. A few first- and second-years are scattered about the tables, studying or looking at scores. They barely glance at me.

I find an armchair in a corner and settle in to clear my mind and eat the bread and cheese I brought with me. I don't know how much time passes. Perhaps I doze off. The next time I look at the clock, I realize with a start that it's time to prepare. I wonder if Marburg is here yet. Probably it's not last minute enough for him. I pull myself out of my chair and climb the stairs back to the third floor, concentrating on taking deep, even breaths. This time I notice nothing outside my field of vision.

"I will return in half an hour. Be ready," the Wolff says.

Whether changing here is to keep me away from Marburg or just a privilege of being the only fourth-year woman, it takes a lot less time than it does in a toilet stall. My hair cooperates on the first attempt. Even my caterpillars feel different, marching in formation with their thousands of tiny feet. The Wolff's influence, no doubt.

"My compliments to your dressmaker," the Wolff says when she returns. "The effect is suitably professional."

"I'll tell her," I say.

She holds the door open for me and I walk out—surely not the last time? I descend the stairs to the waiting lounge with her silent, solid, infinitely reassuring presence behind me, and yet I sense another presence beside me, too, and when I take a seat in the waiting lounge with the Wolff to my left, the chair to my right does not seem empty.

I'd considered bringing my father's photograph with me, but decided not to risk it. I didn't need to, after all. He is here.

To my surprise, Oskar, the page-turner of last year, is here, too, waiting for us. He leaps up when we walk in.

"I have my old job back," he says. He seems nervous around the Wolff and quickly resumes his seat on the other side of the room.

Herr Grimmelshausen arrives in the lounge a few minutes later. He nods to us and to Oskar and settles into a chair, where he looks at his pocket watch every few minutes, a gesture I've long since come to associate with people who are scheduled to perform with Marburg. We're barely fifteen minutes from curtain time when he strolls in. Herr Grimmelshausen is visibly irritated.

"You have warmed up, I presume?" he says.

"Yes," Marburg says with unusual deference, and busies himself unpacking his violin.

They say no more until Herr Schädler sticks his head in and points at them.

"Good luck," I say to Marburg as he passes. I keep my voice cool and even.

He looks down as if he hadn't seen me until that moment. "Er—thanks," he mumbles with a glance in the Wolff's direction, and then the room is empty again.

How odd that he should perform his recital in Madame Kurtz's light blue morning dress.

"Warm up," the Wolff says. I unpack my violin and bow, put the mute on and run quietly through a set of drills. The provost's voice filters in. After this, applause; Marburg has made his entrance. Another pause, and then he begins.

I don't pay much attention. I continue my warm-up and imagine myself walking out on the stage alone in a little over an hour, holding myself tall, my stride radiating confidence and grace, the lace overlayer of my gown floating behind me, my necklace sparkling. I see myself stop precisely in the center, bow to my audience with dignity and reserve, raise my violin, place my bow, center myself, and begin.

A few passages of the Bach fugue. Tricky bits of the Bruch. Trickier bits of the Paganini. My caterpillar army marches back and forth in fancy drill patterns. Caterpillar sergeants bellow orders and caterpillar troops turn crisply this way and that. The Wolff watches me impassively. I forget she's there.

Marburg's violin in the distance switches from Italian Baroque to something Mozartian with piano. He misses the occasional note, but recovers. After Mozart comes something floridly Romantic. The time passes quickly. He finishes; the house applauds enthusiastically.

"He is not without talent, that one," the Wolff says, echoing my thought. "It is only discipline he lacks. And a professional attitude."

"He told me—that night—he's going to audition for the Berlin Philharmonic this summer."

"You don't say."

"I suppose he'll get in."

"It is less a question of whether he will get in than whether he can stay in."

A few minutes later, the three of them reappear in the waiting lounge.

"Congratulations," I say.

The Wolff glances from Marburg to Herr Grimmelshausen, one eyebrow raised.

Marburg mumbles something. Herr Grimmelshausen pokes him in the ribs.

"Er—thanks," Marburg says. He packs up and leaves.

"A man of few words," the Wolff says.

"A fine young protegé," Herr Grimmelshausen says. His voice, I notice, is rather high. "Not unlike your own. Good luck this evening, Fräulein."

"Thank you, Professor," I say.

Then he, too, is gone, leaving us with Oskar, who retreats back to his corner.

The Wolff shakes her head. "He's done you an enormous favor," she says.

"How? He didn't insult me."

"He's given the audience something to compare you to," she says. "You may recall his previous treatment of you at will. Now might be a good time, in fact. But mainly he has been merely competent. Pull your things together. Herr Schädler will call us soon."

In fact, Herr Schädler calls us almost immediately and the three of us head for the stage right wing, where we sit down again.

It is so familiar now, this ritual. For the last time, Herr Schädler points to me. For the last time I rise, step into the wing and await his signal. I touch my necklace, its smooth pearls, tiny diamonds, delicate gold. I feel its power radiating down my arms into my fingers. I think about touching the core of what it means to be human. He points to me again. For the last time I step out onto the stage.

I hold myself tall. I walk with confidence and grace. The lace overlay of my gown floats behind me. Applause buoys me—my shoes seem not to touch the floor. I stop precisely in the center. I bow to my audience. The applause quiets. I raise my violin, place my bow, center myself, and begin.

Bach's opening Adagio. Music for a long walk by a river, for thinking deep, sinuous thoughts that rarely resolve before giving way to new ones. It centers me, readies me for the Fugue, in which my audience, riveted and utterly still, mirrors the intensity of my focus through its intricately woven lines. When the Fugue at last resolves and another pause leads into the slow, graceful Largo, I hear them exhale with me as one person. The final Allegro feels jubilant under my fingers and—I didn't expect this—like a gift from me to everyone who has helped me come this far, living, or dead.

At the final flourish, applause bursts out, solid and enthusiastic. It seems to last a long time. I feel a bubble of exultation growing in my chest.

They're with me.

The Wolff takes her place at the piano without ceremony, with Oskar beside her. I wait while she adjusts the bench. When she nods to me, I turn to my audience and lift my violin for the Bruch.

From the orchestral introduction, from the first long, low note from the violin, I do indeed feel invincible. When the first movement finally boils over at full volume, we ride its currents precisely together, faster, slower, separately, in unison. If the Bach felt like a gift, the Bruch feels like the essence of being alive. Bruch's Romantic exuberance, so different from Bach's ascetic intricacy, makes me want to shout for joy—but of course the music itself is my shout. Every note, every phrase, every passage contains its own identity, its own space and time. My hands take on a life of their own. A few strands of hair work their way out of my French roll. The slow second movement sings. In the third, the bow bites at the strings, trading full-throated themes between piano and violin, its final passages the most virtuosic of all, its final flourish a moment of complete, full-bodied exhilaration.

I take my time lowering my bow, willing the moment to last.

When the applause finally ends, we begin the Dvořák *Romance*.

After the towering heights of Bach and Bruch, the *Romance* is sweet and intimate and doesn't pretend to be anything else. I see Joseph's smiling face in my mind, as I always do, his expression kind and warm, his eyes a place of safety. Minor keys do make themselves felt at times, but intertwined with the themes, as if to say, *such things happen in life. Don't be afraid, all will be well.*

As we've rehearsed the *Romance*, I've felt a genuine affection growing alongside my deep respect for the Wolff. I still know nothing about her life outside of the Conservatory, but she plays as if she knows something about romance, about life. So, I play the *Romance*, not only for Joseph, but for Maria Anna Wolff, the consummate musician from Vienna who has given me so much of herself for the last four years. And when the last high note fades into silence, it may be this small gift has found its way, for as the applause rises, I turn to acknowledge her and she is smiling at me, a rare gift in itself, and her expression seems to mirror my own feelings.

She exits with as little ceremony as she entered, with Oskar behind her carrying her score. I stand alone again, to close with the Paganini Caprice No. 1. Once more, the hall stills.

The last time.

I take a moment to focus my concentration, looking at the wooden floor of the stage. Take a few deep breaths. Look up. Lift my violin and my bow. One more breath. For an instant my father stands beside me.

I begin.

I was right when I chose No. 1 last fall: I will never need another lesson in ricochet bowing. For over two and a half minutes, the bow bounces rather than slides across the strings; it is more difficult if played a little slower, so I do. It's marked *andante*, walking, after all. Though I learned early on not to hold my breath during this bravura morsel, I imagine my audience does, as my bow skips across the strings in seemingly impossible combinations. But they aren't impossible. I've put a hundred hours or more into these two and a half minutes and every hour has been necessary and worthwhile.

The final chord peals out across the hushed hall. The reverberation hangs in the air for one impossibly long second and then the applause thunders out in earnest. I bow twice. Take a step back. Bow twice more and then stride off the stage, where the Wolff and Oskar are applauding in the wing.

Herr Schädler points to the stage. I float out for another curtain call. Applause continues to rain down. I've done it. I've finished. I've succeeded.

I've made it through Conservatory.

✦ ✦ ✦

I follow the Wolff back up the stairs to her studio, where I pack up my violin and she locks her door behind us, then back downstairs again and out into the foyer. The marble surfaces reverberate with voices. Dozens of people I don't know congratulate me as I head toward my family and friends. They're all here: Felix, Franz, Arnold, Robert, all their families. The Dietrichs. Mother and Anni. Johanna and Heidi. Ros. Herr Kurtz and Katerina, over with the Marburgs, where Reinhold is taking his share of compliments. Everyone talks at once. Someone slips a cup of punch into my hand. Even Mother looks happy and excited.

"Really amazing!"

"Your father—"

"Well done!"

"Who knew four little strings could make all that noise—"

"But do your hands hurt?" Heidi says.

I tell her only a tiny bit and only for a little while, like how your legs feel when you run hard. I don't want to discourage her, after all, by admitting that by the end of the hour I thought they might actually fall off.

"Not bad for a squeaky miniature instrument!"

"Hello, Christian," I say. "Thanks for coming."

"Wouldn't have missed it," he says, taking my hand and, to my surprise, raising it to his lips.

"I may be only a lowly third-year violist," he says, "but I predict you'll go far. Let me know where I can come hear your professional debut."

"I, ah—well, if I get one, of course I will!"

He bows over my hand again and melts into the crowd in the direction of the refreshment table.

Gerda Dietrich is significantly pregnant.

"When—?"

"I haven't seen you since Christmas Eve," she says. "A lot can happen in six months. Come see us, now you're going to be finished. We'll tell you more."

"Right," I say, trying and failing to avoid staring at her midsection.

"Stupendous program," Herr Dietrich says. "I'm surprised your fingers aren't down to bone."

"They are, but don't tell Heidi," I say. "I should introduce you to her. She might need the best teacher in town one of these days."

"I think that honor goes to Professorin Wolff," he says. "Speaking of whom—"

The Wolff is striding toward us accompanied by an old man with white hair and a luxuriant white mustache and beard. An artistic director, perhaps?

"Professor, allow me to present Fraülein Adler. Fraülein, this is Max Bruch."

My jaw drops in what I'm sure is a highly unprofessional manner. The old man takes my offered hand and kisses it in a very courtly way.

"Pardon my interruption, Fraülein," he says. "I wish to congratulate you. I have seldom heard my concerto better played, particularly by someone so young. You actually reminded me of Joachim, who premiered it back in '67. I trust you'll have the opportunity to play it before an orchestra soon. Not that Professorin Wolff's piano reduction is second best, by any means!"

"Hardly the same thing," she says.

"I hope so, too," I say. "I'm honored that you approve."

"Quite approve, Fraülein," he says cheerfully. "I don't mean to keep you from your public, however. Perhaps we shall speak further later on." He bows over my hand again and strides away. I stare after him.

"My God, I'm glad I didn't know he was here," I say to no one in particular. "I'd have been an absolute wreck."

"Yes, that was fortunate," the Wolff says. Her face, as usual, reveals nothing. "Come upstairs when you're ready to leave. I'll be in my studio and you can change out of your gown. You may leave your things overnight if you're going out. They'll be quite safe there."

"Notes at nine o'clock?"

"Naturally," she says before she walks away.

"That was Max Bruch," I say, still staring at the spot where he disappeared.

"So I gathered," Herr Dietrich says. "The living composers do turn up from time to time, you know. It's the dead ones turning up you want to watch out for. Quite a coup that he liked what you did."

"But what was he doing here?"

"Listening to you play his concerto, you ninny," Gerda says. "Look, we need to go. Come visit soon, all right?"

I promise I will and they disappear, to be replaced by Herr Kurtz and an effusive Katerina, who is dragging Otto by the hand.

"You did it!" she squeals.

"Congratulations, Fraülein," Otto says.

"Thanks to the generosity of Herr Kurtz," I say.

"Thanks to your own dedication, Fraülein," Herr Kurtz says. "It was a worthy investment. You're still considering a solo career?"

"I hope so," I say.

"I have no doubts," he says. "In the meantime, I trust you'll still be willing to continue teaching Katerina. She would be heartbroken to lose you."

"I'll be there Saturday morning."

"We shall expect you, then," he says.

Katerina kisses me on both cheeks, Otto nods politely, and the three of them stroll back to the Marburgs.

"Do you have plans?" I didn't hear Joseph coming up behind me.

"No," I say. "Party tomorrow. Tonight, I'll go home and fall over, I suppose."

"Have you had dinner?"

"Sort of." The bread and cheese seem like yesterday.

"Let me take you out. I know a quiet little place that's open late and the food is excellent. I'll take you home after. Nice necklace, by the way."

"You've convinced me," I say. "When we're done here and I've changed clothes."

I feel weightless and carefree, even though the Wolff's notes tomorrow will last all morning. For once, I'm not worried about the future and how to reach it. Because, for once, this moment, right now, is enough.

Joseph's quiet little restaurant turns out to be French, quite elegant. I regret changing out of my gown, which would have fit right in, though of course I still have on his necklace under my day dress, if that counts for anything. Over champagne and *boeuf bourguignon* we talk of the recitals, mine in particular, my mother's health, Anni's prospects, his plans for the summer (work, mostly), and mine (unknown). Even serious subjects seem less burdensome here.

We're enjoying our dessert of fresh berries with cream and coffee when he asks me to marry him.

Not right this minute, he hastens to add, turning quite red. But consider it. Think about it. Think about how I deserve a stable home so I can perform whenever and wherever I have engagements. Whenever I choose. How we could be happy together. How there's no hurry. But just think about it.

I'm sure I look as though I've seen a ghost. I stammer something incoherent, assure him that I'm deeply honored and I will indeed think about it. We finish our coffee with a sort of silence between us and emerge again into the evening, still warm even though the sun set hours ago. He takes me home on the streetcar, clasping my hand as we stand under the trees outside the door of my building.

"Until tomorrow, then," he says. "I hope you're not angry."

"No, no, of course not. Just overwhelmed—you've given me a lot to think about," I say.

"I should have waited," he says. "I just didn't want anyone else to get there ahead of me."

"There's no queue, I promise you," I say. "I'm honored. Truly, I am. I'll see you at tomorrow's recital, then."

"I'll save you a seat." He smiles down at me, gives me a small kiss, and waits to turn away until the building's front door shuts behind me.

Tired though I am, it takes me a very, *very* long time to fall asleep.

✦　✦　✦

When I arrive at the Wolff's studio at nine o'clock the next morning for my notes, Herr Bruch himself is occupying the chair in front of her desk and the two of them are chatting away as if they're old friends.

He rises to greet me, kisses my hand again and pulls up another chair for me, all the while explaining that he was only fortunate enough to attend my performance because he happened to be in town visiting family, but plans to stop in Bonn on his way back to Berlin. There he intends to speak to his old friend Herr Biedermeyer, the artistic director of the Bonn Orchestra, about my auditioning to perform the concerto there, for he hears that Herr Biedermeyer is looking for new solo talent and is open-minded about women musicians, if they are *very* good. If I'm interested, of course. Maria—that is, Professorin Wolff—suggested that I might, in fact, be interested, and is that really the case? For he must hear it from my own lips; it's not his way to push people where they do not wish to go.

"Audition to solo with the Bonn Orchestra?" I repeat, not really putting the meaning of the words together in my stunned surprise and sounding, I'm sure, very thick indeed.

He nods cheerfully and sits back, waiting for me to speak.

"Yes!" I manage to squeak at last. "I am. Very interested! It has been my dream to be a soloist."

"Excellent!" he says. "And what else may I tell him you have in your repertoire besides my own humble concerto?"

I think back over the last four years, naming the quartets, the sonatas—

"No other major concerti?" He looks slightly disappointed.

"Not yet," I say, flashing what I hope is a confident smile. "Now that my recital is finished, I plan to begin, ah, expanding my repertoire in that direction." I cast a sidelong glance at the Wolff, who sits, silent and impassive, watching to see if I can manage this very gentle interview without falling on my face.

"Excellent!" he says again. "I will sound immodest, I fear, if I say that one can make a good many rounds of the concert circuit with my concerto.

It is far from the greatest work of all time, but it has proved reliably popular. Still, the more work one has at the ready, the better, I'm sure you'll agree. Do you plan to be an Austro-German specialist, then?"

"I love our repertoire, of course." The Wolff coughs, which might be covering up something else. "I also love the music of other countries and I wish to master all of it. Well, as much of it as possible."

"A proper answer." Herr Bruch nods approvingly. "Each informs the other, don't you agree, Professorin?"

"Of course," she says in a tone that suggests they've had this conversation before, which in turn suggests they didn't just happen to meet for the first time yesterday.

"Very well." Herr Bruch stands up and reaches for his hat on the rack by the door. "When I see Herr Biedermeyer tomorrow, I shall urge him to contact you through the Conservatory. Will that be satisfactory?"

"I—oh, very satisfactory, yes. That would be fantastic!"

"In the meantime, I shall let you get on with your notes, of which I should imagine there will be very few, eh?"

"Professorin Wolff always finds room for improvement," I say.

He laughs, a large, booming laugh. "That scarcely comes as a surprise." He bows to us both as he steps out the door and closes it behind him.

I stare after him, wondering if I just imagined the whole thing and will wake up soon. "Did he—did he just—"

"We shall see what Herr Biedermeyer has to say," the Wolff says in precisely her usual tone, as if she were discussing my practice schedule. "Now then. Warm up for ten minutes and let me have the Bach. The Fugue in particular had some points that require attention . . ."

When we're done, I offer her back her Bruch score, but she says to keep it in case I need it for my audition in Bonn.

"I shall expect you to keep in touch," she says, handing me her calling card and another thick score. "Here is another arrow in your quiver. You know how to study it, I should think. But you may ask me for assistance if need be."

It's Mendelssohn, his E minor concerto, also thick with penciled notes.

"Another essential warhorse," she says. "Once established, a soloist can branch out, forward or back, into the lesser known, the obscure, or the, ah, dangerously avant-garde."

I put the scores in my bag and thank her several times. We both neglect to mention that, technically, I'm no longer her student and have no right to her time or her resources.

By evening I'm still walking around in a kind of trance. Arnold plays his recital with a sweet purity that edges even his most brilliant passages. I wonder if Alma knows her young man's true love is his cello—or perhaps Alma is his muse and he's playing just for her. Robert plays with a combination of technical brilliance, masculine force and lyrical tenderness that will leave men weeping and women fainting, or vice versa, wherever he goes. Both are mobbed afterward. I can barely elbow my way in to offer my congratulations.

Instead, I talk, or rather listen, to Tante Hanne, who rhapsodizes for several solid minutes, and exchange a few words with Herr Walter, who appears to have enjoyed himself. I tell Oma Judith about my encounter with Max Bruch. She raps her cane enthusiastically on the marble floor.

"We'll take Bonn by storm!" she says. "You keep me informed. We'll have a grand time, you'll see!"

"Do you think his being here was a coincidence?"

"Doesn't matter, does it?"

"No," I say. "I just begin to think the Wolff is more devious than I gave her credit for."

"Be glad she's on your side, then," Oma Judith says. "Be glad I am, too, for that matter."

Just as with the Wolff, I can never tell when Oma Judith is joking.

By the time I arrive at the Walters', a sense of unreality has replaced yesterday's euphoria, as if my body, wandering around the Walters' crowded sitting room, is now being occupied by someone else. Practically everyone I know is here, all talking and laughing, eating and drinking. Anni and Franz carry on with their animated private conversation, Mother sits in the most comfortable armchair and lets Tante Hanne fuss over her. People occasionally sit down at the piano and play something for people to sing along to, though I notice Robert isn't one of them.

"I had that thing growing out of my fingers for the last six months," he says. "I'm willing to share."

Tante Hanne drafts Joseph to help serve. I try to help, too; she won't hear of it.

"This is your party, dear, go and celebrate!"

Joseph says the same. So, I circulate from group to group. Arnold's family, whom I've never really talked to before. The extraordinarily shy Alma, who says she and Arnold have been in love since their first year of primary school and plan to marry as soon as possible. Franz's father and stepmother, who radiate quiet pride in Franz's accomplishment. I thank Herr Herzberg for making my beautiful necklace, which seems to please him very much.

Felix, Arnold and Franz discuss their upcoming auditions for the Köln Sinfonia and what they'll do if they don't get in. Robert tells Herr Apfelbaum of his plan to travel around Europe for a while before beginning auditions, sounding completely confident that opportunities will await him whenever he wants them.

Mindful of Johanna's instructions to act the part of a successful professional artist, when people ask about my plans, I say I'm hoping for a solo audition with the Bonn Orchestra, as if I might actually have a chance. It feels a little untruthful, but this room is as safe a place as any to see what acting successful might feel like.

Joseph finally finishes carrying platters back and forth to the kitchen and joins me in my rounds. I tell him about my morning and he seems very excited by the prospect of coming to hear me play in Bonn.

"I haven't got it yet. Don't jinx my chances!"

"I think your chances are excellent," he says. After that our conversation turns to other subjects, though it studiously avoids the topic of marriage.

The Apfelbaums take Mother home in their taxi when they leave. Joseph takes Anni and me later on the streetcar. On the hard wooden seat my week suddenly catches up with me. I lean against him while Anni talks animatedly about her fencing club, her upcoming summer fencing camp and her job in the bakery. Joseph listens with his usual serious attention and offers comments and suggestions, but I don't hear much of it. I only wake up when he pulls me to my feet to get off at our stop.

✦　✦　✦

After that everything is a blur. Other classmates give their recitals. At our graduation ceremony the provost speaks for what seems like hours about how exemplary we've been and what an asset to the musical world we'll become. We receive diplomas hand-written in such elaborate script that we can't read our own names. I wonder if I imagined meeting Max Bruch. The more days pass, the less I believe it really happened.

Two weeks later a letter arrives, forwarded from the Conservatory, inviting me to appear in Bonn on a date in late June for an audition with Herr Biedermeyer, artistic director of the Bonn Orchestra, to play the Bruch Violin Concerto No. 1. An accompanist will be provided. Would I be so kind as to please confirm my intentions in writing as soon as possible? Yours most sincerely, Georg Reisenholm, secretary to Herr Rudolf Biedermeyer, artistic director of the Bonn Orchestra.

The Future:

1910-1911

23

DEBUT, JULY 1910–APRIL 1911

July 1910

I stare at the letter, my mouth hanging open, my heart racing, and try to think of what to do next. Answer the letter, right. Say, *Yes, I'll be honored to audition*. But how to prepare? Where to stay? What to wear? What if I can't play it anymore? What if I can only play it with the Wolff and not with someone else? What if I can't play it with a real orchestra?

Gradually, my incoherent panic grows tired of banging around in my head and two thoughts emerge. First, I need to talk to the Wolff. Doubtless she knows already. She probably forwarded the invitation.

Second, I need to talk to Herr Dietrich. He'll know how to avoid beginner mistakes with an orchestra. And Gerda did ask me to visit. It's early enough in the day to do both. So, I do.

✦　✦　✦

"I've been expecting you," the Wolff says. "Let me see your letter."

I hand it to her. She glances over it and hands it back.

"Herr Bruch is a man of his word. Have you answered?"

"I wished to consult with you first," I say.

"You are in doubt?"

"No, Professorin. As to the specifics. What should I say besides 'Yes'? How much money should I ask for? What should I wear to audition? How should I prepare?"

"Ah. Say, 'Yes, thank you very much,' and ask him to recommend a hotel. Reserve a room and go down the day before. For rehearsals and performances, they will book you a room. Assuming you succeed at the audition, they will offer you a contract. It should be fair enough. As a new name, just out of school, and a woman, you will have less negotiating power than a better-known man. Unfortunate, but true. When you become famous, you can name your own price. Wear your black gown to audition and one of the others to perform. And practice. Judith Čápová will be your chaperone?"

"Yes, Professorin."

"Well, you'll have an interesting time."

"That, er, does seem to be the consensus, yes."

The Wolff smiles, almost.

"I will be here during business hours through July if you have further questions," she says. "Administrative work is unglamorous, but necessary."

"Thank you, Professorin," I say, rising to leave.

"One more thing."

I turn back.

"Remember that you are not a student asking for permission. You are a professional—a young one, to be sure, but a professional nonetheless—and you have a right to be where you are. You will communicate this with your bearing, your conduct, your clothing, your hair, your ability to look them in the eye. Men, it seems, are born understanding this. Women must learn it. Come see me before you go."

Exactly as Johanna told me. But I don't feel like a professional, yet. I'll have to be an actress.

"I understand, Professorin," I say. "I will."

✦   ✦   ✦

"Four more weeks," Gerda says. Her hand presses into the small of her back when she stands and she sits back down again as soon as possible. "Honestly, I'm not sure how many more times I want to go through this."

Thomas sits on my lap to name all the parts of his current favorite toy, a wooden caterpillar on wheels.

"Do most four-year-olds know words like 'antennae'?" I say, momentarily distracted.

Gerda laughs. "He's a precocious one," she says. "But wait till he discovers real caterpillars don't have wheels."

"I was his age when my father began teaching me violin. Has he started yet?"

"Not yet. He wants to be like Papa, but he lacks the coordination and the patience. Plenty of time yet."

"Plenty," I say, remembering how there was plenty of time, until there wasn't. I hope these children will be luckier.

"What's it like, being finished?" Gerda says.

"Oh! That's why I came, actually. I need advice."

"Hm! Personal or professional?"

"Professional. Er—well . . ."

"Wil will be home any minute for the professional part. What's the personal part?"

I feel my face turn bright red.

"Joseph proposed?" she says.

"He just asked me to think it over," I say. "I said I would."

"Does he expect you to give it all up, now you've finished school?"

"No. He promised me a stable home to return to between engagements."

"Did he, now? Perhaps you ought to snap him up before someone else does."

"Herr Dietrich didn't expect you to give it all up, did he?"

"No, I chose to. I'll return to nursing one day. But I always wanted a family. And a garden—" She sighs, looking around her tiny kitchen.

"I remember."

"I'm halfway there, at least. But can you imagine two children running wild in this flat? The neighbors will be at us with pitchforks. Soon enough, we'll have to move and then I'll get my garden. The children will grow up. There's always a need for nurses. If Joseph allows you to be who you are, he's one man in a thousand. Do you love him?"

"I don't know what love is supposed to feel like," I say. "I feel safe with him. Is that love?"

"It's one kind. A very good kind. I thought you might have dedicated your *Romance* to him—you played with great feeling. Ah. I hear Wil's key."

"Is there coffee?" Herr Dietrich says as he clatters past, loaded with case, bag, coat, and several other things.

"Of course," Gerda says. Thomas wriggles off my lap and runs after him. When Herr Dietrich returns, Thomas snuggles contentedly in his arms.

"So," he says as he sits down heavily at the table. Gerda sets a mug of coffee down in front of him and sits down heavily also. "Anything new?"

I hand him my letter from Bonn. Gerda reads it over his shoulder.

"Congratulations!" he says. "You accepted, of course?"

"It only came today," I say. "I wanted to talk to you first, and the Wolff."

"You hardly need our permission," he says with a laugh. "Though if it will make you feel better, go, my child! I give you my blessing."

"How do I make a professional orchestra respect me?"

"You do what you've done every day for four years. Look everyone in the eye and behave like you've earned your place there, because you have. Respect the music above all and they'll respect you. That simple. Who's your chaperone?

"Felix's grandmother said she'd go with me."

"How sweet!" Gerda says.

"Well, you'll have an interesting time," Herr Dietrich says.

"Everybody says that. I don't know whether they mean I'll end up in jail or on a boat to North Africa."

"Always hard to say," he says.

"Stay for dinner?" Gerda says.

"I should get back. My recital wore Mother out, so I'm trying to be around more. Be more helpful."

"You'll be glad you did," Gerda says.

"Answer that letter," Herr Dietrich says. "And now you're going to be a famous soloist, you may call me Wil, if you like."

"Maybe after I get the engagement," I say, wondering if I could ever be so familiar.

"Admirably cautious," he says. "And now I really should gobble my dinner, as there's a performance tonight. I suppose you're not coming? A pity. It's a soloist from France and Mahler's First."

"I'll be on my way, then," I say.

"I look forward to telling people I knew you before you were somebody," he says as he and Thomas see me out.

"Right," I say. "Good luck tonight."

"Thanks!" he says. "With Mahler, you take all the luck you can get."
I wave goodbye to Thomas and take my leave.

✦　✦　✦

My first trip to Bonn. My first travel without my family, and my first of any kind since my father died. My first stay in a hotel. I feel daring and cosmopolitan, never mind that Bonn is only thirty kilometers away from Köln by a local train that stops absolutely everywhere. Once the outskirts of Köln give way to fields and orchards, I ask Oma Judith why people think she's so dangerous.

"I say what I think," she says. "It used to get me in trouble. Now I'm old, people assume I'm crazy but harmless, so I can say what I think even more. I lived in a commune, you know, outside of Prague, when I was young. We were penniless and creative and there was a fair amount of sex. You might say we were the real Bohemians. I started as a painter, but I got to be better at poetry. Lidia had the real gift for painting. You've seen her work in the house. She's looking forward to going back to it now Ros and Felix are grown up. So, I wrote poetry, and stories, too, about being Czech, and about being a woman. I was honest, so people thought I was scandalous. Out of bounds, unfeminine, improper. It's that simple. I'm not going to kidnap you or drag you through the taverns, or anything like that, in case you were worried."

"I wasn't worried," I say. "Not much, anyway. I'd like to read your poetry. The Wolff said I should find it in translation."

"I translated it myself," she says. "I didn't trust anyone else. We have copies around somewhere. And don't think I raised Lidia to be a wild animal. She studied painting with Louisa Piepenhagen and one or two other people. She was getting quite a reputation when she married Marcus. I hope she can get it back. It's dangerous to step away for so long."

Many stops later we arrive in Bonn. Much as I resent spending money on a taxi, I have too much luggage to walk, but at least Oma Judith insists on paying half. The Hotel Bonn isn't opulent, which is good, because I can't afford opulent. It's pleasant, with a small restaurant where we have dinner before we head upstairs for a quiet evening of me practicing Bruch with the mute on and trying to think of calming things, and Oma Judith reading a book.

In the morning, after a light breakfast I have a hard time swallowing for all the caterpillars doing warm-up exercises in my stomach, we walk the short block to the concert hall under linden trees in full summer leaf, past planter boxes bursting with flowers. The Beethovenhalle, named for Bonn's most famous native son, stands on its own square, a white Neoclassical temple with a large statue of Beethoven in front. My instructions direct us to a small side door that opens onto a long, narrow stairway.

"Welcome to the glamorous world of the arts," Oma Judith says.

"Right," I say.

We climb up, and up, and up. Finally, at the top, we reach an office in which a man sits behind a large desk covered with papers.

"Fraülein Adler? You're early, excellent," he says. "I'm Georg Reisenholm, Herr Biedermeyer's secretary. And your companion?"

"Judith Čápová," Oma Judith says.

"If I might warm up somewhere and change into proper attire?"

"Of course, Fraülein," he says. "I'll show you to a dressing room and I'll come for you when it's time. You'll have half an hour with the pianist to review the score before you play."

"Excellent, Herr Reisenholm," I say, pretending to be a confident professional violinist for all I'm worth.

The bowels of the Beethovenhalle remind me strongly of the Conservatory basement. Perhaps the underbellies of all musical institutions look the same. Herr Reisenholm leads us to a dressing room and departs. As his footsteps click away down the corridor, my caterpillars shift from calisthenics to a general riot.

"This is big," I mutter. "March in lock-step today, all right?"

"What?" Oma Judith says.

"Nothing."

Very little time seems to pass before Herr Reisenholm returns. He leads me to the stage and Oma Judith into the hall. I'm ready: I've dressed, warmed up and run through a few passages. Just for luck, I picture Reinhold von Marburg tripping on the hem of Madame Kurtz's light blue morning dress. My caterpillars give an angry little salute, and begin to march.

Yes, I'm nervous. But I'm ready.

The hall itself is narrower and deeper than Sinfonia Hall, with galleries along the side walls. Herr Nofziger, the pianist, looks about sixty, with a bushy gray beard and a curt, businesslike manner. He's clearly skeptical of a young woman just out of Conservatory. Fine. We rehearse while I continue doing my best impression of a confident, professional violinist.

Herr Reisenholm returns in half an hour with a very round man: Herr Biedermeyer, the artistic director.

"A pleasure, Fraülein," he says. "Herr Bruch was most enthusiastic about your recital in Köln. Are you ready?"

"Yes, Herr Biedermeyer," I say.

When they're seated, I take several very deep breaths, nod to Herr Nofziger, and the orchestral introduction floats out of the piano and into the hall.

"Herr Bruch was not mistaken," Herr Biedermeyer says afterward as he climbs laboriously up the steps to the stage. "We shall be delighted to offer you an engagement. In September or October, I should think. Four days of rehearsal should suffice; you are quite prepared. If you will come up to the office when you've packed, we can discuss terms."

"Very nice, Fraülein." Herr Nofziger extends his hand.

"Thank you," I say, extending mine.

Professional. Not student.

"I'm coming with you," Oma Judith says as we leave the stage the way we came in.

"Good. If I get us lost down here, two can shout louder than one," I say. But, in fact, it seems less labyrinthine than before. And better lit. Funny, what a difference an hour makes.

✦　✦　✦

October 1910

When I return to Bonn, it seems almost no time has passed, but I walk to the first morning's rehearsal under a shower of red and orange leaves falling to the sidewalk.

My caterpillars don't normally turn out for rehearsals, but they have for this one.

Heads turn, whispers ripple through the sections when Herr Biedermeyer introduces me. Stay calm, I tell myself. Surely, they knew their soloist was a woman? Surely, they've had women soloists before? Perhaps they didn't expect one so young. Perhaps they think Herr Biedermeyer engaged me for my looks, or as a favor for his friend Bruch.

Well, then, I'll just have to earn their respect, as the Wolff said, by making it clear that I belong here and, as Herr Dietrich said, by respecting the music above all else. As I'll have to earn everyone else's, every single day for the rest of my career.

Herr Biedermeyer, as I suspected, is also the conductor. Once he is settled on the podium, a brief discussion of dynamics, tempi, and interpretation precedes the downbeat. And yet when the downbeat comes, the orchestra plays the first movement too slowly—not horribly too slowly, just enough to drag. I have to tap my foot to keep from getting ahead of the pace, unlike with Herr Nofziger, whose tempi matched the Wolff's— and Bruch's. When we reach the end of the Prelude, I take a deep breath.

"Herr Biedermeyer, the Prelude is marked *allegro moderato*, 116 to 120 beats per minute. We are playing it, I believe, around 110. May we try it again within the range of the marked tempo?"

I hear feet shuffling.

Herr Biedermeyer looks indulgently down from the podium. "Are you quite sure?" he says.

"I have the full score here to check," I say. Herr Biedermeyer, I note, is conducting from memory.

He glances at the Wolff's score.

"So it is. The 110 feels right to us. However, if you wish to attempt it a little faster, we can certainly accommodate you."

"I played my audition at the marked tempo," I say, very, *very* politely, because I suspect I'm being tested somehow, or possibly just patronized, and I need to tread carefully. On the other hand, not playing the work as the composer intended won't do me any good at all.

"Perhaps you would care to tap out your preferred tempo?" he says, still very indulgently. More feet shuffle behind me.

I tap out two beats a second.

"Well, then," he says and raises his baton.

It goes much better. At the end, I hear a bit more murmuring behind me.

"Do you need to repeat any of this movement?" Herr Biedermeyer says.

I check my score and name a starting measure. He lifts his baton and we do the passage again. I name another measure. We repeat the process four or five times.

The second movement, by contrast, is too fast. Not drastically too fast, but I keep having to rush in order not to fall behind. It's marked *adagio*, slightly over one beat per second, and the orchestra is playing it at nearly one and a half beats per second. The feeling is quite different. I grit my teeth and scamper along with the orchestra.

"Herr Biedermeyer, the tempo . . ."

We have the same conversation. I tap out a beat per second. We do it again. I check a few cues.

"You are ready for the third movement?" he says.

"At the high end of *allegro energico*, as marked. About 150 beats per minute, more or less."

I tap it out.

"Are you sure? That is quite fast." He looks concerned. I can't imagine why; he *heard* me do it at my audition two months ago.

"I believe the composer intended it to be quite fast, Herr Biedermeyer, so that is how I have prepared it."

"Well, then." He raises his baton.

He actually pushes the tempo past 150. Either he has an imperfect grasp of the composer's intent or he's trying to trip me up. I've worked on the piece for so long—a year since I began it—that I stick with the orchestra like a rider on a galloping horse. But it's obviously rushed. When it finally boils to a finish, I feel a sort of grim pride: I didn't miss anything, even at the orchestra's excessive pace. I think fast. I have to get him to slow it down, but I don't want him, or the musicians, most of whom are more than twice my age, to think it's because I'm not confident at that speed.

"What do you think, Fräulein?" Herr Biedermeyer says, looking down at me with a paternal smile.

"It is exhilarating at that tempo," I say. "If that's your preference, I have no problem with it. It is faster than marked, however."

"You would prefer to take it slightly slower?"

"I would prefer to play within the marked range. However, the tempo we just played is fine, if that is your wish. Only the expression suffers. Because even though it's quite fast, it's also expressive, as you know."

"I see," he says. "Well, we may have fallen into a bit of a habit, I suppose. Let us try it a little slower this time, then. You said 150? Very well."

He raises his baton again.

It's better. I check several measures for the timing of my cues. At last, we take the whole thing from the beginning, without stops. Herr Biedermeyer sticks with the correct tempi, thank goodness. The work sounds better. I hope the musicians behind me think so, too.

"We will see you at the same time tomorrow, then, Fraülein," he says when we're finished. "Our afternoon here will be devoted to the remainder of the program. You're most welcome to stay, but I'm sure you would like to explore our lovely little city with your chaperone."

I debate for a moment whether to sit in the hall and watch, but the morning promised to become a lovely fall day and I would quite like to be out in it. So, I thank the musicians, pack up my things in the dressing room, and Oma Judith and I make our exit.

"What did you think?" I ask her as we walk back to the hotel.

"I think you held your own," she says. "Managed not to make him look stupid. A good trick but not always easy."

"Why did he play the wrong tempi? He heard my audition. The pianist was right on. Was he trying to trip me up?"

Oma Judith laughs. People turn to stare.

"Don't give him too much credit," she says. "He only heard the beginning and the end. You put him right to sleep! So today he just played it out of habit, the way he remembered it."

"He was *asleep*? But he said Herr Bruch was right about me. And he gave me the contract!"

"Reisenholm, the secretary, heard you. He's a musician himself, you know. I got him talking to me afterward. I'm betting he pretty much runs the Bonn Orchestra. He jabbed his employer in the ribs at the right time and whispered in his ear. Biedermeyer took it from there. Biedermeyer's a good conductor, just lazy. He doesn't have enough energy to be malicious. I don't think you'll have trouble with him after this. Most importantly, the musicians know you're serious. They may think you're an upstart, but they saw what you can do. They were struggling in the third part, too, though you probably couldn't see it. You'll be fine after this."

"I hope so. I can't believe it—asleep! I hope I don't have that effect on the audience."

"You won't, unless people in Bonn spend as much time eating and drinking as he does. Now let's get your violin stowed and find someplace to have lunch. I want to visit Beethoven's house."

The next days' rehearsals focus on phrasing, dynamics, and interpretation. Herr Biedermeyer doesn't test me anymore, if it was a test. The morning of the performance we rehearse the last remaining trouble spots and then repeat the whole thing. My anxieties have subsided and my excitement is growing. I'm nervous, but also eager to show what I can do, to get started on this life I've dreamed of leading.

✦ ✦ ✦

Oma Judith stays with me in my dressing room, reading the program someone has placed there while I prepare and warm up. The blue-green gown and black slippers. Joseph's necklace. The French roll. Scales. Arpeggios.

A soft knock on my door. We exchange looks of surprise. It's not time yet, surely? I open the door to see Herr Werner, the white-haired concertmaster, standing there in his formal concert clothing. I feel a small stab of anxiety. Have I forgotten something?

"Pardon my intrusion, ladies," he says. "I only wanted to wish you good luck this evening and to let you know the orchestra members have been most impressed with you this week. Clearly, you are the master, or mistress, I should say, of your instrument. I hear you are a recent graduate of the Köln Conservatory?"

"This June," I say.

"All the more impressive," he says. "Well, best of luck tonight." He bows, steps back and continues on down the corridor.

A few minutes later, there comes another soft knock. This time it's one of the cellists, who says much the same thing. After him, the first oboist, and then one of the horn players, all saying they've enjoyed working with me, all wishing me luck. In all, at least ten musicians knock at my dressing room door. I begin to feel like an equal, which I should anyway, but that thirty-year age difference has kept getting in the way.

When Herr Weber, the stage manager, knocks on my door for places,

Oma Judith and I exchange a look as she pulls herself laboriously to her feet.

"You'll make your father proud," she says. She kisses me on the cheek and limps out to take her seat in the hall, her cane tapping on the floor.

I wait by the stage manager's desk, my strings tuned, my bow adjusted, my hands warmed up. My caterpillars parade about my stomach in elaborate formation behind their leader, who brandishes a tiny flag with a violin on it. Reinhold von Marburg appears in my mind wearing Madame Kurtz's light blue morning dress and then vanishes. I think of Anni, who suggested the strategy in the first place. I think of my mother, who has made the journey to see me play when she would far rather have stayed home. I think of my father. I think of touching the core of what it means to be human.

I'm ready.

Herr Biedermeyer appears at my shoulder.

"Full house tonight," he says. "Everyone in town is eager to hear the lovely girl soloist. Not that I want to make you nervous!" He chortles, which makes him jiggle.

"I'm fine," I say. Actually, I wish he would go away, but as we're about to begin, he'll be gone soon enough.

The house lights dim. The orchestra tunes. Herr Weber signals. Herr Biedermeyer enters, threading his way between rows to the podium. He ascends the podium, bows to the audience, turns and raises his baton.

If I expected a solidly German program in the Beethovenhalle in Beethoven's birthplace, I underestimated the sophistication of its audience. The concert opens with Rossini's Overture to *The Thieving Magpie*, a short, lighthearted romp from an opera in which the villain is a bird, but I don't hear much of it.

A big Italian finish, enthusiastic applause. Herr Biedermeyer threads his way offstage.

"*Bravo, Maestro*!" I say as he passes me. He laughs.

"Always nice to start with something short and sweet," he says. "Now they can let in the latecomers and shuffle the chairs around for the Bruch. All ready?"

My caterpillar army is on the march behind its tiny banner. I feel my father's presence beside me.

"Absolutely!"

A minute later, Herr Weber gives his signal. I pull myself to my tallest height and stride out onto the stage, Herr Biedermeyer a few paces behind me.

✦   ✦   ✦

This is how flying must feel to a bird. As the Bruch progresses from its first long, low note through its passionate Prelude, its deep second movement to its virtuosic conclusion, the orchestra is the wind lifting my wings as I soar above it, twisting and turning on its currents. The energy of the audience is electric; no rehearsal could match it. Every cell in my body and brain focuses on the music: following the conductor, hitting the cues precisely, breathing with the phrasing and the bowing, knowing when I'm in charge, when the orchestra is in charge. Most of all, *feeling*: feeling what the music is expressing, emotions for which no words exist, making them real through the mechanics of creating sound.

As long as it lasts, nothing exists outside of this experience. There is only the orchestra, the conductor, the audience, and the music. They are all mine, all subject to the commands of my bow.

It is magnificent, and when it's over, I feel as though no time has passed at all.

A beat of reverberant silence passes while I hold my bow high, waiting for the echoes to fade, before I lower it and the hall erupts in applause. I exhale. Not that I thought they wouldn't, but it's powerful applause, a real ovation. I take my bows, extend my hand to Herr Biedermeyer, who kisses it, turn to Herr Werner, the concertmaster, who does the same. I applaud the orchestra—my colleagues—and stride briskly offstage, Herr Biedermeyer behind me.

"Well done," Herr Biedermeyer says. "Herr Bruch was indeed not mistaken."

And then we are onstage again for another round of bows. Herr Weber appears, threading his way through the orchestra to hand me a large bouquet of deep red roses, which I didn't expect. I'll check for a card when I return to my dressing room, though I suspect I know who sent them.

This time, when we exit the stage, the applause fades and the house lights come up for intermission. I pack away my violin and bow as musicians begin to stream past me. Some pause to say something. A few raise my hand to their lips. When the corridor is clear, I take my case and my bouquet back to the quiet of my dressing room. I back the door shut, set everything down and study my reflection in the mirror: my hair in its French roll, my blue-green gown, my necklace. My beautiful necklace.

"You did it," I say to the mirror.

I've made my debut. I've succeeded. It went well, maybe even better than my recital. Not perfect. Nothing will ever be perfect. But worthy. I earned my place. I belong here, in this world, playing my father's violin. My violin. Ours.

My reflection smiles back at me.

I want to savor this moment forever.

✦ ✦ ✦

Of course, Joseph sent the roses. Considering this is October, he must have paid a fortune for them.

When Herr Weber calls places at the end of the intermission, I return to the wing to watch the second half. Herr Biedermeyer stands ready, waiting for the orchestra to tune.

"You've recovered?" he says, his round face all smiles.

"Mostly," I say.

The oboe's mournful A cuts through the mutter of instruments.

"Onward!" he says. Herr Weber gives his signal and Herr Biedermeyer enters to applause. I settle back in my chair to listen.

It's *Scheherezade,* by the Russian Rimsky-Korsakov, inspired by the Arabian tales of *A Thousand and One Nights.* As a child I loved those stories, full of men in white pantaloons, veiled women, and most un-German magic. Most of all I loved Sultana Scheherezade, the goddess of storytellers, whose intelligence and courage saved her own life and redeemed her bitter Sultan, murderer of brides. What nerve she had, when the slightest mistake would be her undoing, to sit night after night and tell tales of magic and adventure to an angry man who wielded over her the power of death.

The nerve of a swordsman. Like Anni.

The concertmaster plays Scheherezade's line, which amuses me, Herr Werner being at least sixty, with a great mop of white hair and a full white beard. But his Scheherezade, like the Sultana herself, is delicate, beautiful and strong. He understands her, clearly, despite their differences.

A far better-dressed crowd than I'm used to fills the foyer when I emerge from backstage with Herr Biedermeyer. Men bow to me. Women in elegant dresses take my hand. Everyone is most kind. Some wish me good luck in my career. No one seems to think I shouldn't be here. I suppose that crowd stayed home. Herr Biedermeyer stands at my shoulder in a proprietary way, as if I were his discovery. Which, in a way, I suppose I am.

My own family and friends hang back, waiting their turn. They're all here, except the Dietrichs, because Wil, too, has a concert tonight and they also have a very new baby, Elisabet, born in August. Mother has found a chair and looks utterly exhausted, but happy. To my surprise, I see Christian Königsmann deep in conversation with Franz and Anni. And—I have to look twice to be sure—even the Wolff is here!

I introduce them all to Herr Biedermeyer, who looks especially thrilled to meet Herr Kurtz, while Katerina kisses me on both cheeks.

"Darling! I want all the details next Saturday!" she says.

I promise to provide them. Perhaps I should invent some, in order to match her glamorous expectations.

"More recent graduates, eh?" Herr Biedermeyer says, turning his attention to Felix, Franz, Arnold, and Robert, and handing each his card. "Come see me if you want to audition. We're always looking for young talent."

Having seen the musicians of the Bonn Orchestra close up, I'd guess the last time they hired young talent was around 1890. But maybe he's talking about soloists. I overhear Robert arranging an appointment for a few months from now. No one will ever say "no" to Robert, I'm sure of it.

"I shall look forward to it," Herr Biedermeyer says. He bows to everyone and moves on to another group.

"Told you I wouldn't miss your debut," Christian says. "I think you improved on your recital, if that's possible."

"I thought so, too," I say. "Having the whole orchestra does give it the most amazing energy. Have you met everyone?"

"Franz introduced me around," he says. "I won't keep you, but congratulations. The first of many, I hope." He kisses my hand, waves to Franz and the others, and strides out the front door into the night.

"Professorin!" I say as the Wolff approaches. "I'm so glad you came! Er—was it decent?"

"Tolerably," she says. "You reflect well on your training."

"Notes tomorrow?"

"Day after tomorrow will be adequate," she says. "After that you can focus on the Mendelssohn." She turns to leave. "Oh, and congratulations," she adds, turning back. "It was a quite respectable debut."

She's out the front door before I can thank her for that extravagant compliment.

"It's just embarrassing, the way she heaps praise on you," Anni says at my shoulder.

"'Respectable' is a new twist on 'decent,' that's for sure," I say. "But I'm pretty sure she means she liked it."

"If you say so," Anni says.

"You're all right?" I ask Mother as I slip into the seat next to her.

"Just tired," she says. "I'm glad I came, though. It was worth it. You looked so grown up, standing up there. Your father would have been so proud of you."

"I hope so," I say. "I'm glad you liked it."

"*Liked* it!" Anni snorts. "She was applauding louder than anyone. Even louder than me."

"I thought of you, Anni, when they were playing *Scheherezade*," I say.

"What, me, marry a murderous Sultan?" Anni says. "He'd never make it to morning and no one would ever find the body."

"Yes, you," I say, laughing. I'm beginning to feel a little giddy. "Because of her nerve under pressure, like a swordsman. Like you."

"Oh," she says, looking quite pleased. "You did, eh?"

"Well?" Oma Judith limps over, her cane clicking on the floor. "What do you think, Sarah? Did I keep your girl safe enough?"

Mother nods. She sags in her chair.

"We need to get you home," Frau Apfelbaum says.

"You're going back tonight?" I ask. "Shouldn't Mother stay at the hotel and rest?"

"She insisted," Frau Apfelbaum says. "You'll have a late night, no doubt, but we promised we'd take her home safe and sound. Don't worry, it's a short train ride and we'll see that she's settled in before we leave her."

"Not me," Felix says. The whole group has gathered around now. "We're staying to take the toast of the town out to dinner. Knowing her, she hasn't eaten since breakfast."

"Lunch," I say. "Oma made me. But dinner sounds like a good idea. I'll change and meet you at the stage door in fifteen minutes."

"Then I'll escort you back to your dressing room so you can pack up," Herr Reisenholm says.

"I'll be home tomorrow morning," I say. To Anni, I whisper, "I'll look after Mother from here on, all right? You deserve several months off." I hug them, Mother and Anni both, long and hard. At the door back into the depths of the hall, I turn and wave. They all wave back to me.

✦ ✦ ✦

We occupy a large table in the hotel restaurant, eating, drinking, and laughing until after midnight. Robert tells stories of his misadventures as a boy in New York City. Oma Judith tells about growing up in Prague and her misadventures in the art commune. I have no misadventures to offer, as sheltered as my girlhood was, and the stories I do have don't fit the mood. And yet, they're all here because of me.

I have my beautiful bouquet of roses in a vase upstairs in my room and an envelope with a very handsome cheque in it, more than I've ever earned in my life, locked in the hotel safe until I can get it home to the bank. I have the applause, the appreciation of so many strangers. The *feeling*—the soaring exhilaration of playing with the orchestra behind me. The magnificent sound of my father's—our—violin, as much a part of me as my own body. The sense that he stood beside me while I played. A glimpse of the future, of a life fortunate enough to contain moments like tonight.

I lean back in my chair, suddenly very tired. Stories and laughter wash over me. The other tables have all emptied and the staff has laid them for breakfast. I catch Oma Judith's eye. She abruptly pushes her chair back from the table.

"Carry on, gentlemen," she says. "At least until the staff throws you out. But the talent needs her beauty rest and so does Marthe."

The table erupts with more laughter. They stand and I embrace each of them, all my brothers.

Joseph is last. "I'll come by tomorrow," he whispers.

I give him an extra hug in reply.

They're still at it when we climb the stairs to our rooms.

The afterglow lasts well into the next day, as I pack my bags, wrap my roses, retrieve my cheque from the hotel safe. Oma Judith and I board the train at the Bonn station and splurge on a taxi home from the station in Köln. I wave goodbye to Oma Judith at the front door to my building, watch the taxi round the corner, open the door, and climb the stairs.

I'm fishing for my door key when I hear quick footsteps inside and the door whips open. Anni stands there, her eyes wild, her face bloodless.

"What—"

"I can't wake her up!" she says. "I thought she was sleeping late, because she was so tired last night. I slept late myself. But—"

I push past her, drop my bags and case and the roses on the floor and run into Mother's bedroom. She is lying in her bed under her eiderdown, her face slack, her skin nearly the color of the sheet. One hand hangs over the edge of the bed. I gingerly take her wrist to feel for a pulse.

Nothing.

I feel under her jaw.

Nothing.

I press on her heart.

Nothing.

I turn back to Anni, my expression, I'm sure, now the mirror of hers.

"I'll go get Dr. Goldmann," I say.

But we both know it's too late.

✦ ✦ ✦

Dr. Goldmann tells us there was nothing either of us could have done, that a massive stroke in the night is a merciful and largely painless end. He returns home to make the necessary telephone calls and comes back to deal with the undertakers. Anni and I sit silent on the sofa, our arms around each other as men troop through our front door with a stretcher and troop out a few minutes later with our mother under a sheet. One of them hands us a card with the funeral home's name and an appointment time.

"To make arrangements," he says.

We nod, not hearing.

Dr. Goldmann asks us if we want a rabbi to come. We exchange a look.

"What for?" Anni says.

"Whom can I call?" Dr. Goldmann says. "You shouldn't be alone."

"The Apfelbaums on Josephine-Lang-Strasse," I say. "And the Walters, on Droste-Hülshoff-Strasse in the Neuehrenfeld." I copy their addresses out of my address book and give them to him. He promises to summon them and leaves.

We stare at each other. In Anni's face I see my own shock and disbelief. Was it last night I played the Bruch violin concerto with the Bonn Orchestra? It feels like that was someone else, in another lifetime.

"Just like that," Anni says.

"Just like that."

"What do we do now?"

"Sit for a while. Hold on to each other. Wait."

The rest of the day is a blur. People arrive. Joseph. Tante Hanne. Frau Apfelbaum. Oma Judith. They busy themselves in our little kitchen. Someone puts food in front of me. I eat it and then forget I've eaten. Anni at some point retreats into her room and slams the door several times. Later, somehow, it is night. Someone puts more food in front of me and again I eat it and then forget I've eaten.

Someone finds my roses and puts them into a vase, but they've begun to wilt from being too long out of water and their petals are already falling.

Then, somehow, it's late and we're to go to bed with our mother's bedroom door gaping open. Tante Hanne announces she's staying, sleeping on the sofa so we won't be alone. In the middle of the night, Anni and I in turn awaken, crying from bad dreams. Tante Hanne is at our bedsides in a moment, holding us, comforting us, stroking our hair and patting our backs. Somehow, we go back to sleep with Tante Hanne singing to us as if we were children and somehow, inexplicably, dawn breaks, the autumn sunrise promising a clear, cold day, bright, but without heat. We wake from a last bit of sleep that felt heavy but restless and look around us, momentarily befuddled, trying to remember what happened to make everything so familiar seem so strange.

In the following days that blur one into the next, Franz, of all people, is unusually present. But it's not so strange, really. He has been where we are and at a much younger and more vulnerable age—ten, when his mother died after giving birth to his youngest sister. He seldom speaks of it and he speaks little now, but he spends an hour or two a day in our flat, just sitting by us—sitting shiva, Tante Hanne says, but he just shrugs and keeps sitting, a quiet and comforting presence.

✦ ✦ ✦

After the funeral, which is attended by very few people, Joseph asks me again to think about marrying him, promising me safety, security, loyalty, and love. I talk it over that night with Anni when everyone has gone, for we're considered able to be on our own now, and in fact we feel only exhausted relief when the last guest departs.

Anni says I would be an idiot to turn him down.

"He *listens*," she says. "Do you have any idea how few men actually *listen*?"

I ask if she would want to live with us. She says she'll think about it.

✦ ✦ ✦

I have no more performances. I'm unable to learn anything new, unable to play for more than a few minutes, just as when my father died. The Mendelssohn concerto I started learning in the summer withers away. I didn't expect to be so flattened. We knew this was coming. Mother said so herself. She wasn't afraid. I thought I would be able to keep going, to channel my sadness into my playing, but it doesn't happen. It takes all my mental strength to figure out the next thing that needs to be done, and then do it.

Slowly, over days and weeks, Anni and I sort through Mother's possessions, in which we find few clues to the person she might have been. We give her clothes, those that aren't too patched and darned, to charity. Her forest green woolen shawl we offer to Tante Hanne, to Oma Judith, and to Frau Apfelbaum. All decline to take it, perhaps fearing it will upset me to see them wearing it. In the end, it, too, goes out into the world where it will warm the shoulders of some unknown woman, one who until now was cold.

We prepare simple meals. Afterward, I can't remember what we ate, or what we talked about. More than once I hear Anni's door slam in the middle of the night and when I reach her room, I have to pick my way over

372

all the things she's thrown onto the floor to reach her bed, where she lies crying.

I, on the other hand, feel like a hot air balloon whose fire has been turned off. I replay the events of that night over and over, trying to find some way I could have changed the ending. I played my debut concert. I saw her in the foyer of the Beethovenhalle. We talked. We embraced. Anni and the Apfelbaums took her home: taxi, train, taxi. They helped her up the stairs. She went to bed. She died.

I sat around a large table in the restaurant of the Hotel Bonn with my friends and Oma Judith and listened to people tell stories and ate, and drank, and laughed. I went upstairs, admired the roses Joseph sent me, washed up, and fell into bed, exhausted but euphoric, where I slept soundly until morning, dreaming, not only the themes of the Bruch Violin Concerto but the strains of *Scheherezade*.

Maybe if I had persuaded her not to come. But I wanted her to see me solo with a real orchestra, to show her I would be all right on the path I chose. And she wanted to come. Anni says she tried to talk Mother out of it, but she insisted.

Maybe if I had persuaded her to spend the night at the hotel, instead of taking the train back to Köln. But she would never want to spend money to sleep in a strange place. She did what she wanted. She went home.

I could not have changed the ending. In any case, it's done.

One night I ask Anni's forgiveness for being so absent and she gives it. Another night she asks my forgiveness for being so angry and I give it. We'll never be those sisters who exchange all their confidences and share all their secrets, but it doesn't matter. Wherever our paths lead us, we will have this bond between us of forgiveness and acceptance.

Though it doesn't seem so just now, we are strong, I believe, tempered in the heat of our shared losses. We're two new trunks growing out of the same fallen tree, even if by our leaves and branches you would guess we're two different species.

✦ ✦ ✦

April 1911

The first crocuses and daffodils are just emerging when Joseph and I are married in the Walters' sitting room by Papa Ernst's employer, the mayor of Köln, under the Walters' own wedding canopy. Anni stands with me, Robert with Joseph. The Apfelbaums are present, including Ros and Jan, Berit, Franz, Arnold and Alma, who are already married, Wil and Gerda with Thomas and baby Elisabet, some old friends of Joseph's.

Tante Hanne, or Mama Hanne, as I must now call her, overflows with happiness that her son is finally married and with the joy of fussing over people. Papa Ernst engages in animated conversation with everyone. The house reverberates with music, laughter, voices echoing good wishes, the clinking of glasses.

The luminous expression on Joseph's face is something I will remember all the rest of my life. The joy of it masks—almost—the silent void that remains somewhere deep inside me, diminished from last fall, but still stubbornly, darkly present. Perhaps, as I've thought before, joy and sadness will always travel hand in hand for me in this way. Perhaps it's impossible to understand one without having known the other. Perhaps that's the business of this life: to ride their currents without drowning in either.

So be it. I look into Joseph's eyes on this day and I feel happiness. It is real and I will treasure it, whatever life brings in the days to come.

I am finally sure: whatever I do, wherever I go, I will always love him.

End Book 1

ACKNOWLEDGEMENTS

No work of art is ever perfect. This story became immeasurably better, not to mention that it exists at all, thanks to the support, encouragement, and contributions of many people, listed here by chronological category in more or less alphabetical order.

My long-suffering teachers in the Grossmont College Creative Writing program: Rich Farrell, Ryan Griffiths, and Karl Sherlock.

My early readers: Lauren Carlton, Anita Orne, and Bennett Spevack, who had no idea what they were letting themselves in for. I hope they find this version much improved.

My team at Acorn Publishing for their initial encouragement and ongoing support, reassurance, patience, and guidance in the arcane process of turning a draft on a screen into a finished work you can hold in your hand: cofounder Holly Kammier, project manager Leslie Ferguson, and editor Laura Taylor. Thank you all for making the publishing experience an education and a pleasure, as opposed to absolutely every soul-crushing thing I'd ever heard about it before.

The dedicated people who bring the Orcas Island Chamber Music Festival to life every August, for allowing me behind the scenes into the world of chamber music: OICMF's visionary founder and artistic director Aloysia Friedmann, executive director Anita Orne, festival manager Linda Slone, and production manager Mary Taylor.

The dozens of musicians who share their gifts with audiences at OICMF, especially its quartet-in-residence, the Miró Quartet, who have answered a thousand questions, inspired me, made me think, taught me, corrected me, and not laughed at my mistakes.

San Diego Opera principal conductor Yves Abel: consummate artist, maestro, teacher, friend.

GLOSSARY OF MUSICAL TERMS

Adagio	A slow tempo, about 66–76 beats per minute (bpm).
Allegro	A fast, bright tempo of about 120–168 bpm.
Allegro brillante	The second term is descriptive. Thus, fast and brilliant.
Allegro energico	Likewise, fast and energetic.
Allegro moderato	Moderately fast, about 116–120 bpm.
Allemande	A traditional German court dance in moderate 4/4 time: **1**-2-3-4.
Andante	Italian for "walking." Thus, a walking tempo, about 76–108 bpm.
Arpeggio	The notes of a chord played one at a time, either ascending or descending.
Baritone	Male vocal range that falls between tenor and bass.
Baroque era	The period in all the European arts from about 1600–1750 AD. Johann Sebastian Bach was its towering musical genius in Germany.
Bourée	A fast-paced seventeenth century French dance in a duple meter: **1**-2, **1**-2.
Bridge	Here, a voice that connects between other voices. Also, the little wooden piece on a stringed instrument that holds the strings in place above the body.
Caprice/ Capriccio	A lively piece of music in a free form. Paganini's Caprices were short show-off pieces, fiendishly difficult.
Chaconne	A courtly dance with melodic variations over a short, repeated bass phrase in slow triple meter: **1**-2-3.
Classical era	From 1750 (the death of Bach) to about 1820. The use of melody and harmony replaced Baroque polyphony (many voices). Masters include Joseph Haydn, Wolfgang Amadeus Mozart and Ludwig van Beethoven.
Concertmaster	First chair of the first violins in an orchestra. Decides questions about bowing, leads the tuning, plays all the violin solos.
Concerto	A large-scale form for a single soloist and full orchestra. A virtuosic demonstration of the soloist's technical and emotional range.

Counterpoint	A type of polyphony combining multiple melodic lines of equal importance, as opposed to a melody and harmony.
Courante	French for "running," a fast-paced dance in triple meter: 1-2-3, 1-2-3.
Double stops	When the bow plays two strings at once.
Dynamics	The range of volume from loud to soft.
Ear training	Essential musical training to identify pitches, intervals, melody, chords, rhythms, etc., solely by ear. Can be grueling.
Flat	A half step below the named tone; e.g., B flat is a half step below B natural.
Flourish	Here, when string players finish with their bows held aloft. The applause doesn't begin until they lower their bows (or until the conductor lowers his or her arms), so that the last notes have a chance to reverberate into a beat of silence.
Flutes (of violin)	The little ribs traditionally carved into the violin's scroll.
Forte	Loud.
Fugue	A specific use of counterpoint in which two or three individual voices chase a theme around and do gymnastics with it, usually on a single instrument. Reached its peak in the Baroque music of Johann Sebastian Bach. Fugues can be very, very difficult.
Gavotte	A bouncy French folk dance in moderate 4/4 meter: 1-2-3-4.
Gigue	French for "jig." A fast dance in compound meter, such as 6/8: 1-2-3-1-2-3.
Greek modes	The Greeks were the first to organize musical notes in a way we recognize. Modes are precursors to our scales, with seven notes instead of eight. Like scales, they differ from one another in the placement of whole and half steps and have different characters as a result. They have wonderful names. From brightest to darkest: Lydian, Ionian (same as a major scale), Mixolydian, Dorian, Aeolian (same as a minor scale), Phrygian, and Locrian. Some composers use modes today. But they won't appear anywhere else in this story, I promise, and there will be no quiz.
Key	The scale, or group of pitches, that forms the basis for a musical composition. Keys are major or minor, depending on the location of the necessary half steps within the scale. The notes, A, B, C, D, E, F, and G, and their sharps and flats, each have major and multiple variations of minor scales.
Key signature	The number of sharps or flats in a given scale, the symbols of which are placed on the musical staff at the beginning of each line.

Largo	A slow tempo, 40–60 bpm.
Legato	Smooth, connected notes.
Lieder	German for "songs." The Lieder of Franz Schubert for voice and piano are perhaps the best known. Art songs are still popular with today's composers.
Loure	A slow French Baroque dance in compound meter, such as 6/8: **1**-2-3-**1**-2-3.
Luthier	A maker of stringed instruments: the violin family, guitars, mandolins, and, of course, lutes.
Lydian/ Mixolydian modes	See Greek modes.
Major	A scale whose steps are: whole, whole, half, whole, etc. Brighter than minor, sometimes described as sounding happy, a gross overgeneralization.
Measure/ bar	The unit of written music bounded by single vertical lines, divided into the number of beats indicated by the time signature.
Menuet/ Minuet	A French courtly dance in triple meter: **1**-2-3.
Metronome	A mechanical or electronic device that produces a regular, repeated, merciless sound to assist in keeping a regular beat. The bane of music students everywhere.
Mezzo-forte	Medium-loud.
Mezzo-soprano	The second highest vocal range, between soprano and alto.
Minor	A scale whose first steps are whole, half, whole, whole, etc. Darker than major, sometimes described as sounding sad or melancholy, another gross overgeneralization.
Modulation	A change from one key to another.
Movement	The different sections of a traditional sonata or symphony. Most sonatas have three movements: fast, slow, fast. Most symphonies have four: fast, slow, moderate, fast.
Musicianship	Knowledge, skill, and expressivity in performing or writing music.
Musicology	The study of music as an academic subject, distinct from training in performance or composition.
Oboe gives the A	The oboe is the hardest instrument to adjust. So, when orchestras tune, the oboe plays an A, and the other instruments all tune to match it.
Oratorio	A large scale composition, usually sacred, for orchestra, choir, and soloists. Not exclusively Baroque, but Bach wrote a lot of them. Probably the most famous is *Messiah* by Georg Friedrich Händel (usually anglicized to Handel because he lived in England).

Orchestration	Expanding a composition written for a single instrument into a work for a full orchestra.
Ostinato	A phrase, usually in the bass line, that repeats over and over, with a melodic line over it.
Overtone	A frequency higher than the fundamental frequency of a note that vibrates simultaneously with it and contributes to the timbre of the sound. Also called harmonics.
Overture	The opening musical introduction to an opera or ballet.
Part	The written music for a single instrument in an ensemble.
Partita	A suite of movements for solo instrument or ensemble whose meter, tempo and style are usually based on traditional dance forms.
Phrase	Analogous to a phrase in language; an expressive unit within a theme.
Pianissimo	Very soft.
Piano	Soft.
Pizzicato	Plucking the strings of a bowed instrument.
Prelude/ Preludio	An introductory section before the main piece. Also used in the Romantic era for a small-scale piece intended to stand on its own.
Quartet	A chamber work for four players; also, the four players themselves.
Quintet	A chamber work for five players; also, the five players themselves.
Razumovsky Quartets (Beethoven)	A set of three string quartets, Opus 59 Nos. 1–3, from Beethoven's middle period, composed in 1806 on commission for Count Andreas Razumovsky, the Russian ambassador to Vienna.
Resonance	When the frequency of vibration in one part of a musical instrument matches the natural frequency of another part, causing it to vibrate also, thus producing a richer and more complex sound.
Ricochet bowing	French for "rebound." Bouncing the bow off the strings instead of drawing it back and forth.
Romantic era	A period in the arts spanning most of the nineteenth century, and later for many individual artists. Romantic music was influenced by nature, literature, poetry, and nationalism, and broke down the old Classical forms in favor of emotional, dramatic, often programmatic works.
Rosin	A solid, sticky form of pine resin that string players apply to their bowstrings to create friction.
Round	A composition in which multiple voices sing or play the same line but start at different times. For example, *Frère Jacques*, or *Row, Row, Row Your Boat*.

Rubato	Giving flexibility to a strict beat in order to give expressive shape to a phrase.
Scale	A consecutive series of notes between any one note and its octave (the note with the same letter, one level up or down).
Scherzo	Italian for "joke." A vigorous, light, or playful composition, usually a movement within a symphony or sonata.
Score	Written music that shows all the voices in the ensemble together, each on its own line. In a quartet, musicians may play from a score to learn the work and then from parts to reduce page turning; in an orchestra, they play from individual parts. Conductors can look at a full orchestra score and hear it in their heads. Absolutely incredible.
Scroll (of violin)	The spiraling ornament at the end by the tuning pegs.
Second violin	In a quartet (one each) or a symphony (in sections), there are two violins (first and second), viola, and cello. In early string quartets the first violin tended to get all the glory, but later, the quartet became what Goethe called "four rational people conversing."
Sharp	A half step above the named note, e.g., A sharp is a half step above A natural.
Sinfonietta	A small orchestra.
Sonata	1. The quintessential musical structure of the Classical era, involving main and secondary themes and their development. 2. A multi-movement piece for one or two instruments, usually fast, slow, fast, composed using sonata form.
Soprano	The highest vocal range, sung by women, and sometimes boys in children's choirs.
Stand-mate	In orchestras, two musicians usually share a music stand.
Strings of violin	E (highest and thinnest), A, D, G (lowest and thickest). Though the violin looks delicate, it is strong enough to withstand the tension put on it by the strings, up to 18 lb. by the E string.
Symphonic/ Tone poem	A large scale, free-form work for orchestra that tended to replace the sonata form symphony in the Romantic era. Sometimes programmatic (like Berlioz's *Symphonie Fantastique*).
Symphony	1. A Classical era form for full orchestra, usually having four movements: fast, slow, moderate, and fast. 2. A synonym for the orchestra itself, comprising the string family (including double bass), woodwinds, brass, percussion, and occasionally other instruments.
Tempo	The speed at which music is played, in beats per minute (bpm).

Theme	Main melodic idea.
Theory	The study of the fundamental elements that make up music and how to use them.
Thirds	Two notes played with a note between them, for example C/E (major third), or C/E flat (minor third).
Timbre	The perceived quality of a musical note or sound. The reason a C on a piano sounds different from the same C on a violin.
Trio	A chamber work for three players; also, the three players themselves.
Vibrato	In strings, winds, or voice, making the sound pulsate slightly in order to enrich it. A complex tool that must be used very precisely and is not always the same.
Virtuoso	A musician with exceptional technical and expressive skill.

LIST OF COMPOSERS

Bach, Johann Sebastian (1685–1750)

German master of the Baroque era who composed in all forms of the time
and brought the arts of counterpoint and fugue to their highest level.
Several of his sons also became composers in later styles. Note
string quartets had not been invented yet, so he didn't write any.

Balakirev, Mily (1837–1910)

One of The Five (see below).

Beethoven, Ludwig van (1770–1827)

German, one of the greatest Classical era composers, who composed in all
forms of his time, including sixteen string quartets. He began losing his
hearing around age thirty, but persisted despite this existential trauma and
his ultimate total deafness.

Berlioz, Hector (1803–1869)

French Romantic era composer and conductor.

Boccherini, Luigi (1743–1805)

Italian Classical era composer and cellist.

Borodin, Alexander (1833–1887)

One of The Five (see below). He was also a chemist.

Brahms, Johannes (1833–1897)

German Romantic era composer with classical leanings.

Bruch, Max (1838–1920)

German Romantic era composer, originally from Köln.

Bruckner, Anton (1824–1896)

Austrian Romantic era composer and organist known for symphonies and
sacred music.

Chopin, Frédéric (1810–1849)

Polish Romantic era composer who lived in France and composed
primarily for solo piano.

Dvořák, Antonin (1841–1904)

Czech Romantic era nationalist composer.

The Five

a group of mid-nineteenth century Russian composers who founded the *Russian nationalist movement* in the 1860s, seeking a distinctly Russian sound using traditional folk melodies and harmonies.

Glinka, Mikhail (1804–1857)

First major Russian nationalist composer.

Haydn, Franz Joseph (1732–1809)

Austrian Classical era composer, long-lived, hugely influential, and famously good-natured. Wrote in all forms of his time, and spanned the cultural change from liveried servant in the employ of a count to free agent in his later years. Known as Papa Haydn, Father of the Symphony, and Father of the String Quartet.

Joachim, Joseph (1831–1907)

Hungarian violinist, among the greatest of his time.

Kreutzer, Rodolphe (1766–1831)

French composer (German father, hence the name) and violinist who composed among other things forty-two études or caprices for violin. Not to be confused with a slightly younger German composer, Joseph Kreutzer.

Liszt, Franz (1811–1886)

Hungarian Romantic era composer and pianist, known for flashy, bravura compositions and performances.

Mahler, Gustav (1860–1911)

Austro-Bohemian composer and conductor, best known for very large-scale symphonies and also songs.

Mendelssohn, Felix (1809–1847)

German Romantic era (but on the conservative, Classical end) composer, pianist, organist, and conductor. Hugely gifted, died at age thirty-eight.

Mozart, Nannerl (Maria Anna, 1751–1829)

W.A. Mozart's older sister, an equally gifted child prodigy, forced by her parents to abandon her career.

Mozart, Wolfgang Amadeus (1756–1791)

Austrian Classical era composer and child prodigy, widely considered one of the greatest European composers of all time. Wrote in all forms of his era; known for sonatas, quartets, symphonies, concerti, operas, and a great Requiem Mass. Died at age thirty-five.

Mussorgsky, Modest (1839–1881)

One of The Five (see above).

Paganini, Niccolò (1782–1840)

Italian Classical era violinist and composer, the most celebrated violin virtuoso of his time.

Rachmaninoff, Sergei (1873–1943)

Russian composer and pianist, the last Russian Romantic.

Rameau, Jean-Philippe (1683–1764)

French Baroque era composer known for harpsichord works and operas.

Rimsky-Korsakov, Nikolai (1844–1908)

One of The Five (see above).

Rossini, Gioachino (1792–1868)

Italian composer best known for operas.

Rubinstein, Anton (1829–1894)

Russian composer, pianist, and founder of St. Petersburg Conservatory.

Saint-Saëns, Camille (1835–1921)

French Romantic era composer, very prolific.

Schoenberg, Arnold (1874–1951)

Austrian modernist composer who eventually abandoned traditional keys in favor of unanchored twelve-tone compositions.

Schubert, Franz (1797–1828)

German Romantic era composer who died at age thirty-one. Very prolific, maybe best known for his Lieder (art songs).

Schumann, Clara (1819–1896)

German pianist and composer, married to Robert Schumann. She gave concerts, raised eight children, and outlived him by forty years.

Schumann, Robert (1810–1856)

Perhaps the archetypal German Romantic era composer, married to Clara Schumann. He suffered from mental illness and died at age 46 in a sanatorium.

Schradieck, Henry (1846–1918)

German violinist and well-known teacher.

Spohr, Ludwig/Louis (1784–1859)

German violinist, conductor, and composer, primarily for violin. Invented the chin rest, among other useful things.

Strauss, Richard (1864–1949)

Late Romantic/early modern German composer and conductor best known for symphonic/tone poems and operas.

Tchaikovsky, Pyotr (1840–1893)

The most European Romantic of the Russian composers, but still definitely Russian. Prolific in all forms, though possibly best known today for ballets, such as *The Nutcracker* and *Swan Lake*.

Wagner, Richard (1813–1883)

German composer best known for operas, in which he attempted to synthesize poetry, drama, music and visual effects into a *Gesamtkunstwerk*, a total work of art. Experimented with tonal structure and audience endurance. His controversial antisemitic writings later made him a great favorite of the Nazis, which ultimately didn't do him any favors.

LIST OF MUSICAL COMPOSITIONS

BEFORE

Music Box

Mozart: "Papageno's Magic Bells", from the opera *The Magic Flute*, K. 620

CONSERVATORY

Year 1

Fall

Haydn: Trios for Violin, Viola, and Cello in G Major, Op. 53, No. 1 (second) and in D Major, Op. 53 No. 3 (first)

Winter

Mozart: Sonata for Violin and Piano No. 17 in C Major, K. 296

Orchestra

Mozart: Overture to *The Marriage of Figaro*, K. 492
Beethoven: Symphony No. 1 in C Major, Op. 21
Schubert: Symphony No. 1 in D Major, D. 82

Spring

Beethoven: Sonata for Violin and Piano No. 1 in D Major, Op. 12, No. 1
Mozart: Quartet No. 14 in G Major, *Spring*, K. 387

Berit's solo recital

Bach: Partita for Violin No. 2, BWV 1004

Ros's solo recital

Mendelssohn: Sonata for Cello and Piano No. 2 in D Major, Op. 58

Year 2

Fall

Schubert: Quartet No. 13 in A Minor, *Rosamunde*, Op. 29, D. 804
Schumann: Sonata for Violin and Piano No. 2 in D Minor, Op. 121

Winter Orchestra

Mendelssohn: Overture to *A Midsummer Night's Dream*, Op. 21
Mozart: Symphony No. 30 in D Major, K. 202/186b
Brahms: Symphony No. 1 in C Minor, Op. 68

Spring
>Mozart: Sonata (unspecified, for balance)
>Schumann: Sonata (unspecified, for balance)

Spring Solo recital
>Bach: Partita for Violin No. 3, BWV 1006

Year 3

Fall
>Beethoven: Quartet No. 7, Op. 59, No.1, Razumovsky Quartet No. 1
>Kreutzer: Études (unspecified)
>Rameau: Dances (unspecified)
>Mozart: Quartet No. 17 in B-flat Major, *The Hunt*, K. 458 (Ros)

Winter Holiday
>Bach: Christmas Oratorio, BWV 248

Winter Orchestra
>Haydn: Symphony No. 50 in C Major, Hob. 1/50
>Beethoven: Symphony No. 5 in C Minor, Op. 67
>Wagner: Concert Overture, *Polonia* WWV 39
>Dvořák: Symphony No. 9 in E Minor, *New World,* Op. 95, B178

Vienna Quartet
>Mozart: Quartet No. 22 in B flat Major, Prussian Quartet No. 2,
>K. 589
>Schumann: Piano Quintet in E flat Major, Op. 44
>Tchaikovsky: Quartet No. 1 in D Major, Op. 11

Spring
>Spohr: Concerto No. 8 in A Minor, Op. 47
>Saint-Saëns: Sonata for Violin and Piano No. 1 in D Minor, Op. 75

Third-year recital—Arnold
>Boccherini: Sonata for Cello and Piano, (unspecified)

Third-year recital—Felix
>Rubinstein: Sonata for Violin and Piano No. 1 in G Major, Op. 78

Third-year recital—Robert
>Beethoven: Sonata for Piano No. 8 in C Minor, *Pathétique*, Op. 13

Third-year recital—Franz
>Brahms: Sonata for Viola and Piano, (unspecified)

Ros's recital
>Bach: (unspecified)
>Paganini: (unspecified)
>Rachmaninoff: Sonata for Cello and Piano in G Minor, Op. 19
>Dvořák: *Silent Woods* for Cello and Piano, B. 173

Berit's recital
　　　　Bach: (unspecified)
　　　Brahms: Concerto for Violin in D Major, Opus 77
　　Paganini: Caprice No. 24 in A Minor, M.S. 25

Year 4

Fall
　　Schumann: Piano Quintet in E flat Major, Op. 44

Winter Orchestra
　　　　Berlioz: *Symphonie Fantastique*, Op. 14
　Tchaikovsky: Fantasy Overture *Romeo and Juliet*, TH 42
　　Bruckner: Symphony No. 7 in E Major, WAB 107
　　　Strauss: *Till Eulenspiegel's Merry Pranks*, Op. 28

Solo recital
　　　　Bach: Sonata for Violin No. 3 in C Major, BWV 1005
　　　Bruch: Violin Concerto No. 1 in G Minor, Op. 26
　　Dvořák: *Romance* for Violin and Piano in F Minor, Op. 11
　Paganini: Caprice No. 1 in E Major, M.S. 25

Debut
　　　Rossini: Overture to *The Thieving Magpie*
　　　Bruch: Violin Concerto No.1, in G Minor, Op. 26
Rimsky Korsakov: Scheherezade, Op. 35